Red Snow

Will Dean

W F HOWES LTD

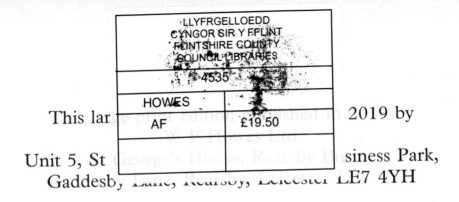
This large print edition published in 2019 by
W. F. Howes Ltd
Unit 5, St George's House, Rearsby Business Park,
Gaddesby Lane, Rearsby, Leicester LE7 4YH

1 3 5 7 9 10 8 6 4 2

First published in the United Kingdom in 2019
by Point Blank

A CIP catalogue record for this book is available
from the British Library

ISBN 978 1 52886 770 2

Typeset by Palimpsest Book Production Limited,
Falkirk, Stirlingshire

Printed and bound by
T J International in the UK

Red Snow

For Alfred. Always.

CHAPTER 1

There's a Volvo down in the ditch and I'd say it's been there a while.

I touch the brakes and my truck comes to a stop nice and easy; studded tyres biting into ice and bringing me to a silent standstill. It's all silent up here. White and utterly, utterly silent.

The display on my dash reads minus nineteen Celsius. I pull on my hat and move the earflaps so they don't mess with my hearing aids and then I turn up the heat and leave the engine idling and open my door and step down.

The Volvo looks like an ice cube, all straight lines and sparkling crystals, no signs of life, not a colour or a feature to look at. It's leaning down hard to the right so I'm roughly level with the driver's side window. I knock. My gloved knuckle sounds dull on the frosted glass so I rub my hand over the window but it's blasted solid with ice.

I step back, cold air burning my dried-out cheeks. Need more creams, better creams, prescription winter-creams. My mobile has no reception here so I look around and then head back to my pick-up and grab my scraper, one from a collection

1

of three, you can never be too careful, from my Hilux door well.

As I scrape the Volvo window the noise hits my aids like the sound of scaffolding poles being chewed by a log chipper. I start to get through, jagged ice shards spraying this way and that. And then I see his face.

I scrape harder. Faster.

'Can you hear me?' I yell. 'Are you okay?'

But he is not okay.

I can see the frost on his moustache and the solid ice flows running down from each nostril. He is dead still.

I keep scraping and pull the door handle but it's either locked or frozen solid or both. My breath looks nervous in front of my face; clouds of vapour between me and him, between my cheap mascara and his crystallised eyelashes. I've seen enough death these past six months, more than enough. I knock on the glass again and strain at the door handle. And then his eyes snap open.

I pull back, my thick rubber soles losing purchase on the shiny white beneath.

He doesn't move. He just looks.

'Are you okay?' I ask.

He stares at me. His body is perfectly still, his head unmoving, but his grey-blue eyes are on me, searching, asking questions. And then he sniffs and shakes his head and nods a kind of passive-aggressive 'thanks but I got this' dismissal which is frankly ridiculous.

'My name's Tuva Moodyson. Let me drive you into Gavrik. Let me call someone for you.'

The frozen snot in his moustache creaks and splinters and he mouths, 'I'm fine' and I can read his lips pretty well, over twenty years of practice.

I pull on his door handle, my neck getting hot, and then it starts to give so I pull harder and the ice cracks and the door swings up a little. It's heavy at this angle.

'You trying to snap my cables?' he says.

'Sorry?'

'It's about minus twenty out here I'd say and you just yanked my door open like it's a treasure chest. Best way to break a door handle cable.'

'You want to warm up in my truck?' I say. 'I can call breakdown?'

He looks out toward my truck like he's deciding if it's a suitable vehicle to save his life and I look at him and at the layers of clothes he's entombed himself in: a jacket that must contain five or six other jackets judging by its bulk, and blankets over his knees and thick ski gloves and I can see three hats, all different colours.

He coughs and spits and then says, 'I'll come over just to warm up, just for a minute.'

Well, thanks for doing me that favour mister Värmland charm champion.

I help him out and he's smaller than me, half a head smaller, and he's about fifty-five. There's a pair of nail scissors on the passenger seat next to a carrier bag full of canisters, and there's a bag

3

of dry dog food in the footwell. He locks his Volvo like there are gangs of Swedes out here just waiting to steal his broken down piece of shit car, and then he trudges over to my pick-up truck.

'Japanese?' he says, opening the passenger side.

I nod and climb in.

'Ten minutes and I'll be out your hair,' he says.

'What's your name?'

He coughs. 'Andersson.'

'Well, Mr Andersson, I'm Tuva Moodyson. Nice to meet you.'

We look out of the windscreen for a while, side by side, no talking, just staring at the white of Gavrik Kommun. Looks like one of those lucky blanks you get in a game of scrabble.

'You that one that writes stories in the newspaper?' he says.

'I am.'

'Best be heading back to my car now.'

'If you go out there again you're gonna end up dead. Let me drive you into town, your car will be fine.'

He looks at me like I'm nine years old.

'I've driven more tough winters than you've had hot lunches.'

What the hell does that even mean?

'And I can tell you,' he says, rubbing his nose on his coat sleeve. 'This ain't nothing. Minus twenty, maybe twenty-two, it ain't nothing. Anyhows, I texted my middle boy three hours ago, told him my location, and when he's done up at the pulp mill he'll come pick me up. You think I ain't spent time in ditches in winter?'

'Fine. Go,' I say, pausing for him to think. 'But I'll call the police and then Constable Thord'll have to come by and pick you up. How about we save him the bother.'

Mr Andersson sighs and chews his lower lip. The ice on his face is thawing, and now he just looks flushed and gaunt and a little tired.

'You gonna be the one driving?' he says.

I sigh-laugh.

He sniffs and wipes the thawed snot from his moustache whiskers. 'Guess I don't got much choice.'

I start the engine and turn on both heated seats. As we pass his frozen Volvo he looks mournfully out the window like he's leaving the love of his life on some movie railway platform.

'Why don't you buy Swedish?' he asks.

'You don't like my Hilux?'

'Ain't Swedish.'

'But it goes.'

We drive on and then he starts squirming in his seat like he's dropped something.

'My seat hot?' he says.

'You want me to switch it down a notch?'

'Want you to switch the damn thing off cos I feel like I peed my pants over here.' He looks disgusted. 'Goddam Japanese think of everything.'

Okay, so I've got a racist bore for a passenger but it's only twenty minutes into Gavrik town. It's never the cute funny smart people who need picking up now, is it?

'Where do you want dropping off, Mr Andersson? Where do you live?'

'Just drop me by the factory.'

'You work there?'

'Could say that. Senior Janitor. Thirty-three years next June.'

I pull a lever and spray my windscreen and the smell of chemical antifreeze wafts back through the heating vents.

'How many janitors they got up there?' I ask.

'Just got me.'

'You get free liquorice?'

'I ain't got none so don't go asking. I'm the janitor and that's it.'

I drive up to an intersection where the road cuts a cross-country ski trail marked with plastic yellow sticks and they look like toothpicks driven into a perfect wedding cake. The air is still and the sky's a hanging world of snow and it is heavy, just waiting to dump.

'You did the Medusa story, eh?'

I nod.

He shakes his head.

'You just about ruined this place, you know that? Good few people be quite pleased to see you run out of town, I'm just saying what I heard.'

I get this bullshit from time to time. As the sole full-time reporter here in Gavrik, I get blamed for bad news even though I'm just the one writing it.

'I'd say it was a job well done,' I say.

'Well, you would, you done it.'

'You'd rather elk hunters were still getting shot out in the woods?' He goes quiet for a while and I switch the heat from leg/face to windscreen.

'All I know is we lost some hard-won reputation,' he says. 'And thank God we still got the factory and the mill to keep some stability. That's all I'm saying and now I done said it.'

As I get closer to town, the streets get a little clearer, more snowploughing here, more yard shovelling, and the municipal lighting's coming on; 3pm and the streetlights are coming on. Welcome to February.

'Suppose you were just doing your job like anyone but we're a small town and we're cut off from everywhere else so we've learned to stick together. I got eight grandkiddies to worry about. You'd know if you were from these parts.'

I drive on.

The twin chimneys of the factory, the largest employer in town, loom ahead of me. It's the biggest building around here save for the ICA Maxi supermarket. Two brick verticals back-dropped by a white sheet.

'Say, you hear me pretty good for a deaf person, don't mind me saying.'

'I can hear you just fine.'

'You using them hearing aid contraptions?'

I feel his eyes on my head, his gaze boring into me.

7

'I am.'

'I'll be needing them myself pretty soon, sixty-one this coming spring.'

I drive past the ice hockey rink and on between the supermarket and McDonald's, the two gateposts of Gavrik, and up along Storgatan, the main street in town. I head past the haberdashery and the gun shop and my office with its lame-ass Christmas decorations still in the window, and on toward the cop shop, and then I pull up next to the Grimberg Liquorice factory 'Established 1839' – or so it says on the gates.

'This okay?' I ask.

He gets out without saying a word and I look around and there are five or six people scattered about all looking up to the sky. This doesn't happen, especially in February. A hunched figure in a brown coat slips on the ice as he walks away. I try to look up through the windscreen but it's frosted at the top, so I open my door and climb out onto the gritted salted pavement. I can hear mutterings and I can sense others joining us from Eriksgatan.

They're looking up at the right chimney, the one I've never seen smoke coming out of. There's a man, or I think it's a man, a figure in a suit climbing the ladder that's bolted to the side of the chimney, climbing higher and higher past the masts and phone antennas attached to the bricks. He's in a hurry. No hat or gloves. I look up and the sky is blinding white, dazzling, and the pale clouds are moving fast overhead, the wind picking up. As I stare up it's like an optical illusion, like the chimneys are toppling over onto me. And then the man jumps.

CHAPTER 2

He hits the cobbled area in front of the factory, in front of the arch, and his head breaks like a watermelon.

One person screams.

One.

A singular howl from a woman standing behind me.

'Get Thord,' I say to Janitor Andersson. 'Get the police.'

But he just stands there looking down at the man on the cobbles and then up to the chimney and then back down to the man. More people are coming out now, fastening coats and adjusting hats and gasping as they work out what just happened.

I see someone head off to the police station all of one minute away so I run into the factory lot and the snow is turning red.

'Stay with me,' I say, louder and more forcefully than I'd expected, but it's no use, he is the most dead person I have ever seen. His limbs are twisted and his arms are pulled in tight to his cracked head like a child in deep sleep. I feel useless. I can't help this broken man, I can't do anything for him.

Thord arrives at my side and takes the man's pulse and moves his cold ungloved hands toward the man's head but then stops because what good would it do?

He leads me away from the body and turns around and after a while an ambulance pulls up.

'Out of our way,' says one of two paramedics.

They get to work and I stagger a few steps back toward the iron gates and half of Gavrik has turned out now; took some of them a while to get their outdoor gear on I guess, their boots and their mittens and their jackets and their bobble hats. But they're here now.

I feel faint so I let my back rest against the railings. I slouch down and notice a speck of pink snow on my boots and I think I'll pass out but I don't. And then I hear scream number two.

A well-dressed woman runs out through the factory arch and throws herself down next to the dead man. The paramedics retreat for a moment like they know who she is and they can't do much anyway.

'Step back, everyone,' says Thord, his arms outstretched, walking toward the street, toward the crowd of ski jacket people. 'Best thing you can all do is step back and return to your offices and your homes. Step back, please.'

And they do. Because they're Swedes and because they can't see much now that the ambulance is blocking their view, and also because it's minus nineteen, maybe less.

An old couple walk off up the street consoling each other.

Constable Thord looks at me.

'You alright, Tuvs?'

I nod.

The woman who threw herself down at the dead man, I'm pretty sure he was the boss of the factory and she's his wife, Anna-Britta I think her name is, she's wailing now, quietly sobbing from behind the ambulance. Chief Björn turns up and says something to Thord and then heads over to the body and pulls off his hat. It's getting dark now, whites turning into greys.

A Volvo taxi drives past slowly and another cop arrives. The new one. She started last week and that story made my front page. I can only see her back right now, black hair under her police hat, a tortoiseshell grip holding it all together. She turns and I see her face in this dull light and her eyes flash to me.

'We're gonna close up the gates,' Thord says, frost in his eyebrows, a red-haired woman passing behind him. 'Need to take photos and whatnot, and also talk to witnesses so maybe you can help me get a list together, seeing as you were here?'

I nod to him. 'Sure. Now?'

'Head over to the station in, I don't know, about an hour, an hour-and-a-half.'

'Okay.'

'Best if you get back to your office now. Sorry you had to see that.'

I photograph the chimney and the ambulance on my phone. After I turn my back on the scene, on the frozen weight of what has just happened, I can still feel the power of it behind me. It's uncomfortable to turn my back, to shun it, the brick factory and those two chimneys and the dead man broken in the snow. The shadow, the shadow of all of it, is stretching down Storgatan, and I follow it for a few minutes, a black Mercedes 4x4 skidding away as if to escape the chimney's darkness, and then I turn left and open the door to *Gavrik Posten*.

The bell tinkles and I step into warmth.

Lars isn't in, he's part-time and he'll be in tomorrow. Nils is back in his office slash kitchen on the right selling ad space to the same people he's been selling ad space to for the last twelve years. Lena's in her office on the left fixing for the print.

I kick off my boots, my stomach queasy, my legs unsteady, and then pull off my coat and gloves and hat. I hang up the coat on its reinforced hook and place the other woolly stuff in my basket.

Lena opens her door. Jeans and a ski undershirt. She has more grey in her afro than when I arrived here in Toytown and I think it suits her.

'Something happened?' she asks.

'Yeah.'

I pull off my fleece and lay it down on my desk.

'Grimberg jumped,' I say.

'What?'

'Climbed up the factory chimney and jumped off. He's dead.'

She covers her mouth with her hand. I'm always surprised and impressed by how affected she gets by bad news, the amount she's seen in her life, in Nigeria, in New York, in Gavrik. There is no blasé in Lena Adeola.

She shakes her head. 'You see him do it?'

I nod and she steps closer and puts her arm around me. Maybe it's because of what I've been through these past six months or maybe because of Mum or maybe because I'm leaving in ten days or maybe it's all of it. She's not normally a hugger.

I shudder at the thought of Grimberg hitting the cobblestones. That noise.

'Get you a coffee?' she says. 'You need a break?'

'I need to give a statement. Tell Thord what I saw and who was around.'

She heads into Nils's office slash kitchen and I catch sight of his tube-socked feet up on his desk and then she pours coffee from the machine into two chainsaw store freebie mugs and hands one over to me.

She sips and looks back to her office.

'We'll have to move things around now,' she says.

'I'll work tonight,' I tell her. 'We'll have enough for the front page.'

'If that's alright,' she says.

I nod and take my winter cream and spread it onto my chapped hands and work it into the valleys where my fingers meet, and my knuckles, and then

14

onto my cheeks and eyelids. My lids are the worst, weeks of dry and cold. The February air can't hold humidity. I look at the clock, ten past four, and I think about that noise. That crack. Why did he jump? What could be so awful that you'd climb up a chimney in February and then end it all? I pull out my aids and switch on my microwave-sized PC and open my stories.

Six leading headlines that will now be trumped by the factory suicide. Valentine's dinner at Hotel Gavrik next week with a secret special guest. That will be dogshit deluxe, make no mistake. I think of the man's head on those cobbles, the snow, the dash of colour, the sound, the life leaving him right then, the exact pinpoint moment of death. I cringe and rub my eyes and open the next story. The local council have called for a Kommun-wide roof clearance effort this coming weekend. They're worried about collapses. They're also warning tres-passers not to approach the abandoned black warehouse behind the Toyota dealership because with all the recent weather they say it could fall down any minute. The pulp mill an hour or so north of here is sponsoring the annual Gavrik vs Munkfors ice hockey match on March 13th. It sponsors the match every year and in most towns this wouldn't be a news story but this isn't most towns. Björnmossen's, Gavrik's largest gun store, is starting its sale on March 3rd. All ammunition half price. Next story: there was a scare last week when a little girl skated into an ice-fishing hole on the reservoir so the owners have cordoned off an area exclusively for skating. Fishing trumps skating, or at least it does here in Gavrik. And finally, perhaps the biggest story until the grisly events of today: the sole full-time reporter at *Gavrik Posten*, yours truly, is leaving after next week's issue to start work at a bi-weekly publication down near Malmö. I got my golden ticket.

I try to dodge the indoor puddles of water that mark every entrance area this time of year, and pull on all my Gore-Tex fleece-lined gear. This is the deal in February in central Sweden. You spend half your time pulling on gear or taking it off, and the other half's spent either digging out your truck or else scraping it.

My hearing aids are still on my desk so I reach over and pull them on, each one uncomfortable on account of my dry crocodile skin, and then head back out onto the street.

It's cold and there's nobody around. The ambulance is gone, the cops are gone, the body's gone. But the factory's still there. Oh yeah, it's still up there on its granite hill, looking down over the whole of Toytown and casting its shadows all the way out to McDonald's.

The cop shop's empty and the new girl's nowhere to be seen. I ring the bell on the counter and Thord wanders through.

'You wanna do this back there where it's warm?' he asks.

'You bet.'

He opens the heavy code-locked door and I step through. I've been back here one time before, when I was interviewing sources about the Medusa murders last October. Place hasn't changed much. Filing cabinets and six desks, three occupied. A kitchenette and a rack for police coats, and photos on the wall of Chief Petterson, Thord's late father.

'Coffee?' he asks.

'I'm good, thanks.'

This is February and that means peak coffee and peak booze and peak TV and peak online poker and that's about all there is until the snows melt away in late April.

'Horrible thing,' Thord says, sitting down at his desk and pointing to the chair on the other side.

I sit down. 'Horrible.'

'What happened before we arrived? Can you tell me in your own words?'

His cheeks are red and sore and his lips are peeling like old bark from a log.

'I arrived about three-thirty and there were maybe six or seven people looking up at the old chimney, the one on the right that never smokes. I got out my truck and looked up. Mr Grimberg was climbing that rusty metal ladder that runs up one side of each chimney, he was close to the top, just past the faint G of the Grimberg Liquorice lettering that runs down to the factory roof.'

'He was the only one on the ladder?'

'I think so. Didn't see anyone else, but it all happened very fast. He got to the top and then,' real quick, he jumped off. It was silent and then I heard a crack and he hit the cobbles by that arch tunnel that runs through the middle of the building. Then you came.'

'Anyone talking to him from below? Any arguments? Raised voices? He look scared?'

'Don't think so, it all happened so quickly.'

'We heard he was being spoken to. That he looked terrified climbing that ladder, almost like he was being chased. Nobody else around?'

I shake my head.

'Spoken to?' I say. 'Chased?'

Thord hasn't made a note of anything I've said, even though he has a chewed biro and a pad of paper in front of him.

'Horrible thing to happen in your last week,' he says.

'It is.'

'You recognise any of the other witnesses? I saw most of them myself, but two old-timers were walking off as I arrived.'

'There was Linda from the newsagent and a woman with bright scarlet red hair. And there was Bertil with the bad knee, used to work out at the sewage works.'

'Bertil Hendersson? The bee man?'

I nod.

'Okay, that's helpful,' he says, standing up. 'Thanks for coming by.'

'Quote for the paper, Thord?'

'Say what now?'

'I'll be needing a quote from the police, please.'

He swallows hard and looks over toward Chief Björn's desk. There's a speedboat brochure laying open by the telephone.

'Well, this ain't like other things, you know that.'

'I still need a quote.'

'I don't mean the . . .' he hushes his voice and sits back down, '. . . suicide, I mean the family, the Grimbergs. They're discreet people and they wouldn't want me saying too much if you know what I mean.'

'I'll be respectful. But I need a quote.'

'Let me talk to the Chief and I'll call you first thing in the morning.'

'Need it for the print, Lena's over there right now waiting for it. Just give me a soundbite.'

'Police say . . .'

I wait but he keeps on looking over at the direction of the factory and then at Chief Björn's desk. There's a stack of cruise holiday brochures next to the speedboat one.

'Police say . . .' I say.

'This was a tragic incident. Our thoughts are with the Grimberg family at this time.'

'That it?'

He frown-nods.

'Okay then, that'll have to do.'

'Don't go meddling with the Grimbergs, Tuvs. They're private people and the whole town relies on them.'

'We have to tell the news, Thord.'

'They're private people and they're not like me and you. They've been in that factory as long as my family's been in Gavrik, since 1840 or some such, and they pretty much built the whole town. If it wasn't for Grimberg Liquorice there'd be no Gavrik so we owe them the courtesy. They've had more than enough tragic deaths over the years. Blighted, they are. Leave them be.'

CHAPTER 3

I step out of the cop shop and ice-cold wind blasts my face.

Why did Gustav do it? Why end it all? And why kill yourself in front of the whole town?

Shuffling, I cross Storgatan, empty of cars and people, and head back to the office. Snow is falling in sporadic flakes, floating down slowly and gently. I look to my left toward the factory and see a flash of warm colour up at one of the top windows. Then it disappears. I cup my hands over my ears to protect my aids, each one worth a month's salary here, or three weeks' worth at my new job, and then I run like anyone runs on an icy road. Ronnie's Bar, now refurbished, opened last week for the first time in years. A new place in a town with nowhere else to go. The office bell tinkles and Nils steps in from his office slash kitchen holding a bunch of white helium balloons.

'Kid's birthday. Happy Meal and all these and a tricycle. Nice day for it.'

I'm not sure if he's being sarcastic about the chimney death, or sincere.

'Have fun.'

He sets the balloons down. They have a lead weight to keep them from escaping Gavrik town, from leaving all this behind, and then he pulls on his huge jacket and hat and mittens.

'See you in the a-m.'

Lena's door's ajar so I stick my head around.

'Thai?'

She signals her approval.

I sit down at my desk, a pine catalogue thing from the early nineties, and pick up my phone and dial.

'Print night?' asks Tammy.

'Good memory,' I say. 'You should count cards in Vegas. Two pad thais, please, fierce as you are, pick up in fifteen minutes.'

'Got it.'

I google Gavrik and there are chimney jump headlines in the regionals and even some of the nationals are running with it. *Wermlands Tidningen* talks about the family and how important they are to the community but they spell Anna-Britta, the widow, they spell her name wrong, and that really pisses me off. *Göteborg Posten* focus on Grimberg Liquorice, Sweden's third largest producer of salt liquorice and seventh largest producer of sweet liquorice. Lots of talk about heritage and secret recipes and other impersonal filler. Nothing much about the man who actually died or the grieving people he left behind.

My right hearing aid beeps so I pull it off and pop out the battery and take a new one from my key fob and then I pull off its sticker and wait a few minutes: a neat trick that gives me extra battery life. I drop in the new one and close it up. The aid plays a jingle as I switch it on.

I look at Gavrik on Google Maps because I want to see the factory's location relative to everything else. The building has an extra pull tonight. It's always had its own special feel, an ancient superiority, but now it's more intense. I zoom into Sweden and into Värmland and into Gavrik and there it is. An industrial lot of three acres or so at the top of Storgatan, north of the cop shop and Hotel Gavrik, its nearest neighbours, and south of St Olov's church ruin.

My Hilux's door is frozen shut so I tug on it gently remembering what Janitor Andersson said about cables snapping. If I lose this vehicle I am one hundred per cent fucked, especially in February. The thing about being a small town reporter in the north pole is that you need a good reliable truck to get you to stories – and even more importantly, to get you away from them.

I pull the door and snow from the roof falls in and settles on my seat. Thord asked if someone was chasing Grimberg up the chimney. Was that even possible? I turn the key in the ignition and switch on the blower, full speed, full heat, all of it focussed on the windscreen, and then set the heated seat to max, and then grab my scraper. It's a routine, like a fighter pilot's pre-flight checks. I scrape the windscreen and mirrors and front windows and spray blue antifreeze on the rear ones. Then I get in and turn the wipers on and release the handbrake and set off. There is no noise and the dash says minus twenty-two.

Three-minute drive to Tammy's van on the edge of ICA Maxi's supermarket lot and I don't see a single person on the way. Not one. Her van's steaming and lit up and it's probably my favourite place in town and the only place I'll really miss.

Everything's white. It looks like God poured a bottle of correction fluid over the whole town, and who the hell could blame him.

Tammy's there leaning out of her hatch with her lumberjack hat tied under her chin, a bag of delicious food in each hand. I stand on tiptoe and kiss her cheek and stick two hundred kronor on the counter and grab the bags and run back to my truck.

I pass seven snow-topped For Rent signs on empty shops on the way back to the office. Seven.

Lena and I eat in silence at her desk. My noodles are glistening and ferocious with chili flakes and they are good. Really good. We both have a can of red Coke from the newsagent across the road and I wish mine had some rum in it. Fifty-fifty would do me just fine. We eat from the plastic containers. I have crackers, Lena doesn't.

'Hell of a day,' she says.

I have a mouthful of shrimp and peanuts so I just nod.

'You ever been inside there?' she asks.

'The factory?'

Lena nods, chopsticking noodles into her mouth.

'Just into the modern bit at the back when they launched some new flavour years ago. Seemed normal enough back there, just with that old building stuck on the front.'

Lena pulls a thread of spring onion from her teeth and picks up her Coke.

'They've got vermin trouble,' she says. 'Monster rats out in the liquorice root barns. God help them if they ever get inside.'

I wipe my mouth.

'Did you meet Gustav Grimberg, the man that died today?' she asks.

'I've never actually talked to him. Seen him in the bank I think, but no.'

'His dad died the same way,' she says.

'Off the chimney?'

'No,' she shakes her head. 'They say Ludvig Grimberg poisoned himself but that was maybe twenty years ago and you know how these stories get out of hand.'

I take a swig of Coke.

'Couldn't stand the girl his son chose to marry. That's the hearsay. Old man Ludvig blamed her for the business getting into trouble. That place has seen more than its fair share of death over the years.' She sucks a noodle into her mouth. 'You all packed?'

'Flat's ready pretty much. I kiss goodbye to the Hilux next week. Then I got to visit . . .' I pause and swallow hard, '. . . Mum's grave, I haven't been since the day itself, and then I'll be gone to the south where the girls are pretty and the boys are even prettier.'

'Nice life.'

I throw my food carton into the bag it came in and tie a knot in the end.

'Gonna send this to the printers in thirty minutes,' she says. 'You gonna have the front-page suicide ready?'

'Will do.'

I head to my desk and my ears are quite painful now, all dry crusty skin at the top where there's not enough fat. I write for twenty minutes. Turns out it's not easy to distil what I saw, what I heard, into headlines and copy. The watermelon crack, the two screams, one from a passer-by, all the sharper for it being so alone, so completely from just one person, and one from Gustav Grimberg's wife. It's not what I'm used to. I wrote about murder a lot last year. Medusa. The deaths in Utgard forest just outside town. This is totally different. A man jumped. There will be un-answered questions and guilt and thoughtless whispers of 'there's always another option' and 'took the easy way out' and there'll most likely be some distasteful chat in the haberdashery store over the road.

I write with an eye on the victims. His family. According to the official online records, God love Sweden for making all this stuff public, Gustav had a daughter, Karin, aged twenty, and a wife, Anna-Britta, the woman I saw, the second scream, aged fifty-three, and a mother, Cecilia, aged eighty-two. I have to be mindful of them. When Dad died the papers made mistakes and that pained Mum for the rest of her life. They said he died on June 26th when in fact he died on June 25th. These mindless errors made things worse for Mum. And, consequently, for me. When Medusa was stopped back in October there was all sorts of nonsense printed. Online and traditional papers. Good ones, even. Mistakes and lies and sloppy journalism and bullshit alluded to, but never quite clearly enough for anyone to sue.

I finish up and fact-check and read it through out loud and then I send it to Lena. She says thanks and I say goodnight.

There's a white taxi outside when I get to my building, a Volvo with its engine idling. Is it Viggo Svensson, the dangerous creep from Utgard forest? I speed up and lock myself into my flat and place a kitchen knife next to the door and then I double-check the locks. Most of my belongings are packed into three big suitcases for me to take on the night train down to Malmö. The train will take eleven hours whereas a flight would take one, but airports and planes are hell on earth if you're deaf. The announcements, the rotten acoustics, everyone in a rush, me trying to hear scary security and police people. I vote trains.

I put my aids in desiccant to dry out overnight

27

and then I get ready for bed. My sheets need changing. I say goodnight to Mum and Dad; the photo beside my bed, the one I can look at straight in the face now that they're both gone. I can look even though she stopped taking care of me after he died. Even though I had to feed us and shop for us and cook for us. Even though she never really asked how I was for all those years. I can look at her photo now. It's a start.

I think back to a guy I studied with in London, a redhead – don't think about the watermelon crack, not now, nothing you can do to help, think about the student – nice guy, never really knew him, safe to think about him, nice neck, nice hands, nice voice. And then I hear the sound of skull bone cracking on cobblestones.

CHAPTER 4

My pillow alarm shakes me awake at seven and I drag myself over to the window and check the thermometer. It's minus six, a mini heatwave. Halle-fucking-lujah.

I get to the office and write for an hour or so, drafting headlines and story ideas for next week's issue. The pile of *Posten*s in reception reduces in height through the morning as Svens and Ingrids drop in to say how awful it was with the, you know, at the factory, just dreadful, he had a drinking problem, no it was drugs, and business worries, but it's the young girl they feel for. Then they take a copy and place twenty kronor in the biscuit tin honesty box and pull on their hats and leave.

I need to visit Mum. I'll buy flowers and one of those long-lasting weatherproof candles from Ica Maxi and drive down to Karlstad and spend time at the grave before I leave town. Maybe I'll go twice. Once seems disrespectful; an obvious, lazy, throwaway gesture.

Lars schlepps in at eleven and my God it takes him an eon to get undressed from his winter gear.

The hat gets un-Velcroed and then placed in his basket. The jacket comes off like an arthritic polar bear freeing itself from a straightjacket. He hangs it up. The boots are pulled off and placed on his rack. Then the fleeces and the static crackles and the big Christmas sweater with the bad stitching and then he says 'morning' and wanders through to Nils's office slash kitchen with his bifocals atop his bald patch to start his coffee and sandwich routine. Honestly though, I'll miss him.

I draft a list of people I'll need to talk to regarding Gustav Grimberg's death. I've never covered a high-profile suicide like this and it's tricky to know where to start. An accident, a car crash or lumberjack maiming, a murder even, or a medical procedure gone horribly wrong, I'd wait the requisite amount of time that Lena taught me was appropriate in a small town like Gavrik, and then, respectfully with condolences, I'd approach the family to see if they wanted to say a few words. Can't do that with the Grimbergs, not yet anyway. Because they're reclusive and pretty much unknown to the whole town, but also because their grieving process will likely be so much more jagged and complex than most. I can't even imagine what the three women left behind must be going through.

I pull on my jacket and boots and cross the road to the newsagent for chocolate. Storgatan's grey with slush and grit and old salt. The factory seems larger today, that disused chimney on the right side staring the whole town in the eye, complicit

30

in a death, responsible by way of its obscene and pointless height.

The store has some new dark-chocolate pistachio special-offer thing but I ignore that because dark chocolate makes me want to bite my tongue off. I buy 500g of Marabou milk chocolate goodness and stick the bar in my deep coat-pocket and head to the police station. The ticker tape queue machine thing says two and the screen above the counter says two so I take the ticket and ring the bell.

'Thought I might see you this morning,' says Thord, a slice of rye toast in his hand with a limp piece of red pepper on top.

'You thought right.'

He takes a bite from the toast and a spray of fine brown crumbs showers down the front of his uniform.

'What happens now?' I ask. 'You still think he was chased? Will the coroner from Karlstad be involved?'

'Already is involved, this one's been fast-tracked.'

'Fast-tracked?'

'Post-mortem happening as I eat this sandwich. And if it's all tickety-boo, they'll release the body and sign off the funeral taking place tomorrow afternoon, cos that's the family's wishes.'

'That fast?'

'Fast-tracked, like I said. The Chief knows the coroner real well, old friends, and the coroner can make it happen. Nothing unusual about the body,

31

so I'm told. The Chief reckons its's tragic but it's an open and shut suicide. We ain't got any other funerals planned in St Olov's cos it's February and cos nobody really gets buried there anymore. So this can go straight to the front of the queue.'

'Poor man.'

'Expecting they'll find cigarette burns on Gustav cos he was bullied pretty bad at high school as far as I can remember.'

'Bullied?' I say.

'Real bad,' he says.

'You asked me about people talking to Gustav before he jumped.'

He stops eating. 'You remember something?'

'No.'

He carries on eating. 'Wasn't nothing. Incitement to suicide is the thing. Karlstad police explained it to us cos we ain't never come across it before. But there wasn't no evidence. No note. No eyewitness reports.'

'Incitement?'

'Happened a few times on internet forums so I've been told. Facebook and the like. Manipulation. Mainly teenagers telling each other to take pills or whatnot, sometimes filming it, live-streaming.'

'But . . .'

He cuts me off. 'Nothing of the sort here, Tuvs. Grimberg had two liquorice coins in his breast pocket and nothing else. There was talk of some old man, some hunched old man with a walking stick and a dog, talking to Grimberg before he jumped.

Some kind of argument, but that could have been anyone. This was just a tragic accident.'

'Accident?' I say.

'Incident,' he says.

I watch him swill his toast down with coffee.

'Which church?' I ask.

'Call the factory office,' he says, taking another bite. He swallows and says, 'Gotta go, police business to attend to.'

He picks up a copy of today's *Posten*, my words all over its front page, the suicide, and also the back page, the ice hockey grand slam, and heads back to the office, probably to 'take care of business'. I catch sight of the new cop back there as the key code door closes. I see her ears and the back of her head. She has excellent hair.

When I step back out a big, black raven swoops down toward me and then flaps its uneven wings and craws and flies high between the twin chimneys of the factory and beyond. I see a man walking through the arch that cuts through the centre of the building and I'd recognise that soft body anywhere.

Why is David Ghostwriter Holmqvist heading into the Grimberg factory on a day like today?

I get to my desk and my left aid's hurting in my ear. What I really need is a few days, no, a week, a whole entire uninterrupted week with no hearing aids. I'd stay silent. It's as much of a relief as going braless, more even at this time of year. Shame my new job down south starts a

33

day after this one ends. I can't afford a gap. I have bills to pay, funeral expenses and arrears dating back to Christmas. Envelopes I couldn't bear to open. Blocked it all out. I didn't manage and now I can't afford a week between jobs. Sucks to be me.

I dial the factory office.

'Grimberg Liquorice, Agnetha Hellbom speaking.'

'Hello, this is Tuva Moodyson from the *Posten*. I'd like to offer my condolences, and if I may, could I ask you a few quick questions about the service tomorrow?'

'Hm-hm.'

'Where is it to be held?'

'Service in the Lutheran church on Eriksgatan. Strictly family only, I'm sure you'll understand what with the tragic accident and all.'

Accident?

'Will there be a public memorial?' I ask.

'Don't know yet, it's only just happened, wouldn't you say? Let's allow Mr Grimberg some respect before we start involving the masses.' There's a pause. 'The burial part will be public. You can pay your respects then if you have any. Will that be all?'

'May I ask where Mr Grimberg will be buried.'

She takes a long breath. 'If you were local you wouldn't need to ask. Family plot in St Olov's, right here next to the factory. Now, this is the one thing the family have asked me to communicate to the public: donations to the Swedish Childhood

34

Cancer Foundation. No flowers. None whatsoever. Anything else?'

'No, that's all.'

She hangs up.

I keep an eye out the window, past the mouse-
nibbled Christmas decorations that one of us
should really think about removing, the nativity
Joseph is quite horribly disfigured, the nose and
ears are almost completely gone, and I keep look
out for David Holmqvist. All I see is a white Volvo
taxi, probably Viggo Svensson's, drop off a girl
dressed in black. She's as thin as a spider leg and
she's wearing a heavy backpack underneath her
coat that makes her look like Quasimodo.

Holmqvist doesn't pass by so I head outside in
all my gear and I reckon I lose about an hour a
day during winter just pulling on and peeling off
the ugly man-made layers that keep me alive. I
buy a ham sandwich from the newsagent, it has a
criminal margarine-to-ham ratio, and walk up to
the factory gates. The one operational chimney, the
left one, is still pumping out aniseed steam. They
haven't shut down production. Through the iron
gates I can see Andersson, the janitor with the
attitude problem.

'Hello Mr Andersson.'

No response. He's pushing sludge-snow with a
shovel as broad as my desk.

'Mr Andersson,' I try a little louder.

He turns to me and tuts and walks over to meet
me at the gates.

'What do you want?'

'Sorry about Grimberg.'

'Yeah, me too.'

'You going to the church service tomorrow?'

'Not invited,' he says. 'Family only. Going to the burial though, reckon half the town will turn out and it's my job to make sure the grave's shipshape tidy. Terrible business.'

'Very sad.'

'He has a daughter, just got back from her fancy art school.' He coughs and wipes his mouth on his coat sleeve. 'I'd do anything for that girl after all that she's been through. Poor Karin.'

And then I notice the snow *skalle*.

I almost step on it.

Fist-sized snow skulls were popular in the town back in the 1800s and they've recently come back into fashion. It's a peculiar Gavrik thing. I wrote about them in last week's *Posten*. Kids make them. Kind of like a Scandi-folkloristic practical joke mixed with good Christmas cheer. The skull is the size of a snowball. It is a snowball. But the cheeks have been smoothed away, and little fingers have been pushed in to make eye sockets and nasal sockets and a gaping mouth. A piece of grit sits in each eye hole. And this one, this grotesque snow *skalle*, has red lingonberry jam dribbling from its cranium and it has toothpicks for teeth. Andersson looks at me looking at it. He raises his shovel and crashes it down on the skull sending pink snow shards flying in every direction and then he says, 'Damn kids, no respect.'

We say our goodbyes and when I watch him get back to shovelling I notice the area he's working on is the area where Gustav Grimberg died. Under the snow and the frost and the slush I imagine scarlet gravel, blood frozen into the grit binding the stones. Perhaps it'll show itself in late April when the town thaws.

I work all afternoon from the office and never see Holmqvist leave the factory. Is there another exit? What's he doing there the day after a suicide?

By four, Lars and Nils have left. Some new reality TV show starts tonight, and Friday night is taco night in Sweden; tacos which bear no resemblance whatsoever to anything Mexican, swilled down with Danish beer and consumed in front of an American Netflix series and all polished off with Swedish salt liquorice from that sad, old place across the road.

'Staying long?' asks Lena.

'Five minutes,' I tell her. 'Story to follow up on.'

She returns to her office and I get my gear on and take my Leica binoculars and my torch and leave. And then I realise that this is my last ever normal Friday at *Gavrik Posten*, so I head back indoors and keep my big boots on – fuck it – and head into Lena's office at the rear of our building.

'Thanks for keeping me . . .' I swallow a big hard dry nothing, 'for keeping me on the level these past years.'

'What do you mean?' she says. 'You're worse now than when you started.'

'I've learnt a lot.'

She smiles and turns back to her screen and I leave the office with a good feeling in my belly. I need to say these things more often. I never said them to Mum, not the things I needed her to hear, even when I knew she only had weeks left. I needed to tell her that I forgave her, or that I at least understood it, that she did the best she could even though that was almost nothing. But I never managed to get the words out. I was too late.

I leave and turn right and pass by the factory and head up toward the pitch-black emptiness of St Olov's ruin.

CHAPTER 5

I pass the factory and it looks like a fancy brick
house. The ground floor is four windows to
the left of the arch and four windows to the
right. The upstairs windows all have net curtains
except for the one directly above the arch. There's
some kind of metal hook over the arch-tunnel
entrance and it looks like a ready-to-strike scorpion
tail in this dim grey light.

I slip and slide as I walk up the shallow hill
to the church; well it's not a church, not like
you'd recognise, it's a pile of old stones. A snowplough passes. It's lit up like a lunar exploration
vehicle, scraping back snow from Storgatan and
dumping down salt from its rear end. The noise
is godawful.

The churchyard is lit from two streetlights but
it is dark within. I've worked about five minutes
from this place for over three years now and I've
never visited. Why would I? I open the gate and
there's a woman there.

'Sorry, are you coming out?' I ask, holding the
metal gate open and standing aside.

She stands in the shadow of a leaning yew tree

39

and I can't hear her words; she's wearing a scarf, and I can't read her in this darkness.

'I'm deaf,' I say. 'I can't hear you.'

She walks through the gate and stands under the streetlight. She looks ancient, a brown fur coat dragging in the snow, its hood hiding her hair. She pulls the scarf down a little exposing a shrivelled mouth painted with bright orange lipstick.

'Sorry,' she says. 'Are you coming in?'

'Yes,' I say. 'Just for ten minutes. Why?'

'Take this.'

She sticks her gloved hand into the pocket of her fur coat and pulls out something and places it in the palm of my ski glove.

'What is it?'

'It's just a piece of bread. If you walk through the graveyard it'll keep you safe. Pop it in your pocket. And . . .'

'Yes?' I say.

'Try to hold your breath when you get deep inside. If not hold, then keep your breathing shallow.'

Mad as a fruit bat.

'Okay,' I say. 'Goodnight.'

I walk in through the gate and she shuffles off down the street. The moon is out and it's waxing three-quarters full but the ice clouds are floating past so the light comes and goes.

There's a large sign in front of the ruin itself telling me the church dates back from 1100 and was roofed and used regularly until the Gavrik black flu of 1917.

The walls are a metre thick in places and topped with lead and moss and leaves and a thick carpet of untouched snow. It's a small building with a large flat stone at the far end where I guess an altar once stood. This place almost feels like nature: a forest or a moor or an unlit bog. Places that terrify me. On the stone someone's graffiti'd a symbol. I step closer and the moon brightens and I see it's an emoji. A sad smiley face in black with huge angry eyes.

I step through the tangled rhododendron bushes, their tight buds wilting and shrivelling from the unending cold, and look at the graves. I'm trying to find the Grimberg family patch because I need to unpick why Gustav died the way he did. I need to unearth the story.

There are little stacks of snowballs piled near many of the tombs and they have candles flickering inside. One is a stack of snow skulls, these ones quite beautiful, the grown-up version, polished to almost clear ice, with no grit in the eye sockets. They look like glass ornaments or expensive crystal paperweights. And they sparkle from the candlelight within.

Poor Mum. She deserves better. There are solar lights on sticks next to some of the stones, generally the newer-looking stones, and they're flickering with the tiny dribble of electricity they've managed to eke out of the Toytown winter sky.

The toughest to look at are the old and the new.

The oldest stones are unreadable, moss-crusted

and pocked. They're not remembered, the people underneath, too many degrees of separation between them and the living world. Most are not quite upright. They're forgotten and they are falling as slowly as anything in the world could ever fall.

And the new. The freshest graves are still mounded with earth or gravel, humps of fresh soil that haven't had time to settle. I give these a wide berth. No logical reason but I just can't walk too close to them.

An owl toots from a nearby tree and I reach instinctively for the old woman's bread in my pocket.

Toward the very corner of the graveyard, the most pristine section, the area closest to the factory itself, I find the Grimberg family plot. It's the largest here and the most grand. A low stone wall surrounds the twelve, maybe fourteen graves, and a short evergreen hedge skirts the wall. The hedge looks black. I get wind feedback in my aids so severe I'm tempted to switch them off, but I don't want to be without them in a place like this.

These Grimberg graves have proper candles, real ones, not electric, and they look like they've been lit recently, their wicks still high in their windproof cases. I see recurring names: Gustavs and Cecilias and Ludwigs. At least two of each. And then I notice it.

My heart stops for a few beats.

There's an area of ground covered with what

looks like the top of a barbecue or half an oil drum. It's smoking from a small chimney at one end. I've read about these. Thought we might have needed one for Mum, although in the end the ground in Karlstad cemetery was thawed enough to dig. But up here it's colder. Up here in Toytown trapped between Utgard forest and hills and frozen rivers, up here in this frost pocket, up here the permafrost runs deep and true and the earth only thaws out properly in early May.

The heating device is connected to two tall propane tanks. The snow's melted all around and I can actually feel the heat coming off the thing and it's comforting even though I hate to admit it. This will be where the broken body of Mr Gustav Grimberg, CEO of Grimberg Liquorice, will be laid to rest tomorrow afternoon.

The surrounding graves have also thawed a little. I can see bunches of wilted flowers with black petals, and piles of mussel shells, and on one, a small one, not an ancient one, I notice a stone carving of a toy truck.

It's like I've been punched in the throat.

'*Lilla* Ludo,' it says, and I almost have to turn away, suddenly aware of what I'm standing on. '1998-2005' it says. 'Beloved and much missed' it says. 'Son of Gustav and Anna-Britta and brother of Karin' it says.

I step back and walk away to catch my breath. It's cooler over here near the perimeter wall, away from the propane grave heater.

Maybe I wouldn't feel like this if it wasn't for Mum, for the fact that I haven't visited her since the burial. I don't really believe in it and neither did she for that matter. When someone's gone, they're gone. But that little boy's grave and that warm plot are altogether more haunting.

I take the chocolate from my pocket and snap off a line and it's hard and frozen solid, but then it thaws on my tongue and the roof of my mouth coats with its cheap cocoa-butter velvet and I feel better. Sugar hits my blood. I take the Leica binoculars from the other pocket and hold them. Should I do this? I'm a reporter and I need to get a grip on the factory death. My last big story. And in a way, doing all that at arm's length is more respectful than talking to them face-to-face. I'm up here at the end of the building, at the right-hand side as you look from Storgatan. Connected to the back of the old factory building, through the archway, is a modern unit. There are nine or so vintage delivery vans, which I reckon must struggle this time of year, and then the old root barns Lena told me about. You see, a hundred years ago this was an important place. The Grimbergs would buy tons of raw liquorice from far-off countries and have the root bundles shipped all the way to little old Gavrik town to be processed into salt liquorice. Our salt cravings probably date back to Viking times, when everything was salted and brined and preserved underground, that's what Lena reckons and who am I to argue. She told me once: too much salt and you die, too little salt and you die. I see a person wearing a huge coat walking out from behind the trucks. I think it's a woman, and the barns look like gallows tonight, small cranes on wooden platforms lit with foggy white light.

I see another figure up in the attic window, maybe two or three figures, all dimly lit by low-watt light bulbs. Rumour is an old woman lives up there, Cecilia Grimberg, dripping with diamonds and pearls, but I don't know, people like to talk. And I might have once asked why a family like the Grimbergs bother with cheap low-watt light bulbs if they're so damn wealthy and then Mum might have said, on one of her better days, she might have said, well Tuva, maybe that's why they're so damn wealthy in the first place.

I don't understand the attic window. It slopes at forty-five degrees and it's not like that through subsidence, it's like that through design. Makes me uncomfortable. I step away and tighten the scarf around my neck and my cheeks are numb with cold. In the distance I can see tower blocks built in the seventies, families in their cubic living spaces, TV lights flashing from the windows; they're all warm up there with their beef-mince tacos and their salt liquorice and their wholesome family lives.

I trudge through snow, more aware of the graves beneath the white, more thoughtful of the souls down there than I was earlier tonight, and head back to the ruin. I have an urge to look one more time, a yearning to see that angry spray-paint smiley, so I step inside the ruin and David Ghostwriter Holmqvist is standing on top of the altar stone.

CHAPTER 6

He's dressed in black.

'David?'

My voice fails me as I try to say his name.

'David?' I try again.

He stays at the rear of the ruin, his pale face glowing against the thick stone walls, snow falling between my body and his.

'I saw you walk up from the street,' he says, like that's a good enough reason to ambush me in this twelfth-century church skeleton.

I pad closer to him and the stillness returns; the heavy lead-topped walls holding back the wind like they've done for a thousand cold winters.

'I'm heading home,' I say, checking the exit. 'Are you okay?'

He makes a kind of 'oh, you know' shrug and I notice the scar above his lip as it lights up in the snow glare.

'New project,' he says.

I want to get back out in the open.

'I'm heading to my car now,' I say.

He nods and tightens his hat strap and joins me and together we wade through our old boot prints to the entrance of the church ruin, the arch so low we both have to duck to walk through it.

Holmqvist looks up toward the factory chimneys.

'I'm not convinced it was suicide,' he says. 'Such a strange choice of death.'

'What do you mean?'

'I've written several suicides and I've researched all the available methods. I've read about them all at some length, and an intelligent person would numb with pharmaceuticals and or alcohol, and then choose an exit both clean and final. And, if she or he was so inclined, a method to cause minimal pain to relatives.'

The owl in the tree hoots once and then hoots twice more.

'Not sure people think that clearly when they decide to kill themselves,' I say.

'I've come close four times.' He looks at me, straight into my eyes to judge my reaction, to read me. 'I was thinking more clearly on each one of those occasions than I usually think, and, as I'm sure you realise by now, I usually think very clearly indeed.'

He steps to the iron gate and swings it open.

'I didn't know,' I say.

'But you do know what I've lived with. You do know I've been a pariah my whole life for no reason whatsoever, so you could have perhaps imagined that I'd have researched an available exit, you could have perhaps thought that through?'

We're on the pavement now, all grey slush and

icicles and myriad footprints with what look like the same tread design. That's what old snow looks like when everyone buys their boots from ICA Maxi.

'I'm sorry,' I say, and I am. For so many things. Holmqvist was the bogeyman the whole town suspected of the Medusa murders. I mean, Jesus, he was arrested twice despite no real evidence against him. If I thought he was evil I wouldn't be talking to him right now in front of St Olov's ruin with not a living soul anywhere to be seen. 'I noticed you go into the factory earlier,' I say. 'I must pay my condolences, too.'

'No, that was . . .' and then I can't hear him because an ice wind has gathered on Storgatan and swept around the front of the factory.

'What? Say that again.'

'Doesn't matter,' he says.

'What did you say? Tell me.'

'I said it was business, the reason I visited. Book business.'

He slips a little as we cross the road by the cop shop so I grab his arm and he kind of pushes me off. Lena has switched on the Christmas lights in the office window. They look ghoulish. If she doesn't take them down by my leaving drinks next Thursday I'll have to do it myself.

'You're writing about the factory?' I ask.

'It's all hush-hush,' he says. 'But to be honest with you it's a rather exciting project. I expect you'll hear more in due time when things are officially announced.'

He looks quite smug now, the mole on his Adams apple rising and falling as he raises his chin to smile.

We get to my Hilux.

'Need a lift?' I ask. I don't want to give him a lift anywhere but I need more information. I need material for my last story.

'I'm parked in ICA,' he says. 'Business, then food. The wrong order, but there you go.'

I unlock my truck and climb in and leave the door open and switch on the engine and the heater. 'Will you be at the burial tomorrow?' I ask.

He shakes his head. 'I'm not welcome, and that's fine, I've made my peace with it. A crowd of Gavrik's masses plus myself is a recipe for disaster. No, I've paid my respects to Gustav, and I'll spend tomorrow working at home.'

I get out and scrape my windscreen and he just stands there watching me.

'Okay,' I say. 'I'm off.'

He doesn't say goodbye or wave or do anything so I reverse slowly, snow crunching under my studded tyres, and pull onto Storgatan. He's there in my mirrors, the man who wrapped his coat around me to keep me warm until the police arrived in Utgard forest last year, the man who had his German shepherd stand guard to keep the elk and the wolves and the God-knows-whats away from us.

The snowploughs have gone and my dash reads minus fourteen. Storgatan is deserted aside from

50

two men standing outside Ronnie's Bar smoking cigarettes and tapping their boots together and moving from side to side. February's hard on smokers. Smoking involves three times as much pulling on gear and pulling off gear than I have to endure, and that's saying something. There's a kid in a bright red jacket sitting at a bus stop outside the haberdashery store and he looks about thirteen. His hockey bag is bigger than he is and his stick's resting against the Perspex wall of the shelter. Winter's tough for kids and old people, tougher even than for smokers. If you're an adult, if you're aged between eighteen and eighty, then you'll most likely have a nice warm Saab and spend about zero time outside in the elements. But if you're very young or very old, if you're the most vulnerable to the cold, if you're the least able to cope with icy paths and freezing temperatures, then you'll be waiting for lifts and hiking along unploughed roads to bus stops in your heavy boots and you'll see much more of winter than you'll want to or need to.

Damp burger-scented air is rising into the sky above McDonald's and hanging there like a fast-food cloud. I pull a left and pass ICA Maxi with its frozen pyramids, its growing Matterhorns of shovelled and ploughed snow, its mountains of dirty white that will linger, protected by trapped chill, long after the ground snow has melted.

There's a Volvo with a trailer parked right out-side Tammy's takeout van like the driver thinks it's a goddam drive-thru. He's parked so close he can probably reach out of his window to the food hatch without getting out of his warm car with its Dire Straits CD and its fluffy steering wheel cover. He drives off and I park and jog over to her.

'He parked up close,' I say.

'And who can fucking blame him,' Tammy says, refilling her toothpicks and napkins, with her white-bobble hat on top of her head.

She mumbles something else but she's turned her back to me and I can't hear.

'When are you closing up?' I ask.

She turns around with a smile on her face.

'Five minutes ago. Let me clear away and we can eat in your truck, deal?'

I nod and watch her chop the last of her spring onions. She slices each one into a hundred micro-scopically thin green-and-white discs with her Japanese Global veg knife. She told me once how much her chef knives cost, even the short-bladed ones, and I thought she was joking. She packs away shrimp and egg noodles, and locks the rings of sliced spring onion into Tupperware boxes.

'Good night?'

'Three thousand, six hundred kronor – or about four hundred bucks or more than half a month's rent or about a tenth of your new hotshot Malmö monthly salary.'

I blow her a raspberry.

'I'll need it,' I say. 'You have any idea how

expensive apartments are down there? I'm going to end up living in a milk carton.'

'It's not expensive down there,' she says as she shutters up the serving hatch. 'It's dirt cheap up here and you've got comfortable with it. That's the problem, clear as ice; the locals never leave because they're locals and they think everywhere else is terrifyingly different and expensive. I was born here – I know. And then every once in a while an outsider like you comes and you get trapped here cos you get addicted to the cheapness.'

She jumps down from the back of her van carrying two white plastic bags and then she locks up and joins me and gives me a hug and a kiss on the cheek.

We sit in my Hilux, her in the passenger seat, heated seat medium, me in the driver's seat, heated seat low, blower at medium speed, the heat focussed on our feet. It's comfortable. Here with my engine running and my headlights shooting out into an endless snowfield, it is bearable.

'Like it?' she asks.

Beef panang curry, hot enough to warm my zero-kelvin heart from all these months of incessant dark and ice; steaming and mingling with perfect rice-cooker white rice and a few spicy crackers. I just smile and make a dumb pleasure noise.

We eat for ten minutes not saying much. A woman skis past us wearing a backpack with a baguette sticking out of it. Yeah, people ski to the supermarket in Gavrik, totally normal, nothing to see here. When the wind turns, my exhaust fumes get blown to the front of the truck so I see the field, the empty flat field that's as white as meringue, I see it through a grey poisonous fog. Any other time of year it would be unthinkable for Swedes to keep their car engines running, un-fucking-thinkable, we even turn them off at red lights, but in February, especially a February as cold as this one, nobody says a thing. Rules change when the mercury sinks below minus ten.

'Guess who I saw tonight?' I ask.

'Don't tell me it was that ratshit taxi driver from Utgard forest.'

'Sorry Contestant Number One, incorrect.'

'Holmqvist?' she says.

'Congratulations you've won a brand new snow-blower.'

'What's he doing these days?' she asks. 'I never hear about him since, you know.'

'Some new book project apparently, something involving the factory. He's creepy but he's not a creep, you know what I mean? Sometimes the weird-looking guy is actually the sweet guy that nobody ever picked for a sports team.'

Tammy bags up her empty plastic container and takes a swig of apple juice straight from a carton.

'Last time we talked about him we were on our way to see your mum. It was the day after,' she says.

'Yep.'

'If you want me to come with you to visit the grave, I will y'know,' she says. 'I'll stay in the car if you like, but I'll drive down with you, I'm happy to do it.'

'Come live with me in Malmö,' I say. 'Fuck this place.'

'Eighteen months of my course left and then who knows. If they need a bridge designing down there, who knows. Careful what you wish for Tuva Moody, it might just happen.'

I give her two thumbs up.

'Might have to visit Stockholm before then.'

'Why?' I say.

'Little cousin getting bullied. Shitty rich kids taking his bag on his way home from school. He's having a tough time. I remember when some rat-face guy used to wait for me after class, used to ask for my number, saying he wanted to be my friend. Scared the hell out of me. Back then my older cousin told that guy in no uncertain terms to back off. So now big cousin Tammy may need to set up some kind of ambush and kick some racist Stockholm butt. Or else just talk to his teachers.'

'Best cousin ever,' I say.

She nods her agreement.

'Many journos here from out-of-town to cover the suicide?' she asks.

'Some,' I say. 'Recognised a pair from Jönköping but they didn't stay long. Too cold for them. Too Gavrik.'

I wait around to make sure she can start her car. I've had to jump her middle-aged Peugeot three times since Christmas. And then I head back home.

There are final red bills and a post-redirection confirmation in my mailbox along with a card from Aunt Ida, Mum's sister, not that they spoke. I open it. It's a Good Luck card and it shows a black kitten playing with a horseshoe on a patch of clover. Four-leaf clover. The kitten has a pendant around its neck in the shape of a wishbone. Her paws are crossed like fingers. No message, just the card.

The entrance mats are sodden with dirty ice-water. I head up to my apartment and take a half-empty bottle of zero caffeine Coke from the fridge and top it up with rum, all the way up, full to the brim, the perfect balance, the perfect dose, and take it to bed. Can you force someone to kill themselves? Why did Gustav jump? To save his family? The factory? His reputation? When is a suicide actually a homicide?

CHAPTER 7

I wake and swallow two paracetamols, then a third, and rub cold water into my eyes. I try to put my aids in but my ears are not having it, no sir. I dig out my cream, the serious one, the fatty prescription one, and rub it gingerly into the thin hard reptilian skin within my ear cavity.

What do I wear to a funeral in February? I collapse on my sofa with a coffee and a microwaved cinnamon bun, the centre still frozen solid, to review my options. Black ski/burglar chic is what it'll have to be, with liberal amounts of underclothes.

I drive to the office. Lena and Lars are here but Nils hasn't come which is to be expected. I lock up and turn to walk up the short hill and the hearse is right there, long and dark and very much not built for Gavrik Februarys.

It looks like Mum's hearse.

I stand still and let it make its cumbersome way up the gritted hill. There's a fresh three centimetres of snow for the occasion and it's brightened up the town and covered the grit slush. It's fitting. It seems as though the factory's operational, like

57

people are working there today. They only close two days a year: Christmas Eve and Midsummer. The smoke from the one operational chimney, the left one, is black, and the air smells of burnt caramel. Bitter. The hearse passes me and I notice Anna-Britta, Gustav's widow, walking behind it all on her own. She's elegant in black with a small red brooch, and it looks like she needs more clothes on. The private ceremony's over. This is the public part. Anna-Britta focusses on the coffin through the hearse's rear window, at the man she was married to since she was eighteen, and she walks, sure-footedly, past the chimney he jumped from, and on to St Olov's.

The town is as quiet as a minute silence.

It's always quiet but today it's reverential; hushed for a man who was fifty-five years old and who pinched the wick of his spluttering candle years before it would have dimmed away quietly.

The hearse's rear wheels skid a little as it turns into St Olov's and I set off to join the crowds of people already in the graveyard. I walk in and skirt the old ruin which looks like the decaying sunken corpse of a church: the bones, the skeleton, but nothing on top, just the uprights, no innards.

I melt into the throngs of people wearing their black ski jackets and fleece-lined hats. Maybe someone here knows why Gustav killed himself? The older people are wearing their best furs and the younger people are sporting their only coats: man-made black windproof things they've bought in ICA Maxi. I can see four examples of the same design from last winter's stock and I'm not even trying.

There's Benny Björnmossen from the gun store and Bengt the hoarder from Utgard forest, and then I spot the pretty cashier from the supermarket. I can see Agnetha Hellbom who works in the factory office. She's wearing a black mink coat with a fox-trim hood. And then Henrik, her husband, the town's hotshot lawyer. He looks as shiny as a dog in a dog show but his posture's terrible. People are paying their respects to him and he looks like he's caught in a wind tunnel he's had so much work done. A short moustache sits atop his plumped lips. His cheekbones are artificially carved and his chin's too square and his skin's been pulled tight behind his ears and pinned in place. I'm looking for the new cop but I don't see her.

'Lot of people,' says Lena, approaching from my side. She looks beautiful in a dark-grey wool coat.

'Good turnout,' I say, and then I instantly regret the stupid words, words I hate, words I never heard at mum's funeral because you can't say that when only seven people turn up.

The gravestones are each topped with a strip of snow, and the east-facing edges of the stones and of the gnarled yew trees are wind-blasted with Hoare frost.

There's a hunched man in the distance, well back

from the other mourners, and his dog's almost as tall as he is.

The coffin comes through. They've carved an avenue through the snow and ridged it up each side so the procession can pass and it reminds me of Moses parting the red sea except this sea is white. No colour. Today is a black and white movie.

And then I notice the daughter. Gustav's little girl, the woman who stepped out of the taxi, the one Janitor Andersson talked about. Karin Grimberg. She's a pallbearer, front left, carrying her father with her own body along with five men. Her face is resolute and matt white and her shoulders look strong like she could carry twice the weight today even though she's a twig of a person.

We, the masses, the uninvited masses, shuffle closer to the Grimberg family burial plot. People nudge forward to secure a good position. The factory looks different in daylight, it looms larger and it looks wet, like it's secreting something; stains of moisture running up the walls and down from the ancient iron gutters.

'Beautiful coffin,' says Lars, beside me, wearing a black Muscovite hat with faux-fur trim. A vegetarian's hat. And he's right, it is beautiful, but it's still a stupid standard off-the-shelf unoriginal funeral remark. Not that I'm doing any better. I glance at Lars and I can tell he's wearing a tie. I can't see it under his coat but his neck's pinched and red like a sausage about to burst out of its skin.

The coffin's corners are curved and bevelled. It's as shiny as fresh-cut coal and it looks nothing like Mum's.

Lena takes my sleeve, not my hand, and pulls me gently toward a better observation space, closer to the ruin itself. I put on my sunglasses. Plenty of other people are wearing them, either because of snow glare or red eyes or because they're a useful shield when you're curious and you want to look. I need to look because next week I'll have to write about all this for my last ever issue of the *Posten*. And because what Thord said about incitement is bothering me. Did Gustav have an enemy? Are they here with us today? Was that public chimney jump the lesser of two evils? My sunglasses tap the tops of my hearing aids and they rattle and it's too loud so I pull them off.

A tailless cat runs over from the factory. It jumps the broad, snow-capped wall and scurries to the family grave, ignoring the throngs of stern-looking people. It sits down serenely on top of lilla Ludo's grave, the one with the stone truck, and it hisses. I have difficulty hearing things in the open air this time of year what with ill-fitting aids and so many people muttering things under their breath, but I hear the hiss clearly. This cat has one ear and it looks malnourished and it is saying 'leave us'.

The priest, a man as tall as an elk, stands by the grave, head bowed, wearing nothing more than a cassock. No scarf, no proper boots. I take my hat off to him, I really do. He talks gently to Anna-Britta

61

who is now being visibly held up by her daughter, the Goth pallbearer, Karin, and gestures for them both to move to the grave. Anna-Britta touches the corner of the coffin. People mutter things all around me and the air is perfectly still and as cold as outer space.

The coffin gets lowered down and this makes me queasy all of a sudden. The sight of dug earth and the smell of my medicinal face cream. It was the same when Mum was lowered; the same smells and the same taking from this surface world, from all of us, from above, and sinking the person down, deep down, deeper than I've ever dug or stood or laid, slowly, smoothly, and leaving the person down there in that other realm. They're supposed to rise but we sink them down.

A boy with frozen snot-trails running from his nose shrieks with delight on the other side of the graveyard, and faces and fur coats turn to him in disapproval. Their furs shimmer in the wind like they're still animal. The boy plays on. He's throwing snowballs except they're not snowballs, they're candle guards, little ice balls made by hand with love and kindness to protect the lights brought here by relatives. He picks another up and throws it at a gravestone.

'He's in a better place,' says a middle-aged man beside me in a grey ski jacket. 'No pain now.' And I wonder where these vignettes of greeting card wisdom come from. How do we know he's in a better place?

The two Grimberg women step gracefully to the grave and I can only see their backs now: one broad and elegant, one narrow and straight. Anna-Britta falters. She lets out a little scream and the crowd, the town, all of us, we hold our breath, uncomfortable somehow with that outpouring of emotion in public, in Gavrik, in Sweden, in February.

My head hurts and I can taste toothpaste on top of rum.

'Mamma has to wait till spring or else it's cremation,' I hear a woman say in front of me. She has elastic straps around her boots with studs to stop her slipping. 'We can't afford this,' she says. 'Normal people can't bury when it's cold like this.' I look around for the propane gas heaters but they've been taken away.

Anna-Britta and Karin each throw earth on to the coffin.

I see mum's oak version in front of me, down in its own hole, my chapped pale hands throwing dirt onto its lid, the final action, irreversible, the returning to nature.

Anna-Britta and Karin each drop a white lily into the deep dark pit.

I hear a low-level gasp, a noise collective but tiny, the sharp intake of a hundred breaths, and it's her, the old woman, Gustav's mother, Karin's grandmother, the lady that gave me the lump of stale bread that I'm holding right now in my coat pocket.

On the other side of the wall. A vision. Cecilia Grimberg is colour, a hundred colours and textures, a tropical bird, a psychedelic dream where tulips merge into flamingos against a turquoise sky. She steps to the wall that separates her world from ours, her lips as orange as they were last night, her hands ungloved, her nails lime-green, and she throws a bouquet of long-stemmed roses, orange and pale pink and white and deep blood-red, into the hole. Onto her son. And then she turns back.

CHAPTER 8

We all watch Cecilia walk back to the arch in the centre of the factory, and disappear. The world returns to monochrome.

The priest comforts Anna-Britta, and I sense people start to retreat in respectful mini-steps, shuffling silently away from this fresh grave, now that what was to be done has been done. It is swine cold and people can't stand still for too long.

The rabble of ski jackets and hats, a mismatch of old-world fur and new-world Thinsulate, head out through the gates of St Olov's and onto the bend of Storgatan. We move as one; hushed and careful not to slip. Black smoke bellows from the one operational chimney and, without anyone announcing anything, without any obvious organisation, we follow each other into the grounds of the factory like a troop of black beetles.

I start to look around for Lena or Lars but I can't see them anywhere. We move past Gustav's death spot and under the brick arch cutting through the old factory. We turn left through a door in the wall of the arch. There's a staircase but nobody climbs it. Two signs point upwards:

one to the office, and one to the 'Receiving Room' whatever that is. We walk without speaking, scraping and tapping our outdoor boots as we go, rubbing them on the extra mats provided, filing into the ground floor canteen.

The room is square with a kitchen and counter on one side, the side closest to the chimney base. We're in the front left half of the building as I'd see it from my office and the ceilings are high and the décor is nineteenth-century convent. Round tables, battered old metal chairs, enamel jugs of water on each table. Everyone's sitting down, unsure why we're here or who invited us but aware that this must have been the Grimberg's intention, despite none of them being here to welcome us.

'Watch it,' a woman ten years older than me says as I approach the kitchen counter.

I look down at what she's pointing to.

'Watch what?' I say.

She points again and then, not looking up, says, 'Step on a crack, break your mamma's back.'

'Sorry?' I say.

'That crack.'

There's a crack on the stone floor, perhaps from when the chimney was used as an exit for furnace smoke rather than just the final stage of the air extraction system to breathe liquorice air out into Gavrik.

'She's dead,' I say.

The woman looks at me.

'My mother,' I say. 'She's already dead.'

She looks down at the crack again and then turns and walks away. Serves her right. But I step over the crack, not on it, no point in tempting problems.

The spread is better than the room. Thermoses of coffee and tea, boxes of Grimberg salt liquorice, slices of kladdkaka chocolate cake. It's all homemade here, well, factory-made I guess, by the kitchen staff in hairnets and aprons. I take a slice of apple-and-cinnamon cake and a cup of coffee and go find a seat.

There's a free spot on Lena's table although not directly next to her. I smile at the men either side of me, and sit down.

The conversation in the canteen is hushed. The high ceiling and the subdued voices play hell with my aids so I turn down the volume. You'd think I was just pushing my hair behind my ears if you saw me. I'll lip-read instead. I don't get one hundred per cent of the words, not even close, but the skill, and the fun, is in the deciphering and the gap-filling. Interpreting body language helps. I take a fork to my cake and the man beside me, I recognise him, I think he's a delivery driver here, I've seen him climb into one of the Grimberg trucks, he sucks air through his teeth.

He looks like a younger version of Janitor Andersson. I look at the hairs sprouting from his nostrils, then turn back to my cake and he sucks air through his teeth again.

'Can I help you?' I ask.

'Nice cake,' he says.

I smile-frown.

'Best not let it fall.'

'What?'

'The cake.'

I frown at him. No smile this time.

'If it falls over the saying goes you'll never marry.'

I knock the cake over with my fork and then I pick it up with my hand and knock it over again and then I eat it in two anaconda mouthfuls.

This place is the reason why Gavrik doesn't have more cafes and restaurants. Lars explained it all to me my first month here. The factory employs over four-hundred locals, if you include the delivery drivers, and they all get fed, for free, on-site. If this factory had fallen down last century then my three years here would have been a lot more tolerable.

I sip coffee, the rum from last night a distant memory, a memory asking me if I'd like another drink, just a couple tonight, maybe three.

People are getting into their stride all around me now. They're talking louder, the hush of dignified funeral etiquette long forgotten, and they're talking freely. There's a pink shrimp of a guy opposite me, mid-forties, parking-inspector moustache, and he says, 'It's old money, all this, they're worth a fortune what with all the artwork, three Edvard Munchs and a Gauguin in the Grand Room upstairs, that's what I heard. Biggest producer of salt liquorice in the country.'

Third biggest, I want to say to him.

And then a woman with auburn hair and a purple ski jacket, the clash is so extreme it kind of works, she perks up without having been invited to join the conversation, and she says, 'It's cowardly if you ask me. Easy way out, off that chimney.'

Double doors with cracked safety glass open to let someone in and now I can see through to the new part of the factory. There are women and men out there in hairnets making jet black liquorice on today of all days.

'They're working,' I say to myself.

The man next to me, the cake man who looks like the janitor, he mumbles something but I can't hear him clearly, his diction's poor and his tongue looks too big for his mouth.

'Sorry?'

He talks again but now he has a mouthful of kladdkaka cake, the shiny chocolate sticking to his gums as he chews, half an incisor covered in cocoa butter and flour and sugar.

'I'm deaf.' I point to my hearing aid. 'Can't hear you.'

He chews and stares at my ear for a while, then licks his teeth.

'You don't look deaf.'

If this wasn't a weird post-funeral coffee party I'd take this guy apart.

'What were you saying?' I ask.

'Only close down two days a year, Christmas

and Midsummer. Today they're working at half capacity out of respect.'

'They might have closed out of respect,' I say.

'Grimberg's wife would never do that,' he says. 'Most ambitious of all of them. Probably celebrating right now, up there counting her kronor. Always wanted to run this place and now she is.'

He gets up and taps his nose and leaves.

Benny Björnmossen's here and he's looking pretty good, like he just got back from Tenerife or someplace. But I can't see the new cop.

'They live upstairs, didn't you know?' says a woman behind me. I can hear her quite clearly, she speaks well, like a regional radio presenter who wants to be heard. 'Huge place, biggest home in the town, palatial, all the luxuries right above our heads.' She sniffs. 'Gold taps. Six bathrooms.'

'You got it all wrong,' says a man to her left. I turn and look at the stoat face on this man, all sparse facial hair and scabby cheeks and little ears set too far back on his head. He is at least half stoat this guy, maybe sixty per cent. 'The family, what's left of them, they live in a big mansion on Lake Vänern. Lovely place it is, all servants and well away from the likes of you and me. Upstairs is just their townhouse is all.'

I stand up and gesture to Lena that I'm leaving. I tighten my scarf and walk out onto the sodden rugs and gaze left up that staircase toward the Receiving Room. Receiving what? The walls are covered in paintings and photos, and the stone steps

70

are carpeted down the centre with a red runner bolted to the staircase with brass rods. I need to get up there and work out this family. Work out why Gustav really jumped. I step out and that smell of burnt caramel hits the back of my throat. A delivery truck enters through the gates. It looks vintage, maybe late seventies. On the side of the truck someone's spray-painted 'soon' in bile yellow.

I zip up my jacket to higher than I like it. My phone beeps so I pick it out of my pocket. David Holmqvist. I open the message.

'Farewell dinner at seven. My house. Bring nothing.'

CHAPTER 9

My dash reads 18:10 and minus fifteen degrees and apparently I'm overdue for a service. Not my problem. I drive behind a snowplough in my fleece-lined jeans, no long johns required with these, and scratchy wool jumper. As I head down Storgatan I notice white glows from second-floor windows, people using their SAD lamps to harvest a little bonus serotonin before they embark on their Saturday nights at Ronnie's Bar or McDonald's.

The town is churned slush and it's sparkling in my headlights. I drive past ICA Maxi and on through the underpass beneath the E16. There's always graffiti under here but now there's new art joining the old and this is fluorescent yellow so it leaps out at me as I drive. CALL HOME it says. I catch it in my rear-view mirror as I drive up and out toward Utgard forest. CALL HOME.

The world darkens but the snow becomes whiter out here, untrodden and ungritted, pure white nothingness in every direction. I see the sign to Mossen village and turn right onto the gravel track. My truck shakes.

I rev past Hoarder's caravan and past Viggo's red cottage. There's a half-finished building project in his garden, maybe a new shed or garage, and his taxi's in the driveway with the 'Careful, Kids on Board' sign up on the roof. I accelerate up the hill and my tyres slide around a little but then they get caught in the grooves. Above this point is just the wood-carving sisters and then the man himself. With so few cars driving up and down the track, there are two deep grooves carved into the hardened snow and I may as well be driving on goddam train tracks because I have no capacity to turn whatsoever. I skid on the top of the hill and drive through the boggy section. It's pretty up here in winter. It's all sparkly ice, perfectly flat on top of the water; uniform, with clumps of reeds poking through, their heads like spiked Swarovski baubles.

The smoke from the sisters' workshop smells good. When I drive around in wintertime interviewing sources or watching ice hockey finals I smell woodsmoke every day. People keep their fires on. Even those with modern fully-insulated houses need to light their log burners in February and it makes the town smell better. The sisters aren't working as I drive past their open-fronted workshop, must have packed up carving for the night.

I brace myself for a confrontation with David's German shepherd or Alsatian or whatever it is when I park up but it's not here, and neither is the chain-link fence spanning each veranda post that used to keep the beast penned in. It's just the house with its mirrored windows, and David's car plugged into the socket on a stick so his engine stays fully charged. An orange dog-collar hangs from a hook. I wrap my scarf around my neck and over my mouth and pick up the bottle of screw-cap Pinot Grigio I bought with me and head to the front door.

Opera music. I knock and wait, shuffling from side to side and blowing into the scarf over my mouth to try to keep my face from frostbiting off.

'You're here,' he says, opening the door, a blast of warm air meeting me like entering H&M in December. Honestly, these temperature variations are ridiculous. Can be twenty-five below outside and twenty-five above inside. Passing through fifty degrees in less than a metre. It isn't normal.

'Thanks for the invite,' I pass him the screw-cap bottle and he takes it like it's a soiled nappy but then forces a kind of kinked smile and ushers me inside. There's a new carpet, a circular grey one right inside the entrance. 'This is nice,' I say, pointing to it.

'Hate the thing but I bring it out each winter to absorb boot drips and save my oak boards.'

I take off my coats and hang them up as neatly as I can. I slip off my boots and place them on his rack.

He leads me into the stainless steel kitchen.

'Didn't see your dog outside?'

He looks at me with genuine sadness. 'It didn't work out I'm afraid. But the good news is that he's living on a farm outside Munkfors and from what the farmer tells me, he's jolly happy to be there. Might even father some pups. All for the best. Wine?'

He shows me a bottle of white Burgundy that looks like it costs more than my ski jacket. Must have ordered it from Systembolaget. They probably had to get it sent over from Stockholm or Karlstad and I reckon my pinot will probably end its short life in a sauce if it's lucky.

'Just one glass.'

He pours me half a glass and tells me he'll give me half a glass of red with the main course because I really ought not miss the red, it's a respectable Bordeaux, very respectable, so I agree and then I notice the penis on the chopping board.

I point to it.

He smiles.

'I'm sorry,' I say. 'I knew you'd be cooking something exotic but I'm not sure I can eat that.'

'You've probably had it before.'

What's that supposed to mean?

'Braised ox-tongue is a winter favourite, a must-eat at this time of year. Would you at least try a little?'

'Tongue?' I ask.

'Tongue,' he says, and then he licks his lips in the way I've seen before, his own tongue, licking to the left like a lizard, then back to the scar in the centre of his lip, then to the right.

'My grandma used to cook it for us,' I say. 'Sorry, I thought it was . . .' I trail off. 'My mistake.'

He passes me a half-full glass of white wine and gestures over to the expensive designer furniture in the living room. We sit opposite each other and his trouser leg lifts a little to reveal a strip of leg so hairy it's hard not to stare. Maybe he gets hairier at winter time? I know I do.

'I asked you all the way out here because of what you said in the churchyard.'

He stops talking and I anxiously try to remember what the hell I said.

He just looks at me.

'Sorry,' I say.

'Exactly,' he says.

'Sorry?' I say again.

He nods.

I open my eyes wider and take a wasabi pea from the bowl on the table between us.

'Nobody has ever said sorry or that they feel sorry for what I've endured,' he says. 'The police didn't apologise for arresting me twice for the Medusa murders. Nothing. But you actually felt bad for me. For me thinking about ending it all. You actually made the effort to tell me in the churchyard. You made me feel like I am not alone.'

I wasn't expecting this level of openness and now I feel even more awkward. Out here in this house in this forest, I feel exposed.

'I meant it,' I say.

He nods and looks up at the ceiling and I stare

at the mole on his Adam's apple. Best view I've ever had of it.

'I have an exciting book deal,' he says, changing the subject.

'That's great, congratulations.'

I'm pleased we're not talking about feelings anymore. I don't do that sober. I can hardly do it drunk.

That crooked smile appears for a moment and then leaves.

'First book to be released in my own name, it's what I've been waiting years for. Its working title is *The Liquorice Factory* and it's really a kind of family saga crossed with some post-industrial history mixed with a little misery memoir.'

'Okay.'

He sounds happy but he looks sad.

'I got the green light from the publisher months ago and Gustav and I have been hard at work ever since, me interviewing him and reading through archive material and so on. Gustav had a lot to get off his chest. He told me once that if you look up toxic masculinity in the dictionary you'd see a photo of his father.' Holmqvist snorts. 'Gustav felt belittled and, what with the childhood I endured, I could sympathise. And then the unthinkable happened.'

I think back to the watermelon crack.

'It was dreadful.'

'Yes, well anyway, now my book's proving rather more challenging.'

I remember being upstairs in this house last year and checking out the guest room, the one with hundreds of white box files, all organised in alphabetical order, all containing reams and reams of graph paper and intricate handwritten notes.

'A book must be the last thing on their minds now,' I say.

'That's as maybe,' he says. 'But there are deadlines. Contracts.'

'They seem to be a closed shop.'

'Oh, you have no idea,' he says. 'You have absolutely no idea. There's a code of silence, you see. The workers in the factory, on the floor, in the canteen, in the trucks, in the office, they all owe a debt to the Grimbergs and the Grimbergs owe a debt to them.'

I frown and he uncrosses his legs and then recrosses them and his oven beeps and he looks over to it and then back to me.

'The average stamper or quality-control taster has been working in that factory since school and maybe their mother was a stamper or worked in the canteen and maybe their father and their grandfather was a delivery driver if he wasn't up at the pulp mill. It's a generational business in the same way as a large coal mine or steel works. It's codependency, if you understand what I mean, they need each other. Excuse me a moment.'

Holmqvist stands up and walks over to the tongue that looks like a T-Rex cock. He gestures to the dinner table, a glass-topped thing, and then he puts a tea towel over his arm and brings out two plates that look like they don't contain any bull tongue. I grab a fistful of wasabi peas and stuff them in my mouth because who knows how much of this guy's cooking I can stomach tonight. The burn in my mouth is pleasing.

I sit down at the table and he pours me San Pellegrino fizzy water and places a bowl down in front of me. Salad leaves with shiny little chicken livers and I can handle that, it's offal and it's very David Ghostwriter Holmqvist, but silently I thank him for not making everything so out of my comfort zone that I go home hungry.

'Duck tongues,' he says.

I look down and yep, they're tongues alright, my mistake, apologies. How many life decisions did I balls up to be in Utgard forest right now staring at a bowlful of duck tongues.

'Quite delicious, don't worry. A gamey, delicate preamble before the main event.'

I cut into one and it's small enough to be unintimidating although the texture is unpleasantly muscular and I get flashbacks to the troll locked in my basement, the pine shin-high figure with its animal tongue, now probably shrivelled to nothing, and a surprise in his pants. I'm still not comfortable with the wood-carving sisters or their creations. Expensive carved trolls with human fingernails and human hair and human eyelashes.

'Delicious,' I say. I'm not lying actually, they're

tasty in their star-anise sauce, but that texture. 'Maybe the Grimberg daughter will speak to you?'

'She won't even look in my direction,' he says, swallowing a whole tongue.

There's something disturbing about swallowing a whole tongue. Tongue sliding down tongue. It's against nature.

'The family are generous to a tee, it is their downfall. Each successive generation is taught from birth that they owe the community everything they have. The company was built on the hard work of the great-grandparents of today's workers and the family would be nothing without Gavrik's residents, they actually tell their children this.'

'I guess it's true,' I say, slicing a tongue in half.

'Quite so, but you see it's a dreadful burden to carry. Gustav and his father refused to modernise the factory beyond that add-on at the back because machines and processing plants would have cut the workforce by as much as sixty per cent. But the company is unviable at current levels, or pretty much unviable. The Grimbergs are accustomed to life's luxuries, you only need look at their Receiving Room to see it. So the book deal is their saviour, one of several windfalls that have helped them over the years.'

'Oh?'

'You'll have to read the book for all the details,' he says with a glint in his eye. 'From now on I'll have to do my best to fill in the blanks without the Grimberg women helping me. The deadline can't be moved, you see.'

I sense an opportunity.

A chance.

CHAPTER 10

This will be my last big Gavrik story and I might just have found a way in.

'I can help,' I say eagerly, the offer crystallising and clarifying in my head as the words pass my lips.

'I don't see how.'

I take a sip of the wine and the oven beeps again so he excuses himself and clears our bowls, mine with three complete tongues, the largest three, hidden deftly beneath a romaine lettuce leaf. He pulls on a pair of thin latex gloves, the transparent kind, I can see his knuckle hair through them, and gets to work with his knife.

Holmqvist brings over two hot plates of ox tongue, his hand protected by a tea towel, and places them down. Mine is sliced thinly and covered in jus and sprinkled with flat-leaf parsley and sea-salt crystals. His is whole.

'Where were we,' he says, savouring his meal, sticky taste-buds clearly visible on the top of his whole tongue like the nubs of some hideous Lego brick.

'I can help you,' I say again.

'No, sorry. I work alone. I don't think anyone can help me except the Grimberg women. I'll have to keep pushing.'

'The more you push the more they'll push back,' I say.

'We have a contract,' he says.

'They'll give you the bare minimum, then. The book will be dull.'

He looks agitated now, squirming on his chair and scratching the back of his hand.

'Let me talk to them,' I say, and he's shaking his head before I've even finished the sentence.

'What makes you think . . .'

'It's what I do,' I say. 'Let me talk to them. Listen to them.'

He squirms and scratches the palms of his hands. 'But I have a routine, a ritual. I can't write with another person. I write alone. Always have.'

'You still can,' I say, working out the details in my head. 'I'll research for you. Freelance. I'll give you all my research notes. You pay me. You write the book.'

'A short-term research contract?'

'Exactly.'

He scratches his neck and then his ears.

'So, in return for you interviewing the three remaining Grimbergs – Cecilia, Anna-Britta and young Karin – I would, rather, my publisher would, pay you?'

I nod.

'I'd have to talk to my editor.'

'Twenty-thousand kronor,' I say. 'Up front.' I feel like a movie gangster but really I need to uncover if Gustav had enemies, anyone with enough leverage to force him to make that fatal jump.

'I'll have to check,' he says.

'I'm leaving town soon,' I say. 'And I am good, David. Very good. I can start on this right away. I'd work on it alongside my *Posten* reporting. And I'll work in the evenings.'

He chews on his lip and looks at me and then looks up at the ceiling and then looks at me again.

'Twenty-thousand kronor,' he says. 'Half on completion of the interviews. Half on publication.'

'All up front,' I say.

'Take it or leave it,' he says, half filling my glass with red wine.

I feel hot in my socks. This is my way in.

'I'll take it,' I say.

He looks at my plate. 'Excellent. Now, eat up, it's getting cold. Bon appetite.'

I have one week left in Toytown and I still have to move out and return my truck and attend a 'surprise' leaving party at Ronnie's Bar, and I have to complete a final print for the *Posten*, one I can be proud of. This time it'll be fixed Friday and distributed Saturday. Only the second time it's ever happened. Industrial action at the printers in Gothenburg; they're striking over working hours. Good for them. Now I'll need to juggle all that with researching Holmqvist's book but at least I can ask the Grimbergs about Gustav's jump. I can dig.

'I'll do a good job,' I say, but he's lost in the art of slicing through his slab of tongue. It's black at the licking end and thick and pink at the throat end and it looks as tough as a saddle. I drink a little of his red wine and keep it in my mouth and then I fork in a thin slice of bull tongue. Tastes a bit like rare, fillet steak, at least when it's masked by wine. I chew and then hesitate, my throat asking me if this is something I really want to swallow, and then I force it down.

'After what we went through with Medusa and all, I trust your instincts,' he says. 'I'm not liked in this town, everyone thinks I'm strange and really I don't much care anymore as long as I can write up here in peace, but I do take this project very seriously indeed. I'm putting my faith in you.'

I'm flattered.

'Email me your bank details so I can prepare the transfer.'

He takes a business card from his pocket and slides it across the table to me.

'Do I get a deadline?' I ask.

His upper lip bulges as his tongue moves up over his top teeth.

'Next Sunday.'

That suits me because after that I'll be living in a hotel by the sea overlooking a clear horizon, near a city with an art gallery and excellent Indian and Lebanese food and a department store and a decent airport. I'll be waiting to move into a nice little apartment and I'll have already paid the first month's rent.

He has a thick wedge of tongue on his fork, the taste buds glistening with sauce, and he places it back down on his plate.

'The Grimberg women don't like me,' he says with a wry laugh.

'They're mourning,' I say. 'Their world has shattered.'

'They need this deal, Tuva. And so do I. You should also speak with the janitor and a few other long-serving employees, they don't open up to me either, and then submit your typed notes and we can all walk away happy.'

'I'll do my best.'

He smiles and rolls up his sleeves and my God this man is half ape. He clears away the plates of tongue and I'm relieved, my stomach unclenching at the prospect of dessert. You can't serve offal for dessert, not even he would do it.

'Raspberries, basil, cracked black pepper and vanilla mascarpone.'

He says mascarpone like it rhymes with Al Capone and I snatch the plate from his hand greedily, happy for something to enjoy rather than endure.

'How was your Christmas, Tuva?'

'Didn't celebrate,' I say, images of Mum's grave in my mind, candleless, weeds working their way up from deep underneath the snow and earth. I think back to the fish fingers I ate for Christmas lunch in front of the TV. Then in bed. Bottle of vodka. No glass. The fish fingers coming back up. The dread that I didn't do enough for her, that I was the one person that could have let her go with a kind word in her ear and I did not. I could've whispered, 'don't worry Mum' or even just, 'I'm here, it's okay' but I did not.

'Wasn't in the mood,' I say.

'It was a horrible end to the year,' he says, misunderstanding me, thinking I was talking about Medusa. 'I couldn't have written such a thing.' He downs the remainder of his wine. 'I don't celebrate either, never do.'

'What are they like?' I ask.

'The Grimbergs?'

I nod.

'They're intriguing, I must say. Kind of quasi-aristocratic and incredibly superstitious, well-read, and that means a lot coming from me. They're all bright, hard-working, stoic to the point of I don't-know-what. You might need to spend hours and hours with them to gain their trust.'

'Actually the biggest story for the *Posten* is Gustav's suicide, 'I say, 'so I'll need to interview them for that. Kill two birds.'

'Ah,' he says, his eyes pained.

'What?'

'Don't call it a suicide when you talk to them, call it "the accident" or "the tragedy" or something like that. They don't think like you and me.'

87

I don't think like you, mate. I don't know anyone who does.

'Fine,' I say.

He smiles an arrogant smile and clears away our dessert bowls; mine wiped clean, his hardly touched.

'Are they tempted to sell the factory now Gustav's dead?'

'The vultures are circling,' he says. 'That lawyer with the stoop and the sculpted face, the one with all the real estate, he's very interested, well he would be wouldn't he? Now that my lawyer's retired, Hellbom has the whole town to himself. A monopoly. And what with his wife working there, they could modernise and make a fortune. But the Grimbergs won't sell. Over their dead bodies. And this book deal should help them keep the place in business.'

He stretches an arm out to me over the table.

'Glad to work with you,' he says.

I reach out tentatively to meet his grasp, his knuckles sliding next to mine. 'Same,' I say.

I pull on my outdoor gear, happy for the unexpected and very much needed twenty-thousand kronor and imagining my next apartment, maybe one with a partial sea-view and a washing machine. Then my hearing aid beeps a battery warning and I rattle my key fob, two spare batteries in there, I never go anywhere without them. I say goodbye and drive away. I stuck to my one glass limit and that feels pretty good. Every evening is a test and I passed this one with flying colours. I drive by the sisters' woodsmoke and head slowly down the hill and as I pass Viggo's cottage I notice lights and exhaust fumes in my rear-view mirror and his Volvo pulls out onto the track and follows me.

CHAPTER 11

Viggo's on a job, that's all, maybe taking someone to Karlstad Central Hospital or to Ronnie's Bar. Big deal. But I accelerate and switch my lights to full and look at my phone because it might be a big deal with this creep, it just might be. He locked me in the back of his taxi once before and scared the colour right out of me.

I'm sweating.

Cold sweat, chills under my sleeves and up my calves. Nobody else around. Empty roads. My mirrors are bright with his headlights and he's too close to my rear bumper. Nobody drives like this on snow, not even on a ploughed asphalt road. If I brake he will hit me. So I accelerate, opening up a small gap, but then I see the bend near Bengt's place and slowly tap my brake, pumping it gently, partly to show the shithead behind that I'm slowing down, and partly to keep a grip on this ice. I skid little skids but I steer out of them and the carved tracks help me to stay on the road. I make the turn and carry on at about fifty kph and then indicate and turn left and judder up onto the main road and accelerate like hell.

He's still following me.

The gap's closing.

Why wouldn't he be driving this way, there's nothing in the other direction, just an empty road leading to a junkyard and then Spindelberg prison. But the distance between us is too small. Unsafe. I spray antifreeze on my rear windscreen and turn my heated seat to low, sweat beading on my neck and my upper lip. I can make out his face and his sallow grey eyes. He turns his headlights to full beam and they flash in my rear-view mirror and now I can't see him back there. I wipe the rear screen and he's coming faster now, no one else on the road. I can feel him behind me, his bumper, my nerves on edge, his Volvo right there, with its 'Kids on Board' safety sign erect on the roof. He dips his headlights and starts flashing his hazards. What the hell is that, some sort of message? Some sort of Nordic distance flirting? My heart races and I put my foot down and nudge one ten which is way too fast on this road.

He dips his beams and switches his interior lights on and I can clearly see his grey, pallid face and I can see the objects hanging from his rear-view mirror. I can't make out detail but I remember from before. A thumb-sized *hustomte* troll. A crucifix. And a Swiss army knife.

I head under the underpass, my hands tight on the steering wheel, my body stiff, my mind as focussed as it can be; the taste of hot dead tongue still lingering on my warm live tongue. And then he turns up and off without indicating and joins the E16 northbound, toward the pulp mill. He's gone. Of course he didn't indicate. The worst men don't indicate. Ever. It's like they feel entitled to turn whenever they feel like it.

I breathe and slow down to sixty.

Seven days, Tuva. Seven days and then out of this place for good. I slump in my seat and rub my eyes. I grab the pack of wine gums on the passenger seat and squeeze it with my hand until it bursts and then I take three and put them in my mouth to get rid of the bull taste.

The colours outside change. It was all white in the woods, all unbothered snow and clear ice-streams, motionless over granite. Here, approaching town, the white picked out by my headlights is grey from exhaust fumes and grit and salt and boot prints, and the colour, what colour there is, is man-made and uncoordinated; bright jarring flashes of windproof sportswear and kid's sledges.

I pass between ICA Maxi and McDonald's and I'm starting to wonder if I'm getting paranoid here in my last week. The chimney suicide unsettled me. And Viggo Svensson was on a job, an urgent pick-up, and he drove from his house to the motorway. That's all.

I could do with a puritanical cocoa-only smug month and maybe I'll do that in March. Or April.

When I park I take the bottle of water from my truck because it'll burst if I just leave it there, and head upstairs to my apartment. There are three empty black suitcases in my living room next to my PlayStation. One's old and I bought the other two in Karlstad for the move. Straightforward. That's my life. No pets, no relationships, no furniture, no heirlooms, no plants. No living things whatsoever.

I unpeel one of those sheet face-masks. This one's peppermint and I reckon I could do with about six consecutive treatments. Just fucking wallpaper me. I look like a horror movie but my skin's hurting which means it's getting a drink. I pull out my aids and pour three fingers of white rum and check the headlines on my iPad. Police ask drivers to be prepared and have a phone and blankets when they travel. Goddam February. Living here is like living in Siberia except our broadband's ten times faster.

I sleep an agitated sleep and wake up and turn off my pillow alarm. Holmqvist asked me to meet him under the factory arch at 9pm and that's where he is when I drive past at 8:55. I park at my office and walk over to him standing right there in Gustav's death spot. Right there.

'Morning,' he says.

'Morning,' I say, not wanting to get too close.

He moves away from the arch and he's got a confidence I haven't seen before, like he's guiding me around a show-home and he's ready to sell it to me, like he's prepared his spiel and he's pretty happy with his product.

'Look from back here,' he says, gesturing to the

railings, razor burns raw under his chin. 'Better view.'

We stand with our arctic coats resting against the iron railings, looking up at the building.

'Let's start with the basics. Built in 1839 from local brick, the tallest non-ecclesiastical structure in Värmland, outside of Karlstad of course, for ninety-seven years. Seven men died during construction. The scaffolding failed.' He looks up at the chimneys and then back down to the archway. 'Most of the site is deconsecrated land.'

'Sorry?' I say.

'It was church land before, belonged to St Olov's.' He points to the ruined church and then back to the factory. 'There are graves underneath us, hundreds of ancient tombs. What you can see here used to be the factory in its entirety. The ground floor left of the arch was the cooling and stamping rooms, and the furnace under the chimney to heat that part of the building. Used to be that the right side of the arch, ground floor, was the shredding and mixing and heating area, big vats of sugar syrup, and a furnace there under that chimney.'

I stare at the death chimney.

'Nowadays all the manufacturing goes on at the corrugated-steel structure at the rear left, behind the old stamping rooms, which are now in fact the canteen, you following?'

'I think so.'

'Upstairs hasn't really changed. Left of the arch:

the offices and archives. Over the arch: the Receiving Room, you'll be working from there mostly. To the right of the arch is the most luxurious part of the whole building: the residence. Which includes the "Grand Room". I hope you'll get access, someone needs to.'

'You haven't been inside?'

'Follow me.'

He walks to the arch and I do as he says. It's not swine cold today, just about minus-seven cold. It is discomfort chilblain cold not death cold.

'This way,' he says, pointing to the staircase I saw after the burial.

I follow him up the stone risers with their red carpet runner and brass poles. The pictures lining the walls are mostly black-and-white, a big house by a lake, wide-angle photos of the entire staff from the thirties and forties, a picture of a small boy with a kitten. Two of the photos are hung upside down and three have sheets covering them. We get to the top and I feel a chill around my neck.

'Offices that way,' says Holmqvist. 'Elegant staircase, isn't it?'

It is. A high ceiling and mustard-yellow wallpaper. Faded. More paintings shrouded with sheets of linen.

'Why are some of . . .'

'The Receiving Room,' says Holmqvist. 'Come this way.'

He opens a heavy door inlaid with old tapestries

95

in the panels, and I follow. He's acting like he owns the place. The room's lit by a sprawling chandelier and the bulbs are flickering like they might all expire at any moment, like they're original from 1839.

'Now, tell me, what do you think?'

I start to answer but then he says, 'Exquisite, isn't it? Finest room in Gavrik, no question.'

Someone coughs in the doorway we just stepped through and now I feel like a nosey babysitter roaming around rooms I haven't been invited to visit.

'You must be Ms Moodyson?'

I approach and hold out my hand and do some godawful little curtsy type-thing I haven't done since I was about seven years old and that I hated even back then.

'My name's Anna-Britta Grimberg, pleased to meet you.'

She has a kind face, all eye lines and rushed make-up and burst capillaries. Her eyelashes are extraordinarily, almost painfully, short. They're practically non-existent and she does what she can with mascara but gets more on her lids than her lashes.'

'I'm sorry for your loss,' I say.

She nods like she doesn't want to talk about that with me. Not now, not ever.

'You're here to assist with the book? You can talk to myself and my mother-in-law and my daughter in this room. You can talk to the employees, wherever they happen to be working, but please, I ask you, do be considerate. My employees need to focus and they're all in mourning so please bear that in mind.'

I thought she was going to ask me to be gentle around her ailing mother and her grieving kid, but no, apparently I need to look out for the factory workers.

She doesn't acknowledge Holmqvist or talk to him or even look in his direction.

'Andersson will give you a tour,' says Anna-Britta. 'I trust that will be okay?'

I nod and try to ask her about her husband but she excuses herself, her well-cut charcoal dress leaving the room and replaced by Janitor Andersson in his overalls and fluorescent-yellow fleece.

'I've got pipes to lag. Let's get on.'

Suddenly the elegance in the room drains away and Holmqvist looks awkward next to Andersson who, like Anna-Britta, completely ignores him.

'Tuva, I'll be getting off back home,' says Holmqvist. 'Call me if you have any questions.'

'Wait,' I say, Andersson itching to leave this panelled room with its Gustavian furniture and the unlit tiled fireplace in one corner. 'You want me to talk to the staff and the family, but what do you need in particular?'

'Everything,' he says. 'They don't, I mean, they haven't spoken to me yet. You need the personal angle, the quotes and the insight into the generations who've worked here.' He looks

97

at me conspiratorially, the mole on his Adam's apple rising and falling as he swallows. 'And whatever you can on the family. Gustav gave me anecdotes, but they were dry and mostly public information. You're excellent at the *Posten* with your human-interest stories.'

I'm floored by the compliment, one of the few I've ever received in this town about my writing.

'The publishers need interesting stories. Details that will sell the book,' he says.

'Pipes won't lag themselves,' mutters Andersson. 'And it'll be minus twenty tonight, that's what the *Posten* says.'

That weather report is taken, by me, from a Gothenburg paper and it's already two days old so he may as well lick his finger and stick it in the air.

'After you, Mr Andersson,' I say.

We walk downstairs and I put my hand on Andersson's shoulder and he jumps.

'What?' he says.

'Why are some of the photos upside down?'

'What a thing to ask on a day like this.'

Is there someone the family can't stand to see in those photos? Someone they're blaming for Gustav's jump? A worker or a distant relative? An ancestor?

'Why are pictures covered or hung upside down?' I ask again. 'Whose face don't they want to see? I helped you back in that ditch. Now you help me.'

He half turns and says, 'I don't owe you or nobody else nothing. Never have.'

We walk out through the arch to the rear yard. Everything on my left is modern: a one-storey steel structure with loading doors and a metal roof. To my right are old wooden barns, open to the elements except for warped roofs that I wouldn't want to walk underneath. I can see the wall of St Olov's beyond, dark yew trees lining its perimeter.

'This is where the workers come in,' says Andersson. 'No car park on site.'

'Why not?'

'Why do you think? Not enough room as it is for the trucks to come through and load up, never mind with all them Korean hatchbacks trying to fit through. You'll be out in a delivery truck tomorrow evening. Mrs Grimberg set it up. You'll get to drive along with our oldest driver, daft goat, he drives truck number one and he can fill you in on that part of the business.' He coughs and points. 'We got parking down the road past St Olov's and workers got to walk round. It ain't convenient in winter time but it works pretty good. And some of them could do with the exercise.

'Keep up,' he says, trudging through slush to a door with a sign above it that says, 'Employee Entrance'. Inside is a room with a desk and a wall-sized clocking-in machine, like something from a museum. Little cards that get stamped and a big analogue clock in the centre.

'Is that machine still working?'

'Just cos things are old don't mean they're bad, you just gotta look after them.' He tuts and opens a door to the right without looking inside.

'Toilets,' he says.

Oh, thanks. Great place to start, Mr Tourguide School-dropout. The room has cracked stained tiles and old white sinks with brown marks where the water hits the porcelain, but it's clean I think, or as clean as you can make an old communal toilet block. There are about a dozen doors at the far end and they're not good cubicle doors, not like you or I would want them to be, these are half-size things so people could stretch up and see your hair or bend down and look at your boots.

He opens another door without looking in.

'Lockers.'

It's like something out of a derelict school. Hundreds of dented locker doors, a long boot rack, coat hooks, drying cabinets humming at one end, hot cupboards for wet clothes that always smell of teenagers.

There's a row of plastic baskets near the door, each basket holding hairnets or shoe covers or face masks or latex gloves, the thin surgical kind.

'Don't just look at them,' he says. 'Put them on.'

'You're not?'

'I got pipes to lag.'

I slip blue plastic shoe covers over my boots and a hairnet over my ponytail and then start to put on a pair of gloves.

'You're not cutting or stamping, you don't need no gloves, come on.'

He leads me to the automatic double-doors and they open and he walks away in the other direction.

I step inside.

The vast room is clean and dry and sterile. It feels like a factory. The floor is rubberised in some way and it extends up the walls on each side about half a metre. I can see stainless steel vats of what I guess must be liquorice being made and stirred with stainless steel blades. Above us are extractors and aluminium air-ducts sucking air up toward the big chimney. There are workers everywhere and they look like drones. Or ants. Or worker bees. White-coated humans with identical hairnets and identical shoe covers scuttling around not looking up and not acknowledging I'm here.

I walk on.

Black liquorice snakes are being extruded through holes onto a conveyer belt and then cooled in a machine. It's alive, humming like some giant cuboidal insect. I read signs like 'Danger: Cooling Zone' and 'High Voltage'.

There are staff everywhere. They're carrying clipboards in this part of the room, reading dials and making notes. In the central area, I see long tables of people elevated from everyone else. Most of them seem to be women but it's hard to tell with these uniforms.

First, the cutters. They slice up narrow black

snakes with a skill and speed I'd expect from a surgeon or a Michelin-star chef. With a scalpel-type blade, they cut the snake into small discs and then the discs fly along the conveyer to the stampers. Each one, there must be eight of them, each one pushes what looks like a stamp you'd expect a nineteenth-century earl to seal hot wax onto his documents with, they push that down into the liquorice to produce the famous 'G' enclosed in a circle on each disc. And now I realise what Holmqvist meant about mechanisation making a difference here. If I were a management consultant or a banker, which thank The Lord Baby Jesus Christ I am not, I'd look at this get-up and visually erase seventy per cent of the workforce, and then visually install three big machines, and then visually write myself a seven-figure pay cheque.

A stamper reaches behind her back with one gloved hand, while still stamping quick-fire, and passes me a liquorice coin. Black and soft. Warm. I take it and thank her and she whips her hand back to work. She has bright red hair under her hairnet; not ginger or strawberry blonde, but bright red like a sports car, dyed red, scarlet blood-red like a shiny murder apple.

On to the quality control area. Lines of people touch sweets with their gloved fingertips and throw misshapen ones into a bin. There are three women at one end who are randomly tasting samples.

Then there's a packaging zone. Tubes and boxes

and plastic packets, the big ones you get in Gavrik cinema on the three days a week it bothers to open. The packaged goods are loaded into crates and the forklifts arrange them on pallets and drive them out of the double doors into a covered loading bay, where the vintage trucks – I got to tell you, I would not be driving a Dinky Toy truck like that on these roads in February, but they do look nice – those trucks take them to stores all over the country.

I open the door with the cracked window and step through into the canteen. A hundred faces look up at me and then look straight back down to their coffees and their cardamom buns and then Janitor Andersson taps me firmly on the shoulder.

'Come on,' he says, holding me loosely by the arm, coughing and spluttering.

I shake him off. 'You left me in there.'

'Now I'm taking you to the old factory. Haven't got all the time in the world.'

He marches out into the yard, me pulling off my hairnet which is stuck in the grip I use to keep my excuse for a ponytail in place. I drag off my shoe covers and place them all in a container by the door.

Janitor Andersson heads under the arch and takes a long key from the jailor's ring hanging on his belt. He unlocks the door directly opposite the entrance to the canteen – the key's as long as a meat skewer – and ushers me in.

'All the good gear in this side, bit cramped now, no computer hocus-pocus; all good Swedish-made steel in here. The family asked me to show you so I am.'

The room's the same size as the canteen the other side. Huge rusting vats sit rooted like redwood stumps here and there next to wooden desks and stacks of dusty conveyers.

'The old offices and lockers,' he says, pointing into the murk.

We walk through, a single bare light bulb buzzing and struggling to light the place. It's freezing. Unheated. Dank and mouldy. I see desks with old-fashioned circular dial telephones and typewriters and filing cabinets and blotters.

'All could be valuable one day, you never know,' says Andersson. 'Old man Grimberg – may he rest in peace, although I doubt he'll ever get the chance – Gustav's father I mean, not popular but he listened to me, asked my opinion, noticed I actually had a brain in my skull, he always saw this as museum potential, an attraction for passing tourists, you know the sort of thing.'

Tourists? Passing tourists? Seriously?

I walk over to the lockers. These are crammed three-high, hundreds in a small space with cracked mirrors on some of their doors and cracked mirrors on some of the walls.

'And that there's the south furnace but it hasn't been hot since before World War Two. Chimney walls are over a metre thick at the base.'

There are two doors the size of my truck doors, latched across.

'Can I look inside?'

He steps over and heaves the latch up and pulls a door.

'Don't go right in, it's not safe, vermin and all sorts with the sugar around this place, just take a look.'

I stick my neck inside and it's like a small room, originally a coal or wood-burning furnace, with the circular chimney base even deeper inside.

We step away and something catches my eye. Something scuttling. A tiny mouse or an over-size beetle. It scurries behind an old stamping table and past a shiny black line.

A wet line.

There's a dark trickle of blood flowing down into the floor drain.

CHAPTER 12

'Look,' I say, pointing to the blood.

Andersson starts to say, 'Come on, I've got pipes . . .' and then he stops. His eyes open wider. We walk closer to the dark shiny line and step around the stamping table.

Cobwebs float in mid-air.

Something very bad has happened in this space. Something irreversible.

The room is freezing cold and it is silent.

We get to the far end of the table and there's a pair of boots. My breath catches and I push myself to keep walking.

A man on the floor.

'Mary, Mother of God,' says Andersson under his breath.

I crouch down to the man but can't see him clearly, the distant light bulb not up to the job.

I take his pulse. His skin is cold.

Nothing.

'Get help,' I say. 'Call an ambulance.'

The dead man has a small puncture wound on the side of his neck. Not a slice, but a small cut. His neck is red with his own blood but it is not pumping out.

'Go!' I say, my voice returning to me. And Andersson goes.

The man's eyes are black. No, wait, they're covered. Each lid is eclipsed with a black disc. Two Grimberg Liquorice coins. But the lids aren't closed. His eyes are wide open and the coins are sitting atop his own black pupils. My own eyes start to acclimatise to the murk. He looks terrified. Like a screaming dead man from a different era with a penny on each eye. Like the myth. Coins to pay his way across the river Styx to the underworld.

There's a noise at my back.

'Move aside,' says Thord.

I step back making sure I don't tread in the blood.

'When did you find him?' asks Thord, his fingers to the man's neck.

'A few minutes ago,' I say. 'He's dead.'

Thord shines his torch at the man's face but the batteries must be dying and the beam comes and goes.

'Did you touch anything?' he asks.

'No.'

The liquorice eyes shine in the sporadic artificial light and I can see the capital 'G' on each coin and I can see the stoat features of this poor, scared man. His mouth is wide open like he's in agony. He has small ears set back and he has tufty whiskers. It's the man from the canteen. Attacked. Bled out. Murdered.

His shirt is soaking wet but it's not bloody. The torch cuts out and we're plunged into semi-darkness. I can hear Thord shaking it, but nothing. Then Janitor Andersson pulls out his phone and switches on the light. He moves closer to the body and Thord grunts his thanks.

The wound is as small as a hernia cut or a mole-removal incision. A neat slice, perhaps a centimetre long. But it is deep. The killer found the artery or the vein – I'm not sure which is which – with all the skill of a cardiac surgeon. There's a shiny line running away from this poor man and there's something stuck in the wound itself. A tooth. It looks like there's a sharpened tooth rammed into the flesh.

Was a dog involved in this attack? A killer and his dog? A wolf?

'What the . . .?' says Thord, pulling on a pair of latex gloves.

I think he's going to extract the tooth, but he moves his fingertips toward the man's gaping mouth and I see what he's really staring at. There's a shining black mass between his teeth like he's biting down on a black cooking-apple that's far too big for his mouth. The janitor moves his phone torch closer. Must be a dozen or more liquorice coins rolled into a black mass, part-melted by the man's saliva acids, grey dribble now running down his cold, still face. His jaw is locked as open as can be. He's trapped in an eternal scream with black on his eyes and black in his mouth and an animal tooth lodged in his neck.

Clouds of vapour hang in the air from Thord's lips. His breathing quickens. He has an expression which says 'this is over my pay grade'. He looks panicked.

'Stand back, give me some space,' he says.

Chief Björn arrives with the new cop. They both have torches and their torches are working. Björn looks at the scene and then he turns to his young colleague. 'Keep everyone on the site, nobody comes in or goes out. Move everyone into the main factory and control the exits. I'll join you as soon as I can.' She nods but her face says 'why is that man screaming?' and 'why is his jaw locked open?' She leaves and she ushers me and the janitor to follow her and all of a sudden I want to flee this factory and this town and never look back.

CHAPTER 13

After two hours trapped inside the modern factory waiting for the inappropriately small police force to search the building and tape up the scene, Janitor Andersson and I are instructed to give our statements to Chief Björn at the cop shop. Thord's already sealed three-quarters of the site and he looks desperate for outside forces to arrive. The Chief is business-like but I can tell even he's rattled. The exactness of the fatal wound, the dog tooth, the liquorice coins sitting atop the man's still-open eyes. The fear on his face. And the fact that a cold-blooded murderer was walking among us. *Is* walking among us.

The victim's name was Gunnarsson. Per Gunnarsson.

Björn takes my statement. He asks me what time I found Gunnarsson and if I saw anyone else around. He asks me about my whereabouts in the hours leading up to the discovery. He asks me if I disturbed the scene in any way. He asks me if I know who killed the victim.

On my way out of the station I ask the Chief a

dozen of my own newspaper questions and he just glares at me and shuts the door in my face.

'Still got them pipes to lag,' says Janitor Andersson, coughing beside me. 'Even with all this evil.'

'Who would kill that man?' I ask.

'Gunnarsson? Plenty of folk. Anyone can kill, I'll tell you that for nothing, anyone and everyone has it in them. And he wasn't well liked.'

I look at him like 'what?' and realise that, even though my heart feels hard and tight in my chest, even though I want to run away from the dead body, still lying where we found it, still unmoved by the authorities, I need to question Andersson. I need to do my job.

'I feel faint,' I lie, as we approach the factory gates, three police cars parked blocking the entrance from vehicles. 'I need coffee.'

'Hotel's open,' he says.

'You live under the factory. Could I come in for a cup? Five minutes?'

I turn my back on the factory and on dead Gunnarsson with his liquorice eyes, and it feels like I'm standing in front of some Eastern-bloc presidential palace, looking down on my subjects, one of them an unknown killer. I have Toytown laid out in front of me like some nightmare version of a kid's roadmap rug.

We pass the new policewoman and she lets us through. Most of the site is closed off, but the new part of the factory has reopened.

'How tall are you?' Janitor Andersson asks, looking up at me.

'Above average,' I say.

'Best watch yourself.'

The factory's built on a granite hill. The hill isn't level so on one side the builders had to create a slanting basement to even off the site. The basement is full height on the far left side, then it peters out like a wedge of cheese under the centre of the building.

'Ain't much, but you can come in,' he says. 'Police already searched it.'

There's a kitchen with a kettle and a two-ring hob and a multipack of cocktail sticks and an old pine table with two chairs. Foil-wrapped pipes cling to the ceiling. A bunch of electrical cables snake from one side of the room to the other and there's a fridge and an old TV and some patio furniture.

'Will you feel safe down here?' I say.

'I got all the keys,' he says, rattling his jailor's ring. He's wearing work gloves, the fitted thorn-proof rubber variety ICA sells in packs of ten. 'Nobody'll bother me. Say, why did Gunnarsson have them coins on his eyes? That the voodoo?'

'No idea,' I say.

'Got a bedroom through there.' He points to the low ceiling area. 'I'll be sleeping with a sharp Norrland knife under my pillow tonight for good measure. And through here's my workshop.'

He leads me in and tells me the Grimberg kids

used to play down here years ago. He says he feels like a protective uncle of sorts to young Karin.

There are bottles of motor oil and square cans of turpentine stacked in the corner. I look around and check the exits, check the corners. Duct tape. A length of blue nylon rope and a pair of bolt cutters and a fine bradawl screwdriver and a multi-pack of salt liquorice and a sawn-off length of steel pipe. There's a blowtorch sitting atop a toolkit and it looks like a gun. I count six posters on the walls. They're bygone adverts for exotic locations like the Grand Canyon and Mexico City and The Great Pyramids.

'I ain't never been,' he says, noticing me looking. 'Not yet anyways. Got eight grandkiddies and another on the way. I'll find a way to take 'em all one day, God willing.'

The edges of the posters are curled and the paper's mottled with mould spores. These are cold, moist posters of hot, dry places. There's a framed photograph hanging from a nail. Janitor Andersson surrounded by his grandkids, a pet dog just out of shot. I can see the tip of its tail. The room is full height at one end and then tapers to about one metre at the far side but that's not even the worst thing. The lower parts of the walls are wet with groundwater. The air is heavy with it.

'Problems with damp?' I ask.

'What doesn't mind, over, doesn't matter,' he says.

'What?'

'You know, you heard the old saying.' He coughs into his elbow pit. 'What you doesn't mind, over, doesn't matter. That's how it goes.'

What?

I'm getting claustrophobic down here in this wet sloping room with no window so I turn to Andersson. 'I'll be back tomorrow. If you think of anything important about Gunnarsson, just let me know.'

He looks at me and tuts like this kind of thing, a suicide and a murder in the same week, is best kept out of newspapers. Best kept buried like poor Per Gunnarsson soon will be.

I photograph a team of crime-scene investigators putting on their white suits and entering the old factory. Anna-Britta calls for me from the canteen doorway.

'Tuva.'

She ushers me inside and walks upstairs so I follow her. She opens the door to the Receiving Room, such a contrast from Andersson's subterranean hellhole, and then she gestures for me to sit down.

'I heard you found him.'

I nod.

'I'm so sorry. Did you see anything strange just before? Anyone you didn't recognise?'

'Not that I can think of.'

'This is all rather delicate as I'm sure you can imagine.'

'Delicate?' I ask. 'A man lost his life.'

Anna-Britta bites her lip. 'Two men.'

'I'm sorry,' I say. And I am.

'Before we go on, Tuva, regardless of whether Gunnarsson was an accident or whether it was something more heinous, will you give me your word that you'll keep the gruesome details out of your newspaper? Andersson told me all about the . . .' she blinks and looks at my neck. 'We need to contain the reputational damage is all. There are livelihoods at risk.'

'First of all, this wasn't an accident. Second of all, I need to report what happened. I can't omit details.'

'Can't or won't?'

'I have a duty to my readers and to the victim, and you know this news will get out anyway.'

'My staff won't talk.'

I raise my eyebrows.

'They will not talk,' she says again.

'Did you know Per Gunnarsson?' I ask.

'I can't say.'

'Can't,' I ask. 'Or won't?'

She sets her jaw.

'Okay.' I try to look conciliatory. 'If I agree to treat this as sensitively as possible, to consider the factory and the town when I'm writing, to reassure locals that you're still open for business, then you'll answer my questions and allow me full access to the factory, including access to your private residence beyond that door.'

She stares at the residence door with its coat of arms moulded above the frame like it's a whole other world back there. She shakes her head.

'That's our home, Tuva. It's already been searched by the police, already been messed around with.'

'I know. And I've interviewed hundreds of people for stories and I can only really write them, and do them justice, if I see their environment. I found a man dead under your home and it was no accident. He was killed.'

'My husband would not like it.'

'But you're in charge now,' I say, forcing a smile to soften my words.

'I'm sorry, Tuva, I . . .'

A figure in black bursts into the room from the residence wearing a veil headband and she has a beauty spot painted above her lip.

'Mother,' says Karin Grimberg, her voice calm and firm. 'I think it's canine.' She stays in the doorway and I try to look beyond her and inside; to take a peek at the Grand Room, but I can't at this angle. There's a dark red curtain in the way. Karin ignores me completely. 'It's dog.'

Anna-Britta rubs her palms up and down her face and I notice that her fancy Swiss rectangular watch isn't working, it's telling the wrong time; it's stopped. She looks unhinged sitting there on a grey upholstered ottoman.

'Karin.' Anna-Britta's voice is brittle and too high. 'Come in, please. Close that door.'

The figure in black, pretty in a kind of first-year-of-university-trying-a-little-too-hard way, steps over.

'I saw you at the funeral,' she says to me, a wooden box clutched tight in her hand.

Anna-Britta locks the door to the family residence.

'Are you working for us now?' Karin asks. 'Did you see the cadaver?'

Anna-Britta looks horrified. 'Tuva's helping with the book,' she says. 'She's going to be interviewing us, for the family history.'

Karin places the box down on a desk and I notice that her beauty spot isn't a spot. It's a spider. Well it *is* a spot, a mole I think, but she's painted it black and there are eight tiny legs, mascara strokes or something, four on each side.

'This might help with finding out who slaughtered Per Gunnarsson,' says Karin. 'The police won't let me into the old factory to check things, but Andersson showed me a photo of what was lodged in Gunnarsson's neck.'

He took a photo? Why didn't he mention that to me?

Anna-Britta looks like she might pass out. 'Do the police know Andersson took a photo?'

Karin shakes her head. 'He said it was accidental, he was trying to switch the torch function on. He took dozens of pictures. And I'm pretty sure it's canine', she says, opening her box. 'These are from my cabinet.'

She holds out a small box, like a jeweller might use to display a range of rings or precious stones; little sockets cut into black velvet. Inside each socket is a tooth with a Latin inscription.

'These are the closest to what Andersson photographed: a fox and a badger and,' she points to a larger tooth, 'that one's a wolf. The one found in the cadaver's neck was a dog's tooth, a large dog. I'd say it came from a German shepherd.'

CHAPTER 14

'A German shepherd?' I say.

'Judging by the size of it,' says Karin. 'Look, compare it to the wolf canines here, they're not that dissimilar. Could be a Doberman but I'd say it's German shepherd.'

All I can think of is David Holmqvist's dog, the one 'adopted' by a farm out in Rednecksville.

'You sure?' I ask. 'Are you studying veterinary science?'

'Sculpture and fine art,' Anna-Britta answers for her. 'But last year Karin completed an online course in taxonomy. And another in pathology. Karin, why don't you wait in my office while Tuva and—'

'I quit my sculpture course, mother,' says Karin looking at Anna-Britta and then slowly turning her head to face me. 'I'm needed here.'

Her mother looks uncomfortable like she has about a hundred things she wants to scream right now and it's damn inconvenient me being here.

A knock at the staircase door and then a face peering around it. Rosy cheeks. Thin '80s hair. It's

Agnetha Hellbom, the office manager and wife of Gavrik's only expensive lawyer.

'Mrs Grimberg,' the woman says, her voice as thin as her hair.

'What is it?'

'The police chief needs a word.'

'On my way,' says Anna-Britta, and then she adds, 'we must help Gunnarsson's family in any way we can, and we must offer the workers counselling.' She's speaking with the kind of fake gravitas any new CEO has to cultivate, and she's looking at me from the corner of her eye, like she wants me to hear this too. 'Can I leave that to you, Agnetha?'

Agnetha scowl-nods and licks her lips and walks back through to the offices.

'Blood-sucking parasitic leach,' says Karin, and all of a sudden I like this young Grimberg. She's a younger version of me. She's weird and she's lost her father and doesn't care for shitty people. I like her a lot.

Anna-Britta glowers at her daughter and I notice how pink-raw her cuticles are. Tiny open wounds around each fingernail like miniscule fragments of raw chicken flesh.

'Tuva, I need to give the police my statement, why don't you eat down in the canteen? Half the site's locked down and will be for some time, but we're allowed to keep the rear factory and canteen open. Chief Bjorn's been very understanding, what with how vital we are to the town.'

I walk downstairs. Is the killer still here in the building? In the attics or a secret store room? In the residence? And when was Gunnarsson murdered? I don't want to be here but I need to find out what's going on. Who killed this man in this way? Why?

The carpet is threadbare and thin, the photos on the walls unnerving because they're all black-and-white and the faces look too pale and the eyes look too dark. I swing a right into the canteen.

I reckon there are a hundred people in here. Whispering. Is the killer in this room? Hiding in plain sight? I take a wet plastic tray with chipped edges and slide it along the steel rails toward the food. A row of stainless steel knives stick to a magnetic rail behind the servers. I look at the blades and then down to the food. Lasagne or salmon. I point to the lasagne and a sodden slab gets deposited on a plate and handed to me, the server not looking me in the eye.

'Thanks,' I say.

Nothing.

I move along and take some bread, the fluffy sugar-loaded polar bread that looks like a circular pin cushion, and then I pick up a glass tumbler.

This is school again. My Stockholm high school was pretty good actually; quiet suburb, good mix of people, interesting kids – but as a deaf twelve-year-old the school lunch part was always tricky. By default, some weird survival technique I seemingly haven't shaken off, I sit with the most awkward-looking people. I'm a thousand miles away from my twelve-year-old self, happy to hold my own in court or in a press conference scrum, but here I'm an ultra-aware deaf kid again, just struggling to hear what's being said in a big room where the mouths are full and the volume's too high.

I sit down and nobody looks up from their food. I guess they're in shock. Or they don't know what to say on a day like this. Or they're afraid for their jobs. For their livelihoods. For their lives.

I pour water from the oversize enamel jug on the table and say hi to the woman next to me and she just grunts and keeps on shovelling.

The lasagne is a trade descriptions breach but I eat it. Let's just say Dr Atkins would not approve of the ratio of pasta, overcooked to the point of mixing seamlessly with the béchamel sauce, to meat. I keep my aids on but I don't pick up much. People aren't talking, they're just munching, and that background noise is difficult to hear through.

A hand on my shoulder.

'Sit with us,' says the red-haired stamper who gave me the coin earlier. I almost retch at the memory of Gunnarsson's throat, at the mass of coins lodged in his gaping mouth.

I stand up and the women on my table look amazed, like I just got picked as a goddam cheerleader or something. I go sit with the stampers.

'You here cos of Gunnarsson?' asks Red.

'No, no, just doing some research for a book, a history of the liquorice business.' It's kind of true.

Red frowns at me and eats her salmon. She has large features and clear skin. She's niche beautiful. Red points to a woman collecting her apple pie at the counter.

'Great White,' she says.

'Sorry?' I say.

I wait for Red to finish another mouthful of her salmon.

'Psst,' says Red to the woman she calls Great White, loud enough for half the room to hear and turn and look at us. Red winks at Great White and Great White smiles a sad, hesitant smile back, and her teeth are sharp and they're bigger than Constable Thord's and that's saying something.

'Great White,' says Red. 'She used to go to school with Gunnarsson. Most people here did and most people here got harassed by him at some point.'

Red eats more salmon and I move my tepid lasagne around on my plate.

'Screw-ins,' says Red, pushing her plate toward the centre of the table. 'Paid for by Gustav Grimberg cos she's a taster. Twelve years she's been tasting so she's got no teeth of her own left, they all went black as liquorice and just as soft.'

Red and I each take a bowl of apple pie with a squirt of canister cream. The room watches us sit back down.

'Gunnarsson had his throat cut from ear to ear,'

says Red, her fingertip scraping across her own neck. 'Head almost came off.'

I don't correct her.

'You've always been a stamper?'

'I'm the fastest here, ninety a minute, maybe ninety-five. Old man Grimberg used to say I was the fastest stamper they've had since my ma back in the day.' She sniffs.

'Old man Grimberg that just died? Gustav?'

'His dad,' she says. 'Ludvig his name was. He was a letch.' She shakes her head and her eyes darken. 'In that family tree like a fungus, that's what ma says.'

'What is?'

'You know what I mean.' She points up and raises her hand above her head and then she curves her finger and points down and lowers her hand so her finger hits the table with a thud. She mouths the words 'they're letches and they don't mind taking the easy way out if you know what I mean.' She looks up at me. 'You met Pissy Knickers yet?'

Oh, come on.

'Works in the office and earns about three times what I earn just for moving papers about. Hair like candyfloss in a rainstorm.'

'Agnetha Hellbom?'

'That's it. Pissy Knickers wants to get her claws into this place, into the money, greediest person in all of Gavrik, so keep your eyes out for her.'

'Why do you call her that?'

'Cos she looks like she just wet her panties, that's

why. Greedy cow, you'd think her and her Ken doll husband might have enough cash by now. You know who he is, do you?'

I can feel the rest of the table listening to every word of this but I reckon they already know the answer. Just like I do.

'Henrik Hellbom,' she says. 'The lawyer with the polished face and that big Mercedes jeep. He bought the Grimberg's lake house, you know that? That in your story cos it should be.'

'I'll be comprehensive,' I say.

'*Advokat* Hellbom and Gustav Grimberg were at school together. Well, Hellbom never had a dad growing up. And he had about as much money as my family did which is to say none.' She scoops up the last of the squirty cream from her plate with her finger and sucks it. 'Poor,' she says. 'Dirt poor, and Hellbom hated Gustav something dreadful. He wanted everything he had.'

I thank Red for the information and give her my business card and take my tray over to the rack and walk out.

I linger at each photograph as I walk back up to the first floor. There's one with a grey sheet over it so I lift one corner of the sheet and it's not a photo underneath but a mirror. I keep walking. I get to the top and step into the Receiving Room. The *kakelugn* stove, the tiled cylindrical fireplace in the corner of the room, is cold to the touch. On the thin mantelpiece above sits an acorn and a small bowl of sea salt.

I make notes from my day: witness names and police details – more for the paper than the book. I check my phone and the hashtags #GavrikKiller and #Ferryman and #LiquoriceMurder are starting to trend. A man died in this building earlier today and it's obscene that the place is still open for business. It's not right.

The window shows a frosty Gavrik with the typical amount of Sunday February traffic which is pretty much zero. I see Storgatan and the back of Hotel Gavrik and the secure car park of the cop shop, and then down the street I can see my office and the cross-country ski store and Björnmossen's gun shop. And then onto the larger lots out of town: ICA Maxi and McDonald's and the ice rink up the hill. I can see apartment blocks built in the seventies: towers like toadstools pushing up through the mulch to stand erect. They might be hideous but at least they're warm and dry, at least my one is, not like this place.

Anna-Britta walks in.

'The pulley hook?' she says.

I look at the hook.

She joins me at the window, pointing to the big, steel joist protruding from the façade with a hook at its end.

'The raw product. We use refined liquorice now, but back then we bought raw roots, the idea was that they could be stored up here. There used to be an identical joist and hook one-storey higher, and that was used to elevate the bales so they

126

could be hauled into this very window. The hook you're looking at weighed the root bales as they came in.'

'The roots weren't stored here?'

'The atmospheric conditions weren't suitable. We're on granite but there's an aquifer, something to do with the water pressure. The root bales were stored down in the root barns.'

Karin walks in with her veil over her eyes and carrying a tray covered with a tea towel.

'Can you deal with those while I talk to Tuva?' Anna-Britta asks her.

Karin nods and I strain to see what's on the tray. Looks like two saucers of milk and a bowl of salt and a pine cone and a feather dipped in something red.

'I meant to ask you,' Anna-Britta says, her voice slightly louder and clearer. 'Can you hear me alright?' She's making odd hand gestures like someone trying to mime in charades. 'I'm sorry, I can't do sign language.'

Yeah, I can see that.

'Neither can I,' I say. 'Not very well, anyway.'

She clears her throat.

'Could we talk through there?' I ask, pointing to the door to the residence.

'No,' says Anna-Britta.

'Okay.'

'The police have advised me not to discuss what happened today. But I'll bring you old newspaper clippings that Gustav . . .' her voice breaks and she clears her throat and apologises. 'That my late husband kept, and also some samples of early order forms and invoices. For the book. We have some interesting customs forms from the 1800s, all sorts of stamps from countries that no longer exist.'

'Fascinating,' I say. 'But David did urge me to focus on the human side of the business, on your family itself, the history of key individuals and so on, their role in the community.'

'I find it difficult to work with . . .' she trails off.

Karin, arranging the pine cone close to the tiled stove, snorts when she hears this.

'You can work with me now,' I say, still thinking about the dog tooth in Gunnarsson's neck. But it can't be connected to Holmqvist, half the Kommun have German shepherds and we don't even know it's from a German shepherd. 'David's not the monster that people make him out to be.'

'I don't wish to discuss him.'

Here we go.

'David's just different,' I say.

'Well, Karin and I are relieved we're dealing with you now, aren't we dear?'

Karin nods and places a saucer of salt under the chaise longue and I can see there's some kind of pointed sculptor's chisel already under there.

'Especially with what happened today,' says Anna-Britta. 'I wouldn't feel secure with that man here every day.'

'Can I just ask, what's with the salt and the pine cone?'

'Precautions,' says Anna-Britta, and then the wind picks up outside because the window rattles in its frame and the chandelier bulbs flicker on and off. We all look out and the sky's turned as dark as lead, and then there's a deep grumble of thunder with no appreciable lightning. Snow starts to fall. 'This is a factory but it's also our home,' adds Anna-Britta. 'Evil visited us today inside our own home. Old evil. Unwelcome evil. We need all the precautions we can get.'

CHAPTER 15

It's getting dark outside. The temperature's dropped and the one-eyed cat I saw on lilla Ludo's grave hisses at me as I exit through the factory gates.

An ambulance pulls up. No flashing lights. Three people in forensic suits step out from under the factory arch and uniform cops remove the police tape. A body bag is brought out and placed inside the ambulance. Sleet-snow falls in broad wet flakes and the whole scene is hushed. There are church bells ringing somewhere close by, but it's half-hearted and they finish soon after they start. Too cold to ring bells in February. I pass one TV news reporter, a woman from Stockholm, trying to film in bad light with a golf umbrella held over her head. I can hear 'suspicious circumstances' and 'police won't comment further at this time'.

I pack my stuff into the truck and, because I have about two microwave ping meals and no drink whatsoever, I head over to Ronnie's. Another deep growl of thunder. I need a drink, anyone would. In London, four years ago, I'd have bought a bottle of something at a corner shop or supermarket. Here the state-owned alcohol shop, Systembolaget, is closed completely on Sundays. The whole damn day. The state think we'll drink ourselves to death on Sundays and I'd say they're just about right.

Ronnie's has two outdoor candles flanking the entrance and the snow's been scraped clear and the pavement's gritted. It looks welcoming. The blue neon sign above the entrance buzzes. I open the door and get blasted with warm moist air and a seventies rock ballad I don't know the name of. Something Midwest American.

The floor's soaking wet with meltwater and the coat racks are bulging with heavy goose-stuffed jackets and fleeces of every colour. Hook failures are not uncommon in this part of the world. The coats, when wet, weigh too much. There must be thirty or forty locals in here and the place has the kind of calm 6pm Sunday vibe you might expect in early February except people are chatting about neck wounds and curfews.

I sit at the bar.

'Tuvs,' says Ronnie. 'What can I get you?'

I love him for asking a normal question. He knows all the crime scene details by now, if anyone does then he does. But he also, as an experienced barman, knows I need a drink.

'Malibu and Coke, please. Strong.'

He pours the drink and stands watching the TV on the wall, some ice hockey game I'll probably need to write about for next week's issue.

'You heard anything more . . .' says Ronnie, and I try to hear him in this place and read him through his blonde-grey beard but I can't.

I finish my gulp. My veins dilate and my forehead smooths and my tight mouth slackens with relief.

'What?' I ask.

He looks at me but someone at the other side of the bar raises his hand so Ronnie serves the other guy.

I like this place a great deal. It smells of beer and sweaty long johns, but the lighting is such that you can hide down here and forget you're in Toytown. I text Tammy to invite her down and she tells me she's working another hour and then she'll shut the van up and meet me. I send three kisses.

I'm in my element: drink in hand, quietly observing the human condition. My specimens are loosened from their mighty Nordic inhibitions by vodka and cold Danish beer. They are talking and playing pool and gossiping like hell. One guy points to his own eyes and then to his throat. I'm watching, but more important than that, I'm reading.

The chats are fascinating. I can't pick it all up of course, sometimes very little, but I can fill in the gaps by scanning their eyes or the way they're standing.

The cashier from ICA Maxi is here, the pretty one. She's with three guys who look like they have a much better skincare regime than me. There's some kind of complex four-way flirt going on and I can't make out the dynamics exactly but one guy is clearly in the lead. He's the trainee mechanic who changes my tyres twice a year.

Nils is in the far corner nursing a beer and a brandy but I don't want to talk to him and I'm pretty sure he doesn't want to talk to me. He's with one of his maximum bore ice hockey mates and they're wearing matching XXL jerseys and Nils's gelled hair is shining in the lamplight from the pool table.

Closest to me, at the table next to the bar, is a guy who went bankrupt a few years back and a woman who used to work in McDonald's but now helps run the summer water-sports place at the reservoir outside town, the one with the caravans. I sip my drink and hear them talk about the body and the fact that Gunnarsson was mauled to death by a crazed dog, apparently, but they quickly move on to discuss snow and how it compares to last year and what the forecast is for next week. The guy says he's getting low on firewood and the woman says she is as well. They agree they'll both double their stores for next winter. Can't get caught out in February. Literally a death sentence. He says he'll keep his kids home from school tomorrow on account of the bloodthirsty rabid dog. Rabid dog? He goes on to tell her about his chest infection and she sympathises but not for long and then she starts talking about her seasonal affective disorder and about the vitamin D drops she's taking and how they aren't helping much. He says he has something in his walls and I don't make it out at first, but then I realise he's got mice living in his walls, and she says, 'Who hasn't?' I finish my drink and order another.

'Sorry we got interrupted,' Ronnie says, scratching his chin whiskers. 'You heard any more about . . .' and then he points in the direction of the liquorice factory.

'Not much,' I lie. 'You?'

He shrugs and glances at the hockey match on the TV.

'Drugs is the rumour,' he says. 'Gunnarsson was mixed up with some people over in Munkfors.' He looks at me. 'The eyes thing was a message.'

'What kind of message?'

'Also heard Gunnarsson had been hanging around Gustav,' he says, ignoring the question. 'Maybe pushed him into the jump somehow, kinda bullied him to end it all; that's what's being said.'

'Not sure you can persuade someone to kill themselves, Ronnie.'

He looks at me and ponders. 'Maybe you're right and maybe you're not. But now we've got a murder scene. Maybe two. I have to think to myself: what if the killer's sitting at my bar or playing pool on my table.' Someone at the other side of the bar wants to order food so he wipes the spill from my glass and goes to take their order. I look at the laminated menu stapled to the pine bar. Toasties. Hot dogs. Nachos. Burgers. Ronnie's carefully curated range of microwaved delights. All one hundred kronor which back in my London university days would have been about ten pounds and would have bought all four items.

I settle back and lip-read two guys comparing the relative merits of various porn websites. My phone vibrates. It's Tammy saying she'll be ten minutes late. And then the new cop walks in.

'What can I get you?' Ronnie asks her.

'Two gin-and-tonics please, doubles, one with ice.'

'Alright then,' he says.

I'm right next to her and this is where I introduce myself and ask her something smart about the murder case. But I can't. I freeze. She doesn't say hi and neither do I. It gets awkward. I can't say hello now, not after all this time. She smells of honey, but also somehow warm, a spice scent like nutmeg, or maybe sandalwood, faint and soothing. And then she steps away with some guy I recognise from the mill, some junior supervisor clown with biceps popping out of his T-shirt. She walks away and smiles back and I reciprocate but I do it too late and I think she missed it and now she's gone.

Tammy, get here now.

I try to act all nonchalant at the bar all on my own in my jeans and fleece and unwashed hair but really I'm discreetly inching my barstool over to where she was standing. I'm breathing in the air to try to detect her scent once more and I manage it, but it's oh-so diluted now, just a ghost of a beautiful smell.

135

I down my rum and Coke and order a shot of vodka.

One of the two porn-website-debate guys is blocking my view of the new cop so I'm forced to listen-read him and he's now moved on to talk about his grandmother who slipped on the ice outside her building and broke her hip. He plans to visit her every day until she gets out, especially if there's a deranged killer on the loose, to give her some peace of mind. I feel empty inside and pathetic for not visiting Mum more when she was alive – however awful those visits always were, however cold – and now for not visiting her grave. Porn-website guy can manage it but I can't? There are long-lasting cemetery candles, the ones you buy from ICA Maxi, two for ninety-nine kronor. Dozens if not hundreds of these candles are flickering in every graveyard in the country right now but Mum doesn't have a single one.

I'm slouched on my stool when Tammy hugs me from behind and kisses my cheek and drops a bag of prawn crackers down on the bar.

'Ronnie,' she says. 'I know, I know. I'm bringing these in from outside and yes it is officially against your policy but it's been a shitty day and these are so gooood.'

Ronnie shrugs. 'Only if I get to share.'

Tammy tears open the bag and Ronnie hands her a low alcohol beer and we finish the crackers in about three minutes flat, me and Ronnie taking most of them.

'How are you?' I ask.

'On the one hand: eighty per cent of my target and, considering the fact that most of my customers are scared, and what with the electrical storm out there, I'll take that. One ratshit customer returning his red curry because it was too spicy for his lame-ass pale taste buds. Well, he did have a point. Overheard him call a girl a whore one time last year. So I spiced up his red curry so much I thought his micro cheese doodle dick might fall off in shock.' She takes a long swig of her beer. 'Perhaps it did. Anyway, hit eighty per cent of my target. On the other hand: there's a psychopath on the loose and I work alone at night in a food van on the edge of the world.' She gestures with a nod over to the new cop. 'Who's the new girl?'

'New cop.'

'We could do with her. How long the last one manage?'

'Six weeks,' I say. 'Not sure she liked the community.'

Tammy laughs.

'Pool?' she asks.

'Sure. You rack them up while I pee.'

I head to the toilets at the back and there's a queue even on a quiet Sunday night. This is partly because there are only two cubicles and it's partly because of the extra time people need to pull off long johns and thermal one-piece merino-wool undergarments but also it's the time they need to improve their hat-hair and their February lizard skin. All those minutes add up. I get to the front of the queue and go in. Is the person in the next cubicle a normal person or a throat-slicer?

Tammy's waiting by the table when I get out. The light above it, one of those low-hanging pool-table things, is sponsored on one side by SPT Mills and on the other side by some Norrland brewery. She breaks.

'Did you see them bring the body out?' she asks.

'Tam, me and the janitor found him.'

She drops her cue on the table and steps closer. She mouths, 'the body?'

I nod.

She places her hand on my shoulder. 'Shit, you okay?'

I nod.

'Why were you in there?' she asks.

'I'm doing book research for David Holmqvist. I was checking out the old factory.'

'Ghostwriter Holmqvist?'

I nod and miss a ball, an easy corner shot I could have made with no adrenaline or alcohol in my blood.

'What book?'

'It's about the Grimbergs.'

'What's left of them,' Tammy says, leaning down to take her shot. 'It's just the three witches left now, right? Course, I haven't ever met any of them because millionaires don't fancy traipsing down to my van for the best food in Shitsville.' She looks at me and lowers her voice. 'You actually see the body? People saying it was a drugs thing.'

'The body,' I whisper, 'had liquorice coins on its eyes and in its mouth, and a dog tooth lodged in the neck wound.'

She misses the white ball and almost rips the green cloth on the table. She steps closer again.

'What the fuck?'

'I'm just glad I wasn't alone when I found him. I know Gustav Grimberg was suicide, but still, two bodies in one place, it doesn't feel right.'

'Ain't right,' she says. 'You think it has anything to do with Grimberg money? People say that place is crammed full of Picassos and marble furniture and grand pianos and all sorts, like a palace or whatever. And the jewellery, they got it all insured for over a hundred million, so they say.'

'I'd say two hundred.'

She looks at me. 'You're shitting me, right?'

I nod and line up my cue and pot a ball.

'I can't eat their liquorice, too salty for me,' she says.

I miss a tricky shot thinking of that coagulated liquorice mass lodged in Gunnarsson's mouth.

A hand comes down hard on the back of my cue and it is purple raw with cold and the finger-nails are painted white and they're chipped.

'Verbal warning,' says the red-haired stamper. 'From Anna-Britta Grimberg herself. For breaking protocol.'

'Sorry?' I say, and I can see Tammy approaching to stand behind me.

'Next time keep away from me when I'm working.' Red has a wine box under her arm, but she's ripped open the cardboard and the internal foil bag is sticking out like the bowels of some unfortunate mammal. 'And keep your mouth shut if someone gives you something for free. You want them to do to me what they did to Ma? Want that on your conscience?' Her eyes are bloodshot and she's spitting her words out. 'Ain't got nothing else to say to you.' She lifts her chin and scratches her neck. 'You show your face on the factory floor again and . . .' she picks up the black eight ball from the table and drops it down a corner pocket and walks out.

CHAPTER 16

I wake up with a mouth like an armpit. My head's ruined and that's a bad way to start a brand new week. I reach over for my phone and try to look at it but my lashes are stuck together. I rub and rub and eventually my phone's lock screen comes into focus and it is 8:10A.M. and I've slept in.

I never do this. Never. I scramble out of bed, my stomach empty and bloated at the same time. Snippets of last night play back to me like short videos. I throw cold water on my face and then I shower and use whatever exfoliants I have left to scrub myself raw.

Breakfast is half a bottle of lemon Fanta with a Berocca vitamin tablet still fizzing away at the bottom like some neon primordial life-force, and two strips of Marabou milk chocolate straight from the fridge.

The whole front section of my skull is throbbing.

I park up and I'm only about ten minutes late but I feel guilty like a truant school kid. There are two photographers working outside the factory. I open the door to *Gavrik Posten* and the bell above

141

it rings. Luckily I can't hear it because my aids are still in my pocket. Benefits of being deaf include not bothering with jarring noises when you're hungover as fuck.

Lena's back in her office and Nils is back in his office slash kitchen and Lars isn't in until later. I take off all my gear and get behind my desk and slip my aids on but keep the volume low. My heart's racing at a pretty unhealthy level and I promise myself to join some kind of iron man open-air beach-gym place when I move down to Malmö; live on spinach juice and organic smug-grass smoothies.

I scroll Twitter and the newsfeeds. The liquorice killer is everywhere, except somehow overnight all the hashtags have merged into one. Or rather one has overtaken the others: hashtag Ferryman. The old myth. The coins on the eyes. Quotes and stolen snippets and locals being interviewed. Nobody knows much. Gunnarsson was a loner with no family and no close friends. My focus will be on the investigation, the case, but I also need to make time for his obituary. I need the records to show that he was a real person before his jugular vein was slit open.

There's one non-Ferryman headline. An elderly couple were found frozen to death in their car an hour's drive north from here. The piece doesn't get much real estate on account of the murder, but on any other day it'd be the biggest story for weeks.

An email arrives in my inbox from a retired schoolteacher who sends me random things. Yesterday she found a deer frozen to death in the centre of a small lake past Utgard forest. She's attached three photos and it looks like a sinister ice sculpture: half a white deer hovering silently above the ice with the other half entombed in solid water, and it'll likely stay that way until the big thaw. I can make out a bird perched on its antler like it may as well be just another tree. Maybe it was being circled by a wolf? Maybe a predator can push an innocent into making a fatal decision? Is that what happened with Gustav? Was a wolf nearby? I have a message from Anna-Britta, and seven emails from David Holmqvist. Anna-Britta suggests I take that guided drive with her oldest delivery driver. He knows everything there is to know about the factory, apparently. I'll do it. He might be helpful. Holmqvist's clarifying the rules of engagement for his book research: what I should delve into and what I can avoid. He's very specific and he wants me to include more information on the Ferryman killer.

I leave Gustav Grimberg's full-length obituary because I don't have time for it right now, and focus on Per Gunnarsson instead. He lived off Eriksgatan in an apartment, I can find that online. He was thirty-seven years old. He was single. He had a terrible credit record. From trawling social media and our own article archives I can tell he was a keen amateur genealogist and that he's been arrested several times over the years, all for alcohol-related misdemeanours.

I sip hot coffee and check in with Thord. He tells me he's busy.

Lars comes in on time. He gets through the door and it tinkles and he takes about twenty minutes to pull off his big grey coat with its faux-fur hood and his ICA Maxi zip-up moon boots. I get restless and itchy just watching. He mumbles 'morning' to me but apart from that, this is a silent movie happening in front of me right now, a movie screening at half-speed. He lumbers over to the window of the office, right by the big stack of *Posten*s for sale to people who drop in, there will be dozens of them, and then he checks the temperature on the thermometer like he does every day.

'Cold?' I ask.

'Medium,' he says, and then he lumbers back to his desk in front of Lena's door and notes down the temperature in his little black notebook. Gonna miss this place.

I pull my coat back on and open the door to the street and they're all there lined up on the other side of the road. It's like a vision from ten-thousand years ago, pagan ancients drawn out of their caves by the sun deity, opticians and hairdressers standing, thermoses in hand, necks bent, faces warming in the morning rays. They're not talking to each other. They're thawing, their thoughts loosening, their skin healing, their hopes returning. I pass between them and buy two Danish pastries and a

144

bottle of Coke from the newsagent. I leave it all on my desk and start walking toward the police station but then I stop, my boots stationary in the grey pavement-slush, and realise that the new cop might be there. I take my phone from my pocket and switch on the camera and look at myself on the screen and grin to check my teeth and then I primp my hair and pinch my big pore cheeks.

Cop shop's empty. Nobody at the desk, nobody waiting. The ticket-queue machine thing reads sixteen and the screen above the counter reads sixteen so I take a ticket and ring the bell.

Chief Björn walks out and sees me and says nothing and turns back.

'Thord,' he says. 'Visitor for you.'

The door closes then opens and I just make out the expensively tailored silhouette of Henrik Hellbom. Judging by the volume of chat there must be seven or eight people with him.

'What's Hellbom doing back there?' I whisper.

Thord's standing with a burnt piece of toast covered in what looks like slices of boiled egg and squeezey-tube Kalles cod roe.

'Morning Tuvs,' he says, then takes a bite.

I gesture for him to answer my question but he just shakes his head and says, 'Doing his job. Taking care of his client.'

A suspect? 'Someone's been arrested?' I say. And then I mouth the word, 'Who?'

He mouths the word, 'No.'

I raise my eyebrows.

'You have information for me,' he says.

'Has someone been arrested?' I whisper.

'I told you already. No.'

'Is the new policewoman here?'

'Noora? Out dealing with the crime-scene guys. Not easy to seal an area and keep the factory working, but we've managed it. Why?'

'I wanted to ask some questions about Gunnarsson and I thought you'd be too busy as you're a senior officer here now.'

He straightens his back and thinks about that. Then he takes a bite and chews and holds up a hand like, 'gimme a sec, sorry about this'.

'Your leaving drinks are on Thursday, right?' he says when he's done chewing. 'Should I bring her along?'

'Only if you want to.'

He nods and swallows and licks his lips.

'We'll all need a drink by then, the way this week's going.'

'The couple' I say. 'The old couple found dead up near the mill. Any police comment for the paper?'

He licks his lips some more.

'I've been tied up, what with the murder right here on my doorstep, but our message is the same every year, Tuvs. If you go out, check the weather forecast first, don't go out if you're not sure, tell someone which route you're taking, be equipped if you do travel, make sure your vehicle is roadworthy, never leave your vehicle.'

'Those two didn't leave their vehicle,' I say. 'Didn't help them.'

He raises his eyebrows and shakes his head.

'They were too old to be out in February. The daughter's in hospital with some kind of bronchitis, bad economy that one. Anyway they thought they'd drive up north and they'd never driven much these past ten years. Not the brightest matches in the box. So they get off the E16 way too early, don't know if they had the dementia or what, but all they'd took with them was some car sweets and thin blankets. Their '87 Volvo skidded straight off the road, which was ploughed and gritted but apparently that didn't help them, and went down a ditch. Dead within two hours, I'd say. Noora found them like two ice lollipops, still looking straight out the windscreen.'

'That's my quote right there.'

'Don't you dare,' he says, one hand on his cuffs.

'I'm going to drive up and photograph the scene if I have time. It's close to the old farmhouse, the one with the grain silo, right?'

He nods.

'Take your phone and your—'

I cut him off. 'I will.'

'You still got that Hilux?'

'Extending the rental contract tomorrow.'

He nods. 'Mind how you go out there, Tuvs.'

I walk out and the sun worshippers have gone back inside now. There are three TV journalists recording short pieces and there's a photographer

I know from *Göteborg Posten* taking shots of the factory arch. I grab my Coke and my pastries and drive by Gunnarsson's apartment building. He lived on the first floor and I try to get in but there's a key-code lock. Can't see anything from street level so I talk to a neighbour briefly and leave.

The E16 is busy as ever. Gavrik is a place the world never really sees, but this motorway links more important towns like Karlstad to the south and Östersund to the north. We're just the liquorice coin on the side of the road that trucks pass by loaded with pine trunks for the pulp mill.

I pass the corrugated-steel strip club and pop two paracetamol from their foil wrapper and swallow them.

The Q8 gas station's doing brisk business. I fill up with a third of a tank of petrol, no sense in gifting money to the rental place when I hand it back, and buy two boxes of tampons and a bag of wine gums and some bright blue antifreeze windscreen-spray.

'Everyone's jabberin' about this ferry-boat driver on the run,' says the woman in the poodle sweater serving me. 'But you heard about that poor old couple?'

'Just up the road,' I say. 'Sad business.'

'Makes you think,' she says, bagging up my purchases.

'Yes, it does,' I say.

I drive up to the exit munching wine gums as I

go, sometimes savouring and letting them melt, especially if it's pear, a white one, and sometimes chewing two or three for a non-alcoholic cocktail. I can't quite remember how I got home last night except I know Tam was there. She looked after me. I'm going to miss her so much I don't know how I'll bear it.

Radio Värmland talks about Per Gunnarsson. All about his age and his hobby researching important family histories, and his job as a quality-control supervisor. There isn't much else to say about the guy. And then they issue some kind of long-term weather warning for the coming week: possible blizzards and ice storms blowing in from Russia, maybe hitting Wednesday or Thursday. Reminders to stock up on firewood and candles.

I pass the farm with the silo. The car's gone but it's left its mark. There are tyre tracks all over, broad ones with a visible tread from rescue trucks and tractors, and normal ones from cop cars and ambulances. And then narrow ones, almost invisible amongst the others, from an '87 Volvo. They look like bike-tyre marks. Could their Volvo have been run off the road by someone? Is that possible?

The grass revealed by the crash scene is dead. It's yellow and flat and the ground is deep-frozen like it'll never be green again. But it isn't really a crash scene, they just drove into a ditch at low to medium speed. And then stopped. And then died. My Hilux would have been out in about five seconds flat but they stayed and maybe they talked about leaving and finding help, or discussed whether to stay, argued or agreed; and maybe they kept the engine running or maybe they didn't. I hope they held hands. I hope they were not afraid. And then they quietly died. Eighty-four and eighty-nine.

I get out of my truck but leave the engine running. There's a wooden cross that someone's driven into the snow but it's leaning because really it needs to be pushed into the earth but that's hard like concrete so whoever left it here must have thought 'best I can do'.

My cheeks burn with cold and my exhaust fumes are lingering low in the air like dry ice in a night-club. I see two bunches of flowers still in their Q8 cellophane wrapping, both discount-price bunches. Small roses in one packet, a mixed bouquet in the other. I see a roll of something under the mixed bouquet and I step over for a better look, my right foot down on the steep white bank of the ditch. It's a pack of Grimberg salt liquorice. The old folks around here love it, they're the main customer base for the company, Anna-Britta told me so.

I photograph it all. Alone. Just my engine noise and my breathing.

Everything here is milky white and the only thing I can see, the only standout feature, is a passenger plane. I can tell by the contrails: four engines, a jumbo, passing silently and smoothly overhead where it's even colder than down here. It's noise-less. There's no air-travel noise in Gavrik because the planes are too high. In a real place like Chicago or Manila or Johannesburg you hear plane noises all day long because important places have airports. We don't. The planes are always high above us and they are always silent as they pass over this unknown liquorice town.

There's a moment where I almost slip. That may not seem like a big deal but slipping somewhere like this can be a death sentence. A man died last year on a farm not far from here when he broke his ankle on black ice, out near his chicken sheds. Had no phone with him. The man was alone at the time; his girlfriend was visiting friends in Munkfors. It was about twenty below. He popped out for five minutes to check on his birds. Just a broken ankle, nothing more dramatic than that, not a single drop of blood spilt, but he was frozen solid when the girlfriend got back home the next day. Mixture of shock and exposure. He shut down. She said he looked like a frightened scare-crow left out in a field over winter; his expression, his posture, slumped and alone, wearing just a robe. A frightened, fallen scarecrow.

I look down and there's a single purple glove at the bottom of the ditch and its fingers are covered in ice crystals and they're hard and frozen and bent this way and that and I have to look away.

I keep Radio Värmland off on the way home

and my headache's almost gone now. It's the noise that gets to me. And the lack of it. The quietness of their death, those two elderly lovers, the man in the old factory with the neck wound, his black-covered eyes, his obstructed throat; and the noisiness of Gustav Grimberg's suicide jump, that watermelon crack. People talk a lot about dignity in death and how some folk fight and battle with cancer and I'm not sure Mum fought it exactly, it's more nuanced than a fight, and I don't see how she lost. It's not a win or lose thing. It's not a sport. She had a miserable life but cancer's a mean twisted fuck and it came to her and then it left her alone and then it took her so fast at the end that I didn't even have time to tell her I'll live on for her, or that I enjoyed my early childhood or that I forgave her. That I loved her. Maybe love's the wrong word. I should have told her that I understood her. That I would survive on my own.

I head to the factory because the family and workers are my best chance for information about Gunnarsson and potential suspects. I decide I'll treat myself to a drive-thru double cheeseburger after my lunch-hour interviews with the Grimberg women and that puts a smile on my flaky little face.

The factory is almost business as usual although trucks aren't allowed through the sealed arch and so they're loading up in the factory lot in front of the cameras. I climb the stairs to the Receiving

Room. Some of the faces in the photographs look familiar so I pause. I don't know these people. I've never met them. But I recognise them from the canteen and the factory floor because, I guess, they're the mothers and grandmothers and great-grandmothers of Red and Great White and Per Gunnarsson. They all stayed here in Gavrik.

I head into the office area.

'No, the incident didn't happen anywhere near our production area,' says Agnetha Hellbom. She mouths 'out' to me and I read her clear as day but I shrug like 'what? Sorry?' and keep on listening. 'It was in a totally different building.' She pauses. 'Yes, we're working around the clock to make up for the disruption. Grimberg Liquorice would like to offer you a fifteen per cent discount on your March order by way of a goodwill gesture . . .' She pauses, her nose wrinkling then says, 'Well, really, I don't think that language is called for.' She puts down the phone.

'Hi, I—'

'You're not supposed to be in here,' she says.

'I'm Tuva Moodyson. I have an appointment . . .'

'I know who you are. You're the newspaper girl.'

'Customer problems?' I ask.

'Go wait in the Receiving Room, that's what it's for, receiving, and I'll see if Mrs Grimberg is available.'

Okay, so she is a bit Pissy Knickers after all.

I walk back to the elegant room with its flickering chandelier and tiled fireplace. The door to

153

the private residence cracks open. I see a striped sleeve and a wrist covered in bangles of different widths and a watch the size of a teacup and nails painted midnight blue.

Then she steps in.

CHAPTER 17

Her hair is as tall as a pineapple but silver-grey. She moves to me with a smile in her eyes and she says, 'Come on, then.' I let her lead me to the door of the residence and she opens it and stands behind me and then she holds her hands firmly over my eyes and pushes me through the curtain.

'What are you doing?' I ask.

'Don't you want to?' she says.

I don't want to be in this building at all, especially not with hands over my eyes. But I need information from her. I need insights. My senses are on high alert and I can't see much through the uneven wrinkles of her fingers. Her hands smell strongly of lemon. The room is large. I think it's a living room or a drawing room, about the size of my whole apartment, no, wait, it's bigger I think, twice the size. The Grand Room lives up to its name.

'Cici,' she says under her breath. 'You can all me Cici.'

'I'm Tuva.'

'Of course you are, I've been watching you for years. You're one of my favourites.'

'Is all this necessary?' I ask, my headache starting to return. I know I can slip her pensioner hands off my face whenever I want.

'They don't want you in here,' she says. 'But my attics are my attics and I can invite whomever I please.'

We're are at the far end now and I've managed to see a dining table and a huge apothecary cabinet the size of a squash-court wall, and a cage in the corner. But I have no details and I'm disorientated. I can hear a high-pitch drone and it sounds like a newborn screaming in the distance.

'What's that noise, Cici?'

'The whine?'

'Yes.'

'Ventilation system,' she says. 'Can't live with it, can't live without it.'

I'm straining to see paintings and ornaments but her hands are too tight to my face. Something's gleaming next to the table, perhaps a silver punch-bowl? She turns me to the left by steering my shoulder.

'You can look,' she says, dropping her hands. 'No peeking back.'

Stairs. She moves to lead the way.

'Come on,' she says, taking me by the hand and walking up.

She's wearing a striped long-sleeved T-shirt with ten or eleven necklaces and a bear-claw brooch pinned in the centre of her back, and a skirt or tutu thing with layers and layers of organza, and spiderweb tights and black boots with a small heel. Her hair is amazing, a kind of '60s beehive, but twisted, with pins and butterfly grips and one of those crazy helter-skelter straws stabbed in the top.

We get to the top of the stairs.

'Welcome to Cici's,' she says, waving her arm around.

I just stand there with my mouth open and gawp. The attics run the full length of the factory, the size of a football field. There are dozens of faded mannequins clustered in groups like they're chatting at a memorial service. Every single one's wearing gloves. Some lace, some velvet, some silk. Apart from a small room at the far end, the only things dividing up the space are the two chimneys at the one-third and two-third points. The chimneys are round like lighthouses.

'Look around,' says Cici. 'Take a tour while I change.'

Change? She heads off to the area between the chimneys, the area above the arch, and I try to take it all in. I've walked past this building a hundred times and I've looked up at this place, and all the while I expected paint pots and fold-away chairs and old ski gear because that's what people store in their attics, isn't it?

There are eight windows pointing forward toward Storgatan, and eight pointing backward to the yard and the root barns. I'm near the end window, the large sloping window I saw from the graveyard, and as I look out now I can see the family plot. Someone's down there, someone in black, probably a hack working on his Ferryman article, photographing the fresh mound of Gustav Grimberg.

'No need to change for me,' I shout.

'It's not for you,' she shouts back.

The place is like the inside of a barn, all exposed pine and rafters and beams that must weigh a ton each. There's no insulation up here but there are dozens of old electric radiators wired in beneath the windows. It's cold, but not freezing cold.

I count fourteen lemons and then stop counting. They're hanging from twine tied over rafters and they're joined by papery garlic bulbs pierced with brass drawing-pins, and horseshoes hanging upward. Obviously. By the slanting window sits a grave candle, the weatherproof kind, and it lights an antique Punch-and-Judy style puppet show complete with painted Gavrik background. I can make out the twin chimneys. Next to it are a pair of vintage ice-skates, red hair twisted around the blades so tight they look like copper coils.

'What do you think?' asks Cici as she walks toward me.

She struts like a sixteen-year-old. I want to ask her about Gunnarsson, and about her own son's suicide, but I force myself to wait. Cici sashays down what must be a homemade catwalk, a length of chessboard linoleum stuck to the floor-boards, and she bares her teeth and smiles and turns.

'Couldn't resist,' she says. 'KK's my only audience since my husband passed and even she doesn't come up here much anymore.'

'KK?' I ask.

'Karin, my granddaughter.'

'You look amazing,' I say, and she does. A floor-length orange jacket with a jagged fringed bottom and blue jeans ripped at the knee and a necklace that looks like three black Christmas-tree baubles, and the same pineapple hair as before.

'Business-casual,' she says, and then smiles again and smacks me on the arm. 'Come on.' She leads me around the attic, her arm entwined in mine. 'This is half my lifetime collection. I've given away the rest. This is my capsule up here, about five-thousand pieces.'

'Your capsule?' I say, and she slaps me again and winks.

'Nothing expensive,' she says. 'If this stuff had been expensive I'd have a three-door pine wardrobe like everyone else. No, this is all beautiful junk, second-hand value: approximately zilch.'

'Well, I love it,' I say.

She bares her teeth and blows me a kiss. 'Knew you would. Can I get you a drink?'

She walks over to a radiator, one of many, and takes the thermos pot sitting next to it.

'Collected it all on my travels over the years. The excellent thing about liquorice, don't touch the stuff myself,' she grimaces, 'is that it grows in the most wonderful places.'

159

'You travel?'

'Did, darling. My husband Ludvig and I travelled three or four times a year. Egypt, Persia, Turkey, China, Indochina, Syria – just the most wonderful places on Earth. To source growers and sign deals, you see. No email back then, Tuva. No fax machines back then.'

I look at her dressmaking tables. At the array of sewing needles and crochet hooks and sharp rotary-cutters. I see her yarn and her felt shears.

'I customise and sew and knit and add a little this and slice a little that until I'm happy.'

'How come I've never seen you around?' I ask.

'All dressed-up and nowhere to go, darling. I like it up here and since Ludvig died, almost twenty years ago, I've spent most of my time in these attics. Oh, don't feel sorry for me, don't you dare. I love it. And I estimate I walk in excess of six miles a day up here so that keeps me young. I've been watching you, you know.'

'You said.'

'I watch everybody.'

A chill runs down my back and I look around the room, trying to check behind the racks of clothes and the peeling mannequins. It seems like we're the only people up here but it's such a disorderly space a half dozen killers could be hiding in the shadows.

She leads me by the hand to a window facing Storgatan.

'Look down there.'

I look.

'That's my theatre set.' She takes a pair of opera glasses from the wall. 'I name the people I don't recognise and I follow them every day for years on end. I tell them where to go, what to do. Sometimes they obey me and sometimes they don't. You were Elizabeth when you first arrived.'

'Elizabeth?'

She shrugs.

'If you look close enough you can work out many, many things. I keep an eye out for old Puss, my grandson's cat, I worry about him getting too close to the road.' She rests her opera glasses against the dimpled glass. 'I even have a friend down there I see from time to time, which is rather nice. Just a silly old ghoul.'

'Ghoul?' I say.

'Just a silly old fool. And I've seen you go into your newspaper office and over to the police station, and driving around in that big wagon, so I knew you were a reporter even before that dreadful business.'

'Medusa?'

'Worst thing to happen to this town since the couple who drowned in their bed.'

'What couple?' I ask.

She adjusts the bendy straw in her hair, hangs her opera glasses back up on the wall.

'You must have heard the tale, the old people who drowned when they built the reservoir outside town.'

Ah, okay.

'Yes, I did hear something, but that was in the sixties or something?'

'Seventy-six,' she says. 'When they flooded the village they made sure and double-sure all the houses were empty. But Sven and Petra Kristersson, they snuck back into their house; they had it all planned, had help, and they weighed down their bed with bricks, put stones on top of their blankets, lead weights, and they strapped themselves in tight together, and they perished right there under all that water.'

'How awful.'

'Well, you say that,' she says. 'But he was in a bad way with his bowels and she was so arthritic her hands looked like seagull claws, poor thing, so really they made a joint decision and although it was sad for their family, I know all about that, at least they made that call together and there's a sad romance in that, don't you think?'

We sit down and she pours tea into two china cups and passes me one and it really is very, very sweet. I can see puppets in the far distance, elaborate antique puppets with rosy cheeks, and their strings are dangling from wooden crosses hanging from the rafters.

'To be helped to die can be a Godsend,' she says.

'I'm sorry about your son,' I say.

'Me too,' she says, her eyes a little older now. 'But it wasn't his fault. I don't blame him one iota.'

She pulls out a pendant from beneath her other necklaces. It's a white rabbit-foot. She caresses it with her manicured finger and looks over her shoulder toward the slanted window and St Olov's.

'I don't blame him,' she says again.

The clouds part and sunlight pours through the attic windows and through the silks and chemises of all colours and makes the kind of patterns on the bleached wood floorboards that stained-glass windows make in a church.

'Do you have any theories about Per Gunnarsson? Did you notice anything unusual through your opera glasses?'

She scratches her chin and mouths 'drugs' and then she says, 'What can you do?'

'Any theories?' I try again.

She laughs. 'Little old me? Well, now you mention it. There was one time about five years ago when I saw Gunnarsson outside arguing with your friend, the one who works from the hot-food caravan. I saw her push him away.'

'Tammy? You saw Tammy Yamnim push Gunnarsson?'

'I did,' she says. 'And now I think it's time for my nap.'

She grabs a long multi-coloured pashmina and we head back downstairs. She ties it loosely around my face and leads me through the Grand Room. Stained-glass effect again, except this time right

163

in front of my eyes; the fabric almost grazes my corneas. The ventilation system screams faintly in the background. We get to the door leading to the Receiving Room and she removes the scarf and pushes me through.

CHAPTER 18

There's a note in the Receiving Room from Anna-Britta, apologising for missing our meeting and saying she'll make it up tomorrow. She reminds me to meet truck number one for a guided drive so I can interview her oldest and most knowledgeable delivery driver. I walk outside and hear voices. From the office: two women arguing in hushed tones. I tiptoe closer to the door. Talk of delayed orders and HR problems. I can't make out many of the words but there's a blame-game deluxe in mid-session.

I dial.

'Tam,' I say.

'*Hej*,' she says.

'Did you ever have an argument, a fight in the street, with Per Gunnarsson?'

There's a pause on the line. 'Hardly even met him. He's ordered once or twice but wasn't a regular. Why?'

'Never mind.'

The sun's going down. We'll have two more hours of dim insipid cloud-light and then the dark freeze will return and a long lonely night will once again shroud the town. I need a drink. I head over to my office and Lars is in so he raises his bifocals to his balding head and says, '*Hej, hej.*'

'*Hej, hej,*' I say, slipping off my gear.

I call Thord and ask about Gunnarsson's post-mortem results but he says they're not ready yet. I'm not in the mood for that double cheeseburger now, so I pull open the bottom drawer of my filing cabinet and retrieve a plastic cup of dry noodles, extra-spicy flavour, even though that's not even a flavour, and head to the kitchen.

'Your last week,' says Nils, leaning back in his one hundred per cent authentic man-made luxury leather PVC armchair. 'Your last week and all this happens.'

'Yep.'

'At least we'll sell copies,' he says. 'Sorry I can't make your drinks on Thursday. Won't be the same without me.'

'You're right about that.'

I pour boiling water from the scaly kettle into my instant noodles cup and stir with a plastic spoon.

'Let me buy you a beer later before I fly off to the Canaries. For old times' sake.'

I look back, spicy MSG steam tickling my nostrils and making my eyes water.

'Okay.'

I eat, slurping, flicking through online apartment ads, watching Lars's annoyance from the corner of my eye. Lars hates anything scented or smoky, he reckons he has a perfumer's nose or some bullshit.

The apartments down south are at least double the monthly cost of my Gavrik place for the same square meterage. I'm moving to another small town, but this one's close to a decent-sized city. Big difference. I shut down the website and slurp the last few noodles and bin the whole thing.

I write for the print, my last print. I take what I need from the latest police statement and integrate it into my story. I focus on Gunnarsson's life. I use what details and quotes I've gathered from colleagues and one I got from his neighbour. My Google alerts flash. Police have released a new piece of information relating to Gunnarsson's injuries. There was blunt trauma to his head from a hammer or a baton or similar. I call Thord.

'Gavrik police. Noora speaking.'

'Is Thord there, please? It's Tuva from the *Posten*.'

She covers the earpiece with her sleeve and the next voice I hear is his.

'Thought you'd call.'

'Blunt trauma?' I ask. 'Thanks for the tip-off. Any weapons recovered? Any suspects?'

'Nothing I can talk about,' he says.

'Come on.'

'You have anything for me?' he asks. 'Two-way street.'

'Rumours of drug problems. Bills not settled. Talk of a dealer in Munkfors sending a message.'

'Anything I don't already know?' he asks. 'Anything true?'

'You checked his school records? I heard Per Gunnarsson was a bully back in the day.'

'We know,' he says.

'I'll call you if I sniff something,' I say. 'I promise. Now, what have you got for me?'

He sighs. 'You'll hear soon enough but keep it to yourself for the time being. The cut to Gunnarsson's throat was from an extraordinarily sharp blade: a medical scalpel or similar. They can tell by the tissue damage.'

'We looking for Doctor Death?'

'You're not looking for anyone. Björn's still sore over your Medusa meddling.'

He tells me he has to go.

I want to focus solely on the murder but locals will still want the old couple-dead-in-a ditch story. Nobody here was close to Gunnarsson whereas the old couple had children and grandchildren and friends and neighbours. They were part of the complex Gavrik spiderweb. I download photos I took from their accident and crop and tidy them up and delete an image of that solitary purple glove and then I check the victims' details online. They had one daughter: the woman they were driving up to meet in hospital. And one son: a firefighter from the local station. I search his contact details and stuff a plastic ICA carrier bag into my coat pocket and walk out to my truck.

Something's perched on my bonnet.

By the wiper blades.

It looks like an innocent snowball but it's not.

I check around and see one woman dragging her ICA weekly shop home in a kid's sledge. I get alongside my front tyre and the snow *skalle* is facing my windscreen, facing my driver's seat.

There's no lingonberry blood on this one but somehow it's worse. It has two liquorice eyes and it has a ball of what looks like chewed liquorice stuck in its mouth cavity. I can't drive with this fist-sized skull on my bonnet. I can't drive looking at those two black eyes. I want to punch it or smack it with a shovel like the janitor did in the factory lot. But I don't. My gloved hand reaches out to it and I hold it gently. It's firm. Icy. I pick it up off my Hilux and there's a small, pointed tooth lodged in its base. My guts weigh heavy inside me and I feel like running away. Am I being watched right now? By Cici? By someone else? The tooth is animal, maybe from a large rat or a mink. Sharp. I think about taking it to Thord. I take out my phone to photograph it but then the white skull falls from my hands and disintegrates on the salted asphalt and its power disintegrates with it. I swivel and look up through a cloud of my own breath, up toward the offices and the Receiving Room and Cici's attics, but there's nobody there. Is this a threat? I watch as Janitor Andersson comes out of his troglodyte basement and nods to me without smiling and heads off, coughing, through the arch toward the root barns.

I start the engine, my heart thumping against

my ribs. Just kids. They probably left snow skulls on all the bonnets in Storgatan.

The roads are busy with cyclists using spiked tyres, and cars with snow-mattresses resting on their roofs; thick slabs of powder that may stay there for weeks if we don't get more sun, and if they don't drive too fast on the E16.

I pull past the haberdashery, which used to be my sanctuary but is no more, and drive between McDonald's and ICA Maxi; past the ice-hockey stands built from local pine, the floodlights advertising SPT Mills, and up round the back. My heart rate starts to normalise. I need to keep asking questions. I need to find out who killed Per Gunnarsson.

Firefighter Johan Linderberg lives near the two-truck fire station that employs him.

His front yard hasn't been shovelled. Can't blame him for that. Deep footprints scar the front garden and a cat, one of those fluffy special breeds, maybe a Maine Coon, is ballet dancing from one footprint to the next because its legs aren't quite long enough. There are miniature snowballs stuck to its undercarriage; white pompoms crusting its fur.

I step in old bootprints just like the cat did, and ring the doorbell. Godawful tune. There's a dead Christmas tree out here leaning against the wall and tiny threads of tinsel are still attached to some of the bare branches. I reach out to touch one and then a face appears at a window next to the door.

The door swings open.

'Yes?'

Stubble rash on his neck. Broad shoulders. Red, barely-open eyes.

'Hello Mr Linderberg, I'm Tuva Moodyson from the *Gavrik Posten*. I wanted to tell you I'm sorry for your loss. I'm writing a piece in the paper to remember your parents and I wondered if you had anything you wanted to say in your own words.'

He blinks and looks me up and down.

'I ain't showered or nothing.'

'That's okay, neither have I,' I lie. 'That time of year, isn't it?'

He nods and scratches his unshaven chin and opens his door wider wearing tracksuit pants and thick wool socks and a Christmas jumper with a big old moose face on the front. He has a craft knife in his hand.

'You want me to say things for you to write up in the paper?'

He looks confused. The TV's muted and there are photo albums scattered all over the sofas.

'If we can just chat about them and I can ask you some questions?'

'I guess.'

He clears space on an armchair and a sofa and I get the strong impression that he'll want to sit in the armchair, it's dented into his shape, so I take the sofa.

'You want coffee?' he asks.

'Please. Black, one sugar.'

He walks away to the kitchen and I pick up a photo album and flick through it. It's from the '80s or '90s. I can see bad hairstyles and proud school-graduation days and an old guy having a birthday lunch with flowers in his hair. One of the girls looks familiar but I can't place her.

'There you go,' he says putting the mug down on the same Ikea coffee table I have in my apartment.

I sip. It's too hot. Kettle-hot.

'They didn't feel no pain whatsoever, that's what the policewoman said.'

I nod.

'No pain or nothing whatsoever.'

'That must be a relief to hear.'

'It is some.'

I sip the coffee but really it's too hot to drink so I just let it warm my fingers.

'Did you know they would be out driving the day of the accident?'

He doesn't say anything, just stares at my head. I get this a lot. He's staring at my ears but trying to look like he's not staring.

'I'm deaf but I can hear you fine,' I say, pointing to my left aid.

'I'm so sorry,' he says.

I get that a lot, too.

'No need to be sorry, I'm fine. Your parents?'

'They never been driving these past ten years, only local to the ICA Maxi store and even then not much. I did it for 'em or my sis did.'

I gesture for him to talk more.

'That's who they was driving to, she's in the hospital in Dalarna with the bronchitis.'

'They were driving to visit her?'

'Like I said, but Mamma couldn't see too good and Pappa's always been a lousy winter driver, so why they didn't just call me and ask me to drive 'em I'll never know.'

'Is there anything you'd like me to include in my piece?'

'They could have just called me. I'd have taken them.'

I nod.

He looks at me, his eyes glazed. 'Just say that we'll miss 'em and we loved 'em. And you can write we're grateful to the factory for all they done.'

I smile and notice a stack of bag-in-box wine containers piled in the corner like kid's building blocks.

'They're empty,' he says, following my gaze. 'For my niece. She makes, well she makes rocket fuel; I can't stand the stuff – she calls it red vodka – but it'd burn my tonsils clean off if I still had any . . .' He opens his mouth to show me. 'She distils it all in her bathroom and she even does a liquorice one to order, Black Evil she calls it. Then sells it in them boxes.' He smiles. 'I ain't much of a drinker.'

This is more common than you might think, especially in the dark months. Home brews, potato moonshine, nasty shit.

'Did your parents used to work at the factory?' I ask.

'Mamma did forty-one years and Pappa done around ten. My sis wasn't so lucky. She had a crappy supervisor, excuse my language.'

'Your sister?' I sip coffee and he switches off the TV and I stop accidentally lip-reading the people on screen.

'Good stamper, one of the best. She was let go years ago and I don't want to go into the details.'

'Okay,' I say, holding up my palms. 'Awful about Mr Grimberg wasn't it. And now Mr Gunnarsson found dead in the old factory. Been a very sad February for the town.'

'Been a sad February for my family,' he says, looking at the photo albums sprawled on the leather sofa with its faux-mahogany accents. 'Real sad.'

'Did you ever work at the factory?

He smiles. 'I'm a fireman, was born to it. But my niece is a stamper up there following in her Mamma's footsteps you might say.'

And then I realise where I recognised that face in the school graduation photo.

'Does she have bright red hair?'

'Like a goddam fire extinguisher,' he says. 'Excuse my language.'

'I've met her,' I say. 'She mentioned something about her mum, your sister. That she's had a hard time recently.'

'Ain't just recent,' he says, shaking his head. 'Been tough for years.'

I stay silent.

'She hasn't got over it. Lost her house, her car,

174

even pawned her wedding ring. Saddest part is that my niece, the red-haired girl you spoke to, she'd not been talking to my parents these past six or seven years. My niece likes to make a fuss, just the way she is, and Mamma and Pappa always told her to keep complaints to herself and hold onto her job, this was years ago, I suppose it's a generation thing.'

I stay silent again but this time it doesn't work.

'You should never not talk to your family. It's too late for my niece now. She didn't get to say goodbye to my folks even though I know deep down she loved them.'

My eyes start to sting and I remember my last words to Mum and they were not ideal, they were not what they should have been.

'Grimbergs got problems up there since the old man passed,' he says. 'Someone'll buy the place soon you mark my words.'

'Buy the place?'

'Expensive lawyer, the one with the Mercedes 4x4, gets a new G-Wagon every other year, he's been sniffing around it. Owns half the shop buildings in Gavrik, probably owns your newspaper office. And his missus works in the office at the factory so I'd say he's got the town pretty much sewn up.'

'Interesting,' I say.

'Damn right,' he says, lifting his grey tracksuit trouser to scratch his dry shin, the flakes showering off him like white sparks. 'If he does buy the factory he'll fire half the people and leave this town as a husk. Town'll be dead like a zombie, a goddam husk.' He gestures an apology for cursing. 'My Mamma and Pappa phoned me. They wanted to talk about something before they had their accident, and I expect it was something about the factory. Mamma sounded agitated. Worried. And I told her I didn't have time.' He looks at me and then down at the photos. 'Reckon they couldn't get hold of my sis on account of her being in the hospital with the bronchitis. Reckon they drove up there to tell her whatever was on their minds. It's my fault. I should have stopped and listened and then maybe they'd still be alive.'

I look at him, urging more words out of his mouth.

'What do you think they were worried about?'

'The factory.'

'Anything specific?' I say, a little too keenly.

'I know they've been walking up there each day, it was part of their exercise route, Doc Stina told them they need to keep on walking no matter how slow,' he says. 'They were both very slow. Anyway, the day Grimberg jumped off his chimney, they both saw the whole thing. I expect they were shaken.' He looks at the sofa. 'You want me to find you a nice photo of Mamma and Pappa for your newspaper?'

'That would be lovely, thank you.'

'Never was no pain, that's what the policewoman said.'

I nod as he looks through the albums.

'Quick and painless,' he says.

I glance over at the sideboard. There's a fire poker and a scrapbook and another stainless steel craft knife and a glue stick. He's been slicing the photos and arranging them in some sort of collage.

He carefully lifts a photo out from beneath its sticky cellophane cover and focusses on it and smiles but then puts it back and keeps on searching and then he looks up at me.

'In a way it's a blessing, don't write this in your newspaper, but it's blessing when you're in your eighties and you've had a good life like they both did, and you get to pass on nice and quiet out in the nature in your own vehicle quiet and painless, d'you know what I mean? I'm no good at explaining things, but like I was telling my niece, it's better to go like that than to die years apart, or to spend weeks in a hospital bed with tubes and wires and bleeping machines and people bothering and picking all over you and running tests. I'd say it was a blessing in a strange sort of a way.'

My stomach feels hollow and hard and all I can think of is mum and the bruises on her hand and the state her veins were in by the end.

'I think you're right,' I say. 'You're a wise man, Johan.'

He bats that away with his forearm and picks out another photo.

'This was Pappa's seventieth down by the reservoir. Sis did him a picnic, real nice spread with cider and herring and all his favourites.' Tears fill his eyes. 'Pappa loved a mustard herring.' A tear runs down his cheek and I watch it land on his shirt. 'Had to have his mustard herring.'

I take the photo and look at it.

'Thank you. It's perfect.'

CHAPTER 19

Systembolaget's window display is full of pink cava and rose wine. Like anyone wants to drink cold red romance drinks just because it's Valentine's on Friday.

The door bleeps and I make a quick sweep of the sterile aisles with their liquor and beer and wine, ordered by price – like the decision to choose a Spanish Rioja over an Australian Pinot Noir is some kind of spreadsheet macro result. There's Linus who got fired from the driving school and there's Great White, the Grimberg taster with the screw-in teeth, and I recognise the distinctive fur hat of Gavrik's resident flasher but I reckon he's retired now or else it's just too damn cold.

I select two bottles of rum and take them to the handsome Sudanese guy with the perfect hairline I usually buy from. It's February-busy so I have to queue.

'ID,' he says.

I give him my national ID card – I take it as a compliment – and he glances at it and passes it back and bleeps the two bottles of Jamaican rum and one carrier bag through his till.

'Four-hundred and sixty,' he says.

I slot my card into the machine and place the rum inside the narrow Systembolaget bag and then put that bag inside the ICA Maxi bag I took from the filing cabinet at work. This should see me through to Malmö, God willing.

An old hunched man walks past me as I step out into the cold and he has his coat hood pulled so tight over his head he must be looking out of a hole the size of a clenched fist. He has a stick to help him walk and the top of it looks like a ball of polished granite.

I leave the bottles in my truck. They won't freeze, the alcohol content's too high, maybe that's the trick, maybe I can learn something.

When I get back to work and strip off my winter gear there's a copy of *Wermlands Tidningen* on my desk.

'How come they knew about this detail and you didn't?' asks Lena, creases on her forehead, walking over from her office, her fleece zipped up to her chin.

'What detail?'

'Complaint filed seven years ago against Per Gunnarsson. Someone claimed they saw Gunnarsson propositioning a minor.'

'He'd ask kiddies for photos,' says Lars from his corner. 'Been rumours about him for years.'

'Can we talk in your office?' I ask her.

I close the door behind me and sit down.

'Who was the minor? Who was the complainant?'
I ask. 'Have the police commented?'

'This is what you're supposed to be telling me,
Tuva.'

'I'll find out,' I say. 'I should have told you something else. I'm juggling a special assignment this
week and I know you're going to hate it but I
promise it'll help me get deeper access to the
factory. It'll help me get the inside story.'

'Special assignment?' asks Lena, crossing her
arms.

'I'm doing freelance research for Holmqvist,
the ghostwriter in Utgard forest. Won't interfere
with my work here, I promise. I'm interviewing
the Grimbergs for him in my lunch breaks. It'll
get me deep inside the story. Assuming that's okay
with you?'

I see her face morph from confusion to fury.

'This is a murder case, Tuva,' she says. 'There
is a sadistic killer loose in Gavrik town and you've
taken on a side job? Call him and quit or I'll do
it for you.'

She hands me her phone.

'Listen. Without this project I can't get access
to the three Grimberg women. And they know
things, I can tell. Let me do the bare minimum
for Holmqvist and it will pay dividends for the
paper. Trust me.'

She shakes her head but it's a shake of acceptance
rather than refusal.

'Do not let me down, you hear?' she says.

I nod. 'Nobody's talking much.'

'Use your techniques,' she says.

'I have to tread softly, they're all mourning.'

'Helps to talk,' she says. 'You're free therapy.'

I bite my lip.

'What are you doing tomorrow night?' she asks.

'I'm moving out of my apartment and moving onto Tammy's sofa. Landlord wouldn't extend my lease for another week.'

'Well,' says Lena. 'The new Tuva Moodyson arrives tomorrow afternoon, not to work but to meet everyone so he can start clean next Tuesday morning at your desk. I know you'll be flat out on Ferryman but we should grab a quick coffee the three of us, okay?'

Poor schmuck.

'Okay.'

I get back to my desk and Lars offers me a coffee and I swear he gets through five litres a day. Swedes are amongst the biggest coffee drinkers in the world, after the Finns, so that tells you just about all you need to know about us right there. We also have some of the fastest broadband and we eat the most sweets and we're almost the tallest and our salt liquorice is the saltiest you can find.

I text Thord about the Per Gunnarsson complaint regarding a minor. Then I email my bank details to Holmqvist and write up the frozen-couple-in-the-car story.

'What do you know about the Grimberg family, Lars?'

He looks at me like a sloth might gaze at an out-of-reach berry.

'They do a lot for the town.'

'Are any of them capable of murder? You actually met any of them in person?'

He thinks about this and then shakes his head and then a snowball hits our office window and it bangs and shakes in its frame and Lars says, 'kids.'

'Know anything about a stamper they let go years ago? Sister of one of the local firefighters?'

He closes his eyes and frowns and I just stare at him. The clock on the wall ticks. He opens his eyes.

'Some talk of an affair,' he says.

'Okay, good,' I say. 'With whom?'

He wrinkles his nose. 'One of the Grimbergs. Not sure if it was the old man or Gustav, may they both rest in peace. Talk of lawyers being involved if I remember right. Some kind of blackmail. Probably just gossip.'

When I leave the office I notice an unmarked cop car parked outside the factory gates. I look up to the attics to try to see Cici looking back through her opera glasses but there's nothing there. I scrape my windscreen and it hits me that tomorrow morning might be the last time I ever do this to my trusted Hilux. I'll drive up to the garage near the sewage-treatment works and I reckon they'll extend my rental for a week but they might try to palm me off with the new model or a demo Land-cruiser. The very idea makes me nauseous.

The rum's sloshing around on the passenger side as I drive home and I'm getting thirsty. I need a drink after that chat with Lena. I'm desperate for it. I call Anna-Britta at the factory office but Agnetha Hellbom picks up. The rum's still sloshing. I can almost taste it. I tell Agnetha that I can't make the drive tonight with delivery truck number one.

Today is goodbye to the flat and tomorrow is goodbye to my Hilux and Thursday night is goodbye to my colleagues and next Monday is goodbye to Tammy at Karlstad train station. So many goodbyes from a place I never wanted to live in to begin with.

I walk into my apartment and lock the door behind me. I stick on some Johnny Cash and take off my clothes, literally pull them down into a hot damp pile. Static crackle. I dump them all on my sofa. I open the rum and remove my aids and slip on my pyjamas and lay down on my bed. My eyes are facing the photo of Mum and Dad, the one from before Dad's crash, before that June twenty-fifth; that black day just after Midsummer, that worst day of every year of my life since I was fourteen. They look happy in the picture, young and in love and uncomplicated, and that just makes me feel more alone here in this barely-functioning life; empty fridge and empty savings account, no partner. I guess their generation grew up faster but I feel a deep and very real fear that I'll be like this my whole life, some transient hack drinking too much with no family whatsoever, apart from the aunt I never knew I had, the one I met at Mum's funeral just before Christmas, the one who looked like Grandma but with better hair. Aunt Ida. Thick scar across her throat from some kind of '70s surgery. Aunt Ida who I now plan to visit someday.

I look in the fridge and pull out one of those party pre-mixed mojito cans. I take my rum and mix the drink. 'Walk The Line' is playing on a loop and I can't hear Johnny but I know he's there.

I'm not a good packer. When I go on holiday I don't iron and fold all my clothes and pack them between sheets of tissue paper with rosebuds and lavender sprigs. I push it all in and squeeze like a professional rugby-forward scrumming businessmen into a carriage of the Tokyo subway. Then I zip up, no regrets.

So I pack my clothes and make-up and all the leads for the obsolete digital cameras I trashed years ago; but the lead may come in handy one day, you know? I throw away a half-opened bottle of shampoo that was medium expensive and turned my hair into an Olympic cyclist's helmet. And then I'm done. Three-and-a-half years of life contained in three black wheelie-suitcases.

I drink and check my email and there's a long message from David Holmqvist. He's appraised my work to date and makes it quite clear that if this book is to sell, and in his words 'sell, it must', then it needs more drama. He explains that even the historical non-fiction memoir of a Swedish industrial family needs conflict and peaks and troughs and challenges and triumphs, and a dozen other buzzwords.

I take a sip and reply that I'm starting gently because the family are in pain. The truth is I'm busy writing up the Gunnarsson murder but I tell him how for ongoing stories I always build trust at the beginning to differentiate myself from other journalists and to get the better story. I tell him leave it with me, I got this.

The flat feels cold so I shower and heat some ready-made rice pudding, the kind that in Sweden gets sold in a condom-style plastic wrapper, and then I pull my aids back on gently and listen to Johnny and his guitar, laying on my bed, my head at the feet end, my feet at the head end, my mind imagining the new policewoman's life, pondering her likes and dislikes, movies and food, the way she brushes her teeth in the morning, how she'd look in a robe, and thinking about her hair and the back of her neck. The light in the room changes. Blues flash off my white walls. I step to the window and see an ambulance drive off toward the reservoir, and then a minute later a cop car sets off from the station with its sirens blaring.

One mojito, extra strong. I can probably still drive. I have to. A cop car and an ambulance together. Could be important. Could be another Ferryman attack.

I pull on the old clothes I'd discarded on the sofa and swill mouthwash and pull on my boots and turn off Johnny Cash and run outside into the night.

CHAPTER 20

I can hardly see through the windscreen. No time to scrape. The blower and the blue anti-freeze start to work but my wipers are fused to the glass. I drive at eighty and slow down for corners like we get taught on our driving tests, the ones with the cardboard elks on frozen ice courses that we're told to miss. Didn't help you though, did it, Dad?

I can't see the ambulance or cop car but there's only one road in this direction. The glass clears and I speed up and take a handful of wine gums from the passenger seat and stuff them in my mouth in a neutron bomb of high fructose flavour. Blue lights up ahead. Please, no more Ferryman victims. No more salty black-liquorice eyes. No more blood.

I dab my brakes into a corner and my wheels slide the wrong way so I steer out of it, the counter-intuitive direction, the 'what the hell am I doing I am steering straight into a ditch' method, and straighten up and carry on. The ambulance is in my headlights now and its exhaust fumes are freezing in this minus fourteen blackness; freezing into heavy, grey clouds and sitting low in the air waiting for me to drive through.

The sirens come on. They're doing this for me, to tell me they're here as if I didn't already know. Then the red brake-lights flash on and off as they dab their brakes and the ambulance slows and the sirens change tempo and they park up pretty much in the centre of the road, and I pull in behind. I can see a police car parked further up with its roof lights flashing and strobing the snow crust of this dry northern tundra.

I get out and pull on my jacket and I step around the ambulance. There's a truck down in the ditch. Again. The cop car's parked so its headlights illuminate the scene and it looks like an outdoor theatre set, spotlights picking out the smoking Grimberg delivery truck, one of the vintage boxy vans with narrow wheels that looks quaint and all but has no place in a Swedish winter.

The cop's at the truck talking at the driver through a mangled door. Reassuring him. Soft words. A dark red smudge on the window. The paramedics join her and then, together, heaving, they manage to release the door. They gently lift out a short man and place him on a stretcher they've had to leave down on the soft powder-snow covering the verge. He looks familiar. Blood runs down one side of his face. The paramedics fit a neck brace. One of his legs is facing the wrong way and they look at it and look at each other and then they cover him with an aluminium foil sheet.

I have my camera in the Hilux and this is one of those journalist moments where what's the right thing to do and what's the smart thing to do are not the same thing. I should be photographing but there are only three of us out here in this minus-fourteen nothingness so the camera can wait.

'Can I help?' I shout.

'Wait in your vehicle,' yells Noora.

I ignore that instruction and watch the paramedics lift the braced man into the rear of the ambulance with all the carefulness and precision of two veteran watchmakers. He doesn't seem to shake or jolt a bit as they load him in and close the rear doors and drive off.

'Get back in your truck and find an alternative route,' says Noora.

'I'm Tuva,' I say.

'This road won't reopen for at least another hour, maybe more. You'll have to reroute.'

She goes to her police Volvo and takes a roll of police tape, blue and white, and ties it around a pine. Lucky the truck didn't hit that tree. Fortunate.

'Tuva?' she asks. 'You said your name's Tuva?'

'Yes.'

'Tuva, do me a favour and return to your vehicle, and if I was to advise you I'd say turn around and drive back home. It's getting late and there's nothing good out here. Go on now.'

Her skin looks moist, not dry like mine. I do as she says.

I complete a three-point turn, my tyres crunching

through hardened snow on each verge, and leave the police Volvo in my mirrors. But then I realise I've not asked for a quote or recorded any details or done anything I've been trained to do. I reverse back slowly on the ice and I hate it, somehow anxious I'll hit the accelerator instead of the brake and run Noora over. Injure her. Kill her.

I get out of my truck.

'Sorry, I should have introduced myself,' I say.

She looks at me like I'm high.

'I'm Tuva Moodyson, reporter at the *Gavrik Posten*.'

'I know who you are, Tuva. Just didn't know what you look like.'

I think I'm blushing but I should get away with it. Could be frost burn for all she knows.

'Thord and the Chief told me all about you,' she says. 'I got a scene to organise and paperwork to do.'

'Can I get a quote for the paper please and then I'll leave you, I promise.'

'Nope.'

She has a small hole under her lower lip. Old piercing scar.

'The delivery driver gonna be okay?' I ask.

I can't see red in the snow but there are holes, fine holes, where warm body temperature drops of something have melted through to the permafrost below.

'I hope so,' she says, blowing a loose strand of black hair away from her face. 'Listen. Off the record.' She pauses and pulls the tape tight around the delivery truck. 'Driver . . .' she says, '. . . this is off the record, okay? Driver wouldn't take responsibility. Reckoned his truck's been tampered with.'

She finishes taping up the scene and sticks the roll in her jacket pocket.

'Tampered with?' I ask.

She looks at me like she regrets ever opening her mouth.

'Off the record,' she says again.

'Who complained about Gunnarsson harassing a minor seven years ago? Do you have a name? Is that an active lead?'

'Can't discuss her,' she says.

Now I know it was definitely a her.

'Anything else?' I ask. 'Any details? Anything I can actually use?'

'Quote you can use?' she says. 'How about reduce your speed by thirty per cent in winter. Driving at night time or in adverse conditions should be avoided unless absolutely necessary. End quote.' She points to my pick-up truck. 'We're done.'

As I walk, I detour around the delivery van. The front passenger side is destroyed, caved-in, and the sign above the windscreen reads 'No 1'.

I feel nauseous.

I should have been in that delivery truck tonight. Down in the ditch. In the caved-in side of the number one truck. If it wasn't for the thirst I inherited from Dad I could have been killed.

I get home and take my bottle of rum to bed.

The morning's dark. The recycling bags take three walks to the bins and I'm left with old beer juice on my hands from a micro-leak. I dry-retch but I don't throw up. They're so heavy I have to drag them down the stairs and across the gritty slush to the recycling containers. I push the glass through and it smashes inside and this is why my aids are turned down low The cardboard is a challenge because the whole goddam container is crammed full with bag-in-box wine cartons, boxes of cheap wine, not even screw-cap wine, that my fellow countrymen live off all year round but have a special affection for during the white months.

I get to work and Lena's in. I say good morning and pour myself a coffee and grab a plastic box full of profiteroles from the fridge below the drainage rack. My mouth's dry and my head's throbbing. I'm a wreck. I take a plastic fork and pierce them one by one and eat them standing next to Nils's desk.

I settle down at my PC and pick up the phone and dial.

'Gavrik Police.'

'Morning, Thord, it's me.'

'Tuvs.'

'Do you have anything on that delivery truck crash last night? Status of the driver?'

There's a pause on the line like he's got his palm over the receiver and talking to someone else.

'Say what now?'

I reposition my ear over the octagonal anti-feedback pad that I attached to the phone the first week I worked here.

'The truck crash last night,' I say.

'Oh, he's alive. It was Andersson, he's the uncle of my neighbour, the kid with the Frisbee thing lodged in his ear lobe. Shaken and beat up, some internal bleeding, I'm afraid to say. Needed putting back together. You was out there at the scene wasn't you?'

'Janitor Andersson?' No, it can't have been. Driving? 'It was the janitor?'

'They got a run of bad luck in that factory.'

'It was the janitor?' I ask again, my heart racing.

'Ran tests at the hospital,' he says. 'Because Noora couldn't breathalyse him last night. Sober as a judge.'

'But was it the factory janitor?'

'One of his brothers so the Chief reckons. Uncle of my neighbour. Bad luck.'

I stare in the direction of the factory. Did someone run that truck off the road? I asked Thord earlier if he thought the old couple had been pushed into the ditch and he told me there was no evidence of it. Just that time of year, he said. But this is too much of a coincidence. And did someone think I was in the delivery truck asking Andersson questions with my digital Dictaphone tight in my hand? Was I a target?

'Bad luck,' I agree, shaking the thought from my

head. I'm being paranoid. It's the hangover. 'The lead you never told me about. The complaint brought by a minor against Gunnarsson.'

'Was never brought by the girl,' he says, cutting me off. 'Complaint got made by an employee who thought she saw something. The girl and her parents cleared Gunnarsson of any wrongdoing. Black gossip, that's all.'

'Okay,' I say. 'You know I'm leaving on Monday, don't you?'

'I ain't going with you if that's what you asking. I'm a Gavrik fella born and raised and I can't stand them big city ways.'

I smile and feel a little better.

'You're not going to elope with me? Imagine how cute our kids would be?'

I hear the same muffled sound as before, his hand over the receiver.

'Gotta go, Tuvs.'

I write up the crash story and jot down a few sub-par headline ideas. The bell over the door tinkles so I look up and it's Nils wearing one of those waxy camouflage baseball-caps with fleece lining and big old ear flaps, they sell them in Björnmossen's right now for 299 kronor on sale.

'Nice headwear,' I say.

He looks up and pulls off his cap revealing a gel-slicked nest of dishevelled, dyed black hair.

'Like it?'

He starts to tussle his hair into spikes.

'When you gonna put away them dusty old Christmas decorations from the window?' he says. 'Get the creeps every time I see them.'

'Why don't you do it?' I ask.

He sticks his chest out and walks over to his office, the salopette shoulder-straps of his outer trousers hanging down by his knees.

'I'm the one who pulls in the dough to pay you three, remember?'

I rub my temple with an extended middle finger and he smiles and shows me gun fingers and then he closes his door and I get back to work organising stories and building a to-do list. His door flies open.

'You ate my chocolate balls?'

I break out into a grin at that.

'Guilty as charged,' I say. 'They're called profiteroles.'

He shakes his head and slams the door to his office slash kitchen.

Number one on my list is 'Gunnarsson allegations' because I still want to find out who made the complaint and who the minor was. Number two is 'post-mortem results' because I still don't have any details as this one hasn't been fast tracked.

It'll help that my next Grimberg interviews will be conducted in the private residence, the Grand Room, because if things start to stall I can refer to an object or a photo, one of Lena's many tricks, and that usually gets people talking.

I might be able to corner them, to get them to open up. The Grimbergs know more than they're letting on.

Lunch is that five-minute drive-thru double cheeseburger I promised myself yesterday. Then I pull up to my parking place and walk over to the factory holding my laptop and Dictaphone.

Parked beneath the arch is another out-of-town police Volvo. Specialist homicide investigators from Karlstad. The car's covering the door to the old factory. I skirt past it and try to open the archway door to the staircase and the canteen, but it's bolted shut and someone's stuck a 'Strictly No Entry' sticker to it so I walk on to the delivery trucks and root barns in the rear yard. The main employee entrance is wide open.

The stampers are working and Great White smiles at me with her screw-ins as I walk by. Her teeth are stained grey with liquorice juice. Red doesn't acknowledge me at all, she's too focussed on her work, head down, hand-punching coins at such a rate it almost blurs. She looks less put together than normal. I realise why. She's just lost both her grandparents. The old Volvo in the ditch. That single purple glove. The fact they weren't speaking for the past six or seven years. I want to reach out and place my hand on her shoulder but I don't. I head through the canteen and up the stairs and into the Receiving Room. Gavrik looks sinister from the window, a lonely Swedish Toytown going about its Tuesday lunchtime business; women on bicycles and men buying ice-fishing magazines and Snus tobacco; a vicious murderer still walking the streets. I turn and approach the door to the private residence and knock.

Nothing.

I knock three times, good hard knocks, and wait with my ear close to the door.

'We'll be talking in here today,' says Anna-Britta from the top of the stairs. 'We'll use the Receiving Room.'

'Must we?' I say.

'He's told you to ask us personal things, hasn't he?'

'Holmqvist?'

Her face screws up as I say the name.

'Here's the thing.' She walks closer to me, her eyes red in the corners, her rose perfume coming off in waves. 'We know the deal Gustav arranged. We'll honour it. The book needs to be a full and frank account. I'll cooperate. But there are some things where I'll draw the line and you must respect that.'

'Like?'

'You know we've got the police in again downstairs, don't you?'

'I saw the car.'

'My daughter can't sleep in her own bed, she's beside herself with worry, exhausted, and I had sixteen staff members call in sick today. Sixteen. They're not sick, they're terrified.'

'Can I make notes as we talk? Can I record?'

She frowns.

'Sometimes I can't hear everything the first time it's said, even when it's someone talking who speaks clearly like you.'

Anna-Britta cringes. 'I'm so sorry, I forget that you're . . .' She touches her earlobe. 'Of course you can record it, go ahead.'

We sit at the desk and I switch on my digital Dictaphone.

'Do you know who would have a grudge against Gunnarsson? Did he have any enemies to your knowledge?'

She holds up her hand. 'I'll talk about the factory, for the book, but not about what happened downstairs. I've told the police all I know. Retelling it'll make me ill.'

'Okay,' I say. 'Let's talk about your parents-in-law.'

She nods.

'Cecilia and Ludvig Grimberg.'

She nods again and her eyelashes are as short and bristly as the fur of a short-haired rat.

'What was your father-in-law like?'

'Ludvig was a complex man.' She says this like it's rehearsed. 'He studied medicine at Lund and then when his father passed away he moved back to Gavrik and expanded the factory building to the rear. He was a man of action despite his back problems.'

'You two were close?'

'My father-in-law didn't approve of me. Ludvig was very protective of his son, you see, because

Gustav's schooldays were so troubled. But Gustav made it clear to his father that his approval was not required.'

There's a bone-handled letter opener on the desk and its pointed end glints in the chandelier light. Anna-Britta takes a jug of water, one of the chipped enamel ones from the canteen, it looks so out of place in this beautiful room, and pours us both a glass. Her cuticles and nails are red raw like they've been grated.

'He was Managing Director until the nineties?' I ask. 'Is that right?'

'Correct,' she says. 'Until his passing.'

'What did he die from?'

She drinks half her water, her eyes on mine.

'Accidental overdose,' she says. 'We're not sure Ludvig even knew he'd taken too much medication. We were at the lake house. He took the pills and then wandered off and died. My late husband found the empty bottles.'

'You think it was really an accident?'

'I don't *think* it was, I know it was,' she says, uncrossing and crossing her legs; the black and grey skirt of her two-piece rides up a little to reveal high-denier black tights. 'Gustav was almost destroyed by his leaving us all like that.'

'Did your husband question whether the overdose was an accident?'

'It was warfarin for goodness sake,' she says to me. 'You don't poison yourself with heart medicine and walk off into the sunset, it's not done. It's not easy or painless; you do it with painkillers and sleeping tablets.'

'Okay, sorry to bring it up. Let's move onto your mother-in-law. Do you two have a good relationship?'

She moves in her seat.

'We're too different for that. We're both very strong-willed people. Cecilia lives in her own world up there, plays by her own rules. When her husband was running things the company did very well. She's never really known difficult times.'

'How is she coping with Gustav's suicide?'

'No,' she says.

'She's not coping?'

'I will not have that word used in my home.' Anna-Britta stands up and walks over to the cold, tiled fireplace and fondles the pine cone and the blood-tipped feather sitting on the mantle. 'I will not have that word . . .'

'I'm sorry,' I say. 'How is Cecilia coping these days, with the Gunnarsson incident and all?'

Anna-Britta turns to me. 'She manages in her own way as must we all. We don't live the same life as other people in Gavrik. We have a lifelong responsibility, all of us, to keep this place alive.'

'Alive?'

'To support the town and make liquorice the same way we have for over a hundred-and-fifty years. We owe it to the people.'

Agnetha Hellbom pokes her candyfloss head around the door at the top of the staircase. She has a needle-shaped silver hairpin stabbed through her perm, like someone's attacked her.

'Sorry, Anna-Britta, the police need two minutes.' She holds up two bony fingers as she says this.

Anna-Britta looks red in the cheeks, heat-rash bumps on one side of her neck.

'Coming,' she says.

'Thanks for talking,' I say. 'Would it be possible to speak with Karin tomorrow, please?'

Anna-Britta looks at the locked door to the residence and then looks back at me.

'We'll see,' she says. 'Karin's not herself.'

CHAPTER 21

When I get back to work there's a box of Grimberg salt liquorice sitting on my desk next to my keyboard. I open the lid. There are two black coins rattling around in the box.

'Who left this here?' I ask Lars.

'You don't want it, I'll take it,' he says.

Someone passes the window wearing a balaclava and stares in. 'Who left it?'

'You don't like the salt?'

The figure at the window's gone. Nobody there.

I throw the box over to Lars and he catches it. Two-hander. Closed eyes. But he makes the catch and looks pretty happy with himself.

Grab some falafel, apparently, from the news-agent across the road but if this is a falafel then I'm a bear hunter with a beard and a Husky and a range of gutting knives.

I write up my Anna-Britta notes. Not sure if the truck crash was her fault in any way – corporate negligence – or if it's just an accident. I told Thord that I was due to ride in the van last night, interviewing the driver, shadowing him for a delivery, and he told me it must have been my lucky day.

'Tuva,' says Lena. 'Sebastian's dropping in after two for a pre-induction chat. That's okay, yes?'

Sebastian? I'm judging this guy already. The name. I'm hating him. 'Can I join at the end? I need to drive up to the truck rental place outside town and extend my Agreement.'

'Your truck can wait.'

I call the rental place out by the sewage treatment works and tell the kid answering the phone, a kid in need of a semester in enthusiasm school, that I'll be thirty minutes late. You might not think an appointment would be necessary for this kind of thing, you might think a garage or car dealership would be open all day, but that's where you'd be wrong. In Sweden these places often close for an important *fika* coffee break and when they're closed they're closed.

The bell over the door tinkles and a young Dolph Lundgren walks in and smiles and for some illogical reason Lars and I both sit up straighter in our seats and stick out our necks and smile back.

'Hi, I'm Sebastian. Here for Lena?' his voice perks up at the end of the sentence.

I stand and lean over my desk and extend my hand over to shake his.

'I'm Tuva.'

Lars shuffles round his desk to greet Sebastian.

'I'm Lars.'

And then we just stand there near the filing

cabinets. He's about twenty-two years old, cheek-bones rendered by Picasso, Cupid's-bow lips about as full as can be, nine maybe ten centimetres taller than me, bronzed from some kind of holiday or solarium, American teeth, smells of Davidoff Cool Water.

'So you're the new guy,' I say. 'My replacement.'

'That's me,' he says, pressing his thumb into his chest. And Lars looks delighted to be getting rid of me and my nail polish and my obsessive reporting style, and replacing me with Cheekbones here.

'Ah, Sebastian, let's walk and talk, shall we?' says Lena, stepping out and pulling on her long, black coat and loose hat.

Cheekbones is one of those athletic types who looks good even in late winter. Don't know what it is really, the exercise making his skin so perfect, or the fact that he can wear a ski jacket and make it look like he's actually off skiing. We walk onto Storgatan.

'What's that place?' asks Cheekbones.

'That, Sebastian,' says Lena, 'is the Grimberg Liquorice factory. 'Biggest employer in town.'

'Locals call it "the factory",' I say.

We walk with me closest to the road and cheek-bones in the middle and Lena closest to the wall, and there's not quite enough room for all three of us so we keep bumping into each other.

'Nice town,' he says.

I don't say anything I just focus on not stepping

205

on a snow-dusted dog turd. They're like evil reverse baked-Alaskas this time of year: frozen on the outside, still warm and soft in the middle.

'Shall we try the hotel?' asks Lena.

'Or McDonald's?' I suggest.

'Let's try the hotel,' says Lena.

The Hotel Gavrik sign is slightly off-centre. There are two garden candles burning by the entrance and star-shaped Christmas lights still light up some of the windows. There's a snowball down by the outdoor candle. I take a closer look at it but there are no eye holes, no lingonberry blood, no toothpick teeth, no gaping mouth. It's just a snowball, that's all. We go inside.

'*Hej*, could we get some coffee, please?' says Lena to the receptionist.

'Card machine's broke,' says the receptionist, a round box of Snus tobacco sticking out from the pocket of her apron. 'You got change? Cos if you haven't got change I can't help you.'

'We have change,' says Lena.

Cheekbones looks like he's visiting a nursing home. We sit down in the corner next to the self-service coffee thermos and tea bags and UHT milk cartons and the untouched tourist information leaflets.

'Coffee?' Lena asks Cheekbones.

'Peppermint tea, please,' he says, and we both look at each other like *what the fuck is wrong with this kid?*

We sit together and talk about his new role as

the sole full-time reporter at *Gavrik Posten*. Lena explains how print media is still important out here in the middle of nowhere, how locals rely on us for news and how we join together a spread-out rural community. She explains how the relationship is reciprocal: Gavrik residents pay for subscriptions and they pay for advertising space that they know will get noticed, and in turn they get a well-written reliable community paper. She tells him how circulation has increased by over a thousand copies a week since I started work and how much of that was down to the Medusa murder investigations and my proactive reporting of incidents.

'I read you found the Ferryman's victim,' says Cheekbones.

'I did,' I say.

'Everyone's saying it was an occult thing because of all the dog teeth left in his throat,' he says. 'Maybe an ex-con sociopath biker, you know?'

'Delete that image,' says Lena in a serious tone. 'Delete it and restart your processor. I'm serious, Sebastian, if you're going to be a good reporter, if you want to be half as good as Tuva and one day get offered a job at a highly regarded *Skåne* journal, then lose the preconceived ideas and the clichés and start treating every person you meet as an individual with their own unique story. First of all, it was one dog tooth. One. And the killer could just as easy be a kindergarten teacher in her 40s as some leather-clad biker. Give everyone their time and listen twice as much as you talk.'

I think back to Lena looking after me when Mum died. How she gave me the time and the space and the silence to manage. How she fed me and how she never asked when I'd be back at work or whether it's time to move on and get back to normal.

'She's right,' I say, sipping my stewed, black coffee. 'Listen more than you talk. Lena knows.'

'I will,' he says, suddenly all back-foot defensive keen.

We both nod and I notice the pinkie ring on his little finger, some kind of crest showing an elk head with antlers.

'I learnt how to talk to people during my studies at university,' he says, his tone higher at the end of the sentence again. Almost a hint of an Australian accent. 'And then in my Masters in Karlstad. We learnt a lot of practical skills.'

Lena and I stifle our eye-rolls.

'You ever lived in a town like Gavrik, Sebastian?' she asks. 'Where do you holiday each year?'

'My family had a summerhouse in Gotland, but in winter we used to go to Thailand.'

Here's a kid who's slid through life on a greased non-friction surface of Teflon privilege and Mamma's kronor.

'Well,' says Lena. 'Welcome to reality, population nine thousand. Tuva, tell him.'

I look at her and then I look around the room for a minute. They're preparing for Valentine's so there are red plastic roses, dusty, on the reception desk. The Ikea tea lights in the Ikea lanterns are blood-red and waiting to be lit. There's a bunch of scrunched red ribbon on top of the menu board but no menu inside yet. Out behind the reception desk there's some kind of eBay fibreglass cherub with a bow and arrow still half-shrouded in bubble wrap.

I wipe my nose on my sleeve. 'Gavrik is cut-off, Sebastian. We're surrounded by dense, elk forests and marginal farmland. It's not as geographically isolated as many places in Sweden, but it's isolated by its attitude. There are no tourist attractions here, not real ones, and the cross-country ski trails are better in a dozen other Värmland towns. Businesses scrape by and most are desperate for some outside investment, some boost. Which never comes. This place keeps going because of the factory and the SPT Pulp Mill just up the E16, you'll visit it soon enough. People who grow up here can't imagine moving anywhere else and, aside from the three of us, most people don't move here by choice. But it's ripe with stories and interesting people and I'd say it's as good a town as any to start your journalism career.'

'My family are in Karlstad so I'll go back at weekends, it's not like I'll be here all the time.'

Seriously? This is what he chooses to say to me?

'Most weekends you'll be talking to sources or eavesdropping in ICA Maxi or writing up head-lines for Lena or else photographing some school play production,' I say with a little too much acid. 'You'll need to get stuck in from day one. Locals need to see you and trust you. You'll have to develop some reliable sources in the Kommun offices and the schools and the police station and the big employers.'

'I'll manage,' he says.

He has that pretty-boy confidence like he's never been turned down by a girl and I envy him and pity him and resent him all at the same time.

'Tuva's right,' says Lena. 'You might think the news here is exciting, the talk of The Ferryman and all, but mostly it's Kommun meetings and writing about new cycle paths. Week one I'll cover your ass like a second shadow. We'll interview together and drive around together and write up your first stories together. Don't worry, you'll get the by-lines. I'll do what I did with Tuva. I'll introduce you to people and tell them to keep you in the loop, and I'll do my best to explain the local ways.'

We pay and leave and the kid has a look on his face as we pass the cop shop and head down Storgatan like he's having regrets, but by the look of the BMW parked in the *Posten* car park I reckon Mummy and Daddy will see him good if he runs home in tears cos Benny Björnmossen called him a college-boy prick, or if he realises there aren't really any restaurants in Gavrik.

Cheekbones and Lena talk in her office and I head off to the Toyota dealership outside town.

I drive past the ice hockey rink and the fire station. My dash says minus three.

There's a mist rising slowly from the sewage treatment plant as I pass and the electricity substation right next to it is buzzing. I see the dealership, all glass walls and beautiful gleaming, brand new fresh-out-the-box estates and pick-ups, and behind it I see the old dealership, the brick ruin, the condemned black warehouse now shuttered up and boarded up and locked up. I wrote an article about it last year. A group of locals think it's unsafe and they want it pulled down.

The door bleeps as I walk in and the room reeks of new car smell. I breathe it in and then I see a teenager in the office with some kind of twisted white-boy half-ass gel-assisted dreadlocks which stick straight up out of his head.

'So, you decided to turn up.'

I turn toward the voice and see Jan-Östnäs walking to me wearing blue jeans a size too small, and a huge belt buckle the size of an iPhone and a suede leather jacket.

'Sorry I'm late, work stuff. I did call.'

'You got the keys?' he asks. 'Any problems with the Hilux, anything I need to know about before we sign off the paperwork?'

'You didn't get my message?' I say. 'I need to extend the rental until Monday, please. Need the truck till Monday.'

He shakes his head and starts probing his gums with a toothpick.

'You think it's one rule for you and another for the rest of us?' he says.

'No,' I say. 'I just want six more days, please.'

'You think your time's more important than mine, is that it?'

Got a dickhead deluxe here.

'I'm sorry I'm late. Can I please extend the rental for a few days? You'd be doing me a huge favour. I'll pay, of course.'

He points back to his office, at Mr Potato Head sitting at the computer. There's an unzipped hold-all next to the desk and I can see one of those long, heavy American-style torches sitting inside with a plastic bag secured to the end with an elastic band. Behind him is a rack of spray paints for retouching bodywork, in colours like Black Pearl and Metallic Bronze and Satin Aquamarine and Sailcloth White and Matt Champagne.

'My boy's taking your Hilux. I promised it to him. You want another Hilux I got six but you'll need to buy it. They're not for rent.'

I feel a rage burn rising from my guts.

'Please, Jan-Östnäs, is there any way I can rent my truck, the one I've had for three years, no accidents, no late payments, for six more days?'

'Not up to me, up to my boy now.'

I sigh and then I wave at the kid and he walks over with jeans that fit but the family must have got a volume deal on those belts.

'Lady here wants to know if she can rent your Hilux for a few days?'

Potato Head just grins and shakes his head. 'My truck now,' he says with a voice that hasn't broken the way it should've. 'Taking it ice fishing with mates.'

'Is there anything else I can rent?'

'Not really,' says Jan-Östnäs. He licks his freshly-picked teeth. 'Suppose I could let you take the Tacoma but you gotta be real careful with her.'

'Her?'

'Ninety-eight Tacoma, runs like a dream but she's an old bird and she's kind of special to me.'

We walk out to the back lot, past shiny new cars with summer tyres stored in their boots. Jan-Östnäs pulls on his gloves. There are discarded toothpicks everywhere out here and they look like pine needles, like matchsticks, like old reptile bones left out in the sun. He points to a white pick-up, one of those old types that look smaller than a modern family-hatchback. The wheel arches are about seventy per cent rust and it has no hubcaps. On the roof sits a thick white blanket of old snow and I can see jump-lead cables hanging down from the bonnet which is never a good sign.

'Why don't you start her up,' says Jan-Östnäs to his son.

Potato Head pulls on a jacket with a mountain-eering cabana attached to the zip. It has a range of knives and car logo keyrings and multi-tools dangling from it. He opens the truck door the old-fashioned way, with the key in the keyhole. How quaint. A ton of snow falls on him from the roof. He swears and moans and then tries to start the engine but it just tells him to go to hell.

'We'll jump it and then you'll need to drive it about an hour to get a decent charge. You wanna take it?'

'Do I have a choice?'

'You can hitch-hike back to town. We have about ten cars pass by this way each day so you might get lucky.'

I shake my head.

'Taxi? I can call Viggo Svensson?'

I shake my head more vigorously.

They jump the old truck from a brand-new navy blue 4x4, one of the muscular American ones that's about twice as tall and twice as broad as my new vehicle. I sign a rental agreement and pay for six days and get in the jumped truck and look back ruefully at my beautiful Hilux, four years old, eighty-thousand kilometres on the clock. I release the handbrake of the Tacoma and pull away.

'She got two decent tyres,' yells Jan-Östnäs from outside. I can read him. 'You look after each other now.'

The truck is a wreck, a corpse, a disaster. No thermometer on the dash, the rev counter won't work; it's automatic but the gears grind like hell, the acceleration doesn't exist and the blower works fine but the seats aren't heated. Kill me now.

CHAPTER 22

The rusty pick-up rattles and the brakes are pretty much unresponsive. Twenty kph crunching down a poorly-ploughed country road with the blower on full and my hands gripping the wheel like I'm cresting the top of a rollercoaster.

You might think I go on about trucks too much and you'd probably be right. But in any northern place where the winters are long and there aren't many people around, a truck is like a family member. It's a thing you rely on, like our ancestors relied on their dogs and horses. I need a good truck and this one isn't it.

The sewage-treatment plant steams quietly to my left and I pull into its car park and keep the engine running. If I switch it off I'll be left truckless on the shit farm.

At least the heater works. But as the cab of the truck warms up it starts to smell like oil rags and overalls, all stale sweat and grease and cigarette smoke. There's an open pack of razor blades on the passenger seat – the kind that come in small paper envelopes. I feel around the steering column so I can work out where all the levers are because I don't want to be stuck guessing out on the E16 at ninety kph. More likely sixty in the slow lane. The cigarette lighter is missing and the stereo's been ripped out and the windows are wind-down ones and there is no back seat at all, just a window to the rear flatbed.

Ahead of me is a representative sample of Gavrik's faecal matter. A swirling, steaming soup of poop made up from the business of Benny Björnmossen from the gun store and Fredrik the shoe salesman and Anna-Britta Grimberg and Janitor Andersson. The snow has melted all around from the manure heat. It's a warm shit pond being stirred like those stainless steel vats of coal-black liquorice in the factory. It's melted all the white around and it's created a noxious fog of its own rising slowly into the cold still air above.

I call Thord.

'Gavrik Police.'

'It's me.'

'Just in time,' he says. 'Forensics got back to us.'

'And?'

'I can tell you ninety per cent. No fingerprints on the body or the liquorice coins. Killer was wearing gloves, they reckon. No fibres of any use, no DNA. They checked for prints in the old part of the factory, but it was a slushy mess and there's nothing clear. The tooth . . .'

'Dog?' I ask.

'Big dog,' he says. 'Big, German shepherd. The

cut to the neck was made by a scalpel or whatnot, and the tooth was pushed in after the victim had died, so they reckon. Told me if the tooth had been pushed in before Gunnarsson bled out then, according to the rocket scientists down in Linköping, the tooth would have been pushed out by the blood flow.'

'Shit,' I say.

'I reckon,' he says. 'Oh, and the head injury. Blunt trauma to the back of the head, happened before the neck attack, most likely a bat or a metal bar.'

I see the janitor's metal piping in my head. The heavy length of piping near his blowtorch and his duct tape down in the basement. But he found the body with me? We were together?

'Okay,' I say. 'Thanks for keeping me in the loop.'

'Chief wants to make an appeal for information in your next paper. Anonymous helpline to call and all sorts.'

'Anonymous?' I say. 'In this town?'

'That's what I said.'

'What's the other ten per cent?' I ask.

'Say what?'

'You said you could tell me ninety per cent. But what I really want to know is the other ten.'

Silence on the line. I stare out at the shit cloud rising from the sewage works.

'Did you notice a wet patch on Gunnarsson's chest when you found him?' he asks.

'Yes, why?'

217

'You see anything else on his chest? Anything strange?'

'Nope.'

'Gotta go, Tuvs. Maybe I can tell you more tomorrow. I'll get Noora to send over the appeal details for your paper.'

I drive away and check the brakes and I reckon the pads need an upgrade because this thing judders when it slows down. I need to stay on guard.

I pull onto the E16 and head north. Was there snow on Gunnarsson's chest? Was he dragged in from outside? Or was there a snow skull sitting on his torso staring into his eyes as his vascular system drained its last drops from that neat neck wound?

There's a clump of wind turbines on a hill and they look frozen. Their blades are turning but only just. I have to really look and they do turn but it looks like they're too cold and too stiff and too achy. White turbines over white snow against a white sky.

The tank's full so I drive all the way past Utgard forest and on to the pulp mill with its mountains of stacked pine trunks and then turn off and loop around and drive southbound toward Karlstad. This was the route I used to take to visit Mum in the hospice. Still is the route I'd take to visit her grave, her and Dad, side-by-side, one stone, some old carved words, some new, space for more, a kilometre or so away from Lake Vänern.

I'm thinking about death more after seeing the panic in Gunnarsson's face, his eyes still open under the liquorice coins, the panic in his expression. That pained transition between life and death. Mum didn't spark it off, the Ferryman did. Mum still feels like the end of a great slow arduous journey, a sad relief, an inevitable and completely predictable full stop. I don't think about death when I think of Mum, I think about how the hell I'm going to avoid her life and live my own and live it well. I know I have control over my destiny and despite Dad's drink problem and Mum's misery, I choose happiness. I just have to figure out how.

Gavrik's getting dark when I arrive back and the faded white 'Grimberg Liquorice' lettering down each brick chimney of the factory is almost invisible. .

'Lars, you still have that trickle charger in your drawer?'

'It's home,' he says.

'Trickle charger?' asks Nils from his office slash kitchen. 'Can I come to the rescue, fair maiden?'

'What?'

'I'll plug you in. Out back?'

I hand him the key. 'Thanks, it's the antique Toyota.'

'You're buying the first drink tonight,' says Nils, pointing across the road to Ronnie's Bar.

'Deal.'

I can taste it on my tongue already.

Nils walks back in. 'Nice lawn mower you got back there.' He says it like he's being funny and expects me to laugh. 'Battery'll take a few hours. Shall we?'

We don't bother to ask Lars because he's a solid-gold bore who has never once said yes. But then I think, what if?

'Lars,' I say. 'Quick drink?'

'Can't tonight,' he says.

Good for him to be honest. He does what he wants. Zero compromise.

We step out and the air's warming up, which is weird as it's night-time. A man limps past us and drags himself up the hill toward St Olov's. I can see patches in the pavement where the snow's melted away and there are tons and tons of salty grit down there, layers of briny granite shards that'll need sweeping up in April.

The neon 'Ronnie's' sign is bright blue and we walk inside and strip off our coats and scarves and hang them all up.

'Beer, please, Tuva Moody,' says Nils, pushing me to the bar.

I order from Ronnie and he has a blue plaster strapped around his index finger.

'Got mice problems,' says Nils. 'Got 'em in the shed, in the roof, in the walls. Feasting and fucking, is how my God-fearing wife puts it. You believe they've nested in our patio-chair cushions? You believe that?' He sips his beer and sighs a big pleasure sigh.

There are ten or twelve people in clusters playing pool or chatting at tables. There's a man in the corner wearing wire-rimmed glasses with tinted lenses and from over here it looks like his eyes are black and oversize and it looks like he's staring at me. I feel out of place. The music. The man. My lack of a Hilux. The mangled delivery truck I should have been strapped into. And the poor guy locked in the morgue with a canine tooth lodged in his neck.

Maybe I'm overstaying my welcome.

'I can't stay out long tonight,' I tell Nils.

'How's about next drink's on the house,' says Ronnie.

He pours us both a shot of tequila. We drink them back with salt and then bite into lemon slices and we both make the kind of sucking noises you make when you drink tequila that way. The salt lingers on my lips. It's everywhere: sodium chloride in the candy and all over the pavements, on the motorway; I can sense it in the air around town. This whole place is salted.

'Another,' I say to the barman.

We drink.

'One more,' I say.

'Hold on,' says Nils. 'I'm not twenty-six. I'll take a beer.'

We both take a beer and sit down at a sticky table.

'Tell me about the Grimbergs,' says Nils. 'You reckon they're somehow responsible for Gunnarsson. What do you think they're up to?'

'Up to?'

'I heard things are falling apart since Gustav jumped,' says Nils, preening his spiked hair as he talks. 'Might be a lawsuit after that van crash. Heard the driver won't work again. Maybe won't walk again. Makes me happy they never gave me that sales job last year. Pay was better than the *Posten*, I can tell you now cos you're almost out the door, but who knows how long I'd survive in that place?' He does a fake shiver. 'People are saying it's all falling down now Grimberg's wife's in charge.'

'Her name's Anna-Britta,' I say. 'And she seems pretty capable to me.'

He sips his beer and checks his phone screen.

'People are waiting for it to collapse,' he says. 'So they can buy it up cheap.'

'Who's waiting?'

'You know who.'

'The hunched lawyer with the facelift?'

'And his brother-in-law, the fella that rented you that piece of crap parked out back of our office. Reckon the factory's worth half of what it used to be on account of all this bad publicity.'

'Brother-in-law?'

'Yeah, Toyota dealer's sister works in the factory, you didn't know that? She's a PA or executive-assistant bookkeeper or something; paper shuffler. And she's greedy and bitter – the greediest and the bitterest of them all, I have that on good authority.'

'Thin blonde hair, thinner than mine, all bunched up on top of her head?'

'That's it. Another beer?'

I nod and he walks over to the bar. My phone vibrates and Tammy says she'll be outside Ronnie's in ten minutes to pick me up and I reply with 'xx'.

The music changes to Elvis singing 'Hound Dog' and I look around the room, my eyes darting to the dark corners, to the guy with the glasses, my hand reaching up to cover my throat.

'You alright?' asks Nils walking back with two fresh beers. 'He messed up the head on these; new barrels.'

I turn down my aids to screen out the music. I'll lip-read Nils instead.

'My lift's here in ten.' I say.

'Perfect,' he says. 'This is a ten-minute beer.'

'Thanks for not being a complete prick these past three-and-a-half years,' I say.

'You're welcome. I think.' He takes a swig of beer and intentionally gives himself a froth moustache. 'Thanks for writing top stories and boosting circulation and making my job easier than it used to be.'

I'm taken aback by this. 'You think I write top stories?'

He nods and wipes away his moustache.

'You handled Medusa like a pro even though it made you no friends and now you'll handle the Ferryman slaughterer like a pro.'

I can't get every word. I never can when I lip-read.

223

But I can guess and extrapolate and read his body language.

'Slaughterer? That what they're calling him now?'

'Or her,' he says.

'Or her,' I say.

'Nah, that's just what I call him on account of the bloodletting. I worked my uncle's abattoir for two summers during school and whenever I hear about throat wounds I think back to them pigs. The iron smell of it all. The squeals.'

'One *Posten* left,' I say. 'Then it's Newboy's job.'

'Pretty-boy-rich-daddy-the-third?' says Nils. 'I'll give him till Midsummer.'

I hug Nils as I leave and his gel leaves a snail trail on my cheek but I enjoyed this drink, drinks, plural. Tammy's car's idling on the pavement so I jump in and it's warm. I kiss her cheek and we drive up toward my apartment building.

'Is there enough space in the car for all your stuff?' she asks.

'Just three cases, should be fine,' I say.

'You've checked all your cupboards, all the high ones?'

'Affirmative.'

'Nothing at the dry cleaners?' she asks.

'Negative.'

'Nothing in your basement storage?'

Oh, shit.

CHAPTER 23

I walk downstairs to the laundry rooms and unlock my storage unit. It's empty, save for one item. I open the door and the unit's about the size of a family bathroom and the troll's sitting right there where I left it.

I approach.

The wood-carving sisters of Utgard forest admitted making it, but they told me it was customised later on. Its face, his face, for it is most definitely a he, is lit from the LED lamp I activated when I walked inside. I can see his tongue, the little animal tongue, maybe a cat's or a weasel's, and it's still hanging from his painted pine lips but now it's shredded. It's been nibbled away. I look around at the corners of the unit and see the doll's eyes that have settled where they fell out last year. The storage unit looks hermetically sealed but the damage to the tongue isn't natural wasting. Something's been eating it.

His stiff pine cock is tight against its sackcloth trousers and I grab the troll around the shoulders and hold it out at arm's length, its protuberance poking the other way. I jog past the washing machines and driers and step outside and look for an appropriate hole in the recycling bin but there is no troll option. There's plastics and metals and batteries and white glass and cardboard and green glass but nothing for demonic little spruce dolls with human fingernails and twig dicks. I place in on top and it just sits there looking back at me, the sackcloth rucked and the swell catching in the streetlight. The tongue is as thin as a line of saliva. I can see tiny teeth marks. I knock it over.

'You ready?' asks Tammy.

I hold up a finger like 'just a sec' and go inside the hallway of my building and I'm acutely aware of the look and sound and smell of the place that's been a kind of home for three-and-a-half Toytown years. I open my postbox and my key dangles from my fingertips for a while and then I drop it. Clunk. I've thought about this mundane act many times in the past years when things have been tough: the ecstatic practicalities of handing in my notice and clearing my apartment and dropping that metal key into that metal mailbox. But all I feel now is empty sorrow.

We drive away.

I have no flat.

I have no truck.

Tam drives and the heavy crowbar she keeps in her passenger-side footwell digs into my leg. I stare out of my window. There are casserole dishes everywhere: heavy cast iron ones left outside front doors with beef stews and fish pies and chunky root-vegetable soups inside. They have bricks on top or else insulation tape to keep the wild things out. The whole town is a goddam freezer.

'How do you feel?' asks Tammy.

Her Peugeot's a stick-shift manual, so I place my hand softly on top of hers and we change gears together until we get to her building. Her hand is strong and clear and knowing and mine's just along for the ride.

I pull out two black wheelie-suitcases and Tam takes the third and together we drag them through salted snow to the entrance of her block.

There's a low brick wall.

And there's a skull.

A snow *skalle*'s perched on the end of the wall and the light from the building glows through it from behind and the eyes look alive.

Tam glances at me and I look around to see if anyone's watching us. Lights move in windows from TV shows.

I use my phone's torch to light up the fist-sized skull.

'What ratshit made that?' asks Tam.

This one has grit mixed in with the snow, it's a dirty-grey colour, and its eyes are not liquorice. This one has doll's eyes, the plastic or glass variety where the pupils move freely. Like the eyes of the troll I just disposed of. The light shines through the snow and through the eyes and Tam and I just stare at it. A thing the size of a grapefruit and yet it has captured us completely.

I move to pick it up.

'Wait,' says Tam, seizing my wrist. 'Look.'

We move to the side of the skull.

There's a medical needle sticking out of the indentation that is the skull's gaping mouth. The needle is almost invisible in this light and the syringe behind the skull is transparent.

'Ratshit kids,' says Tam.

She doesn't know about the meltwater on Gunnarsson's chest. Or the skull at the factory. Or the one on my truck. She doesn't know.

'We can't leave it here,' she says.

I photograph it and then I pick it up carefully and we step to the door.

'The code's 1289,' says Tammy. 'We changed it yesterday. New code's 1289.'

Gavrik residents are once again changing their building door-codes.

We go in and ride the lift up to the third floor. Its eyes move as I walk. Like it's drunk or entertaining a small child. I hold it away from me. The last thing I need is to trip on a patch of meltwater and pierce myself with its needle.

I must have been to Tam's place twenty times in the past years but now it feels different. I'm seeing it through new eyes. Clean, tidy, food in the fridge, the fire in the modern log burner laid and ready to go. It seems perfect. But there's also a demonic snow *skalle* with moving eyes and a needle for a tongue slowly melting away in the stainless steel sink.

★   ★   ★

When I wake the next morning Tam's not in bed. We slept head to foot last night like two thirteen-year-olds, even though she has a small spare bedroom. Tam's gun rests on her bedside table. I reach over to her side of the bed, to the warmth, and then I pull on my aids.

'Breakfast's ready,' she calls from the kitchen.

I pad through flat-footed and see the fire lit in the corner and the coffee steaming from its pot.

'I should have moved in years ago,' I say, double-checking the door locks.

She blows a raspberry and beckons me over.

'Semla,' I say, neither a question nor a statement, just me saying the word to myself and letting it rest on my tongue.

'Not homemade,' she says. 'But they are luxury lux-deluxe.'

I stare down at the sweet bread bun filled with fresh cream and sprinkled with cinnamon.

'Hot milk or hot chocolate?' asks Tammy.

'What do you think?'

We both pour lukewarm hot chocolate, the milky Swedish frothy kind not the thick rich Mediterranean kind, onto the Semla bun and let it soak up. Then we attack with spoons and drink coffee and say very little and it is hands down the best breakfast I've had in years.

We know there's a needle on the sink sitting atop a folded tea towel. We both know it. But we need this moment, this food, this togetherness, this brief escape.

'I'll tell Thord first thing,' I say, gesturing toward the sink.

'Why here, though?' she asks. 'Because of you? A pissed-off reader? Who knew you were moving here?'

Lena knows. Nils knows. Lars probably knows. Other than that?

'I'll ask around, probably kids trying to scare everyone,' I say.

'Too late,' says Tam. 'We were already scared.'

She explains to me how she can only handle the harsh artic conditions of her food van, the obnoxious no-tip no-chat customers, the darkness of it all, the inherent danger, if her apartment is warm and comfortable. She suffers this time of year, I know she does, even when there are no killers loose in this small, marginal town. It's months with no decent light and no decent heat. It's an endurance sport just making it through to May even in a good year.

Tammy drives me to the office. I'm glad she keeps a crowbar in her Peugeot and a gun in her van and a lock knife in her pocket. She needs to be careful and I feel especially protective now I'm about to leave her all alone in this Godforsaken town. As we pass Björnmossen's gun store she tells me her profits would double or maybe even triple if the liquorice-factory canteen ever closed down. And if the Grimbergs ever do sell up that's the first things any new owner would do.

I drive off in the Tacoma to ICA, it opens at

7am on weekdays, and park up. In other towns the supermarkets are open twenty-four hours a day, but this isn't other towns. ICA's empty, apart from pensioners and bleary-eyed nightshift technicians from the pulp mill. I recognise a council worker who repairs potholes, usually alone, she never seems to stop working, strong as a bison, wavy hair to die for. She nods 'hi'.

I fill my basket: one window wiper on a stick for condensation and one very faux-cashmere steering-wheel cover and one portable car-charger starter thing with crocodile clips. 1,980 kronor.

The stack of papers for sale in the office is getting low by the time I get back. The Ferryman is the kind of story that non-subscribing occasional readers will trek through slush to buy.

I open a folder for Cheekbones and deposit the things I've kept behind for no-news weeks, we get plenty of them, stories about the local blood-sucking tick population or the elk-hunt quotas. They might help the new boy in the next weeks or months, or most likely his entire goddam career when local people won't open up to him. At least I look semi-redneck with my scrappy ponytail and my part-Saami nub of a nose and my extensive supermarket fleece collection. Cheekbones looks like a Gant catalogue and that is not going to work in his favour one bit.

I get to the cop shop and there are three grey-haired women standing at the counter. They're all wearing dark fleece jackets and they all have the fur-lined boots that I see on sale in the shoe-shop window each morning.

'Muzzles,' one of them says to Thord. 'Make it the law.'

'I don't make the law, Mrs Alfredsson,' says Thord.

'If there's a dog out mauling folk to death and chowing down on necks the least you can do is make muzzles the law,' she says, her two friends nodding their agreement. 'You got to round up the dogs or make the owners buy leather muzzles, I don't see no other ways round it.'

He explains that there is no killer dog prowling the snowy streets of Gavrik, but she doesn't back down.

'I'll have a word with the Chief,' he says, finally, and that appeases them. They turn and leave at the same time, a mass of dark fleece and red cheeks.

He looks at me and shakes his head.

'I found this outside Tammy Yamnim's building last night,' I say, placing the rolled up tea towel on the counter and then unrolling it to show the needle.

'Drug users?' he says.

'It was embedded inside a snow *skalle*,' I say. 'It was poking out of its mouth. All melted away now apart from the needle and them.' I point to the doll eyes on the towel.

'I always thought the Gavrik skulls were cool as a kid,' he says. 'A town tradition that made us different from Munkfors or Malung, something just for us. But these aren't cool. I'll talk to all the headteachers and we'll have stern words. Leave this with me.'

'You don't think it's the Ferryman's work?' I ask.

He looks at me and gathers together the needle and the eyes in the towel and turns to walk back through the keycode door.

'Kids,' he says. 'Leave it with me, Tuvs.'

I step out and turn to the factory.

The sky is white today, white as new snowdrop petals, and the smoke from the left chimney's rising in a diagonal line linking the factory to the clouds, the earth to the heavens.

'You'll have to go round,' says Janitor Andersson as he shovels slush from the arch entrance. 'New security measures. Police advice. Go round the back like . . .' he stops to cough, one of those rasping full-torso coughs you associate with life-long smokers. 'Like everyone else.'

'I'm sorry about your brother,' I tell him.

'He's alive,' says the janitor.

'Do you think he's well enough to speak with me?'

'How would I know, ain't spoken to him myself for twenty-two years.'

'But you both work here?'

He shrugs and coughs and spits into the gritty slush at his boots. I might not have noticed the phlegm except it looks like extracted liposuction fat and it's speckled with red and it seems ungodly melting through the clean white snow.

'Shouldn't be driving that quick in them old wagons, that's the truth of it. They got the drivers speeding up to make deliveries to make up for delays. Nobody round here listens to me. You just can't drive that fast when it's bad out. Ain't safe.'

So the guy I once found half-frozen in a ditch is now preaching to me about winter road safety?

'I agree,' I say, but he's already turned away to shovel the rear yard.

I walk through the arch looking up at the brick-work and the green mortar and the metal hook poking out of the front of the factory. A flock of white geese or swans, I can't tell which, flies over St Olov's and on toward the reservoir. They look graceful up there, white birds on a blank sky with no colour or counterpoint at all.

The factory floor is busy and I can see laminated checklists stuck to various walls and machines, cleaning instructions and fire-safety notices. There's also an A4 poster appealing for information regarding Per Gunnarsson. It shows the anonymous phone hotline. And someone's scrawled along the bottom:

DO NOT WALK TO YOUR CAR ALONE. GO IN PAIRS.

I pass through the canteen.

The staircase mirrors have been uncovered and I catch glimpses of myself as I walk up the steps and it makes me almost lose balance. The Receiving Room's empty. I knock on the door to the residence, eager to get inside the Grand Room after so many setbacks, but nobody comes. I try the handle. Locked. I walk over to the offices and see figures talking in a glass-walled room.

'Tuva,' says Anna-Britta, opening the door. 'Take a seat and wait five minutes would you.'

The office is dated with a stained tile carpet and a water-cooler machine with no bottle on top. There's a small toilet cubicle with a unisex sign on the door. The figures move inside the glass office and I can see them better now. It's Chief Björn talking to Anna-Britta and if I try real hard I can just about read him, but not her, not from this angle.

'More serious than . . .' I get some words but it's not easy. There are reflections on the glass. 'Talked to the national forensic unit in Linköping . . .' then the Chief wipes his mouth and I lose track. Anna-Britta says something but I can't hear her or read her. 'They have your truck,' Chief Björn says, 'may have it for some time. The brake lines were worn through.' I see Anna-Britta raise her hand to her head. 'Could have been wear and tear,' the Chief says, 'or rats. They'll eat anything they can this time of year. Or could have been someone with criminal intent to harm or damage property.'

Anna-Britta goes on and on, Björn nodding. I focus on his lips so I don't miss the beginning of the next sentence.

'CCTV, a proper check-in system, and keep that arch door locked permanently from now on. I already told Andersson as I came up here. Have all visitors file through that back door, the one by the lockers. A single entrance you can keep control of. You say the janitor stays on top of the van fleet?'

She nods.

'Well, I'll have a word with him but I want you to get the other vehicles checked out, Jan-Östnäs out at the Toyota garage can do it for you, he's got reliable mechanics but he isn't cheap. And I hear right now his economy's in such bad shape he's taken in a lodger – that's between you and me – so he could use the business.'

I'm reading his lips but I can feel someone else's eyes on me. I don't want to look away from Björn but I glance quickly to my left like an animal keeping track of two predators. Karin Grimberg's watching me from the top of the stairs, wearing a floor-length black dress and black gloves that stretch all the way up to her ashen-white armpits.

CHAPTER 24

She looks like a young Galician widow and her dress is so long I can't see her feet. She turns and glides into the Receiving Room. I follow.

'Mother says I'm to talk to you.'

I pull out my digital Dictaphone.

'How long have you used them for?' she points to my hearing aid.

'Since I was a kid. Meningitis.'

She keeps on staring at my ear.

'Do you mind if we talk through there,' I say, gesturing to the locked residence door. 'Anna-Britta said it would be okay.'

'Are you sure you want to?' she says, her attention still on my ear.

What's that supposed to mean?

I nod to her.

'If you're sure,' she says.

'Is it safe?' I ask, checking the doors and windows, checking the shadows.

Karin shrugs and stands up and I reckon she must rub herself with talcum powder she's so pale, so unnaturally dinner-plate white.

She takes a key from her pocket and inserts it into the lock.

'I'd be grateful if you don't tell your friends about the Grand Room. We're private people.'

I nod, eager to see the paintings and furniture in this quarter of the building, that silver punch-bowl sparkling by the table. Lena told me on my first week at the *Posten* that details matter, they add meat to the story.

The door opens without a creak. Karin looks back at me and pushes through the heavy velvet curtain just beyond the door and steps inside.

'This is the Grand Room. You'll have to excuse the . . .' she trails off.

It is like no room I have ever seen before. I mean, I've been here, with Cici's lemon-scented hands over my eyes, I know the proportions. But I never expected this. And in the context of a room so large it seems all the more absurd.

'Where is all the . . .'

'The stuff?' she asks.

I watch her walk over to the tiled stove in the corner, a cylindrical wood-burner twice as tall as I am. I join her. The stove chimney feeds into the main factory chimney on this side of the house, the huge industrial suicide-chimney that dominates Gavrik along with its functioning twin.

'Precautions,' says Karin, picking up three cinnamon sticks. I look at them and then at her white face with its beauty spot, no spider legs today, and then I notice the hairs. Each cinnamon stick has hair threaded through it. One with white hair, one with brown, one with black. There's a stack of cinnamon sticks on the mantelpiece, next to a box of matches, and they all have hair threaded through their hollow centres.

I have about five-hundred questions I want to blurt out but I swallow them down. Important to gain trust. Slow and steady.

'Impressive room,' I say, my voice echoing in the empty space.

She laughs a silent laugh.

The long wall, the wall facing town, is bare. The bricks are slick with moisture and the mortar joining them together has a green sheen. It's odd to see this indoors. There's a vein pattern on the bricks, like a fine-boned vine making its way up and across the wall, tiny spider-thread lines branching up the bricks and across the wood of the window frames. The ventilation system is screaming its pale screams and the ceiling vents look like gaping mouths.

'Refurbishing?' I ask.

Karin shakes her head and points to the window.

'The frames are as wet as undersea sponges,' she says. 'There's no point in replacing them because they'll just rot again. The glass could fall out of them all at any minute.'

'And the wall?'

'They ripped out the plasterboard when Ludo and I were young. It was thrilling. The men carried it out; Father hired workers from the other side of the country, never anyone local, and each board was sodden with dirty water. They needed four men for each dripping board they were so heavy.'

I frown at her.

'They couldn't burn them,' she says. 'They just would not burn, even when Ludo and I poured petrol and engine oil all over them with Father; we loved to see the coloured flames, it was the most exciting thing Ludo or I had ever done. The accelerants burned off it well enough but the boards just stayed there.'

'Jesus.'

'He has nothing to do with it,' she says. 'So now we live like this, keeping ourselves to ourselves and taking extra precautions. The fireplace doesn't work. We'd all die of carbon monoxide poisoning if we ever lit it. I was at college until recently and I had a dry little room and I suppose that was better, at least on paper. Do you take coffee?'

'Please.'

'I'll be back. We have a thermos in the kitchen.'

I stay put. My eyes are everywhere, checking for people hiding, people watching. This is not a domestic room, it's a weird mix of aristocratic proportions and industrial minimalism. And that wall. The front of the building. Soaking wet. I see a hutch with its straw bedding and a water bottle and a food bowl. I walk over and there's a rabbit the size of a pit bull sitting there munching away.

It turns and lollops over to the bed area and I can see that it has three plump white feet. And one stump.

'That's Agamemnon,' says Karin walking through with a tray to the long bare table in the centre of the room. 'Aggy for short.'

The only other object in the room is the apothecary cabinet I saw last time I walked through, glancing between Cici's citrus fingers.

'Interesting home. Beats a radhus semi-detached.'

'You think?' asks Karin. 'I never brought a schoolfriend here, you know. Father was always so private.'

'Everyone in town thinks it's a palace up here with chandeliers and gold taps.'

'It almost was, back when Granny was young, but now all the best stuff's in the Receiving Room to keep up appearances. It's not pride, I don't think. It was Mother and Father not wanting the workers to worry about their jobs.'

'What's behind those doors?' I ask.

She points to each in turn. 'Granny's room next to the big chimney, then Mother and Father's room. Then the door to the attics.' She points to the other wall. 'Then my room over in the corner, I'm working on a clay figure at the moment or I'd show you.' We sit down at the long table and there's a tiny contact-lens case looking back at me, one side white, one side blue. The only plastic thing in the room. Karin pours coffee. 'Then the bathroom and the kitchen. I moved into the corner room after Ludo died so I could see him when-ever I wanted.'

I frown.

'His grave. I have windows facing to the rear root barns and also to the side, so I can see our family plot in St Olov's. Now I can see father down there too.'

'I'm so sorry for what you've been through.'

She looks weary. 'This place takes its toll.'

I move my chair and kick something. There's a clank. I look under the table and there are a line of kitchen knives leading from one end to the other.

'You have knives under the table,' I say. I thought it was a silver punchbowl under there? I hadn't expected this.

She looks at me. 'Nine knives for nine lives.'

'Sorry?'

'Precautions.'

'But what do you mean by "precautions"?'

She ducks under the table and lifts up a knife, it has an antler handle and an engraved base, and then she puts it back into place so it's in line with the others.

'Have you ever said "touch wood"?' she asks.

I nod.

'Have you ever wished someone a safe flight? Or avoided walking under a ladder?'

'Of course.'

'Well then,' she says. 'You take precautions just like we do.'

She offers me sugar.

'You need to ask about my family, for the book?' she says.

'If that's okay?'

She looks up to the lamp above the table, which seems to have dead grass strands hanging from it. She reaches up and touches the grass.

'Precaution?' I ask.

She bangs the table with her knuckles three times. 'Bindweed,' she says. 'For the family.'

Of course it is.

'Granny had a different life to us,' she says. 'That's why she and mother have such violent frictions, you see. Granny never really had to worry.'

'Worry?'

'Back when Grandfather was in charge the factory did rather well. Monetarily, at least. The man did nothing for morale or reputation. We've been in decline ever since Grandfather.' She pauses and looks at me. 'Ever since he left us.'

Karin looks up to the ceiling, mould spores spreading toward the centre from each corner.

'You hear that?' she asks.

I can't hear anything but I can feel vibrations. 'What is it?'

Karin smiles and she has Cici's smile, all teeth. 'Granny's up there strutting about.'

I take another sip of coffee.

'She's a character,' I say.

'Granny takes more precautions than all the rest

of us put together and maybe that's why she's okay. She manages to live her own life up there, dressing her mannequins, carving faces from florist oasis, stitching her outfits, playing with her puppets. Isn't that wonderful?'

'It is,' I say. 'What's that?' I ask, pointing to the huge apothecary cabinet.

'That's everything you'd need to destroy this place,' she says, staring at me. 'And half of Gavrik, too.'

CHAPTER 25

Karin leads me to the cabinet. The hem of her dress brushes across the floorboards, dust fluff sticking to her like a grey angora fringe.

'It's my most precious precaution,' she says. 'My cabinet of life.'

She opens one door and then the other and I can see her breathing quicken. Her cheeks flush. The cabinet is dark wood, mahogany maybe, and it must weigh as much as a hearse. Inside is a collection of drawers and shelves, all polished and well-kept, all labelled in fine Gothic print, all veneered with small tusk-like handles.

'My grandfather started this collection. Many of the oldest items he brought back from the Levant.'

I reckon David Holmqvist might just have enough material for a decent book.

'What's inside the drawers?'

She opens a mid-size drawer on the bottom left and brings out a glass vial with a screw cap.

'The venom of an inland Taipan,' she says.

'A snake?'

'The most venomous snake. Fifty-thousand mice.'

'Sorry?'

'This is enough to kill fifty-thousand mice, some say two-hundred-and-fifty thousand. Or maybe a hundred full-grown women.'

I stare at it and wonder how thin the glass is and what would happen if she dropped it. Is it still potent?

'Put it back,' I say. 'It's making me nervous. What else is inside?'

She places the vial back on its black velvet cushion and closes the drawer. She doesn't pull the other drawers, just points to them.

'Fauna on the top. There's a pufferfish spleen and the dried head of a black mamba. A scorpion, or the remains of one, and then a jellyfish thread coiled like a spring. Next is a shrivelled little poison dart frog, hardly bigger than my thumbnail, and then the tentacle of a blue-ringed octopus. I have two marbled-cone snails, and the carapace, the beautiful fragile miniscule carapace, of a black widow.'

'Amazing,' I say, lost for better words.

'Isn't it? There's a certain power holed up in this old cabinet; a certain force. Next row down are fungi specimens. I'm missing so many but I'll tell you what I have. Okay . . .' she points at the left box. 'Death cap, obviously, then a destroying angel and an abrupt-bulbed Lepidella. Such a beauty.' She smiles at me. 'Then fool's mushroom, ha, then an ivory funnel and an autumn skullcap and two deadly dapperlings, one found by me in Utgard

246

forest when I was eleven-and-a-quarter-years old. I have a deadly parasol and that larger drawer at the end is stuffed full of men-on-horseback.'

'This is a life cabinet?'

'It's a cabinet of life,' she says. 'Next layer down is flora. You've probably seen most of these: deadly nightshade, poison ivy, blah-blah-blah, then digitalis, then poison hemlock and white snakeroot and cobra lily. I'm a bit thin on this level so there are four empty drawers.'

'You don't feel in danger having all these in the residence?'

'Quite the opposite,' she says. 'Because it's here. With us. It's on our side.'

She pushes her black fringe from her eyes, it's as straight as a ruler, and opens a low cupboard door.

'What are the doorknobs made from?' I ask.

She turns to me and grins a Cecilia grin, like a Doberman in attack mode but they manage to make it almost pretty.

'Grimberg teeth,' she says. 'No tooth fairy in our family, we could never afford her. The knobs are the milk teeth of me and Father and all of Grandfather's other descendants since way back when. We have a thing for teeth. It's sweet, really.'

It is fucked up and a long way from sweet.

'And then at the bottom are perhaps the most peculiar items of all.'

She bends down.

On the black velvet cushion sits a pill the size of a peppercorn.

247

'Cyanide,' she says. 'Old and probably useless, but it is cyanide.' She places it back and points to the other drawers at the base of the cabinet. 'Various bullets and shotgun cartridges, a knuckle-duster Grandfather brought back from China, some very potent chloroform, a mustard-gas canister, also ancient, a chisel-tipped Japanese razor that was used to execute a POW, rat poison, a World War Two incendiary device that could burn down half of Gavrik, a lady's flick knife from Andorra.'

'Is something missing?' I ask, pointing to a long, empty, velvet cushion.

'Cosh,' she says.

'Sorry?' I say.

'Cosh,' she says. 'A truncheon, a cudgel, a night-stick, a bludgeon, a blackjack, a mace. Mother keeps it under her bed, I think. It helps her sleep.'

'Ah,' I say. 'You have quite a collection.'

'Now you've seen it,' she says. 'Now you've seen inside.'

'Who do you think is behind the recent events? Gunnarsson and then the truck crash,' I pause. 'Your father.'

'What?' she says.

'It just seems that too many awful things are happening in and around this factory, that's all. I wondered if you had any theories? If you think the deaths are connected?'

'I hope you're not looking at me when you ask that. I wasn't even here when Father had his accident. I was in art college.'

'Of course not. I'm not saying that at all. I just wondered what your view is.'

She looks me up and down and closes her 'cabinet of life'.

'Let's leave,' she says. 'Let's finish up in the Receiving Room. I think that would be best.'

'I didn't mean to upset you,' I say, passing through the curtain into the elegant room.

'It's Mother,' she says. 'She doesn't like people in the residence.'

She adjusts her long black gloves.

'It's not straightforward living above the factory.' She touches the beauty spot above her lip. 'We've had tragedies. More than our fair share. And we have our burden to carry. But we try to take adequate precautions and we carry on for the sake of the town.' She doesn't shiver but she looks cold now, like she needs a coat. 'I've been told this ever since I was five years old, praying by father's bedside each night for the workers and the consumers of our liquorice, praying they'd be able to keep on stamping and eating, praying individually for sick workers or their children, people we'd never met; Ludo and I kneeling there for half an hour some nights on this damp granite outcrop praying for the whole damn town but never ever for ourselves.'

CHAPTER 26

I walk downstairs and the eyes in the photo-graphs, the dark sepia eyes of workers now long-buried, judge me as I pass them. There's a hand-sized oil painting of a small boy stroking a cat with one hand, and holding what looks like a dagger in the other. Probably just a harmless letter-opener. I peer closer and there's either a snowball by his feet, or else it's a snow skull. Grimberg family tradition? A door slams some-where close by. I turn left at the bottom but then remember the arch exit is bolted shut now, new security measure, so I turn right through the heavy wood door and head to the canteen. The place smells of ammonia and meat sauce. There is no chattering here, only whispers, secret conversa-tions, people scared and vigilant. The big doors in the factory are open for forklifts so I short-cut outside and the scarred cat hisses at me and the fur stands up at the back of its head and he stands his ground. I keep close to the wall.

It's warm. Not warm-warm, but maybe a degree or two above zero. There is no sun in the sky, only marbled whiteness. I look down at my feet to see if I can detect the faint red of Gustav's blood in the sandy cracks between the cobblestones, but I can't see anything.

'Watch it or you'll get crushed,' says Andersson. 'Got trucks coming through for pick-ups now the police have opened it back up. We're behind. Watch it lingering under the arch.'

I walk with him to the door of his basement residence and he coughs and splutters and holds up a cracked palm of calloused skin to apologise and then he coughs some more.

'You should get that seen to,' I tell him.

'Strong as a bear,' he says, spitting onto the cobbles below. 'Constitution . . .' he coughs again, a deep wheezing cough, '. . . of a brown bear.'

He looks up at me and wipes his mouth with the sleeve of his overalls.

'How are the family?' he asks. 'I know you speak to them.'

'They're okay,' I say.

'I worry we're in trouble but they don't tell me nothing. I'm part of it, you know, have been for a long time. They ought to . . . I don't know. I got my whole life tied up in this place. Everything. They owe it to me to keep me updated, what with everything that's gone on, with a killer walking about, free as a bird, but nobody tells me nothing, been the same my whole . . .' he coughs, '. . . life.'

'Seem to be okay, considering,' I say. 'How's your brother?'

'I know someone who can save this place. New lease of life and we'd all walk away better off, but will they listen to me?'

I look at him.

'They will not,' he says.

'How's your brother?' I ask again.

He shrugs. 'Breathing. Least that's the word round here.'

'You think he's up to a visit? I'd like to talk to him for the paper.'

He shrugs again. 'Why you keep asking me? Don't ask me, ask him.'

It's ten past three and I can see the janitor's grandson through the window of the basement. He's sucking on a pale blue inhaler and he looks like he could use a steak and some broccoli and a beach holiday even more than I could.

I want to give Tam some cash toward the bills for the week, so I head down to the bank on the corner of Storgatan and Eriksgatan. The cross-country ski store is doing decent business and I can see two women outside Systembolaget each carrying a bulging carrier bag with the unmistakable cuboid shape of a bag-in-box. Maybe a Chilean Merlot or a Spanish Grenache, something sloshing about in a bin liner, strapped into a cardboard box with handy plastic tap. More like a petrol pump than a beverage.

The bank has a queue of three. Benny Björnmossen, owner of the town's largest gun store, is being served and rumour is his profits are soaring thanks to locals stocking up on ammunition and combat knives and door locks and amateur CCTV systems and shiny new rifles. Behind him is some woman I recognise from Pilates down at the Lutheran church, the one and only time I tried it, what a pile of Lycra bullshit that was, then behind her are the wood-carving sisters.

I don't want to tap their shoulders so I clear my throat and the talking one turns around.

'Hello, girl.'

'Hi, how are you both?' I ask.

'Girl wants to know how we are, Alice,' says Cornelia, the talking one. Alice, the quiet one, smiles and Cornelia says 'We're alive, girl, can't complain.'

Alice is growing her hair out but her left eye has no lashes.

'You're leaving us up here with this Ferryman killer, leaving us for the big city, that's what we heard, ain't it Alice?'

'Yep,' says Alice.

'Leaving on Monday,' I say. 'Actually, I'm having leaving drinks at Ronnie's on Thursday night. Tomorrow night. You're both welcome.'

Cornelia looks to her sister and her sister looks back. The number on the screen over the cashier counter changes and I realise I forgot to take a queue ticket so I grab one.

'Not our scene, girl,' says the talking one. 'And watch yourself. There's old evil on the loose.' She touches the side of her neck. 'You doing some book work for Davey Holmqvist, that right?'

I nod. 'Just research. About the factory.'

'Well,' says Cornelia, elbowing her sister. 'Mind how you go.'

'Sorry?'

The talking one pulls up her rainproof elasticated trousers with one hand. 'Most car accidents happen on the last stretch of the journey when you're relaxed and heading back home, ain't that right, Alice?'

'Yep,' says Alice.

'What do you mean?' I ask.

'You've had a good run, especially with what happened last year.' She cringes. 'But don't go pushing your luck just as you're about to go start life someplace more suited to your lifestyle and all that. It ain't safe round here. Old evil. Don't fall at the last jump.'

'I've got less than a week,' I say. 'I'll be fine.'

'Mind how you go in Utgard forest,' says Cornelia, turning to face forward as she gets to the front of the queue. 'If you visit Davey, mind the road. It ain't what it used to be. Ain't maintained. You watch yourself, girl.'

The quiet sister looks at me for a while longer, nodding thoughtfully, then turns to the cashier and presents her numbered ticket. Benny Björnmossen walks back past us with more swagger than a double-jointed cowboy. He nods to me and then to someone else. It's Henrik Hellbom, the lawyer with the bad posture and the stretched face, looks permanently startled, the man with all the real estate, the brother-in-law of Toyota guy.

The cashier peers up and gets all flustered and then she says something to the wood-carving sisters and pulls down a roller blind real quick that says, 'Please bear with us, we will be with you shortly.'

The quiet sister makes a 'humph' sound and then the blind pings up, except now there's a cardboard sign behind the window that says 'Private Banking' and the cashier's trying to tell the sisters they'll have to wait while they serve Henrik Hellbom. They snort and complain but then back off and let him through.

Cornelia, the talking one, looks back at me with more poison than Karin has in her cabinet. She wants to punch Hellbom right between the eyes and I can't blame her. The cardboard sign comes down and the sisters are ushered to the front again and Facelift gets led back through a double-locked door to some manager's office. But it's not like the sisters are going to change bank now is it, seeing how there's a grand total choice of one.

What's Hellbom doing here? Arranging finance so he can make an offer for the factory? Selling stocks so he has enough cash? Is that how it works?

I turn to the cashier, a girl I recognise from a high-school-handball story I ran my first year here, and I tell her I'm changing address, moving down south, and she basically looks at me and says 'so'. I ask what I need to do and she tells me to inform my new branch, nothing she can do about it, 'next please'.

I withdraw cash from the machine and wait outside the bank.

Shivering, I try to avoid eye-contact with passers-by, all of whom I know or know of, all of whom will have some crackpot theory about the Ferryman, and then Hellbom steps outside in his fur-lined black coat and his fur-lined black boots.

'Mr Hellbom?' I ask.

He looks me up and down and frowns and blinks about six blinks in fast succession. He has a sword-shaped Gavrik Chamber of Commerce badge pinned to his lapel and his nostrils flare as he breathes.

'Yes?' he says.

'I'm Tuva Moodyson, I work at the paper. Can I ask you a quick question please?'

He looks around as if for help and then swallows and says, 'I'm late for an appointment'. His voice is deep and he pronounces all the letters in his words, or over-pronounces them, even the two 'ts' in appointment.

'What do you think about the news that a consortium of businessmen from Stockholm are bidding for the Grimberg factory?'

He scowls at me and looks at the factory and he looks worried. My lie has done its job. He wants the factory, I can see it. He wants the factory very badly indeed.

'I must go now,' he says, smiling as an afterthought.

'Police are investigating a criminal conspiracy, a plot to reduce the value of Grimberg Liquorice. Criminal damage to Grimberg trucks, possible connection to the Gunnarsson murder.' I'm watching him closely for any signs, any clues. 'A plot to force the Grimbergs to sell up. Any comment?'

His gloves are fine calf leather, a rich shade of tan, and they are tight on his hands. A second skin. He pulls up his collar and touches the sharp lapel pin and then he blinks five or six times. Sweat is starting to bead above his short moustache.

'Who did you say you were?' he asks, mock calm in his deep, clipped voice.

'Tuva Moodyson,' I say. 'T–U–V–A.'

He looks down and sniffs and spits into the snow and walks away from me.

I head back to my office.

'You working for me or Holmqvist,' says Lena as I step inside and pull off my coat. 'Which is it?'

I look at her like 'ugh?'

'Three days till your final copy. After all we've been through do not short-change me, Tuva.'

'I'm doing Karlstad this afternoon, interviewing the injured delivery driver in hospital.' I pause. 'For the paper.'

She retreats back to her desk.

I call Thord.

'Thord Pettersson.'

'It's me.'

'No time,' he says.

'About Gunnarsson,' I say. 'I need that other ten per cent of your information . . .' But he's already put down the phone.

I check my emails and write up what I remember from the lunch appointment with Karin. I'm not sure how much of my research Holmqvist will use, but as someone who interviews people all the time, I find this family fascinating. There are plenty of Gavrik residents who think their toy soldier collection is interesting or their rebuilt Corvette is interesting and they're all pretty much deluded. And then there's the Grimbergs who think they're normal as cloudberry pie and in reality they're the most darkly exotic people I could ever imagine.

The drive south is a pain in the ass. I usually love this route, straight down the E16 and then the E45, stereo on, heated seat on, cruising past delivery trucks and pulp wagons at a smooth one twenty. Not today. The Tacoma hasn't got a working stereo. Potato Head, the garage owner's son, proud recipient of my Hilux, told me the electrics got damp so they ripped out the unit. Well, thanks for nothing, pea-brain. The fluffy, steering wheel cover does its job but I still hate it. If I drive faster than about ninety the whole truck starts shaking on its axels and if I breathe too much I need to keep wiping the windows with my wiper-on-a-stick. It's a rust box on wheels and the blower's weaker than the final warm breath of a grandpop with emphysema.

Karlstad looks good. It's a handsome city with grand old buildings and a decent department store. There are people here. Life. I find the central hospital and park up. It's not where Mum died, this isn't a palliative hospice. Mum was here years ago for her first cancer and I visited a fair few times, but those were hopeful times, not palliative times. I should have come more. I park and pay and go in. The circular doors move slowly and I shuffle inside and the place is hot and it smells of bodily decay and alcogel.

I pull off my coat and slip blue shoe covers over my boots. It's not mandatory but everyone does it. I ask about Andersson and follow the stripes on the rubberised floor to a lift and take it up and find the ward. He's in a room with one other guy and I have twenty-five minutes before visiting hours are over.

'Hello,' I say, smiling, peering my head round the door.

The guy closest to me is on a ventilator and he looks asleep. The guy nearest the window peers up from his hunting magazine.

'You here for my bag?' he says.

I step inside and shake my head.

'It's full,' he says.

'I'm Tuva Moodyson,' I say, edging my way to the end of his bed. 'I'm a reporter at the *Gavrik Posten*.'

He frowns at me and closes his hunting magazine and I can see a man on the cover with a dead wolf slung over his shoulder.

'*Gavrik Posten?*'

'Yes.'

I take a look at the name next to his bed. It's the right guy.

'You want to talk to me?' he says.

'Just for a minute, if that's okay? I wanted to hear about your accident.'

He grins. 'You're my first visitor.' He points to the heavy, pine chair beside his bed. 'Come and sit down. Moa, you say your name was? Have we met?'

'Tuva,' I say. 'You want me to get the nurse for you, about your . . .' I point to his general midriff area.

'No, no,' he says, sitting up straighter in bed. 'That can wait. Thanks for coming to see me, it's nice to see a friendly local face.' He points to ventilator guy. 'He isn't one for small talk.'

I smile.

'What happened to you that night?' I ask. 'Mind if I record this?' I place my digital Dictaphone on the bedside table next to some indigestion tablets and his glasses case.

'I don't know,' he says.

'I'm deaf, you see.' I point to my hearing aid. 'Want to make sure I don't mishear you.'

'You ain't really deaf. You can hear me speaking.'

I point to my aids again. 'Not without these I can't.'

'You're hard of hearing is all, same as my wife was before she passed.' He raises his voice. 'It's called hard of hearing.'

I clench my teeth.

'What happened that night, Mr Andersson?'

'My crash?'

I nod.

'Well, I was heading back from Munkfors, was supposed to have some kid with me asking questions but she cancelled apparently, too busy smoking the weed drugs most likely, and it was night-time you see, and my night vision isn't as good as it used to be, I'll be honest about that, and I was quite tired, I'm fifty-eight next winter, so I was driving, minding my own business, I told the police all this already, mind, so I'll tell you what I told them, I was driving at a decent speed, and . . .'

I nod, some desperate plea for him to get to the point.

'And it wasn't that cold, I reckon minus twelve or so, long-john weather, not like today, I can see the thaw out my window, all them dead bushes out there, isn't much of a view is it? Anyway, like I was saying, I was driving empty, end of my shift, and there wasn't no warning or nothing, well there wouldn't be on our trucks, you seen 'em, have you?'

'Your trucks?'

He nods and takes a sip of water from the plastic cup on his table.

'Yes,' I say. 'They're quite . . . vintage, aren't they?'

'Well, you could say that. I mean they look nice

261

and everything, all part of the Grimberg brand, but they're not much fun driving in February, roll on spring, that's what I say.'

'But the crash, what actually happened?'

He looks over to ventilator guy. 'Policeman he is. Retired. Robocop I call him.'

I almost laugh but thank God I hold it in.

'The crash,' I say. 'When you came off the road?'

'My brakes were working okay that day, maybe a little unresponsive on the country roads but I was used to that, some of the trucks have worse brakes, they all got personalities you know, I drive number one but we got twelve trucks these days, an even dozen.'

'And they failed?'

'What did?'

'The brakes.'

'They sure did, didn't they? I braked going into a bend and maybe I was doing forty, something like that, maybe fifty, no faster, mind, I told the police all this, and nothing. It was over in a flash. I didn't see my life flash before my eyes or no white light welcoming me to St Peter's Gates or nothing like that. I just crashed and it all went black. Then I woke up here.'

He touches his bandaged forehead.

'What do you think caused it?'

'The brakes, you mean?'

I nod and nudge the Dictaphone closer to him.

'People reckon it might be rats or critters, it wouldn't be the first time, damn janitor don't do his job properly, the lazy old swine. Too busy daydreaming about moving to Spain or Thailand or someplace. He's obsessed with hot countries and he thinks he's in charge of the Grimbergs – well, he ain't.' He sniffs and takes a sip of water. 'He's in worse shape than me, you know that? Desperate to take all his grandkiddies away on a trip of a lifetime, I heard the lads laughing about it, reckons he's saving up for one last big holiday with his grandkiddies before . . .' He drags his finger across his neck. 'Anyways, you know them old root barns in the yard, well they got no roots in 'em anymore, they import it all refined now, but they still store waste product in them barns. If you go there you'll see big containers packed full of old sugar residue and them rats feast off it like you wouldn't believe. I reckon sometimes they go after our brake lines.'

'Maybe you need an exterminator?'

He looks confused.

'Someone to kill the rats.'

'I got two rifles and one air rifle and I offered about ten-thousand times; big nest it is, but they want that old tomcat to fix them. Well, he was quite handy back in the day, but now I reckon the rats beat him up, you seen the state of him, he looks worse than Lieutenant Robocop over there.'

'Can I ask you some general questions about the factory and the town?'

'Sweetheart, you came all the way down here to visit me, you can ask me anything you like.'

I smile and point to the water jug and he shakes his head.

'Did you know Mr Grimberg?'

'You mean Ludvig's boy, Gustav, the one that fell?'

Fell?

I nod.

'Not very well I must admit, but I spoke to him a few times. He always looked so, I don't know how to put it, so tired. Pale and skinny like he was worn out before he even got started. Rumour is that he was caught with a married woman over in Utgard forest a few years back, some cab-driver's wife, but you know how people talk,' he makes his hand resemble a mouth opening and closing. 'His father was much more of a forceful fella, all deep voice and no nonsense despite his hunchback.'

'You must have been shocked when he jumped from the chimney.'

He shakes his head.

'Really?'

'It's in the bloodline, Moa, just like that bent spine all the Grimbergs get. Well, old folks, older folk than me, they'll tell you Ludvig died of the septicaemia or too much pain medicine, or whatever they say, but he poisoned himself with the rat poison and then walked off to die. Terrible back pain, you see. He was a tyrant and most folk said good riddance even if they didn't say it out loud.'

'I didn't know that.'

He taps his nose like now it's our secret.

'This is all on the record, Mr Andersson, that's alright isn't it?'

'Good that it's all being recorded, you can hear me okay? You want me to speak up?' he points to Ventilator Guy. 'He won't mind.'

'Did you know Per Gunnarsson?'

He wrinkles his nose.

'Kept himself to himself. Dreadful bully in his schooldays and nobody ever forgets a bully. Not many friends, young Gunnarsson. Terrorised half the town back in the day, had a thing for putting his fags out on other kids, almost forced my wife's nephew to leave Gavrik town altogether.'

'What's his name?' I ask.

'Who?'

'Your wife's nephew.'

'Hellbom, he's a lawyer now. Might end up a bigshot judge here in Karlstad city, if he plays his cards right. Reckons all that bullying by Gunnarsson made him a fighter, you know, in the courts.'

I nod.

'Do you know the other Grimbergs?'

'Madame Cecilia, that's what we all call her, she's a strange one. People reckon she likes controlling events from up in her attics but I don't know, folk love to gossip, well they ain't got nothing better to do have they. She lives in her own little world that one with all her jewels and her puppets. She made them herself, you know, some of them modelled on local people so they say. But she's mad as an old stick, has been ever since her best friends died in the reservoir accident back in the seventies.'

'Her best friends?' I say. Why didn't Cici tell me that in her attic?

He nods. 'Madame Cecilia was seen chatting to the couple that very morning. People used to say she talked them into it, pushed them into hiding in that bed together all weighed down, but nobody knows for sure. And most people from back then are either dead or else they're too potty to remember, my brother included.'

'Tell me more about Cecilia,' I say.

'Ludvig used to dote on her. Course, he used to dote on lots of women.'

'He was a bit of a player?'

'Fathered more than a dozen bastards, that's what they say. His family tree would look like half a forest, if you know what I mean. Got 'em scattered all over Gavrik, there's Grimberg kids running around; most of 'em probably work in the factory these days what with them being the biggest work place in town.'

He's in full flow now and I'm silently hoping no nurse steps through the door.

'Ludvig was planning on running off with a stamper young enough to be his own daughter. Like I said, it's in the bloodline. But he backed out last minute. Broke her heart and Madame Cecilia's heart and almost split the family down the middle.'

This is the reality of small-town life. Pretty much everyone has some kind of history with everyone else. I gesture for him to keep talking.

'He'd have hated all this, would Ludvig. He'd turn in his grave with a non-blood Grimberg running the factory, I mean . . .' He sucks air through his teeth. 'A woman. Ludvig would not have liked that one bit.'

'You mean Anna-Britta, Gustav's wife?'

'That's it. She used to be together with Hellbom back in high school. Sweethearts they was. Gustav stole her away what with his fortune and all that. Hellbom, my wife's nephew he is, well he didn't have much money back then. Not like today. I ain't said much to Anna-Britta face-to-face but she seems bright enough. Not like that black one.'

'Sorry?'

'Not like that, I ain't racist, I been to Egypt. No, I mean she wears black, she's one of them devil-worshipping atheists, you know the ones.'

'Karin, the daughter?'

'Karin, that's it, my idiot brother dotes on her but I can't think why. Killed a whole family of hedgehogs back when she was a tiddler. Took them out one by one. They covered it up as a bonfire accident at the lake house so as not to get problems with the school.' He looks at me. 'She's one of them Gothic people.'

'So?' I say.

He frowns at me and I hold in my words because I need to find out more.

'Do you think she's dangerous?' I ask.

'I've had two operations and got two more to go,' he says.

'Is Karin dangerous?' I ask again.

'She's dressed in black all the time, that's all I know. Takes after her old man, rest his soul. Anxious people, you know, nervous. On edge. I remember she got in trouble at school for controlling the other kiddies. Maybe she got that from her granny, who knows? Manipulating them to do what she wanted, just like she did with her old dad, may he rest in peace. I heard young Karin was calling up Gustav on his mobile phone twenty times a day before he jumped off that chimney. Ain't normal. Whereas her brother was a sweet kid, he used to love our vans, it was the same fleet back when he was alive, he used to come out with his little model trucks and want to sit in our cabs and turn our steering wheels. He was a good little lad was Ludo.'

'What did he die from?' I ask.

'The masts,' he says. 'It was the phone masts that killed Ludo.'

'Masts?'

An orderly steps inside with a stainless steel trolley full of drink cartons and jugs of water and then a nurse follows him in.

'Time for your wash and change, Mr Andersson,' says the nurse in a rushed but kind tone. 'Behind schedule today.'

'It's my bag that needs changing,' he tells her. 'Full to bursting it is.'

'I'll go,' I say, slipping my Dictaphone into my bag. 'What kind of masts were you talking about?'

The nurse looks agitated.

'Mobile telephone masts,' he says. 'Up the chimneys.'

Nurse looks like she might throw me out of the window any second.

'Thanks for talking with me, Mr Andersson.'

He looks over to ventilator guy, then back to me. 'Safe drive.'

CHAPTER 27

I have an ache to visit Mum and Dad so I head to the cemetery, the small one near the out-of-town DIY stores.

There are no other cars at the graveyard. The ground snow has thawed because it's a good five degrees warmer here than it is in Gavrik. The Karlstad daffodils burst up a fortnight before ours do. Plastic watering cans hang from hooks and a brown compost bin sits with its lid open like some stout lonely creature waiting for its snack.

The plots are well-tended but it's February so nothing looks good. I pass old graves, overgrown with weeds and long grass, and newer graves, all black sparkly marble and gold script. I skirt around the newest graves, the ones with gravel mounds still waiting to settle. I can't look at them straight on. It's too much. I can walk over ancient graves and old graves but it's not right to step on a fresh mound, it's just not.

Mum and Dad up ahead, side-by-side. A space next to Dad for yours truly. That'll be it, the end of the line, the original trio. Mum's relatives are buried someplace up north near Umea and Dad's parents are in Stockholm.

I approach them.

Dad's side is clear and level: dead yellow grass and a candleholder standing empty at an angle. June 25th, that awful day, the worst day of my entire life, is carved into granite forever. Mum's side is a mound. One of the freshest here. The awful swollen shape of it. A hill of pink-grey gravel, coffin-shaped, obviously. It's two metres long and eighty centimetres wide and it's almost as if she's pushing up from below.

It's warm down there. I researched it. When I saw that weird propane-heater tank sitting on Gustav Grimberg's plot I went back and looked it up. The top thirty centimetres or so freezes solid in winter, but underneath that things are always warm.

Dad's stone looks almost new and Mum's is gleaming. Hers has an inscription on it, a few words she gave to her lawyer years ago, the same words I spoke out loud at the funeral and that I will not read again now I'm facing them on her headstone. I can't. I focus on Dad instead. I consider taking a flickering candle from some ancient nearby grave, some person who died in the fifties maybe, someone who won't really miss it now, who's settled right in, right down, a level grave.

This family, this oh-so-small nuclear family, one member still breathing, is a stark contrast to the

271

Grimbergs. Although I suppose they're only three now. But they're not. Because they're the whole town, an entire workforce, a deep lineage of industrial nobility. And we're just three: Mum and Dad down there, and me up here.

There are flowers on the next grave: a pack of Q8 carnations still in their cellophane, wilted from the bitter cold, frost glazing their petals like crystallised sugar. I apologise to Mum and Dad in my head for not bringing them anything, but then I almost laugh because they wouldn't care, they don't care. I start to imagine Mum down there, her hair still growing, her nails still growing, and I have to stop myself. When I see Mum's stone I think of the janitor's brother lying in hospital, grateful for me visiting him even though I was just doing my job, and I feel a concrete weight in my belly for not seeing Mum more when she was still around. I look at her stone and silently apologise and tears push from behind my eyes. They come much easier to me since the funeral. I'm so sorry, Mum.

When I'm back in the truck I automatically check for the temperature but there's no reading on the dash of the Shitmobile and that makes me feel like a sailor without a compass. Thermometers are the navigation aids which help guide cold country people through the whiteness to the spring; the tiny incremental changes offering hope when hope is thin on the ground.

Missed call from Holmqvist on my phone so I

sync with my hearing aid and drive off to join the motorway.

'Yes?' he says.

'David, I missed a call from you.'

'So you did. Tuva, we need to rendezvous today or tomorrow to look through your notes. I need to know what you're including about the Ferryman so I can integrate it into the existing narrative. Can you make this evening?'

It's already dark and I'm tired and I can almost taste the warmth of rum on my tongue.

'How long will it take?' I ask.

'Oh, two hours, maybe more.'

'Tomorrow night okay? I have plans tonight.'

Write up my notes, then drink till the world fades.

'Very well. I could invite you for dinner, perhaps. Tomorrow at seven sharp?'

'Could we do six? I have my leaving drinks tomorrow at eight.'

'Six? For dinner? Well, I suppose I could dine like a savage for the sake of a non-fiction bestseller.'

'Can I bring anything?' I ask.

'A comprehensive and well-organised set of printed notes, double-spaced in Times New Roman, size fourteen or twelve if you must.'

The air's moist with sleet. As I approach Gavrik the factory chimneys dominate the skyline like the towers of some permafrost Soviet research-facility deep in the Urals. I pass ICA Maxi and look for the mobile-phone masts Andersson referred to, but I can't see detail from this distance. I wonder if Cici's spying back at me through her opera glasses. I wonder if the Ferryman's spying on her spying on me.

At five I say goodbye to Lena who's rearranging my back-page sports stories using her fancy editor software. I've arranged to meet Tam at McDonald's for a nugget beast-feast at seven so I drive to her place for a quick shower. Tam has a thing for scented candles. I count five. There are cushions piled on top of cushions and the fire's set for someone to light it. The fridge is full of Tupperware boxes with lock-on lids and her cupboards and knives are so clean I'm scared to touch them.

I shower and drink a rum and Coke and then roll up on the sofa with my knees under my chin. My aids are looking back at me from the table and I suppose I could light a small fire, one that would last an hour or so, just burn one log? I've never had my own fireplace so I leave it. I try to imagine life near Malmö, and promise myself to live a little more like Tammy if I can.

I drive out to McDonald's and park in my usual space, nice and broad, no reversing required to drive out afterwards. Ninety per cent of February diners choose drive-thru so there are plenty of spaces.

I order a coffee just to keep me going until Tam gets here. The place is pretty empty: one old, hunched guy with a heavy stick drinking something hot, two tired-looking parents with a kid sleeping in its fleece-lined buggy, and a table of teenagers, all of them wearing those headphones that look like DJ headphones with the wire hanging out of one end.

I sit with my back to the tills facing Tam's van so I'll see her approach when she's done.

Halfway through my coffee a hand taps my shoulder.

'You're early,' I say, looking around. But it's not Tammy. I straighten myself. It's Noora, the new cop. 'Oh, sorry, hi, I thought you were . . .'

'Anyone sitting here?' she asks.

'No.'

She's wearing a blue fleece, royal blue, with a yellow zip-toggle, and dark jeans, the fleece-lined ones they sell in ICA.

'Thought I should say hello properly as you're the famous local journalist and I'm the new girl.'

'I'm not famous,' I say, my cheeks on fire. I pull off my scarf and lay it on my lap.

'Not what Thord and the Chief tell me. Let me try introducing myself again. I'm Noora Ali.'

She holds out her hand. I shake it and it is soft, not like mine, smooth moist skin and that'll be gone by next winter here I reckon, doesn't matter how much fancy cream you use.

'Good to meet you properly.'

'They're bringing over my food,' she says. 'Apparently fast food in Gavrik isn't that fast.'

'It's made to order, though,' I say. 'When so few people come in they don't leave burgers and nuggets under the lamps to go limp, they make them fresh. It's better, actually. How do you like it here?'

She smiles and pushes a strand of black hair behind her ear and I try to keep eye contact but I have to look away. How old am I, fifteen?

'It's different,' she says. 'That's unfair. I don't know. I've only seen Gavrik in mid-winter so I'm sure it's not always . . .'

'Shit?' I say, and she bursts out laughing like my lame one-word joke uncapped a whole pressurised canister of pent-up frustration.

'Yes!' she says. 'It's . . .' she looks around to make sure we're not being overheard. 'It's a really small town, no?'

'It is,' I say.

'Thord explained to me that it's evolved this own way because of the location,' she says. 'He says people have grown up and married and passed on the same beliefs and superstitions because they never seem to leave.'

'Maybe,' I say, and then her meal arrives. Two cheeseburgers, large fries, can of sparkling lime-flavoured water. Nice choices.

'Help me with these,' she turns the carton of fries to face me.

'No, I'm fine, thanks.'

She shrugs. 'Mind if I eat?'

I shake my head and then watch her. She has a certain way. She unwraps each cheeseburger and then kind of rewraps it with the paper and then nibbles at it. She takes a few fries and bites them and then, I don't know, she eats elegantly somehow, not like me or Tammy. Next to her food is her set of keys. She has a mini torch on the ring along with a sheathed nail file.

'You talk.' She part-covers her mouth with her hand while she chews. 'Tell me what I need to know. I'm off-duty and I'm eating. You talk, please, go on.'

'Okay,' I say, awkward. 'Well, you probably know about me. I'm twenty-six. Reporter. I'm deaf, have been since childhood.' I watch and she nods and she doesn't frown or stare at my ears. 'I've been here almost four years and actually aside from the Medusa murders which were pretty intense, and now this new nightmare, it's been fairly quiet. I have a great boss, have you met her?'

She shakes her head.

'Lena Adeola. I'll introduce you. She used to work in the US. Taught me a lot. Now I'm moving down to join a bi-weekly journal focussing on regional stories and migration.'

She raises her eyebrows. 'My parents are immigrants.'

I nod.

'From Iraq in the eighties.' She dips a cluster of fries into a ketchup puddle. 'I was born here but if you ever need an inside perspective on life as a second-generation Swede you know who to call.'

'Be careful, I might just do that.'

She smiles and unwraps her second cheeseburger.

'Do you mind doing all the talking?' she asks.

'It's fine.'

What a perfect question. No man I know would ask that question.

'Great,' she says, sinking her teeth into the burger. She has a scar from an old piercing below her lip and three more in her right ear.

'Chief told me you got a new lead,' I lie.

'Got two,' she says.

I stay silent but my eyes scream 'tell me what you know'.

'Too early,' she says. 'Nothing firm. Even had one old-timer asking us to question you, can you believe that?' She waves a fry at me like it's a judge's gavel. 'Old timer with a big dog, not someone Thord recognised, lives up by the sewage works, he reckoned you've been at the scene of too many of these incidents so it's likely you're involved and have we checked out your alibis.'

'What?' I say. 'You serious? I was with the janitor when Grimberg jumped and I was with him again when we found Gunnarsson.'

'I'm not questioning you, Tuva,' she says, smiling. 'Relax.'

I spot Tammy outside walking toward me with a bobble hat and a deep frown. She's talking, she's talking a lot, but I can't read her lips through the glare of the window.

'My friend's coming,' I say. 'I'm meeting her for dinner, I'll introduce you.'

Noora looks up enthusiastically like she desperately needs friends in this town.

'Tammy,' I say, standing up. 'Meet Noora, she's police, off-duty.'

Tammy says hi and then stands glaring at me.

'Join us,' says Noora, moving in along her plastic bench. 'Please.'

Tammy orders for us both and then sits down. She doesn't say much. She's tired. I know she's exhausted after a full day cooking in her van, serving ungrateful customers in huge coats who buy from her every week of the year and yet just grunt the order and leave, never any conversation, never any 'how are you'.

I sense Noora doesn't feel too welcome and she makes her excuses and leaves. As she walks away from the table I breathe in through my nose and manage to smell her, to capture her scent. Vanilla and something else?

'That's your Valentine right there,' says Tammy.

CHAPTER 28

Tammy's already gone when I wake up, but she's left a note and a stack of pancakes in the kitchen. I'll get her a cactus in a decent pot and I'll make it up to her at my leaving drinks tonight.

The office is quiet.

A guy who used to work at the pulp mill had an accident yesterday. He had a fight with his wife about Christmas decorations, that's what his neighbour told me, a vocal argument about how come they were still up in February. So the guy took his ladder and raised it up to his roof to remove his illuminated sleigh but the ladder wasn't secure at the base and, long story short, he broke both legs. I got quotes and a statement from Thord about safety around the home and a few photos. Bread and butter.

At eleven I pull on my winter gear. It's crisp and bright outside, and there are more people out than I've seen in weeks. I turn right and notice a van parked under the archway in the centre of the factory. It has 'trap-a-rat' written across the back doors.

I squeeze past it to get to the yard. Stacks of summer tyres, the narrow kind that fit the Grimberg trucks, have been taken from the root barns and piled up near the wall to St Olov's. I think these guys are humane vermin exterminators? Humane exterminators? That even a thing? They're setting up elaborate runs and clear Perspex boxes with trapdoors at the end of them. The old tailless cat with the missing ear is watching them from the wall close to the family grave.

I sign in and walk through to the factory floor. The mixing and heating zone looks like it always does but when I reach the extruding machines I can see the liquorice snakes are a deep shade of red. Glossy. Each fine line of sugar paste and flour and aniseed flavour and liquorice and salt and anti-crystallisation agent is as red as my blood. As red as your blood. The stampers are pounding their little hand tools down onto the scarlet coins like border officials at some stamp-happy bureaucratic country. Valentine's is coming.

The canteen's filling up and staff are pulling chairs down from the tables where they've been resting upside down to allow the cleaners, two white-haired guys who look like twins, to mop underneath. I swing left and open the heavy door to the staircase. I can hardly move it, it's so thick. Must be half a tree. The door has a new 'keep closed at all times' sign screwed to it. I walk up.

There are about forty stairs because the ceilings of the ground floor are industrial high. I walk up past hundreds of suspicious eyes, and one of the mirrors has a fine hairline crack in one corner and I wonder whether or not to tell Anna-Britta. It's the kind of thing that might be important to her.

The Grimberg office is quiet, even quieter than the *Posten*; at least we get drop-ins and phones ringing, this place is a mausoleum. There are four individual offices, but I've only ever seen Anna-Britta in hers and candyfloss Pissy Knickers in hers.

'Tuva, you're going to think I'm avoiding you,' says Anna-Britta, opening her office door wearing a navy dress with matching cardigan. And her broken rectangular watch.

'It's your book,' I say.

'It is not,' she says, an appalled look on her face. 'I'll have Karin talk to you again today. I have visitors in downstairs, you probably noticed, and this is a very busy time for production, second only to pre-Christmas.'

'Is Karin in the Receiving Room?'

Anna-Britta nods and I see that the bags under her eyes are darkening, the skin thinner and more creased than before, like my uncared-for elbow skin.

I find Karin sitting cross-legged on the Gustavian sofa playing on a Gameboy, a boxy grey thing I used to play on as a kid.

'Retro,' I say.

She looks up and narrows her hooded eyes. 'I

like it,' she says. 'Ludy and I used to play Mario all the time, it's very addictive.'

You should try *Grand Theft Auto*.

'It stops me from thinking too much,' she says. 'Helps me forget.'

I know exactly what she means.

'Can we go through again?' I ask.

She looks at me and walks over to the residence door. She opens it and gestures for me to go in.

The room looks like it did before. The exposed brick wall, the slime wall, is dark green in hue and all the furniture is positioned well away from it. I see the cabinet, it looks innocent enough with the doors closed, and I see the table with the gleaming knives lined up underneath.

'What's that?' I ask.

Karin looks at the fruit bowl on the table, the one full of pine needles with a snowball the size of a bowling ball planted on top.

'Granny's thing,' she says.

And then I hear a whistle.

The acoustics up here are awful. Some sounds get lost in the space of the room and some get amplified out of proportion. But I can hear whistling like sitting next to a fireplace on a stormy night. And then I hear it again.

'She wants you,' says Karin, looking over toward the attic.

I walk slowly to the base of the stairs, my Dictaphone in one hand, my handbag over my shoulder. I open the door.

'Come on up,' says Cici. 'Come on.'

She looks like she's been crying but she takes my hand and leads me up the stairs to her attics. It's mild up here now, the frost patterns gone from the window panes.

'Wait there, or not, do what you like. I'll be just a minute.'

She trots off to her changing area between the chimneys and I look at her, impressed with her mobility considering she's in her early eighties. She moves as well as I do.

There are mannequins up here, dozens of them. They're not the figures you see in H&M, these are old, maybe 1970s, all yellowed plastic and sad tired eyes and bad joints. One has false eyelashes and red lips and beautifully-painted pale green eyes, but the tip of her nose is missing. Like it's been gnawed away. Some of them are dressed and some are half-dressed and one's naked with a crispy dried-out daisy chain swinging around her neck and it's so long it reaches her caved-in navel.

Music starts. It's not loud but it's there: tinny speakers playing something I vaguely recognise. Cici looks from behind the conical brick chimney and then springs out and walks down her linoleum catwalk jutting her hips and when she gets to the end, to within about two metres of me, standing here like a dullard with my handbag and my wool jumper and my Dictaphone, she bends down to show me her peacock-feather wings and looks up and bares her teeth and blows me a kiss.

'You should be in Hollywood,' I tell her.

'They should come here,' she says.

I walk with her around the perimeter of the attic space and she's staring at the roof itself, at the wooden beams and trusses and joists. They're old wood, hard like steel, and they are littered with bodies. I make out bees, three of four types, and wasps and lapwings and moths and spiders. The bees and wasps are sleeping, hibernating, and so are the horseflies and bluebottles. Their furry thoraxes are pulsating and their breathing rate has slowed to what looks like a human's breathing rate, their tiny lungs inflating and deflating inside them at the same tempo as mine; and that is unnerving.

'Never wake a white moth,' she says, in a serious tone. 'Or a sleeping bee. Another month and they'll start making their way. I provide safe harbour up here. I find them quite an inspiration, just look at the blue of that housefly.'

She points to an average-looking bug and I look closer and it's black-blue and it has a metallic hue. I move my head to see it in better light. She's right, it is beautiful.

'I like you, Cecilia, if you don't mind me saying.'

'Well,' she says. 'I like you. Do you knit?'

She walks off toward her changing area, which has heaps of discarded dresses and boots and strings of multi-coloured plastic beads.

'I used to,' I say.

There's a sewing and knitting area up here on a big table and her sewing machine is one of those foot-powered types from the fifties. A slow-burning grave candle flickers next to it.

She waves her arm around at the sewing kits. 'I mend everything,' she says. 'That's how I earn my keep now I'm an attic dowager. If KK has a hole or Anna-Britta's grey-on-grey two-piece gets bobbly, I can sort it.' She taps her fingers across her embroidery scissors and knitting needles, all stabbed vertically into a florist's oasis sponge, vaguely face-shaped, one of those stiff green ones you can't help but push your fingertips into.

'Can I ask you a delicate question?' I say. 'It's something that's cropped up with the book.'

She holds up her palm. 'Delicate, delicate, delicate.' She walks over to a long stainless steel rack of boleros and capes. 'Delicate, delicate, delicate.' Finally, she pulls on a new thread of beads, these ones are amber with green aquamarine stones in between, and she looks at the mirror and squeezes her lips together and re-organises her bracelets.

'I'm ready,' she says, turning to face me.

'Per Gunnarsson. The man who died. Do you remember, about seven years ago, that someone complained he was talking inappropriately to a young girl?'

Her face hardens. 'It was dealt with. He was allowed to keep his position here on the basis that he kept away from her. On the basis that he kept himself to himself.'

'Her?' I ask. 'Who was the girl he was talking to?'

'Keep the past in the past,' she says. 'It was dealt with.'

'You can tell me.'

She narrows her eyes. 'I said it was dealt with.'

'Alright then,' I say. 'What happened with your grandson, Ludo?'

'What happened?'

I nod.

'Lilla Ludo was such a little tyke, one of those fun children, not one of the scared, timid ones. He had a backbone and a flame in his belly. He and KK were inseparable, they used to play up here as children, with the puppets and dressing up.'

'It must have been dreadful, losing him.'

'Always incredibly hard to lose a little one,' she says, turning one of the amber beads in her lemon-scented fingers. 'But I believe very firmly in your time. You know?'

'Your time?'

'When it's your time it's your time. Lilla Ludo had leukaemia, dreadful disease, and he didn't suffer much until the very end, thank goodness. As awful as it sounds, it must have been his time. Because that's the only way I can cope with it all. I have to accept it was his time, otherwise I'd be long dead. And so would his mother. We all would.' She looks older now. Her back's curved and her chin's dropped. 'It was dear Gustav's time, although nobody around here will accept it except KK.'

She scratches her chin and I notice her rings.

She has one grey pearl carved to look like an eye. Next to it she has a razor-blade ring with a strip of cork on each edge. There's a huge pink rock on her little finger and it has an insect trapped inside it, a mosquito I think.

'Next time you come up I'll have a whole rack for you.'

'Okay,' I say. How do I respond to this? 'Thank you.'

'Lilla Ludo was treated in Karlstad by excellent doctors. They did all they could with their medicines, and we did all we could with our precautions. But it was his time. He died in his own bed in this very building, which is how, I think, he would have wanted it. My son blamed his stupid antennas up there.' She points through the roof to where the right chimney stands. 'He blamed himself but all the experts said there's no connection. The antennas give off less radiation than holding a telephone to your own ear.'

A hum starts up near the walls.

'Heaters,' says Cici. She walks to the window and looks east out of the slanting window toward the ruin of St Olov's. 'Weather's coming, just look at that.'

There's a grey cloud approaching on the horizon and it's like I can see the actual weather front they show on TV. It's moving in.

'Well, it has been mild,' I say. 'Why didn't the mobile phone company take the antennas down?'

'Oh, they wanted to,' says Cici. 'Turns out the

chimney isn't as good as a steel mast anyway, so they wanted to. But Gustav talked them out of it, he was smart like that. He renegotiated the deal and they're still up there transmitting inane conversations all around Gavrik Kommun. We're the beacon, the central messaging station. If your bus is running late or you want your daughter to pick up potatoes at the supermarket or your friend just got killed, then that message will be relayed via our chimney stack.'

CHAPTER 29

I'm driving past ICA Maxi on my way to Holmqvist's house. I explained I have my leaving drinks at eight so he told me he'll provide a light pre-supper and a non-alcoholic cocktail, a mocktail, one of his own invention.

The snowfall's light but when I look up through the windscreen the low sky looks as though it's holding a whole winter's worth of snow right above my truck. My tyres work okay but I drive slower than I would in my Hilux and I take corners as incrementally as a cargo ship.

I call the cop shop and Thord picks up.

'You have two leads,' I say. 'Let me help.'

'No comment,' he says.

'Bullshit,' I say.

'Listen. One lead. One. A dark blue or black 4x4 vehicle seen driving away the day of the murder. Witness – I ain't saying who and it don't matter – he reckons a guy walked out from the arch and he had a hat pulled down and he had his collar pulled up.'

'The lawyer,' I say. 'Hellbom has a Mercedes 4x4.'

'Hellbom's got a cast-iron alibi. Chief checked it out.'

'What alibi?' I say.

'If you want to help us then put the 4x4 information in your next paper. And if you see a dark SUV acting suspicious, photograph the plates for me, but keep yourself safe. And if someone says something to you, anything, you bring it to me before you take it to your editor, you hear me?'

'I hear you.'

Was Facelift at the scene of the crime? Or was it any one of a hundred other Gavrik residents who drives a dark 4x4?

There are white rectangular lights visible through windows. SAD lamps. Plumbers and nurses and pulp-mill engineers, all desperate for a quick serotonin fix. I pull into the gas station before I drive under the motorway. I buy snow chains, just one set for the rear tyres, a hit to my overdraft but there's no way I can be trapped deep inside Utgard forest when it's snowing. They're a necessity, not a luxury.

My wipers are inadequate. They scrape back wet snow but then it builds on the edges of the glass and by the time I pass the digger yard near Utgard forest my field of vision has narrowed like I'm peering through a telescope. It's pitch black and my headlights are cheap torches.

A few hours with Holmqvist and then rum and hugs and goodbyes. I can do that. Utgard forest is a glacier on my right hand side, the overgrown pines blasted with snow, and the only green visible in my headlights as I turn onto the rough gravel track is the undersides of drooping branches, each tree laden with tons of snowflakes, the cold green needles almost black. I pass Viggo's red cottage and the construction project in his garden looks like some kind of garage. One of those flimsy half-permanent ones with a corrugated, Perspex roof and a concrete base. The whole structure's covered with tarpaulins against the snow. I get flashbacks to the time he parked in the digger yard and locked me in his car. Nothing happened, I know, but he locked me inside and played a song and lit a tea-light candle for God's sake. I haven't been inside a taxi since.

My body tenses as I approach the big hill. I want to rev but not too much, some speed, but controlled, it's a fine balance in this two-wheel rust bucket. At the top my wheels skid and if I was doing more than twenty kph I'd probably be in a ditch or face-planting a seventy year old spruce trunk right now.

The track is narrow here, no passing places, no orange plastic poles to mark the ditches like they have on public roads. I keep slow and central and pray for no oncoming traffic. I drive past the wood-carving sisters' open-fronted workshop. Empty. There's a brace of stiff, dead pheasants hanging by their front door. Who needs a fridge? The fire in the stove's still glowing red. The smell of it doesn't seem so weird now because everywhere I go in Gavrik Kommun I smell woodsmoke. When it gets down below minus twenty like it did a week ago, people need old-fashioned fires to top-up their underfloor heating. When the cold beats the warm, people return to the simple ways: they light actual fires inside their actual houses. Fires. Indoors. I know it's normal but as I grew up in an apartment in Stockholm with no fireplace I still find it unsettling that people set intentional indoor fires.

Between the sisters' place and the ghostwriter's place the snow is deep and the grooves are starting to harden. I have no thermometer but I'd guess we're at minus five and the snow's coming down hard now. It's not movie snow, big individual flakes falling slowly, almost floating down; this is a white-out, a blizzard, a frozen sandstorm. I have less than a kilometre more to drive and I can't see a damn thing. If I wasn't in this forest I'd probably just stop and, I don't know, walk? But not here, not with dozens of wild elk out there, desperate, tall as rhinos, and the foxes so hungry they're almost dead; not with wolves and bears outside.

So I drive at about five kilometres per hour, my senses on high alert, nerves sparking, my hand gripping the condensation wiper, a plastic stick with a pivoting piece of material, wiping the inside of my screen, fridge-cold water dripping on my face.

I remember the turns up here, the hard left and then slow, uphill right. I'm close now. My eyes are straining in their sockets and I'm desperate to see his house, desperate for 'safe harbour' as Cici calls it, and then I laugh because six months ago who'd have thought that I'd ever consider David Holmqvist's house a safe anything.

It's his car that I see first. I pull in and turn around so I can leave quickly later if I need to. There are wires leading from his bonnet to the wooden post with the weather-proof plug socket. At least I know I'll be able to recharge if necessary. I know I'll be able to make it to Ronnie's Bar on time.

I open the truck door and an icy gust blows me back in. Struggling out, wet snow intruding down the back of my neck, I take my lever-arch file of notes titled, 'Grimberg research' and then I pull up my hood to protect my aids and walk over to the front door. That brief thaw was misleading. Tricked us. I haven't walked through deep fresh snow like this for days. David hasn't shovelled or gritted his property; no use when it's coming down this hard. I step like a children's entertainer, like a short cat, like a puppet on a string: lifting my feet up to knee level and then sinking them back down into the white depths. Ghostwriter's house is well lit, security lights beaming out from the veranda posts.

'Didn't know if you'd make it,' says Holmqvist, opening his front door. 'Please do come inside.'

He's wearing a black roll-neck sweater and grey flannel trousers and he looks like a geography teacher on a first date. I can smell some eighties fragrance. His socks are cashmere.

'I've been looking forward to this,' he says. 'What state is the road in?'

'Bad,' I say. 'Getting very bad. That hill's a struggle. When will the ploughs come?'

'Tomorrow if required,' he says. 'When the Carlssons managed the road maintenance and the hole-filling, Hannes might have called in one of the local farmers tonight to get it clear, those tractors can get though anything. But I'm afraid our means have been diminished what with one fifth of the village no longer living here.'

'The Kommun won't help?' I ask.

'Oh, goodness me, no. Private road,' he says, taking my coat and hanging it up and showing me exactly where to place my boots. The circular rug absorbs most of the slush. 'The Carlssons paid the maintenance bill of around, I think it was almost two-hundred-thousand kronor last year, but the four remaining householders can't quite match that. I hope to chip in some more from next year assuming the Grimberg book sells.'

'I thought you already had a deal?'

'Yes, but that's just an advance, you see. The rest is paid out as royalties depending on sales success. If it's a big enough hit I may well move myself to the Dordogne or perhaps a little place in the Loire valley. Somewhere I'll be free from harassment and gossip. Change my name to something French and escape all this.'

We step inside and he hands me a red drink in

a glass filled with crushed ice and a straw and one of those little plastic mixer sticks.

'Spritz,' he says. 'Summer drink, but I thought we needed something bright on a dull February day. Aperol, prosecco, sparkling water.'

'I'll drink a third,' I say. 'Have to drive to my leaving party at half seven.'

'I mixed yours weak,' he says, pointing at my huge glass with his hirsute index finger; his knuckles are tufty. 'Yours is ninety per cent San Pellegrino. Are you hungry?'

'No,' I say, a little more abruptly than I'd intended, the thought of that ox tongue still fresh in my mind. 'This will do me fine.'

He lifts cling film from a large serving plate. 'These are just crisps with sour cream and red onion and *löjrom* caviar, nothing special but I thought we might nibble as we work?'

I love him for this. No tongues or brains or intestine soufflés, just crisps with salty red fish eggs.

'They look great.'

'Let's take them up to my research room.'

I follow him upstairs, his fuzzy cashmere socks at my eye level. Under my arm is my lever-arch file and I'm sipping my Aperol Spritz as I walk. It is delicious.

'Come in,' he opens the door to the first guest room. 'You haven't been up here before. This is my research library.'

I have been up here before.

There's a trestle table, one of those thin pine things for wallpapering, and it's covered with a table-cloth. I place down my file and take a walk around the room. Three shelved walls, each containing hundreds of identical white box-files. I pass San Francisco and Salt Liquorice and Sistine Chapel and Swedish industrialisation 1800–2000 and Soviet weaponry.

'Amazing library,' I say, sipping my spritz.

He nods, his Adam's apple catching on the fold of his roll neck, the mole on the apex sinking beneath the fabric and then emerging again.

I pass Vertebrae and Virology and Vatican City and Vertigo. David's organising his paper into piles. I sip and look at Pyramids and Pyromania and Papua New Guinea and Pablo Picasso. Mammoths and Mayan Empire and Medusa and Mexico City.

'Let me begin.' He offers me a crisp and it's lost some of its crunch, what with all the sour cream but it is good. Partly because it's a relief to eat anything normal here and partly because it just tastes savoury-fantastic. 'As you know, over half of the book will be centred on the historical context of the family. I think people will find the dynasty compelling, what with their position in the community and their history. I have a few outstanding questions, and I thought perhaps you might have some answers.'

'I'll try,' I say, placing another crisp into my mouth, this one with too much of the red-orange caviar. Too salty.

'Before we delve into the Grimbergs: anything new on this Ferryman business? Any arrests made?'

'Not that I know of,' I say. 'Lots of police around still.'

'I hope this won't stop you from finishing your research. I hope it won't jeopardise the book.'

'If anything people are talking more now than before. People open up when they're afraid.'

'Good,' he says. 'Well, first things first, the outside shareholder.'

'Didn't know there was one,' I say.

'Gustav mentioned it. I think it slipped out one time. The Grimbergs still own ninety per cent of the company as far as I can glean, but the outside investor owns ten per cent. It's curious.'

'Curious?' I ask.

'You can't do a whole lot with ten per cent. It's usually a gift or a strategic investment in a public company. But in Grimberg Liquorice, in a private firm, you wouldn't be able to sell to outsiders, you wouldn't be able to insist on dividends, you'd have very little say on how the company is run, and your money would be locked in. Potentially forever. Usually the only opportunity to cash out is if someone buys the entire company. So, you see, it's curious as to why anyone would own ten per cent.'

'I have no idea,' I say. 'I can look into it?'

'You mean, ask the Grimbergs?'

'I can try. I can also investigate using tax returns and company files. I could dig.'

'Please do,' he says. 'Next: the market share the Grimbergs enjoy has been in steady decline since 1979. All of their competitors have sold up to international firms or else merged together and moved into one modern unit and slashed the workforce and modernised. Have you heard from Anna-Britta? Does she have any plans to merge or sell?'

'To be honest,' I say. 'I haven't gotten very far with Anna-Britta.'

He looks disappointed.

'She's been busy talking to police and increasing site security, and I get the impression she's working herself ragged to keep the place going.'

'She's extremely ambitious,' he says. 'And she's tougher than she looks. Gustav told me she's always thought she could run the place better than any Grimberg. She even asked old man Ludvig for an executive position back in the day, a seat on the board. Apparently, he laughed and patted her head.'

'Fool,' I say.

He gives a flat, almost pained smile, and then asks, 'What about Cecilia and the young girl?'

'Both more open, but I'm not sure they're involved with the running of the company.'

He nods and takes a crisp, letting it sit on his tongue for a while before closing his mouth and then his eyes. He chews slowly. He swallows. The mole grazes his sweater. He opens his eyes.

'Have you seen Henrik Hellbom in there, the lawyer who owns half of the town?'

I shake my head.

'Right,' he says. 'Just tell me what you do know.'

The snow outside is sticking to the window and the thermometer attached to the window frame reads minus nine. I open my lever-arch file to the contents page.

'I start with Ludvig and Cecilia. Information about their travels and her perspective on Gavrik life back in the seventies. I touch on his death, it's kind of a running theme, but I think we need to tread gently.'

'Of course,' he says.

'Ludvig may have died by suicide. Poisoned himself. I suspect some sort of cover-up because of the stigma over suicide back then. Gustav took over at the age of twenty-two.'

'Quite the responsibility,' says Holmqvist.

'And now Karin has quit, I think, or is considering quitting her sculpture course to move back to Gavrik. She's worried about her mother. The pressure. The Ferryman.'

He swallows. 'The police will catch the culprit soon I imagine. Most criminals are idiots. Now. What's the residence like?' he leans in closer to me. 'The Grand Room. Have you been past the door yet?'

I nod and his eyes light up, his pupils growing smaller.

'Pretty normal, quite Spartan really. Huge rooms.'

'Huge?' he asks.

'Huge,' I say.

'Paintings, sculptures, fine furniture, things that can be auctioned off if necessary?'

Suddenly I feel defensive of the Grimbergs' privacy which is outrageous considering I'm being paid by Holmqvist to research them and I'm being paid by Lena, one last time, to write about them for this week's issue.

'I'm no expert,' I say. 'Some big pieces of furniture, smaller things would look ridiculous in that room.'

He makes a little 'huh' noise and my right hearing aid hurts in my ear.

'I've got material on lilla Ludo,' I say. 'And his leukaemia, poor kid. Then how many jobs would be on the line if they ever closed down or moved. All three women refer to their duty and how it's been drummed into them. Did you know Cecilia is a muse for herself, a living mannequin?'

He squints. 'What do you mean?'

'She has an enormous clothes collection in the attic, nothing valuable, just interesting pieces she's picked up here and on her travels. I don't think she's bought anything for years but she customises and alters and cuts and sews up there. It's what keeps her going.'

'That and superstitious nonsense.'

I scratch my eyelid. 'Some of that, too.'

'How is the girl coping without her father?' he asks.

'As well as can be expected. I've kept her out of it as much as possible because she's so young. I think we need to respect her privacy.'

'There is no "we",' he says, the scar on his lip glowing in the glare from the table lamp. 'This is my book and I'm paying you to research. Paying you well. I need everything and then I'll decide what to exclude on grounds of privacy or sensitivity. That will be my decision.'

'Sure,' I say. 'I'm just the researcher.'

He looks more relaxed now. Apologetic, even. I down the remainder of my watered-down Spritz, the crushed ice shards freeze-burning my throat on the way down.

'Do they talk much of their old house?' he asks. 'The Herrgård manor house on Lake Vänern?'

'Not much,' I say. 'Obliquely, they reference it. But not much.'

'What about the wings?'

'The wings?' I ask.

He looks at me. 'The big fire.'

CHAPTER 30

'The wings burnt down?'
He walks toward the door. 'Let me get you a top-up.'

I follow him downstairs and notice the hair tufts at the back of his collar and dark shadows behind his ears. He turns suddenly and I feel like a peeping Tom.

'How about that mocktail?' he asks.

'You said someone burnt the wings down?'

He smiles and licks his lip from the centre scar to the left, then from the scar to the right.

'Someone, or, if you listen to some Grimbergs, something. Now, mock mojito or mock negroni?'

How old am I, ten? I can taste a real mojito in my mouth when he says the word and I need to stop tasting it right now.

'Mojito, thanks,' and then I add, quickly, too loud. 'Mock. Mock mojito.'

He takes limes and sprigs of mint from the fridge and takes crushed ice from the bowl he used for the Spritz. He makes a show of filling two tall glasses and breaking up the mint leaves with a pestle and mortar, and rolling and squeezing the lime.

'The wings weren't connected to the main house; they were some twelve metres away from it. One was guest accommodation and one housed Cecilia Grimberg and half her collection, the pieces not stored in the factory. Ludvig Grimberg would buy her masses of clothes. Perhaps a form of bribe, or an arrangement, because of his philandering.'

'When was the big fire?' I ask as David passes me a glass with half a mint plant scrunched into the top of it.

'Tell me what you think?' he asks. 'Honest opinion. This isn't one of those pre-mixed monstrosities, this is my own concoction.'

I sip it and it tastes just like a pre-mixed non-alcoholic supermarket special.

'It's really good. What year was the fire?'

He looks pleased with himself but then I see him pour a small measure of rum into his glass and stir it with the plastic mixer and I want him to do the same to mine.

'February 2011. Nobody was hurt, no major heirlooms lost, but the investigators were baffled by the fact that both wings went up but not the main house. One wing could have been an accident. All three buildings could have been an accident. This looked like mindful arson, but the family eventually received the insurance money despite much delay. Some blamed it on "old evil" whatever that is. Gustav told me he suspected teenagers from the nearby sailing camp and apparently

Cecilia blamed lake sprites or whatever it is she calls them.'

'She lost half of her clothes collection?'

'It was moved to the factory a week before the fire,' he says.

I raise my eyebrows.

He nods.

'I'll ask more about this tomorrow,' I say. 'They've never mentioned it.'

He snorts through his nostrils like they haven't mentioned a lot of things yet.

'Coffee?'

I look at my phone screen. No reception. Five past seven.'

'Quick one. I don't want to rush through this snow and I really shouldn't be late for my own leaving drinks.'

He breaks up a slab of 90% cocoa dark chocolate, the sort that tastes like black slug pâté, and arranges the shards in a ramekin. He places a cup of ristretto espresso next to it and then looks out the window.

'Take it easy down the hill,' he says. 'My thermometer says minus eleven and that's a good thing, it's minus two you don't want. The colder it is the better the grip. How are the tyres on your vehicle?'

'Don't ask,' I say, taking a micro-bite from the bitter chocolate. It has salt flakes embedded in it. I wash it down with the coffee.

'If you have any problems just get Viggo to drive you. His Volvo can get through most weather.'

Not in a million fucking years.

David Holmqvist taps the coffee scoop into a silver bucket he keeps under the gleaming machine. The bucket's a large wine-cooler complete with French logo.

'Compost,' he says. 'I add this to my pile, the lilacs adore it.'

I excuse myself to use the bathroom. I skip upstairs, the over-sweet mojito still coating my teeth, and step onto the landing. The door to the first guest room, the archive room, is open. His bedroom door is also open, mirrors all over the walls. His second guest room door is closed. I look down the stairs and then step toward it. I open the door. There's an old mahogany desk with green ink blotter and a huge-screen apple computer with ergonomic keyboard and weird-shaped mouse. The keyboard's raised on a little shelf and behind the desk is a bookshelf with dozens of titles, some translated. Three are about the Medusa murders from last year. None are in David's name.

An innocent room.

My imagination has a lot to answer for. I close the door gently and slip into the bathroom. It's above average, with a rain shower and decent tiles. Lena taught me to notice these things. I finish up and then wash my hands, my dry face looking back at me. I touch the edge of the mirror and open the cabinet it conceals. Shaving foam, razors, toothpaste, deodorant, heel balm. I shouldn't intrude. I have to. There are five bottles of pills and two boxes of condoms.

I head downstairs.

'Just a few more days of your research left,' he says, my coat loose in his hairy hands. He holds it up. 'Then I'll be quarantined here finishing the first draft.'

'How many books have you written?' I ask.

'Twenty-three and zero,' he says. 'This will be my twenty-fourth but most importantly it will be my first, the first with my name printed on the spine. The Holmqvist name would die with me if it wasn't for this book.'

'I'm sure your parents would be very proud,' I say, my back to Holmqvist; my left hand trying to find the sleeve.

'Why would you say a thing like that?' he says.

'Your first book in your own name.'

I'm still struggling to find the sleeve hole with my hand, my forearm thrashing about deep inside the folds of goose-down padding, my body getting hotter and hotter.

'They read my early work,' he says, still behind me, still holding the coat, adjusting it so I can find the sleeve. 'Before their accident. My mother said "I suppose it's a start" and my father told me "don't give up the day job". I was seventeen years old.'

'Parents,' I say, turning, both arms now in my coat sleeves.

'Don't disappoint me, Tuva,' he says, his lip

307

quivering slightly. 'Do the best you can and I'll include you in the acknowledgements. You'll have your name inside the book, your actual name. In print. I need as much information as you can extract from the family. You must promise me you'll do your best.'

I look at him and sweat starts to bead at my temples and I have a strong compulsion to get outside into cold, dry air.

'I'll do my best,' I say.

He opens the front door. The veranda covers us completely but my boots sink into snow blown over by the wind. I say goodbye and trudge to the Tacoma and the security lights brighten everything around me. Dazzling fresh snow in the air and on the ground and all over my truck. I walk around to the dark side, the driver's door side, conscious that I'll need to be gentle with the handle, Janitor Andersson's words clear in my ears, but I can't even get the key inside the lock. Where the hell is my Hilux with its bleeper? Potato-head is probably cruising around in it right now boring some poor girl to tears and talking at length about his own opinions and his own lame predictable favourite movies and I can't even open my own door.

'Dead?' says Holmqvist, suddenly beside me.

'Frozen lock,' I say.

He steps into his house and comes back with a pen torch in his hand. He's back-dropped by the dog kennel, unoccupied, ready for removal or burning or sale, and he's wearing a woolly hat.

'Can't get the key in,' I say.

He shows me the little de-icer bottle in his hand and I curse myself for leaving mine inside this truck like a Grade A idiot. His breath clouds in between us and he squirts at the lock and takes my key from me and focusses the pen torch and slowly pushes the key into the lock and the truck door opens. An avalanche of snow drops onto my seat.

'There,' he says. 'I expect I'll see you at the factory tomorrow. Drive safely now.'

I get in and he walks back indoors. I turn the key in the ignition and the weak headlights beam out at the road, which doesn't look like a road just a white absence of spruce trees. I scrape and wipe and pull out slowly onto the track, my wheels crunching through deep powder, the undercarriage of the Shitmobile scraping the high snow between my tyre grooves.

The one saving grace is the overhanging trees. I drive at twenty, my eyes on high alert, my aids switched up to a volume I don't usually like. It's freezing cold and I'm leaning forward so my head almost touches the windscreen.

I trundle down past the wood-carving sisters' workshop, their fire still glowing, their razor-sharp tools glinting in my headlights. I drive on toward the hill. I'll be late for my drinks, maybe fifteen minutes late, but that's acceptable. Twenty wouldn't be, not in Sweden, but fifteen I can get away with.

The snow gets deeper up here with the trees spread further apart and the forest is as dark as the bottom of a cave. I speed up to take a small incline, the one before the big descent, and my tyres make a screaming noise. I try to steer out of the skid but it doesn't work and I slide, my hands tight on the wheel, the slow-mo inevitability of it all, the powerlessness, down into a steep ditch.

I come to a rest at an angle, the truck chassis shaking on its wheels.

Shit.

I drag my fingers over my cheeks. Consequences flash before my eyes: explanations and apologies for being so late, and then I see the disappointed faces of guys who've sacrificed a big ice hockey game on TV to dress up and toast me and my new job and my new life in the south.

My foot presses down on the accelerator, my window more open now. Zero traction. Nothing. I'm tilted in this ditch and I can't move. I climb out and slip a little and then I pull my hood over my head. There are no people here, but just about every wild animal you can imagine is a few trees deep watching me, waiting. There are bears in this part of the world. There are moose, unpredictable moose, hundreds of them. There are bats and polecats and wolves. But there's nobody to help and my nose is starting to freeze. I try to attach the snow chains to my tyres but how the hell do these work? I sweat and swear and manage to get one on straight and the other half on and I'm so exhausted from this, just from this. I get back in the truck, snow everywhere, my hands red raw because I couldn't attach the chains wearing gloves. I try to drive up and out.

Nothing.

I am stuck solid. No phone reception. No traffic. Silence.

I almost cry but then I mentally slap myself in the face. Leaving drinks. There must be a way. I have maybe twenty people waiting for me at Ronnie's and I'm not the kind to get stuck in a ditch and just die quietly. I am not that person.

I clamber out of the truck, more positive now, snow falling down the back of my neck, and then I wade through deep powder, knee-deep snow, it's exhausting to walk through, you know, and I break off two pine branches. I saw this once in a film. I lay the branches around my tyres because I need traction and pine-scented traction will do. I scrape again. My windscreen's covered in splodges of snow that have dropped from nearby branches. I floor the truck and it just skids on the spot.

I wave my phone around looking for a signal.

Nothing.

Must be minus twelve or thirteen, the kind of minus where everything starts glistening with transparent panko-breadcrumb Hoare frost. The forest creaks and crunches. My cheeks are cold, not frostbite cold, but red-skin-that-won't-clear-for-a-few-days cold. My mouth tastes like over-sweet mint, like too many sugar-free gums chewed all at once, and if I had a bottle of something in the truck right now I'd open it.

About a kilometre downhill to the taxi driver's house – him and his covered garage-project and his terrified little boy – or two kilometres uphill, deeper into the wood, backward, the wrong way, to the wood-carving sisters.

What a choice.

I choose uphill because there is no way in the world I want to be stuck out here with Viggo Svennson. I lock up my truck and take my torch and get walking.

After fifteen minutes my legs ache from the unnatural gait I'm using. I have to lift my boot to knee-level before taking a step, and it hurts. The snow is colder now and sometimes the hardened crust on the top holds me so I can walk like Bambi on a frozen pond, but most of the time it doesn't hold and I kind of tentatively step, then fall through to the depth of my shin or even my knee.

I walk on.

Utgard forest is a different kind of terrifying now than it was in October. It's a silent killer now. There are no bugs, they're all frozen solid. Deceased. I can't see any evidence of elk or deer or badger, but they're all here, just deeper in the woods.

There's a noise.

A snort somewhere deep in the trees. I stop dead. My pulse is racing. I swing my torch left and right, trying to look into the solid pine walls each side of me. An elk? I see a flash of green above, something behind the clouds, an aurora maybe, but I've never seen one properly, not a good display. I keep looking up to see it again but there's nothing up there and now I doubt if I ever saw any colour up there in that heavyweight sky.

My skin's scorched with cold and my breaths have stopped clouding because I'm frozen on the inside now.

I keep seeing snow skulls, dozens of them, staring at me from each side of the track, some laughing at me, others wailing, their mouths gaping open. But they're not skulls. They're snow-topped rocks. I walk faster.

Every now and then there's a whoosh noise as a mini avalanche rumbles down a branch onto the track in a white explosion.

I go on.

I have no weapon. I have a phone and my emergency chocolate, unopened, and my wine gums, half gone. They're frozen hard like some kind of fad confectionary.

I stop every hundred metres and look and listen and shine my torch. My heart's pounding and there's an elk out there somewhere. There are dozens of them.

I can't see a single thing. There are noises from behind me, from the track not the trees. Footsteps? A man? Is Viggo somewhere behind me? The Ferryman? I think back to that neck wound, that neat slice, that canine tooth. I turn on my axis and the noise stops. The footprints stop. I pant and I stare into the dark white nothingness. Waiting. It's just your imagination, Tuva. It's nothing. And then I turn around and keep on going. My heart is a steam train fighting a steep incline and my mouth is completely dehydrated.

Woodsmoke.

The sisters' workshop becomes clearer as I round a bend. I slip over, the deep snow cushioning my fall, and then I see their dark grey van. It has a dent on one side like it's nudged another vehicle. Maybe they can pull me out with a tow chain? I start to check out their tyres when a voice calls from an upstairs window.

'What you looking at, girl?'

CHAPTER 31

'Can I use your phone, please?'
She burps from the window. I can't hear it but I can see her blow air from her cheeks and then recoil slightly.

'Phone's out,' she says.

I look up at her. Everything around us is wild silence. When I shuffle my feet I can hear cracks and dull screeches, as ice crystals scrape against each other but when I'm still and she's still and all the beasts around us are still it is absolutely noiseless here.

'Out?' I say.

'The snow. Phone lines are out. Be back in the morning I expect.'

'How can I call a tow truck?'

She laughs at this and reaches out and closes the window. I wait, comforted by the smoke hanging in the clear ice air and by the lit house in front of me. If there'd been a power cut as well as a phone outage I may have lay down and died. The door opens and it's Alice, the quiet sister, in a nightie and long johns, wrinkled all the way down to her quite shapely ankles like two concertina pipes. She's wearing thermal slippers and a big red ski jacket. She waves me inside.

'Thanks,' I say, stepping past her.

This is new to me. I've never been inside their home, just the open-fronted workshop.

'Can't get no tow truck up this track tonight, girl,' says Cornelia, the talking one. 'You ain't seen the drifts?'

'I slid into a ditch.'

'Don't know why you're out driving on a night like this, do you, Alice?'

'Nope,' says Alice, pulling off her red jacket.

'You'll take the sofa. We're heading up in fifteen minutes,' says Cornelia. 'Cocoa?'

I'm taken aback by this. Not because they're offering me 'safe harbour', Cici's phrase, but the cocoa. They've never offered me a drink before, and now it's as if we're a trio in some odd short-lived way. Perhaps because of what happened last year. That awful thing. And now with all this snow. Uniting us.

'Yes,' I say. 'Thanks for taking me in.'

'Ain't got no choice, have we Alice?'

Alice shakes her head.

'You go out there, you'll die, won't she Alice?'

'Die,' says Alice, pouring milk into a saucepan and placing it on the hob.

'We'll give you blankets and we'll build up the fire. We always keep the fires in when it's this bad, one down here and one upstairs. Not been like this since '82 but that was back in Norway.'

316

Alice exaggerates a shiver and pours thick cocoa into two mugs, one for Cornelia and one for herself, and into a teacup for me. There's a range of tools on the sideboard. Gougers and plains and blades, all sharpened and oiled.

We stand by the range sipping, these two in their insulated nighties, both with long johns the colour of old dishwater, and me with my keys and no truck.

'It's my leaving drinks tonight.'

'Your what, girl?'

'I'm moving south next week and tonight should be my leaving drinks in Gavrik, all my colleagues and friends are waiting for me.'

'You said about it before at the bank,' says Cornelia, pointing to the window. 'Just look outside. They'll know why.'

I think I'm getting kindness from these troll-carvers, these women with sparse eyelashes, with toenail clippings they store in a glass jar to use on their demonic, sick little dolls. And it's unnerving me.

'Why south, girl?' asks the speaking one. 'Not enough news up here?'

Alice grins and two of her teeth are missing: one from the top and one from the bottom.

'Better job,' I say. 'More scope.'

They both make a 'humph' noise and Alice raises her eyebrows like I just told them I shit gold nuggets.

We drink up and they show me to my executive

single for the night. They both check the front-door lock and feed the log burner directly opposite my sofa with moss-covered birch logs and then they go up to bed and I remove my aids and unclip my bra under my shirt and drag it out of my sleeve and pull the blankets up to my chin and stare at the fire.

When I wake up my eyelids are glued together and I smell bad. Sleeping in my clothes next to a fire under a heap of blankets will have that effect. Cosy but there's a price to pay. I stretch and swivel and my neck aches from the penknife position I slept in. I switch on my aids and see things in the room I missed last night: knitted trolls and elves, a heavy wooden mallet that looks like it's just been repainted, a family pack of Grimberg salt liquorice, a bowl of sanded-pine splinters, a rectangular mirror smashed in one corner as if by an air-rifle pellet.

'Porridge?' asks the kitchen.

'No, I'm fine, thanks. Is your phone working?'

'Nope. Come and have porridge, we made it for you so you eat it.'

I stagger through, rearranging my hair and rubbing my eyes as I join them. I feel like a wreck and I'm not even hungover. Alice and Cornelia are both wearing zip-up micro fleeces under fleece-lined overalls. Fleece on fleece.

'You sleep good, girl?' asks Cornelia, spooning some brown abomination into three bowls. What the fuck is this, *Goldilocks*?

318

'Fine, thank you. Really, I'm not much of a break-fast person.'

They both look up at me.

'Eat,' says Alice.

I sit down. The porridge is wholegrain brown and it's salty as hell. Like everything else around here. But I am grateful.

The sisters eat like they're synchronised perfectly. It's odd. They both drop two Grimberg salt liquorice coins into their porridge and stir, the heat softening the coins and staining their gruel grey. One will lift her spoon to her mouth and then I'll look over to the other and she'll be there too, spoon tipped, liquorice-laced rye porridge and oats slurped in. They'll both chew in unison, staring down into their bowls, then take another mouthful. There is no talking while this happens. I eat half my portion.

'How they doing up at the factory?' asks Cornelia.

I swallow and say, 'Managing. I think.'

Alice blows air out of her mouth at that.

'Baby-face lawyer keen to buy it out from under their noses, ain't he Alice.'

'Yep,' says Alice.

'We knew that sort back in Norway,' says Cornelia. 'Factory never gave Baby Face any legal work. Baby Face don't like that one bit. Never forgot it. Now him and his partners scheming to make a grand fortune.' She snaps her head around and then scrapes the last of her gruel from the bowl. 'Phone's back in.'

'How can you tell?' I ask.

'Cos I ain't deaf,' she says. 'Receiver buzzes when the connection comes on, don't it Alice?'

Alice nods.

'You'll want Magnusson, number's in the book. Tell him you're here.'

I make the call to some gruff old voice that never introduces himself or even confirms that he'll come. I ask about the price and about time and he just huffs and puts down the phone.

'He was friendly,' I say.

Alice shakes her head at me and Cornelia says, 'you don't reckon he's busy enough as it is after that blizzard, girl? You reckon he owes you something cos you drove around here with your fancy ways when the snow was falling like that? Well, I'm not sure you have any right to be upset with Magnusson. He's coming ain't he?'

Twenty minutes later I've washed my face and tidied the sofa and then an almighty noise rumbles outside. The window darkens. I open the front door and the sisters are already working at their benches, sanding and gorging, sewing God-knows-whose-hair through a patch of leather, a tiny scalp, and there's a huge blue tractor parked outside with a snowplough bolted to the front.

'You called on the telephone?' he says.

'Yes, thanks for coming.'

'Follow me,' he says, driving off slowly in the direction of my abandoned truck.

I thank the sisters and follow the tractor. The

snow gets scraped away and the brilliant white daylight clears my head. I love this tractor rumbling and ploughing in front of me with its horsepower and its heft. It's a goddam pleasure to walk behind it. It's a privilege. There are fresh animal-tracks everywhere to my left and my right. He attaches his tow chain to the chassis of my truck and drags it out like an adult lifting a flailing toddler from a paddling pool.

'Thank you so much.' I could kiss this tall miserable farmer even with his his dangly-icicle nostril hairs. 'How much do I owe you?'

He shrugs and mutters something and pulls off the chain and loads it into his tractor and drives off.

Hero.

I check my phone and I have twelve per cent battery and barely a bar of reception. Eight missed calls, seven of them from Tam. I hold my key close to the ignition and I cross my fingers. Maybe finger crossing counts as one of Karin's 'precautions'? Maybe we all take 'precautions'? The engine starts which is a miracle. I scrape and brush snow off the roof and then I drive off down the ploughed hill. Creaking. The tyres squeak on flat compacted snow. On each side of the track there's a ridge of ploughed powder as tall as a horse. I'm driving down a gulley, a gutter, a carved channel, a bowling alley, a bobsleigh run. My hand reaches down for the stereo but there is none. I pass Viggo's house, the taxi diligently dug out by hand hours ago, and then Bengt's house containing a town's worth of hoarded crap. And then I swing a left onto asphalt.

The main road's been ploughed and salted so it looks black again. Frosted, gritty, but black. I sync my phone to my hearing aid and call the office.

'It's me, I'm on my way, be there in twenty minutes.'

'What happened?' asks Lena. 'You okay? Are you alright, Tuva?'

'Blizzard. Snowed in. Nightmare. I'm really sorry I missed it all.'

There's a pause. 'Doesn't matter so long as you're safe. Everyone was worried about you. Your truck working?'

I miss her so much already and I haven't even left yet. The fact that she asks these questions and she really cares. Every single time, she really cares.

'Fine, actually.'

I drive up Storgatan between McDonald's and ICA Maxi, and the twin chimneys of the factory look down disapprovingly from their high granitic plinth. The town's full of snow, ploughed hills dotting the car parks and roundabouts. People look at me as my truck splutters up the street, exhaust gurgling, windows poorly scraped, hubcaps missing, and I feel as if I've let down the whole town. It's like when I used to visit Mum in the hospice after a missed weekend. I suppose it's just me being extra paranoid, extra sensitive, but I always got the impression from the nurses that Mum had been talking, that they thought maybe I could do a little more for my poor old mother, maybe a few more visits and some more enthusiasm, would that be so much to ask?

There's new graffiti on the wall that separates the cycle racks from the road: a spiked upside-down horseshoe with a trademark sign at the top right-hand corner. When I get inside, Nils flies out of his office slash kitchen, the door banging against the filing cabinet where we keep Kommun news.

'Hours they waited for you, hours,' he says. 'There was a bet going, that's what Ronnie's mate told me, was it a new fella or were you pissed in a ditch or was it some hot girl or was it the Ferryman or did the Grimbergs adopt you as a stamper?'

'Ditch,' I say, pulling off my coat, sweat smell hitting my nose. 'Pissed in a ditch.'

Lena opens her door and gives me a thumbs up or thumbs down or thumbs sideways gesture and I reply with a thumbs up and she winks and shuts her door.

I make a note of what David told me last night and list questions I still have for Anna-Britta and Karin and Cici. Most importantly: how did the big fire start at the lake house? But also: who owns the minority shareholding in Grimberg Liquorice?

I walk up to the factory, snow already greying, already salted and grit-speckled, and walk through the arch. The stampers' eyes are down but I can feel each pair flick up after I pass. I head upstairs and get to work interviewing Anna-Britta. She gives me short, unhelpful answers, and then she leaves to visit the bank and I go to the bathroom stuck between two offices, a tiny cubicle not unlike the bathroom at the *Posten*. I hear sirens. I hope it's not another frozen body, another dead gaping mouth, and then I walk back through and Holmqvist is sitting there in a chair with his smartphone in his hand waiting for me. We talk about the blizzard and me sleeping at the wood-carving sisters' place and how I should have stayed at his place on the sofa. He asks me if I can get him some more details about the Grand Room, about the furniture and the artwork, and then there's a piercing scream from the staircase like someone just got stabbed.

CHAPTER 32

I run out to the top of the staircase, Holmqvist close behind me.

'Oh my goodness,' he says.

I dash down the stairs with their frayed red-runner carpet. Cecilia Grimberg is lying at the bottom in the foetal position, completely silent.

She looks like a dead bird. A tiny, broken, fallen fledgling.

I turn to David and tap his arm, 'Call an ambulance.'

Her long skirts, some multi-layered floral thing, are wrapped around her legs and splayed around her like wings.

I check her breathing.

'Can you hear me, Cici?' I almost shout at her. 'Cecilia, can you hear me?'

She stirs.

I can't see any blood but I don't want to move her in case she's suffered a spinal injury.

'It's me, Tuva. You're okay. Stay with me, the ambulance is on its way.'

But it's not on its way.

Holmqvist is trying to get through the locked

arch door because the chimney base right next to us is too thick for him to use his mobile. He dashes over to the heavy canteen door and heaves it open and a hundred voices flood our staircase. He closes it behind him.

I'm holding Cici's fragile hand, her bangles disarrayed, one of her beads smashed and hanging by a thread. She doesn't say anything but she squeezes my fingers.

'You're alright, Cici,' I say. 'I'm here with you. It's Tuva. Help's on its way.'

I move grey hairs from her face and even though she's been disassembled, she is still a piece of art, still a composition, still beautiful. It's as if an installation has been air lifted from a distant gallery in some cosmopolitan place and then dropped from a great height.

'Oh my God,' shouts Anna-Britta, bursting through the canteen door, faces behind her, hats and hair nets and eyes on Cici. 'Oh, no. Not again.'

'She's okay,' I say with no evidence of this whatsoever apart from my gut instinct and the need to calm down Anna-Britta.

'Is she? Is she conscious? Oh, God.'

Anna-Britta looks like she might faint.

'David's calling an ambulance,' I say. 'It'll be here any minute.'

'That man,' says Anna-Britta, and then she looks up toward the top of the stairs.

Karin's up there, her hand over her mouth, her feet teetering on the edge of the top step, the eyes of a hundred ex-workers watching her and watching me.

'Karin, come down,' says Anna-Britta.

We crouch around Cici like three protective elephants guarding a fallen elder. And then the sirens are here and the arch door unlocks and opens and it is bright and cold and Janitor Andersson's standing there holding a length of steel pipe in one hand and his huge jailor's ring of keys in the other.

'Out of the way,' says a paramedic, a guy I've seen late-night shopping in ICA Maxi a few times. 'Give us space.'

We scatter. Karin and I climb a few stairs and Anna-Britta stays close to Cici.

'Watch her neck,' says Anna-Britta. 'Her neck.'

'What's her name?'

'Cecilia Grimberg.'

They work like medical ballerinas, probing and asking questions and checking Cici's pulse and preparing a stretcher and fastening a neck brace.

Cici's trying to speak now. She's moving her lips and her eyes are both open.

'Don't worry Cecilia,' the guy says. 'We're going to take care of you.'

The other paramedic, a Viking with a beard and tanned arms and a broad neck plastered with tattoos, says, 'It's okay'. He's talking to us three, looking at us all in turn. 'We'll look after her now, you did the right thing not moving her. Who's coming with us in the ambulance?'

Anna-Britta touches her finger to her collarbone and the paramedic nods and the two men lift Cecilia gently onto the stretcher like parents with a newborn. They lay blankets over her and walk out through the arch door. I follow them and the cat's out here, the battle-scarred tailless old cat with one eye. He's not hissing today, he's just sitting in the snow watching us.

They climb into the ambulance. I put an arm around Karin and she's as rigid as a rake handle, all shoulder blades and elbows, not ceding to me one iota.

'I'm alright,' she says. 'And Granny will be fine. It's Mother I worry about.'

Cici's sitting up inside the ambulance now, her tall grey hair all over the place, her shirt splayed open. Their voices are raised. Cici's pleading and the paramedics are pleading and Anna-Britta is pointing out toward Storgatan.

Karin and I step closer to the open doors of the ambulance.

'I will not leave,' Cici says, a lump and a bruise growing on her cheek. 'I will not leave Gavrik.'

They're all saying how she'll be back in a day or two and how they need to get her to a hospital and have her X-rayed and keep her under observation and they say she has nothing to worry about.

Cici notices us. One bedraggled journo who slept on a sofa last night and smells like a dumpster, and one granddaughter as dark and stiff as her cabinet of life. She beckons us over.

'Tell them, KK.'

'Granny will not leave,' Karin says. 'She's made a solemn pledge and she has precautions to take care of. You'll need to treat her here.'

Anna-Britta's shaking her head. Cici's nodding. 'I'll call our doctor,' says Karin.

She makes a call and there's a small crowd outside the gates now: Ronnie, and Viggo Svensson in his Taxi-Gavrik uniform, and half a dozen more. If it wasn't minus fifteen there'd be thirty of them.

The doc, Stina Johansson, my doc, their doc, most people's doc, arrives and parks right in the arch under the big steel hook. She ignores me and talks to Cici and the paramedics. They come to an understanding after ten minutes that Cici's too frail for the drive to Karlstad, which is nonsense but I guess it ticks a box, and Doc Stina will look after her at the factory residence. The paramedics look at each other and shrug and say they need to phone this in but Stina is not the kind of person you say no to. I can see that expensive Mercedes 4x4, Hellbom's 4x4, parked over the road. The paramedics carry the stretcher upstairs and Cici looks quite bright now, save for the red bump on her cheek.

Karin and I walk up behind them and we go into the Receiving Room and Holmqvist is there by the door to the Grand Room.

'We can take it from here,' says Karin, to the medics. 'Thank you, both.'

The paramedics look at each other like 'what?'

Doc Stina says to them, 'Tuva and I can carry the stretcher. I won't leave until I'm satisfied that Mrs Grimberg is out of danger. Thank you both for all your help.'

The paramedics take Stina aside into a huddle and the three of them chat in whispers, Cici's stretcher resting on the Gustavian chaise longue and Anna-Britta holding her hand.

'Call us, any of you, if there are any changes,' says the tattooed Viking paramedic. 'We'll pick up the stretcher later.'

They leave.

'Thank you,' says Anna-Britta to Holmqvist. 'We need to be alone now, I'm sure you understand.' She points toward the stairs.

Karin has her key in the door to the residence, and Anna-Britta and I each have an end of the stretcher. I can see a faint line of blood circling Anna-Britta's gnawed index fingernail and it looks like a pink halo.

'Go,' says Cici to Holmqvist.

He does as he's told, his eyes on the door to the Grand Room, the locked door, as he turns to walk down the stairs.

We pass through.

'Excuse all this, excuse all this,' says Anna-Britta to me. 'Excuse the room, don't look, just please don't look.'

I stare down to the floor and we walk to the closest bedroom, Cici's bedroom, the one by the chimney.

'I want to see the family,' says Cici. 'If I'm to be in bed for days and I can't reach my attics then I want to see the family.' She looks to Karin, whose laser-straight fringe is covering her eyes. 'Can I borrow your room, KK?'

Karin smiles a sad smile and nods.

We walk to the far end, to the corner bedroom at the rear. I glimpse Anna-Britta's bedroom and see Gustav's trousers and shirt hanging over the back of a chair. His brown-leather shoes are tucked underneath. I shiver and look away. We slide Cici carefully onto the bed and then the doc asks us all to leave so she can talk to Cici and examine her.

'Don't look at all this,' says Anna-Britta, her eyes tired and red. 'It's not how it's supposed to be, please just ignore it all.'

'I won't write about the residence,' I say. 'I won't describe it.'

She closes her eyes tight shut, her hand on my arm, her other hand on Karin's shoulder. She almost cries but she doesn't.

Anna-Britta busies herself in the kitchen and then we sit at the long table with knives at our toes and we sip sweet tea from repaired china.

'I hope she'll be okay,' says Anna-Britta.

'She has to be,' says Karin.

'She will be,' I say.

'It's those damn heels she wears,' says Anna-Britta, almost laughing. 'Heels at eighty-two. Higher heels than I would ever dream of.'

'It's that old carpet,' says Karin. 'It's tripped me up a dozen times.'

I suspect it may have been Cici's layered skirts actually, but I don't say anything. Her skirts are long and irregular shaped and I wouldn't be able to wear them. There are two slices of white bread in front of me on a small tray, no plate, and a pair of scissors.

'What's that for?' I ask.

'For Granny,' says Karin. 'We'll take three hairs from the top of her head and lay them between the slices and then feed it to a dog. It'll help her regain her strength.'

She says it like it's the most normal thing in the world. Like she's saying, 'oh, it's just two ibuprofen for the swelling, and a glass of water, we'll take them through to her soon'.

Anna-Britta sips her tea but before I can digest, bad choice of word, the hair-bread-dog thing, Doc Stina closes Cici's door and joins us at the table. She's been inside here before, else she'd be staring at the wet wall like I want to do, or at the knives lined up underneath the table.

'I'll leave her to rest for a while,' says Stina. 'I'm confident nothing's broken but she's badly bruised and I think she's sprained her ankle. I've left anti-inflammatories and painkillers in the room and I'll be back tonight to check on her. Keep her hydrated and let her rest. It's a shock when you fall like that. Quite a shock.'

We thank her. Somehow I feel like a family

member and although this is the most fucked-up family I've ever known, it is touching how gentle they are with each other.

Karin sits playing with a mini-blowtorch-style lighter. She's burning pine needles, the ones that used to cushion a large snowball, while Anna-Britta and I talk about mundane things.

'The red liquorice looks delicious,' I lie.

'Second busiest time of year,' says Anna-Britta. 'After pre-Christmas. Should help make up for all the delays.'

'Someone mentioned to me, I can't remember who, that you have an outside investor. I was thinking maybe they could help more now you're running things on your own, what with Cecilia being bed bound and you being so busy.'

She laughs, no bearing of teeth like Karin and Cici, just a soft laugh.

'He helps in his own way. But, no.'

'Could I talk to him?'

Anna-Britta looks at me and realises I don't know the identity of the investor. Then she bends down and picks at a wad of chewing gum stuck to the floorboards.

'Who told you we had an investor?' she asks, rubbing the tacky gum-residue between her fingers. Then, before I can answer, she retrieves a large metal canister of lighter fluid and a ripped cloth from the kitchen. She rubs at the gum with the cloth.

'I can't remember off the top of my head,' I say. 'It might be in my notes. I can find out.'

She puts the metal canister on the table and looks at Karin and then back at me. The air is thick with fumes. 'I think we should check on Cici,' she says, standing back up. 'Thanks for calling the ambulance earlier.'

'Oh, that was David.'

She clenches her teeth.

There are two doors next to each other: the bathroom and Karin's corner bedroom. Anna-Britta opens the bedroom door a crack and I can smell incense. There are posters pinned to the walls: death-metal bands, *Trollhunter* movie prints, photo collages and a *The Towering Inferno* promotional movie poster.

'Do you mind if I pop in to see her with you,' I say. 'To say goodbye?'

We knock on the open door and push it and Cici's propped up in bed playing with her rings and rearranging her bracelets. She looks up at us.

'I didn't fall,' she says in a clear adamant voice, sliding her bangles higher up her wrist. 'I was pushed.'

CHAPTER 33

I walk out through the factory floor and people are whispering and they look afraid. Workers with clipboards are ticking things off and then looking over their shoulders. Quality-control supervisors visit the bathroom in groups. I go past the forklifts and the lines of stampers and tasters and then I get to the stirring tanks. It's all back to black now. No more red. Today is Valentine's Day so we're back to black salt.

Somebody pushed Cici? I don't like to doubt her because I think people should be believed, they should be listened to, and I happen to like her a lot, but I was maybe ten metres away from that staircase when it happened. I was chatting with Holmqvist and nobody else was around, and who the hell would push an old lady down the stairs?

The clocking-in machine looks like it might clock itself out any minute and I wonder if any other industrial company in Sweden still works with this steam-age technology. Most are all gleaming white offices and free baby crèches and hot-desking and electric company cars and flexitime and Skype meetings. Not here.

The root barns are surrounded by towering piles of ploughed snow, and the vats of waste syrup are an unnatural shade of red. I pass through the arch, a delivery truck squeezing past me, and walk out through the gates. Gavrik looks almost normal. The February chill makes everything sparkle. Easterly wind. I can see women and men on rooftops shovelling snow onto the pavements, safety cones placed beneath them, harnesses looped around chimneys, icicles dangling precariously from gutters like glass daggers.

Instead of going back to work, I turn right. The sky darkens two shades and I open the door to Gavrik police station. The ticket machine reads '28' and the screen above the counter says '28' so I take a ticket and ring the bell.

The door opens and it's Chief Björn.

'Twenty-eight?' he says.

What do you think? I hold up my ticket and Noora walks through from the office behind. Both Björn and Noora are drinking from scarred mugs and they both look exhausted from all the Ferryman work.

'How can we help?' says Noora like we've never seen each other before. Björn watches every move she makes.

'I wanted to report an incident at the factory.'

She takes a biro and pad and Björn rests against the wall, his gun stiff on his belt.

'Go on,' says Noora, unsmiling.

'Cecilia Grimberg fell down the stairs earlier

today. She's okay I think, just shaken. But she says she was pushed, that it wasn't an accident.'

'She's okay, you say?' asks Noora. 'No knives involved? No blow to the head? Can she come to talk to us herself?'

'She's ninety-five,' says Björn with a bored expression.

'She's eighty-two,' I say. 'And she's resting. The doctor will visit her again later tonight. No knives, just a push. What would this be? Attempted murder? Assault? Could it be connected to Per Gunnarsson?'

Björn steps closer and points to the key-code door to the rear office. Noora drops the biro and follows his instructions and leaves us.

'You say she's just bruised?' says Björn.

I nod.

'Your report has been officially filed. And don't go spreading rumours we don't need about this being the Ferryman. Nothing to connect these two incidents and the last thing we need in this town is the hysteria. I'll talk to Anna-Britta Grimberg and we'll take it from there.'

'But—'

He looks at me and I can see dry skin on his neck and on the top of his chest, red scaly winter skin.

'Between you and me,' he says, 'I tell you this because you're almost out the door and I don't need any more trouble, so between you and me, Cecilia Grimberg has claimed similar things before.

337

Been pushed, been defrauded over insurance money, been verbally abused in the street. She's not all there.'

'She is all there, Chief,' I say. 'She's as clear-thinking as you and me.'

'Last time she reckoned she got pushed she told me she knew who did it but couldn't tell me. I said couldn't or wouldn't and she said both.'

'Did you follow up?'

He sighs and says, 'She's looking for attention because she never got much from her husband. That's about the size of it.'

He drains the last of his coffee and opens the key-code door and leaves me alone in reception with its vertical strip-blinds and the bolted down chairs.

I cross the road and it is vicious cold, like minus twenty, too cold to snow, and I do a I-don't-want-to-break-my-neck shuffle over to the office.

'Three hours till the print,' says Lena, sitting at my desk. 'You going to file on time?'

'Sure,' I say, catching a whiff of last night's stress when I pull off my ski jacket. 'I'm here now. Three hours.'

She looks at the clock on the wall and then heads back to her office.

I spend an hour writing up stories a little faster than I'd like. It's not easy to do Per Gunnarsson justice as he didn't seem to have much of a life past his schooldays. He had one job and one apartment and no friends or family. So I fill in with details of school achievements and his travels to Norway and Thailand. I fill in with a quote from his elderly neighbour about how he helped her put out the garbage, and about how he drew up comprehensive family trees for the town's most important families, and about how he once fixed her TV. I try to give him some closure and some justice in my paltry, insignificant way. I try to give him a narrative. A decent send-off.

In between the Ferryman stories and the appeal for information regarding that dark blue 4x4, I insert a slice-of-life piece on a record-breaking pike caught by two teenage girls out ice-fishing on the reservoir. Poor wording by me but Lars's photos are great and that's all anyone will really be looking at: the two red-haired girls with broad smiles and the monstrous pike held between them, with its gills flapping open and its lower teeth sticking out of its mouth like some abominable freshwater crocodile. There's also a broken-pipe story. Damage to an old house off Eriksgatan. Looks like seven ineffective ice-rinks, one in each room. All mediocre Toytown bullshit, but it's what my readers want. I learnt that last year. They don't want a paper full of homicide analysis. The front pages, yes, but not the whole thing. They'll read it and they'll all mutter 'must be an out-of-towner, a drifter' and then they'll turn to the rest of the news. They need a few articles that make them feel safe and at home here in murder town.

There are questions niggling me. The identity

and motive of the Ferryman killer is number one, and whether it is, despite what the Chief says, connected to Cici's fall. The Grimberg investor is number two, but then also the mobile-phone masts, and the big fire at the lake house, and the real story behind Ludvig's death. And then there's Gustav's suicide. The coroner was too quick. Are these random incidents or is someone behind them all? I cannot leave this town with a killer on the loose. I can't do that to Lena or Tam or Noora or anyone else.

I try to access the Bolagsverket website, the national record of companies and their share-holders but my password's stopped working. They say they'll email me a new one.

'Lars,' I say, leaning back in my wheelie chair.

Nothing.

'Lars,' I yell.

He looks up, his bifocals not quite straight, his teeth stained grey with liquorice juice.

'Do you know much about the individual Grimbergs?'

'Less than you,' he says.

'You've worked here for twenty-thousand years. If you were still doing my job, who would you talk to about the factory in the eighties and nineties?'

He sniffs and fiddles with the cardboard liquorice box.

'Svensson.'

'Which one?'

'Taxi Svensson, don't know his first name. Told me once when he picked me up from the airport at Karlstad, it was Lanzarote that year, for my psoriasis, didn't help it much, haven't been back, he told me his dad or his uncle used to work there. I'd try him.'

Viggo Svensson? Nope. Not a chance.

'Anyone else?'

He shakes his head and gets up to start photo-copying something.

I cannot interview the taxi driver. I will not.

'Oh,' says Lars, turning to me with a handful of warm paper. 'The ICA Maxi girl, the ex-model one. She's got some kind of connection to the place. Her mum, maybe?'

I email what I have to Lena to keep her off my back and then drive straight to ICA. I can't see the parking-space lines under all the white so I just park where I like. The cycle racks are heaving with bikes with spiked wheels and most have red-and-white ICA carrier bags wrapped tight over their seats. Cars and people look the same this time of year: uncared for. Most Gavrik residents don't shower much in the dark months because it's too cold to go outside semi-wet, and once your hair's under a hat who's going to notice anyway? The plants are dead and the cars have no hubcaps because they have their winter tyres on. Everything's uncared for.

Extra mats have been laid out in the entrance area. The trolleys are soaking wet and some have icicles. Shoppers look relieved that there are hot dogs for sale here and face cream and DVDs and XL multi-packs of strong Swedish coffee.

'Can't talk to you now, I'm with a customer,' says the pretty cashier when I arrive at her till.

I wait, but then there's another customer adding pre-shaped taco shells and minced pork to the conveyor so I run off and grab a can of Norrland beer, the 3.5% stuff, the strongest you can buy outside of Systembolaget, and put that on the conveyer.

'Can we talk?' I ask.

'You got a loyalty card?' she says.

'No. What do you know about the Grimberg family?'

'What?' she looks up at me for the first time. 'Twenty-nine kronor, cash or card?'

I stick my card in the machine.

'Someone told me your family know the Grimbergs. Is that true?'

'Is this about the Ferryman killer? I already told the TV guy and he didn't even broadcast my clip. It's an out-of-towner cos there ain't no ferries in Gavrik town, not a single one.' She rubs her tongue over her teeth. 'My mum used to work at the factory before she quit to take care of Dad. A taster, she was. Don't know who killed that man and put coins in his eyes.' She shudders. 'Grimbergs make liquorice, that's all I know, and it's too damn salty, I know that too.'

'Can I talk to your mum?'

'Better off talking to Uncle Viggo, he knows all about that place.'

'The taxi driver?'

'It's declined,' she says.

Shit.

'Sorry, it's a new card,' I say, and she looks at me like, yeah, whatever, I've heard that one about a hundred times before. I try my other card.

She nods. 'Receipt?'

I take the receipt.

No way I'm driving back into Utgard forest in the Tacoma on Valentine's Day, no way in the fucking world. Viggo Svensson is a Class A creep and I will not be alone with him in a private place.

I walk out to my truck and throw the can of beer on the passenger seat. I turn the key and switch on the heat and make the call I don't want to make.

'Viggo, it's me. Tuva Moodyson from the paper.'

'Hello, Tuva,' he says in a neutral voice. 'What can I do for you?'

'Can we talk?'

'Any time.'

'McDonald's at seven?' I say.

'It's a date.' He calls off and I want to vomit and throw my phone out the window but McDonald's will be safe. Even if he's the Ferryman, if he cut Gunnarsson's vein and stuffed liquorice coins down his throat, McDonald's is public and it's the busiest place in town. It's safe. I'll be fine.

CHAPTER 34

Gavrik's nine-thousand residents will be reading my words tomorrow morning over their coffee and their salted rye porridge, one day late, an eight-day news week thanks to the printer's strike. But right now it's me and Lars typing and it's Nils trying to finalise wording for Benny Björnmossen's gun-store promotion and for the Toyota garage ad, which is a touchy subject because Jan-Östnäs is late with his payments. It's that time of year. Bank accounts are lean and old stock needs clearing out. February means the discounting of unsold ammunition and last season's cross-country skis.

'I need that wording,' shouts Lena, and Nils bangs on his side of their partition-wall in response. He's on the phone so a bang suffices.

'You got a date tonight, Lars?' I ask.

'Oh, yeah,' he says, looking over with a broad grin, his bald patch reflecting the fluorescent ceiling strip-lights. 'Table for one at my sofa, the front door triple-locked, *Arachnophobia* on Netflix, one of my top fifty, Quorn tacos, tub of Ben & Jerry's, a six pack of craft beers.'

'Who says romance is dead,' I say.

He closes his eyes and kisses his fingertips. I actually love him right now.

I email my final stories to Lena. It's dark outside already and I'll leave myself forty minutes to get home and shower before interviewing Viggo.

Lena appears at her door threshold. 'Where's the other factory news?' She looks furious. 'You've written the Ferryman but what about the insider Grimberg stories, that's the stuff our readers want.'

'It's all there,' I say.

'No it isn't,' she says, her eyebrows high on her forehead. 'Don't mind you moonlighting for Holmqvist this last week but I need my fair share, Tuva.'

'You've got the obituary and the truck crash and the red-Valentine's-liquorice story and the piece about Anna-Britta being nominated for the Gavrik chamber of commerce.'

'The old lady who got pushed down the stairs?' she says. 'Readers want to know more about that family.'

I shake my head. 'I told you all about it but it's a private incident inside a private residence, it's not news.'

'Will it go inside his book?' she asks.

'I won't be writing about Cecilia's fall, not for the paper or the book. Off-limits.'

She walks back into her office and slams her door.

'Don't upset her on your last week,' says Lars. 'References.'

'I already have a new job, Lars.'

'Small world,' he says.

It is up here, no shit. It's an actual snow globe. Hermetically sealed.

I take a call from the woman who runs the water-sports place down by the reservoir. Reckons she's seen an old homeless guy going in and out of the condemned black warehouse behind the Toyota garage. She reckons he 'looks like a Ferryman' and I ask her what exactly does a Ferryman look like and she tells me 'like he's bent double and he's out to do harm'. I tell her it's not really a story and that she should call Thord and maybe help the guy find some temporary accommodation.

The temperature on the window thermometer says minus sixteen when I leave. A kid wearing an all-in-one snowsuit crosses in front of me dragging a sledge and he looks like a shrunken astronaut. I pull my hood tight around my head to minimise the air gaps, to trap my stale heat, and then I start the Tacoma's engine. Starts just fine. I complete all my pre-flight checks and scrape the polar crust from each window. Hotel Gavrik glows pink in front of me, all the ground-floor bulbs changed for red ones like a cut-price brothel from hell.

I get to Tammy's flat. She has deluxe bathroom stuff whereas my shower is, was, stocked with ICA Maxi unscented budget shower-gels. To prevent both eczema and also bankruptcy. I turn up the heat and let my head loll on my shoulders, the water pummelling the bony hump at the back of my neck. I lather up with Tam's scented fancy-pants shower cream and it feels good. I smell like a peach. I use the cream on my forearms and face so I'll be able to enjoy the scent myself later. And then I regret it. What the hell was I thinking? I regret sending this signal to Viggo. I shouldn't care, I know that. I shouldn't have to think twice about what I wear or how I smell but still I rub at myself with the water, scrubbing the scent away, scratching it off my skin. But it's there and it's staying.

I pick out the least romantic thing I can see in my black suitcase: a pair of unwashed Mum jeans and a big, cotton sweater the size of a barbecue cover. I put on my least favourite bra, a non-underwired thing, lovely shade of grey, which manages to flatten my breasts into pretty much nothing. What a hideously distorted world this is where I have to be so conscious of all this nonsense, while he and every other man just lives their lives never having to worry.

The fire's laid in the log burner but Tam won't be back home till late because this is one of her busiest nights of the year. In Gothenburg or Jonköping, couples might be cooking something for each other, or meeting at their favourite brasserie, or sharing a delicious super-hot curry at the Kashmiri place down near the town hall. But not here. Tam works for hours to dish up plastic boxes of superb Thai food; and men, it's usually men, pick up the boxes and shiver and maybe buy a red rose, fifty kronor each, she orders them from ICA every year, they reserve three-dozen just for her. Happy Valentine's.

I park in McDonald's, my bonnet almost touching a ploughed snow mountain. The place is medium-busy and they've put heart-shaped corporate balloons by the counter where you pick up your cardboard ketchup thimble and your drink straws. There's a poster appealing for information regarding the murder of Per Gunnarsson, but no reward is mentioned. That's what you get when you're a loner. If someone stabbed me in the neck and implanted a canine tooth in my jugular vein I doubt anyone would offer a reward for that either. I order a coffee and choose a seat where I can observe the front door like some paranoid gangster boss in a movie.

Five past seven, no sign of Viggo. A young couple, both maybe sixteen years old, sit opposite me. He's got two Big Mac meals and she's picking at a McSalad and grazing through most of his fries. They're wearing headphones, the airline-pilot kind, and they're both watching their phones. But it's not a bad thing. From the Formica upward it's all 'things aren't what they used to be' and 'millennials have lost the art of conversation' but beneath the Formica their feet are entwined, and their trainers, matching brand but different colours, are caressing each other back and forth. It's *2001: A Space Odyssey* at eye level but *Brief Encounter* down by the floor.

'Happy Valentine's,' says a voice behind me. The words rustle the fine hairs on the back of my neck. Hints of stale coffee and breath mints. I turn around.

'Where did you come from?'

Viggo's smile collapses. 'From there.' He points to the unisex toilet and I notice the water in his combed hair. He reeks of supermarket cologne and his grey Taxi-Gavrik cagoule has been pressed or ironed.

He hands me a heart-shaped McDonald's balloon attached to a small weight.

'Take a seat,' I say, pushing the balloon away to the next table.

'I thought you might call eventually, before you move down south, but I never expected this.'

'What?'

'Valentine's.'

He sits and his smile is back, his thin-lipped smile that I never saw that time in his parked taxi because he was in the driver's seat with the tea-light candle on the dash and I was behind locked in the back.

'I'd like to talk to you for a story, Viggo. This is not a date.'

'Whatever you want to call it.'

'Why don't you get yourself a coffee?'

'We're not eating?'

'I've eaten already.'

He licks his lips and looks over to the next table. A kid with curtain hair, quite long, is sitting

349

in his ski gear and the tips of his hair, the ends which must have strayed out from under his hat, are wet and speckled with snowflakes. The rest, the hair on the top of his head, is dry. Curtain-hair kid is inhaling chicken nuggets.

'Mind if I eat?' he asks.

I shake my head.

He's back within four minutes carrying a tray. Filet-O-Fish and carrot sticks and an apple juice. Says it all.

'One of your family members used to work at the factory?' I ask.

'Six of my family members used to work at the factory,' he says. 'Uncle Sven was the quality-control manager at the start but he ended up as Ludvig Grimberg's right-hand-man. He was smart with business, contracts, good head for figures. No need to pay a lawyer with Uncle Sven in the office, he must have saved them a fortune over the years. And then five more, two in production, one of them tasting them liquorice coins, and one cleaner back in the canteen. It's fair to say the Grimbergs have been using the Svenssons for decades. And what do we got to show for it?'

'How did . . .'

'And then there's my wife, you see,' he interrupts, rubbing his knuckles against the side of his head. 'Ex-wife. That's the worst of it. Factory boss played games with my own ex-wife. Gustav Grimberg, I mean. Mind games.' He taps his temple with his finger and then he grits his teeth and stares at me.

'Your wife?'

'Ex-wife,' he says.

'What kind of mind games?'

He shakes his head for a full ten seconds and then he pulls out a small Swiss Army Knife, the one that usually hangs from his rear-view mirror, and he cuts his burger in half. 'Not going into the nitty-gritty, not digging all that emotion up again, no way. Old man Grimberg was never with his wife you see, not really. And Gustav was just like his daddy.' He pauses to wipe the blade of his knife on a napkin. 'And I'll say this. If I saw a Grimberg on fire I wouldn't even spit on him.'

I let him eat and cool off.

'Can I ask you a few questions about the individual family members?'

He chews his fish and bun combination, a drop of mayonnaise lingering on his lower lip before he licks it back inside his mouth.

'Fire away.'

'I've heard from several people that there are more owners than just the immediate Grimberg family. Any idea who the outside shareholder is?'

He nods, his cheeks full of processed cod flesh and gherkins.

The ceiling lights flicker and dim but they stay on.

'Who is it?' I ask.

'Mikey's staying up, you know,' says Viggo. 'Babysitter's taking care of him tonight. Older boy from the next village. I told him you might want to stop by for coffee or ice cream, so he's staying up just in case.'

'Who's the other owner, Viggo?'

'You fancy seeing little Mikey?'

'Let's talk about the Grimbergs first, I've got deadlines. The minority owner, the investor, do you know their name?'

'Investor!' he says, laughing. I can see fish mush on his tongue. 'He isn't exactly an investor.'

I stick out my bottom lip like, 'really? Tell me more'.

'You seen the little guy, the caretaker so-to-say?'

'The janitor?'

'Ten per cent owner. My uncle Sven set the whole thing up.'

Viggo puts two narrow carrot sticks in his mouth and chews like a jack rabbit.

'The janitor?' I say again.

He chews and then he starts to talk and I can see unnaturally orange pulp swooshing around on his tongue.

'Caretaker used to live out by the reservoir, big place with room for a horse, that kind of thing. It was his wife's parents' farm if I remember right and he sold it when his wife passed. Caretaker made a lot of money on the sale and had no place to go and no wife so Uncle Sven suggested he invest in the factory. And he did. Ten per cent, not sure what it cost him, probably everything he had, but ten per cent and he gets a dividend payment once a year.'

'And he can—'

Viggo interrupts me, shaking his head again. 'My uncle expected a bonus for arranging it all. Saved the company he did. Maybe thought he'd be able to leave some money to me and Mikey one day so I wouldn't need to drive every hour of every goddam day, out in all weathers, but he didn't even get a single extra kronor from the Grimbergs.'

I try to look understanding.

'The janitor can live in the basement as part of the deal?' I ask.

'Don't reckon that was part of it,' Viggo says, crunching another stack of neon nuclear-orange perfectly-identical carrot sticks. 'Too damp down there to live, or so Uncle Sven used to say, he should be living out someplace else. Sven reckoned the caretaker wasn't too happy with how it all turned out, reckoned he got more bitter with every year that passed. Nobody likes being ignored. What are you wearing?'

'Sorry?'

'Your perfume, that roses or peaches?'

'Not me,' I say, dragging my sleeves further down my wrists, covering as much skin as possible.

Viggo pierces the little foil cover of his apple-juice carton and sucks through the straw, his thin lips puckered like he's blowing me a kiss.

'Smells real good,' he says, slurping the last of his juice and sniffing the air between us. 'Real sweet.'

I scratch my dry eyelid and try to focus on my job.

The caretaker isn't the one pulling the strings,' says Viggo. 'He ain't clever enough.'

'Pulling what strings?' I ask.

'My ex-wife reckoned the caretaker has someone telling him what to do. Janitor was this close . . .' Viggo pushes his thumb and index finger together, 'to moving away someplace warm with palm trees instead of locking his money up with the Grimbergs for a measly ten per cent. My ex-wife reckoned it was some old man, she said she saw them in a truck out by the Toyota garage. Talked him out of moving abroad, made a case for being an industrialist.' Viggo shakes his head and rolls his bloodshot eyes. 'Uncle Sven explained all the risks in black-and-white but the caretaker's mind was made up. Don't know who that old man was, never did find out.'

'Did your uncle ever mention the Grimberg summer house on Lake Vänern?'

'The Herrgård?'

I nod.

'One of the best houses in the Kommun. Five-hundred square metres even without the wings.'

'The wings that burnt down?'

'Sure did, didn't they. Uncle Sven reckoned. Say, what do I get in turn for all this information, ain't no such thing as a free dinner, especially on Valentine's.'

'How old is Mikey now?' I ask.

'He's almost eight.'

'The Herrgård?'

354

'Yeah, so my uncle reckoned a kid burnt the wings down, you know, the strange girl with the dyed-black hair. He reckoned she wasn't messing around, wasn't being bad. He said she heard about the insurance and she was trying to help out her dad.'

'But she was so young back then,' I say.

'Never underestimate kids,' he says. 'My Mikey can do more difficult sums and writing than I can. He can do all that already. And he loves your friend's Thai food, he can eat it even spicier than I can. Anyway, Uncle Sven reckoned the Grimberg daughter overheard her parents talking. Him about the insurance and her about how she always hated the place and how Gavrik was her home. I got my own theory, though, because people used to say the young girl was furious with her dad back then cos he let Gunnarsson stay in his job. My uncle saw them two, the young girl and Gustav I mean, he saw them have screaming rows over it. The girl reckoned Gustav put the factory's interests ahead of the family.'

'Karin Grimberg was the minor?' I ask. 'The girl Gunnarsson was talking inappropriately to?'

'Never was proven,' says Viggo, wiping his mouth on a paper napkin. 'One of the stampers went to HR, went to the lawyer's wife, but nobody lost their jobs over it, the Grimbergs never let anyone go.'

Karin was the girl?

'The Grimbergs never stayed in the Herrgård lake house much after the big fire, that's what Uncle Sven told me, so they sold it to the lawyer, Henrik

Hellbom his name is, real good economy that one, even though he was born with nothing. Never knew his pappa, you know that? Ain't nothing these days but back then it was a real scandal. Rumour is Hellbom bought a family crest a few years ago and commissioned someone to research his roots to see if his ancestors were nobility.' He rolls his eyes again. 'Hellbom knocked that lake house down and built one of them glass boxes. He always gets what he wants in the end, even if it takes him years of work. You just gotta look at his face. You know he gives himself the Botox? Him and his wife went on some kind of course is what I heard. They inject his face with the Botox needles, do it all from home. You believe that?'

My hearing aid beeps and I notice McDonald's has emptied out. There's one girl at the till and one couple at the table furthest away. I look back at Viggo and he's watching me watch the room.

'You think the Ferryman's here?' he says with a flat smile.

'Why would you say a thing like that?'

Viggo shrugs. 'Let's go and say hi to Mikey, he'd really love to see you.'

'I can't do that, Viggo. But I really appreciate you talking to me.'

'Listen.' He looks flustered. 'I've been working out, can you tell? Reckon I been pushed around long enough and now I've drawn a line.' He straightens up. 'I'm showing Mikey how to be a man and I'm making amends for the past. New rules. Now, why don't I drive us to my place and make you and Mikey some ice cream, just the three of us, you'd make his day.'

'I have a date,' I say.

He looks at me like I'm cheating on him.

'Who with?' he says.

'You don't know him,' I say. 'He's coming here in ten minutes, works up at the mill.'

Viggo half closes his eyes and points his fingertip down into the Formica until the flesh bends and his nail turns red.

'You doing mind games?' he says.

I shake my head.

'Grimberg played those games with my own ex-wife and now your new job's gonna take you away from me?'

'Maybe I'll stop by and say bye to Mikey this weekend before I leave for the south,' I say. 'How's that?'

'Saturday dinner, seven o'clock?' he says.

'I'll call you and we can set something up. I'll do what I can.'

This placates him.

I say goodbye and he stands up waiting for a hug but I stay seated and shake his hand. He walks over to the door and pockets his Swiss Army Knife and then he glances back at me and flashes another thin-lipped smile and pushes the door open. Noora brushes past him and steps inside and the music changes and then it's like he never even existed.

CHAPTER 35

Noora's wearing a hoodie and somehow her hat hair looks good. It's been conditioned. Dried properly. She looks at me and then walks to the counter.

My stomach's queasy. Her awkwardness at the cop shop and the truck crash. I walk to the counter and stand behind her and the back of her head pulls me closer. She smells of good things. In this ice-cold town. The sounds in the restaurant dim and Noora's voice becomes crystal clear. She orders a Big Mac Meal. She has a coupon.

When she goes to pay, to place her card in the machine, her hoodie pulls tight across her back and I see the faint outline of her bra strap, the line of her back, the shape of her body underneath all this winter protection. I'm aware of my pulse. She takes her tray and thanks the server and walks off.

'Next, please.'

I just stand there staring up at the back-lit menu that I know off by heart, my head a soft clump of overcooked pasta.

'Erm.'

'What's your order, please?'

'Big Mac Meal,' I say.

'Drink?'

'Coke.'

'Fifty-nine kronor.'

I pay and pick up the brown tray with its informative paper placemat. It's wet around the edges and my fries look underdone. I fill up my Coke cup to half, because that's what I always do, and then I peer around the room.

She's reading a book.

I walk past her to make sure she sees me and then I sit down at the next table, my back a little straighter than it normally is, my chin a little higher.

She smiles.

My mouth dries out completely, zero saliva, a sandy desert. I see better than I have ever seen, the black crow outside by the bins, the couple in the corner looking away from each other, the faint waft of oily steam rising from my underdone fries.

I'm fifteen years old again.

I can't fill my Coke cup here, not like I usually do, not with her right there. I want to but I can't. I eat a handful of limp fries. Too salty. When I really was fifteen, without a dad, but with a mum who couldn't cope, when I was fifteen I got crushes in newsagents. A lot. I'd go in after school to buy gum or a bar of chocolate. I'd see a guy or a girl over the central aisle looking through magazines and I'd fall in love in a fraction of a split-second. Properly in love. Powerfully. Forcefully. Mind, body, and soul. My stomach would sink toward my bladder and my heart would contract hard like an unripe avocado. I'd watch her or him from the corner of my eye, thrilled. Overwhelmed. Delighted. I'd be in love, watching their hair and their wrists and the way they blinked.

This is the same. Right now.

Noora reads with one hand on her book. Her thumbnail isn't painted but her fingernails are, some kind of French manicure, self-done.

I look down and up, eager not to scare her.

She grips her Big Mac with her right hand. Small slivers of iceberg lettuce fall out into the cardboard carton. She's poised, her elbow pivoting on the Formica, her mouth dimpling on one side as she chews.

I sip my Coke.

My breathing isn't normal. It's shallow, laboured, awkward, stifled, hot.

Noora finishes her burger. I haven't touched mine. Then she wipes her mouth with a napkin and looks around to me and licks the corner of her mouth and nods to the bench opposite her.

I point to my chest like 'me?' and she smiles properly and her dimple looks like a stitch pulled tight behind a piece of fine silk.

Oh God.

I scooch over to her table. Her hoodie is unbranded and it looks very soft, maybe fleece-lined.

'I hate Valentine's,' she says.

'Me too.'

'Card shops and candy companies,' she says. 'It's not made for people.'

I nod and unbox my burger and for the first time in my life I'm conscious of how I'm going to eat this thing right in front of her. It's grown in my hands to the size of a family sponge-cake, and now the middle layer is pushing out from its rightful position, threatening the integrity of the entire structure. I put it down.

'Not hungry?' she asks.

'Not really.'

'You missed your leaving drinks,' she says.

Oh my God, she was there? She came?

'You were there?' I say. 'You came?'

Noora nods her head and a black hair thick enough for me to see floats down and rests on her shoulder, one half hanging down near her collar-bone, the other half hovering in mid-air above her hood. 'I was in Ronnie's bar with Thord. He fills me in on faces in the town, that sort of thing. Big group in there for you, they got quite worried, even asked us if there'd been any emergency calls or any more Ferryman sightings.'

'I was stuck in the blizzard, that's all.'

She nods. 'I heard. Bloody Värmland weather.'

'Have there been sightings?' I ask.

'Oh, yeah. I estimate there's about thirty Ferrymen psychopath dog-owners in town according to what I've heard today. We had one grizzly dude tell us it'll be a foreign dog with rabies that killed Gunnarsson, he told us it's a common thing in

361

foreign countries, and now it's here in Sweden and we'll need to do a cull. He said he'd help. And we've had lots of people reporting weird snow skulls all over, and seeing dark 4x4s cos there's plenty here in Gavrik.'

I nod.

'When are you leaving?' she says.

'Leaving?' I say, looking at the door.

'When are you leaving town?'

Never, I am never leaving. Ever. How come I meet Noora now? When I'm on my way out?

'Monday.'

She nods and in her eyes, in the colour around her pupil and the way her lids close, I detect some faint regret or some 'what might have been'. But it's almost definitely just me imagining it.

'My new paper prints every other Monday so they want me to start on a Tuesday. Break me in gentle.'

Noora looks at her cup and says, 'Why doesn't McDonald's sell liquor, eh? They'd triple their Nordic profits in year one.'

I reach into my coat pocket and pull out my plastic Coke bottle.

She narrows her eyes.

'I'm a police officer,' she says. 'I could lock you up.'

I pour rum into her half-empty Coke cup and then I fill mine. She raises her cardboard cup and smiles that one-dimple smile and we chink cups except they're cardboard so the chinking is silent, more of a denting really.

We drink.

Her shoulders slump and she looks down into her cup and mouths 'thank you' to me. She hasn't asked about my hearing aids yet and I could kiss her for that. We're just two women on a non-date in McDonald's on February 14th.

'Have you seen Henrik Hellbom in the police station much?' I ask.

'Botoxed lawyer?'

I nod.

'Few times. Thord reckons he's selling the Chief a timeshare or something. Lots of paperwork. Heard the Chief talk about a "failsafe investment" – like such a thing ever exists. What is it with men and money?'

I think back to the speedboat brochures. The cruise catalogues. Is Hellbom offering Chief Björn a piece of the Grimberg action in return for a smooth sale? Does the Chief have that kind of influence?

'Talk of an internal investigation,' she says. 'This isn't for your paper. I don't know anything for sure. But talk of protocols not followed after Grimberg's suicide.'

'Police protocols?' I say, my voice low.

'Coroner,' she whispers. 'He's connected to the Grimbergs somehow and they asked for it to be done double-quick so they could bury Gustav. Might be an internal investigation.'

'How did—'

She cuts me off. 'I can't say more. Nothing

concrete yet anyway.' She dabs her mouth with a paper napkin and changes the subject. 'Where are you moving to? Going far?'

I eat a few fries, relaxing now with the rum numbing my tongue.

'Just outside Malmö. Small town, but I can get to the big city in twenty minutes.'

'Well, if you get stuck you can always give me a call and I'll tell you my story. Might need to clear it with the Chief first, but should be okay?'

'Your story?'

'Parents both Iraqi medics. Mum was a cardiologist and now she's a cleaner. She's a cardiologist cleaner. Dad works in an out-of-town DIY store. I joined the police as soon as I could and started training with dogs but what I really wanted was to help with gang problems and minority hate-crimes. And they sent me to Gavrik, where everyone's lily white and there is no crime.'

'We had some crime this week.'

'Don't I know it,' she says, her eyes tired.

'And last year,' I say.

'I heard. Björn says you shouldn't have got involved, should have left the Medusa case to the professionals.'

I let my eyes roll up in their sockets.

'Thord thinks you did great, though. He's got a soft spot for you.'

'He's alright,' I say.

'He's out right now cautioning a woman about her homebrew. She's built a distillery in her bathroom.

Makes 90% proof vodka and sells it to the locals in rinsed-out wine boxes. Slices a tiny hole in the bags, she does. Fills them with rocket fuel and then seals them back up. Thord thinks the woman could blow up half her street.'

I remember the firefighter's house. And his niece, Red, the stamper.

Noora sips her drink. 'You really think the old Grimberg lady got pushed down the factory stairs?'

I shrug and shake the remaining fries from the cardboard pouch onto the tray. 'No idea. She's old but she's as sharp as a hypodermic needle. I'll talk to her tomorrow.'

'Björn thinks the old Grimberg woman could just as well be the Ferryman,' she says.

'Björn's an asshole.'

She scrunches her chin into her chest and giggles. Her giggles turn into a cough and she drinks more rum and Coke to stop it.

'No comment,' she says.

'Are you close to making arrests?' I ask. 'What was that second lead?'

She shakes her head like 'sorry I can't go there' and then she changes the subject and says, 'Chief reckons Ludvig Grimberg had some problems years back. Chief met with him in the factory offices, something about an anonymous letter trying to extort cash. Some old family secret, a big scandal they wanted to keep quiet.'

'They ever find out who was behind the letter?'

She shakes her head.

I lean in close and ask, 'Off the record, are you pursuing any other lines of enquiry, anything?'

She leans in as well. 'There is one thing,' she says. 'I'm only mentioning it cos you might help, quid pro quo.'

I move in even closer.

'Gunnarsson was a bully back in his school-days,' she whispers, our faces so close together I could kiss her. 'He was notorious. We're looking at kids from his school, anyone his age or younger, anyone he targeted back then. Could be a motive.'

'Any names come up yet?' I say.

'Nope,' she says. 'We identified two bullied kids so far: one taxi driver and one car salesman, but they were both at work the day of the murder.'

'Revenge?' I say.

She stands up and shrugs.

'You leaving already?' I ask.

'Aren't you?'

We both place our detritus in the appropriate bins and holes and gaps in the wall like responsible Swedes, and then we walk outside. It's swine cold now, full-on wild-hog swine cold, with ice crystals glistening like fake diamonds, and the snow mountains casting shadows away from the white-light street lamps.

'Ronnie's?' I say.

'Too busy,' says Noora.

'Cinema's already locked-up. They'll be halfway through *Dirty Dancing* by now. Hotel has no bar and the restaurant's fully-booked. There's just Ronnie's.'

'I have an hour or two before I can go back to my apartment,' she says. 'My flatmate's got a date.'

'Ah,' I say.

'We could go for a drive in your . . .' she looks at the Tacoma, 'Limo?'

'You want to come to my place for another rum and Coke?' I say. 'My flatmate, well, she's not my flatmate, I'm just crashing at hers until I leave, she'll be back in a few hours but we could drink there?'

She looks at me, really looks at me, and I'm not so cold anymore. It's maybe minus twenty and my scarf isn't around my face because I'd look stupid and I'm not cold.

We drive to Tam's and park and go up without really saying much to each other. She's behind me as I walk and I feel her gaze bore into me and warm me. We go in.

'Lovely place,' says Noora. 'You picked the right flat to crash.'

I light the log burner. It smokes for a while before the column of cold air in the chimney clears and the fire gets going. Dad told me about this before his car got hit by an elk. He told me how the column of heavy frozen chimney air needs to shift before the fire can thrive and the smoke can escape. I close the blackened glass doors and think of Dad's face and then I mix us both a drink.

Noora strokes my hand. She says, 'New beginnings.' Then she clinks my glass, they actually clink this time, and I realise I've asked her nothing about her new life here.

'How are you settling in?'

She scrunches her eyes tight and falls back into the deep sofa and pulls a cushion onto her lap and then drags a blanket up close by her side.

'It was tough to arrive in late January but I'm figuring things out. It's a weird little town but I'm looking forward to summer.'

'It's just as weird in summer,' I say.

She smiles. 'Please don't say that. I'd rather you just lie.'

I sit down next to her and pull another blanket over my knees. It's soft and pale blue and it has tassels all along each edge. We sit and watch the fire, our knees almost touching. The yellow reflects around the room and the fire softens and warms the white walls.

'Nice fire,' says Noora.

'It's not bad,' I say, and then she shuffles closer to me so our calves touch under the blankets. I daren't move. I thought my senses were heightened earlier but now I can hear her every breath and I can feel it on my skin. I can smell her. The pressure of her leg against mine, the light pressure, I'm consciously thinking of it, her skin, drinking it all in, her leg against my leg, her knee on my calf.

I don't move a millimetre.

Noora reaches out and leans her hand against a cushion. I can see soft down on her cheeks, like the fluff of a newborn chick, the slightest fuzz. She smells good. Her breath is rum and sugar and it's hot on my neck. She moves closer. She bends down and rests her head on my shoulder. Is this the move of a friend or a lover? Her arm's at my back. We're slowly tangling together like climbing roses. But I'm much slower. I am terrified to jinx this probably imagined thing. She's just cold. Or tired. I move my chin and rest it softly in her hair and the scent is dizzying. The fire flickers in the corner. I move my hand in tiny increments so it rests on her shoulder. I look at my fingers. I make my breathing slow to match hers. We rise and fall in the fire warmth, the blankets covering us, me inhaling her shampoo and her skin and all of her.

CHAPTER 36

The front door bangs open. I rub my eyes and I'm hot, Noora wrapped around me, the blankets still on top of us, the fire glowing faintly in the corner of the room.

Tammy walks inside.

She looks tired and cold; big blue Ikea bags full of Tupperware boxes hanging from her hands. When she sees I'm not alone on the sofa she looks at me and her face hardens. In the dull light I can make out her molars grinding, that telltale bump on the side of her face enlarging and contracting, her eyes on me. She doesn't even look at Noora.

I put my finger to my lip. 'She's asleep,' I whisper.

Tammy walks through to her kitchen. I can hear her putting her chef knives away and she isn't being too quiet about it. The fridge door slams and then a few minutes later I hear the bathroom door slam.

Noora moves, stretching like a sun-kissed cat on a warm rock. She has a cluster of freckles on her cheek like some recently discovered distant galaxy. She sits up and strokes my hair.

'What time is it?' she says.

'Midnight.'

She fixes her clothes. I feel centred and good but I also feel like everything's at risk.

'You leaving?' I ask.

'I have to.'

I sort my clothes out and throw off the blankets and we stand there near the front door looking at each other, dishevelled, smiling like idiots, our fingers entwined.

'Happy non-Valentine's,' I say.

'That was yesterday,' she says.

I kiss her and she pushes her lips to mine. Our fingers stay meshed, tightening, squeezing, stroking. I feel a glance of her tongue and then she walks out the door.

When I wake up at seven, Tammy's already left for the day and the bottles have been tidied away. I shower. My skin's a hundred times more sensitive than before, every touch noticeable and alive and electrified. I don't look or feel hungover. But I am ravenous-hungry.

Bacon and scrambled eggs. I even use Tammy's chives and slice them finely with her Japanese knife into tiny green rings. I can't cook for shit but this is delicious. I wash up and head down to the truck.

The beer can from ICA has exploded. Not exploded really, more burst in slow motion and then frozen into some weird misshapen light-brown ice sculpture. It looks like the can has fallen asleep and spewed up its guts in the middle of the night; like it choked on its own vomit and swallowed its own tongue and then quietly froze to death.

I walk into the office. The door tinkles and Lena's at her desk but nobody else is here. Lars doesn't come in on Saturdays and Nils has booked off a four-day weekend to ice-fish for perch in some lake I've never heard of. Carve a hole in the ice, drop a line, sit for seven hours, pull out a fish the size of a roll-on deodorant that will for sure 100% guaranteed taste of mud. I don't get it.

I leave the beer can in the sink to defrost and melt away.

'You want coffee?' I ask Lena through her door gap.

No answer.

I step inside.

'I don't ask much of you, Tuva.' She pauses and looks at me. Right at me. 'But I do ask that you do your job the best you can.'

I'm itchy in my jeans and my hands are sticky with cold beer.

'I know.'

'And the best you can do is better than the best most people can do, you understand?'

I nod. Can she smell the beer?

'Your last paper was your weakest. You filed most of your copy late and I suspect you prioritised your ghostwriter assignment because he pays you more than I do.' I try to answer but she holds up her hand. 'This,' she holds up the freshly-printed copy of the *Posten*, today's copy. 'This isn't worthy of your name.'

'I'm sorry,' I say, the words catching in my throat.

She sighs out of her nose.

'Sit down,' she says.

I feel like crying but I don't. 'There's one thing I might be able to do.'

She narrows her eyes.

'Let me write you a story, free of charge, from down south. Maybe next week or next month, whatever you think. I'll write a piece comparing the two places, something the Gavrik people would be interested in, an insight into down there from the perspective of up here.'

She scratches the groove above her top lip, thinking it over.

'You'll need to clear it with your management.'

'I will.'

We drink together in her office, something I've never really done, and I feel like I might just be able to salvage my relationship with Lena. She tells me how Johan, her hydro-electric-engineer husband, the guy from Toytown she met in the US, the guy she left all that for, she tells me how he cooked her elk loin and lingonberries last night, and then they watched *Predator* together because that's their movie.

'*Predator?*' I say.

She shrugs.

So I tell her about my date. Lena listens but it's like a gap has grown between us. I don't mention that my date was with a police officer, or that she's a she, or that it was a non-date in McDonald's, but she knows me well enough to fill in the blanks. Lena raises her coffee mug.

'To romance.'

I raise my mug but say nothing.

When I get to Tammy's she isn't there. What is there is a huge graffiti tag on the side of her food van. Bastards. It's a picture of a brown face with large black eyes, each one with a G motif.'

'They did that with me inside the van.'

I turn around and Tam's there and she looks small in her ski jacket with her bobble hat.

'What?'

'I think there were two of them, I'm not sure, might have been just one. They pushed something heavy against the door of the van and the hatch was already locked up for the night.' She swallows hard. 'And my phone was in my car.'

'They locked you inside?' I say.

Tammy looks at her food van. Her face says 'I never want to be in there again'.

'It was all over in five minutes. But yeah, someone locked me inside. I screamed and hollered. Nobody came. Maybe it's the same ratshit that's been following me these past few nights. Maybe it's the Ferryman.'

'Following you?'

She shrugs. 'Some guy I keep seeing, huge hood,

can't see his face, he's always some distance from me but I keep seeing him. I'm not imagining it.'

'Why didn't you—'

'Think it's best if you spend your last nights in the hotel if you don't mind, Tuva. I'm not feeling too well right now. Might take some time off.'

'Is it because I brought someone home? They didn't stay over, you know.'

'Do you mind?' she says.

'I'm sorry,' I say, reaching out for a hug. But she folds herself tighter and steps back. The air is ice cold and the sky's as white as Karin's antique cyanide pill. There's nobody else around this early, just one stooped guy in the distance walking his dog and both he and the dog look like they want the walk to be over as soon as possible.

'Tam, please.'

'I can help you pay for the room if that's a problem. I need some time alone and I need to know there won't be strangers in my flat.'

'I can pay,' I say. 'I'll be gone this afternoon.'

'Okay then,' she says, and then she walks away to her car.

A deep pain in the pit of my belly. A rip. Half of me is love, or maybe just infatuation, warm and at peace. The other half is fire and ice at the same time, winded at the thought of hurting Tam, of losing her.

Maybe she just needs time. How would I feel if after a tough, freezing workday, when some pinhead locked me inside my own truck, how would I feel if I got home in the middle of the night and my part-time no-rent lodger was hooking up with a stranger at the exact moment I needed safety and a hug and tea and for my home to be my sanctuary. How'd I feel? I'll talk to her later and patch things up. She's my one real friend here and I'm not leaving with things sour between us. I can't.

I walk fast up Storgatan, my cheeks burning in the swirling wind. There are corpses in the salted snow, deflated pink balloons and red hearts with ribbons attached. Some are on top of the slush but some have been churned into it by this morning's plough like raspberry ripple ice-cream. When I walk past Ronnie's Bar I'm careful to step past the frozen puddles of Valentine vomit, irregular ice sheets of half-digested hot dog and cheese toasty and beer.

The death factory looks dark today against the sky. Its chimneys are moving toward me just like they did on the day Gustav died, the wind blowing from the east, the clouds passing over me, the bricks leaning. There is smoke billowing from the one working chimney, the left one, and I can see trucks queuing under the arch to be loaded with crates of salt liquorice coins.

I walk through the factory floor. I recognise everyone and nobody. And then the dazzling red-haired stamper sees me and she stamps even harder, her instrument punching down repeatedly, powerfully, flattening the liquorice coins and imprinting each one with a capital G.

Karin's sitting on the top step of the staircase.

'Hi,' I say.

She smiles but her eyes are red and her mascara's run down her alabaster cheeks in grey lines.

'What I wouldn't give for your life,' she says.

'How's your grandma today?' I ask.

Karin stands up and wipes her eyes with her sleeve.

'She's fine, but Mother . . .' The mascara streaks look like insect legs cupping her cheeks. 'Soon it might just be me left.'

I step up and touch her arm but she recoils.

'Don't say that,' I tell her.

She points to the portraits and photographs on the staircase walls.

'Mother has to walk past them all every day. Grandfather Ludvig, who loathed her, who never wanted her here, who thought she wasn't even qualified to be an owner's wife.' The painting she's pointing at shows a man with grey hair and a twisted torso and small, neat moustache. 'I can't even imagine what he'd have thought about Mother running it all. Don't you see?' She looks at me, blinking, agitated. 'They're the problem.' She points to the photos lining the staircase, her voice louder now. 'And them, the untouchable workers. We can't let them down even if it means we all wither in the process. Father couldn't stand it and now Mother has to walk past all of them; each pair of eyes, a family still dependant on us keeping this place alive.'

'Did Gunnarsson make inappropriate advances toward you, Karin?'

She looks at me, her teeth gritted.

'No comment.'

CHAPTER 37

The Receiving Room is an airlock between the public and the very private: a staged portal connecting two worlds. Karin unlocks the door to the residence and pulls aside the curtain. We step through. The Grand Room is lit by shallow afternoon sun and the brightness doesn't do it any favours.

It's white light this time of year, dental-surgery light, near-death-experience light, and it is bleached of all warmth and nuance. The cabinet of life has its doors wide open and it's glaring at me. Like it's making a threat. My hearing aids lose some of their power because of the high ceilings. The wet wall has a darkness. There are more knives under the long refectory table than last time I visited: carving and bread and filleting and butchers and grapefruit and steak. There's the one made from antler with a capital 'G' stamped or engraved into its base. In some places the blades are spread double-height, knives on top of knives, all pointing out at the world.

'You don't leave home much, do you?' I say.

'There's a maniacal killer on the loose,' she snarls. 'Haven't you heard?'

I don't say a word.

'I go out when I leave town,' she says. 'But I can't exactly hang out at the local café in Gavrik, like you people.'

There is no café, not unless she means the seating area in ICA Maxi.

'Why not?' I ask.

Her eyelids appear heavy beneath her fringe. 'Because we're not like you, Tuva.'

'I have to ask you again, Karin. Did Per Gunnarsson scare you when you were a teenager? Did he make advances towards you?'

'Who told you?'

'I heard he was almost fired,' I say.

'Almost,' she says.

I want to ask her more questions but she knocks on the door of Cici's convalescence room and then she turns and walks off.

'Come in, you,' says a faint voice.

I look back toward Karin but she's gone so I pass the three-legged rabbit and step into the bedroom.

'It's just me, I'm afraid,' I say.

'I know who it is,' says Cici. 'Come inside and let me have a good look at you.'

I walk in self-consciously. Why the hell didn't I bring flowers or grapes like a decent human person? Noora would have brought flowers. Peonies.

'You look radiant,' says Cici, pushing down with her palms flat to the bed sheet to lift herself, just like Mum used to do. 'Have you taken a new lover for Valentine's?'

What? She doesn't know. How could she know?

'Hearty breakfast,' I say. 'That's all. Can I get you anything? Water? Sweet tea?'

Cici shakes her head.

'These are our last days together. Will you come back and visit?'

I nod and straighten her blankets and then I see the mirrors.

'For your make-up?' I ask.

She smiles but this is a smile I haven't seen before, it's paler, it has more patina, she isn't baring her teeth at me. It's an older thing altogether.

'Come here, darling.'

I crouch beside her bed and she still smells of fresh lemons somehow, she must rub the zest into her skin.

'Now, look.'

The mirrors, there are six of them, are arranged in such a way that Cici can watch the street from her bed. She can look at a mirror, a big one, at a comfortable angle; she uses her opera glasses but I can see fine, and there's Storgatan, people heading to ICA to pick up sweets for their Saturday-night TV marathons. And if Cici looks at the other mirror, an oval-shaped antique with ornate gilt frame, she can see the churchyard of St Olov's. The mirrors on the window are angled down, and Cici can look at where her in-laws and her son and her grandson rest in sub-zero silence.

'Isn't it magic?' she says. 'Dear KK set it all up for me this morning, she's such a little bug.'

'It's wonderful,' I say, regretting to the very depths of myself that I never thought to do something like this for Mum in her final weeks. I never told her I loved her or liked her, or told her I'd be alright on my own and I never rigged mirrors so she could see Lake Vänern, beautiful Lake Vänern, the frozen sea with its dozens of ice skaters scratching smooth lines all over the frosted glass surface. She'd have liked it, I think. And I never even thought of it.

'Can you tell me what happened to your lake house?'

She nods and looks wistful, her gaze turning from me to the mirrors set up to view the graves.

'It was a good home to us all, that place. Like a shield. It was mouldy in places but nothing like this old sponge. We had cows nearby, not ours of course, and the marshlands were buzzing with dragonflies each August.'

'You must have been sad to see the house go.'

'No,' she says. 'No regrets. I may have a hundred years left to live or a hundred seconds. No regrets whatsoever.'

My eyebrows rise up into my forehead.

'I mean it,' she says. 'It was time for the house, so the house went. When it's your time you shuffle off and it's the same with houses and it's the same with all my treasures upstairs. I gave away a lot of it, everything made of wool or silk, I gave it all away to the people who needed it, you know, the Kosovans, the Syrians, and whoever had just arrived. They come here and it's so incredibly cold. They're the ones who needed it not some bony, old thing vogueing about in her attic. I gave away half of it all. Gone. No regrets.'

'You're stronger than me,' I say. 'I have regrets and they follow me everywhere.'

'Oh, I'm not strong,' she says, tapping my wrist with her index finger. 'I am terrified. This is the only way I know how to live and I'm eighty-two so I hold onto what works. It helps me. No regrets works. When you lose a father-in-law and a husband and then a son and a grandson and you're still alive, you need a shield of granite. When a man gets slaughtered in cold blood, mere metres below where you lay your head each night, you need that shield even more. Me believing that your time is your time, that is my granite protection.' She looks through the mirrors to the family plot in St Olov's. 'I'm behind granite right now.'

'I lost both my parents,' I say, the words pouring out of my mouth like water from a tap. 'In a way I lost them both when I was just a girl.' I look out at Storgatan through the other mirror. Still crouched by the bed. 'I thought both deaths could have been prevented. They were taken from me. Snatched. A shield like yours would have helped me to move on.' I think about Aunt Ida and her scar and the fact that she made the effort to send me a good-luck card. I look at Cici. 'You might

not think you're strong but you are. I think you're
. . .' But my breathing stops and I can't get the
words out.

She smiles and her teeth are there like last week
and it fills me up from the very bottom of my feet
with pure distilled happiness.

'When you're better,' I say. 'Perhaps you and
Anna-Britta and Karin could go away on holiday
for a week or two. If you come to the south this
summer we could meet up for lunch.'

'Holiday!' she says, like I just suggested we drink
weed killer on the moon. 'We've never taken a
holiday, never, not once. My honeymoon was spent
in Turkey sampling roots and signing import
agreements. What would our employees think if
we took a leisure holiday?'

'They take holidays.'

'Of course they do, and they bloody well need
them and deserve them. But we're different, we're
needed here to keep this place in check. And what
with this maniac covering a dead man with our
liquorice, we'll need to work harder than ever.'
She rubs the rabbit foot around her neck. 'If we
went on a holiday we'd come back to a heap of
sodden bricks and liquorice pouring down
Storgatan like a thick black river, and four hundred
people out of work.'

I'm quiet for a moment, that image in front of
me, that river, my eyes on the mirror pointing
down Storgatan. It's getting dark.

'Tell me about Karin and Per Gunnarrson.'

She narrows his eyes. 'Oh, so you know, do you?'

I nod.

'Peculiar,' she says. 'But no harm done. He was a loner and he had no social skills, Gunnarsson, but really he was just chatting to KK out in the open in broad daylight. We handled it internally and no one lost their jobs, thank goodness. KK was upset with her pappa, and Gustav was upset with the stamper who made the complaint in the first place. Her grandparents helped resolve the whole thing. They mediated. No harm done in the end.'

No harm done? Really?

'Can I ask you, Cici. Have you ever been pushed down the stairs before?'

'No,' she says.

'Oh,' I say.

'Not here,' she says.

I bite my lip.

'Back at the lake house. I was pushed, must have been six or seven years ago. But I was stronger back then I suppose because I only fell a few steps. Hit my head on the banister. No permanent damage. To this day I have no idea why I was pushed.'

'Do you have any idea who pushed you?' I ask.

She looks up at the ceiling. 'There is one thing you could do for me, if you have the energy,' she says.

'What?'

'Would you mind trotting up to my attics? I'd

be so happy if you could grab a few huge armfuls, pot luck, Russian roulette, game of chance. Take from different racks and hat boxes, bring jewellery and the most colourful sneakers you can find. Two big armfuls, and bring them down to me, would you mind?'

I stand, my legs numb from crouching, and leave the room and open the attic door and peer up. I don't really want to go up there all alone. It's too big and too shadowy. There are a hundred corners for a Ferryman to hide in.

A sprig of dried rosemary is pinned to each riser. The air cools. I see the bees and moths sleeping on the roof joists and I feel wary but also privileged to be up here alone with them.

Which racks? The space is a cathedral nave, as long as a football pitch and almost as broad with just those two huge circular chimney-stacks breaking the space. Radiators hum under windows.

'Hello?' I call out.

Nothing.

I walk to the front of the building and the sun's setting over Utgard forest in the far distance. It looks like an infected eye closing slowly and painfully for the night. People are walking into the *Posten* to buy their weekly copy and drop twenty kronor into the biscuit-tin honesty box and then they're heading over to Björnmossen's gun store to check out the discounted bowie knives.

I head to the far end of the attic. My footsteps echo into the roof space. The grave candle's here and it's still flickering next to Cici's sewing machine. It has a weatherproof lid with vent holes and it looks like it might go on burning for days. There's a rotary cutter like the one Mum used to trim fabric, back when she still had hobbies, and next to it rests a stack of spare blades and a pair of dressmaking shears. I keep walking. I've never been this far into the attics before. There are stacks of round hatboxes arranged like towering wedding cakes, and there are piles of loose fabric and embroidery work. A mannequin with black eyes and peeling plastic skin watches me, her body just a metal pole beneath her mink stole. Shoe racks line one wall. I pull down a dusty pair of trainers and they're patent red leather and I think they'll fit Cici's requirements.

The floor creaks beneath my feet and I stop and turn on my heels and look into the dark places behind the clothes racks. My heart pounds and I force my breathing to be shallow and quiet.

I move on.

Necklaces are draped over the long stiff necks of three gloved mannequins and they're also looped over steel nails that have been driven into the walls. I can see puppets hanging from their strings. Some have beards and some have rosy cheeks and some have their strings tangled so badly they look like they've hung themselves. I can see one that looks like Lena and one that looks, ponytail upturned nose and all, a little too much like me.

I gather up a mid-length dress with growling wolves stitched on the base, each wolf chasing the next, and I take ten or twelve necklaces with different-sized beads and crystals and amber nuggets. I think they're all plastic. There's a chair near the linoleum catwalk and I drape everything on it and head over to a rack of trousers by the back wall. Looking out of the windows here you'd think it was night already. The snow glows grey underneath me and stirrers and tasters and quality-control supervisors leave work from their one exit in their ugly ski jackets and oversize moon-boots, trudging back through the arch and round St Olov's ruin with their hats pulled tight around their faces. There's a mannequin on my left with her head too far round and it's like she's in pain. The shadows that she and her lifeless colleagues cast are not okay. They move. They glide over the walls as I walk. A bluebottle stirs and buzzes a lazy buzz and then settles on a window. The rear yard is quiet, but then I see a figure run out from behind a truck carrying a plastic can or box. And then I see light. I see flames.

CHAPTER 38

The wall of St Olov's glows pinkish yellow and there's nobody down at ground level to witness the fire.

It's just me up here. Me and a hundred comatose wasps.

I drop the clothes and the beads to the floor, one set breaking, marble-sized balls scattering over the floorboards and rolling up the linoleum catwalk. I run down the stairs two at a time.

Cici can't help.

'Anna-Britta,' I yell, trying not to sound alarmed. 'Karin.'

Nothing.

I run past the cabinet of life, its heavy doors still open, past the table with its lamp adorned with bindweed, past the rabbit, past the knives, and I look inside Anna-Britta's open door and Gustav's clothes are still there. But there's something else on the chair. A photo. There's a photo of me on Gustav's chair.

I pause, startled at seeing myself, and then run again, past the tile stove and the corner bedroom. I get to the Receiving Room.

389

'Anna-Britta!' I yell, louder now. 'Fire!' and then I'm at the top of the stairs. I find the 'Fire: break glass' alarm above the light switch and push it with my finger. I've had my finger hover over these things a dozen times before, at school mainly, when others were busy playing hockey or handball and I was hiding in some dark corner ready to press the button, for help, for attention, for an exit, but never actually doing it. The glass cracks and the alarm sounds. I get pain in my ears, like dentist-drill pain, and pain in my finger, like a knife slipped slicing a pear. There's blood. I hold the wall. A red smudge on the faded wallpaper. And then I reach up and reduce the volume in both aids to almost nothing and the blood wets my cheek as my fingers brush past.

'Tuva,' shouts Anna-Britta from the bottom of the stairs. 'You're hurt.'

She runs up but I shake my head and point to the residence. 'I'm fine, but Cecilia's still in there.'

She looks at my bleeding finger and sees Cici's amber bracelet on my wrist, the one I tried on in the attic just minutes ago, and she stares at it and then back up to my eyes.

'Help me,' she says.

We run through to the Grand Room.

'Don't look,' she says as we pass the cabinet and the knife table.

We get to Cici and she's propped up in bed but her covers are off and I can see her orange leggings and her striped knee-length '80s socks.

'What is it?' Cici asks.

'Fire in the root barns,' says Anna-Britta. 'Fire brigade on their way. We need to get you out.'

'Where's lilla Karin?' asks Cici.

Anna-Britta looks at me.

'I don't know,' I say.

We lift Cecilia using what Anna-Britta calls a fireman lift. It's a mess, we can hardly walk straight, but we get her out to the top of the stairs where two real firemen take her down like she's a pigeon feather.

The workforce is huddled at the fire assembly point aka the car park of Hotel Gavrik. A few have ski jackets but most ran out in their aprons and their hairnets, and now they're bunched together like emperor penguins enduring a storm at the South Pole. The authorities will have to send them someplace warm soon or else people will start turning blue.

Anna-Britta's talking to the fire chief. Two guys are making sure all the buildings are empty and an army of overfed rats are screeching and scurrying over each other to get away from the heat.

'The upstairs residence is clear, Tuva and I checked,' Anna-Britta says to one of the guys about to run through the unlocked arch-door. 'No need to check it, all clear.'

The guy ignores her. Two women are tackling the blaze. The fire truck can't fit through the arch so it's parked on the Storgatan side and its powerful lights bathe the scene with white light and the hoses attached to the water mains are snaking back to the yard.

I think about the rodents caught in the traps. Not so humane now, are they: the see-through boxes affording each imprisoned rat a widescreen view of its own downfall, a last supper already consumed, a clear trap from which to watch relatives flee in terror.

Heat on my cheeks. The fire is leaping higher and higher, fed by stacks of stored delivery-truck summer tyres and vats of sugar waste. The air smells like burnt pans and hot rubber and it sticks to the roof of my mouth. The night air is thick with it.

'Medics!' yells one of the firefighters, pointing to the wall of St Olov's.

Two paramedics approach the fire hesitantly and together with a firefighter they manage to pull out a burning body from the flames.

It's a woman.

Someone behind me gasps.

Most of her clothes have blackened and her hair has burnt away. Her arms look like overcooked hams. The paramedics rush with the stretcher, past us, past the crowds, toward the ambulance. She's moaning. Her skin is smoking into the cold, dark air. The Chief leaps into action and starts to move people back, to allow the ambulance space. I see paramedics put an IV into the burnt arm of the woman. Morphine? Her charred arms are bent like claws but her teeth are still bright. I recognise them. It's Great White. It's the taster.

I don't have my real camera so I take photos and video with my phone.

'Search it all again,' yells the fire chief.

They can get closer to the heart of the fire now and it's clear there are no more victims. They continue to pump ice-cold water onto the flames.

'Everything's bone dry this time of year,' says the fire chief. My aids are back up to normal levels now the sirens and the alarms are off. 'No humidity,' she says.

Flames are jumping and flicking up every now and then like white snake-tongues and I can hear faint non-human screams. It's distant and it's at ground level. Mice or spiders or hibernating hedgehogs. Insects maybe. Or trapped rats.

'It's under control,' the fire chief tells Anna-Britta. 'You can send your people home now. Don't want them getting frostbite.'

Anna-Britta leaves through the arch and I see Karin greet her and touch her shoulder, their two bodies framed by the brickwork. Storgatan is grey and twinkling behind them.

Noora and Chief Björn join me and the fire chief.

'Under control now?' Björn asks.

The fire chief nods. 'Looks worse than it is,' she says. 'Thirty minutes and it'll be out to nothing. That woman was unlucky.' She coughs into the smoky air. 'We can liaise with Constable Noora here. No need for everyone to be out in this cold.'

Chief Björn nods and then says, 'Gut instinct: accident or design?'

The fire chief shrugs. 'My guts don't work that good no more.' She sniffs the air and flares her nostrils. 'Must have had a big nest in there. Had calls from all over town of rats running around scaring dogs and cats. Big nest, I'd say.'

I look at Noora and mouth 'Okay?' and she stiffens up and straightens her back and turns to Chief Björn. 'I'll collect witness statements,' she says to him. 'And I'll photograph everything once the fire crew gives me the thumbs up.'

Björn's teeth are chattering. He nods to her and then to the fire chief and ignores me completely and walks back to talk with Anna-Britta.

'Hell of a fire,' I say to Noora.

She says nothing. The water jets stream from the hoses and the two firefighters stand bracing each other. The flames are different now, smaller, smokier, blues and greens splitting the yellow.

By nine the fire is out and the red truck's left the factory yard. Noora's taken statements from seven or eight people and she's photographed every angle of the scene but she'll have to do it all again tomorrow with proper light. She doesn't look at me during all this, she just makes her notes.

'Damn ink's frozen,' she says, pulling a spare pen from her uniform pocket.

The arch is cold now. The heat from the corner, where the root barns have stood for over a hundred years, is gone.

'You saw the fire start?' she asks.

'Yes. Are you okay, Noora? Have I . . .'

She looks straight at me, her eyes wide, her lips pursed, and then she looks around.

'Just tell me what you saw, please.'

My stomach feels wrong like I've screwed something up and I don't even know how.

'I was in the factory attics, above the old part of the building. I was helping Cecilia Grimberg with her clothes, because of her fall.'

I think about the rat traps again. Perspex. The plastic boxes melting onto the rats like some awful pre-cooked vacuum-packed delicatessen nightmare.

Noora writes something down then looks up at me. She's looking at my mouth.

'Will that woman be okay?' I ask.

'What did you see?' she asks.

'I was facing the yard and the windows up there aren't very clean, and the glass is wavy, that old rippled glass, and I thought I saw a person running from the root barns. They ran behind one of the vans carrying a container, like a plastic can.'

'Did you recognise the person?'

I shake my head.

'A man or a woman?'

I look over to the smouldering cobbles, the snow gone, the tyre stacks melted down to liquorice-coloured stumps.

'I couldn't see them clearly. Looked normal-size but could have been anyone. I think the box was a small petrol tank like they sell in the Q8 petrol station outside town.'

'What did you see them do exactly?'

'Run away. And then I saw the flames start.'

'What time was this?'

'Maybe three minutes before I set off the fire alarm. About five-ish. Can we chat after your shift is over?' I ask.

She shakes her head slightly. 'Who else was in the yard? Who else did you see?'

'Nobody,' I say. 'There were factory workers leaving just before that, but when I saw the figure run from the root barns there was nobody else around.'

Two firefighters check the ash in the yard to make sure the thing is completely extinguished. Then they allow Cici and Anna-Britta and Karin to enter their archway door. Ten minutes later, once my chat with Noora is over, forty or so people march up to the archway and queue underneath it.

'What's this?' Noora asks Anna-Britta.

'It's called a night shift,' she says.

Noora frowns.

'I've got orders to fill, suppliers who are relying on me. There's a chain. I can't just break it.' She points to the smouldering corner. 'Cordon off the root barns, tape it all up if you need to, but we have a night shift to work.'

CHAPTER 39

'What a February this is,' says Janitor Andersson as he helps support Cici up the broad staircase, his ring of keys rattling on his belt. I assume he's talking about Gustav's suicide and Gunnarsson's murder and now the fire, but he says, 'Never known one like it, not this cold.'

Cici cringes with pain as she hobbles up the stairs, Andersson on one side and me on the other. She insists on walking. Karin runs ahead to open doors and move furniture out of the way. We're a wide load.

'It was bad in '82,' he says, coughing. 'More snow than this, the drifts and all, but not as cold,' he says, as if performing a monologue on stage. I can see he's wearing some kind of bright orange Hawaiian shirt under his overalls. 'Well, at least the fire dealt with some vermin.'

We shuffle into the Receiving Room.

'We can manage from here, Andersson,' says Karin.

'I can help,' he says.

'We can manage,' says Karin.

Andersson looks disappointed to be left out. He nods solemnly and then he leaves.

'Are you in pain, Granny?' asks Karin.

Cici shakes her head and takes the rabbit foot hanging round her neck and rubs its fur along her upper lip. 'I'll live,' she says. 'Until I won't.'

Karin looks at me and then we start to help Cici past the door and through the velvet curtain.

'Does Andersson come back here?' I ask. 'When you need things fixing, I mean.'

'One day I dare say he'll need to come through that door,' says Cici. 'But so far he hasn't.'

'But he's been the janitor for decades,' I say.

Cici bares her teeth at me. 'I'm pretty nifty with a cordless drill, you know.'

Anna-Britta's moving bedding and pillows from Karin's corner room.

'I'm not dead yet,' Cici says to her.

'Chief Björn says it'll get down to close on minus thirty tonight,' says Anna-Britta. 'I can't have you in a room with two exterior walls, you'll perish.'

'When I go,' Cici says. 'I'll go with a flash-bang, not a whimper.'

Anna-Britta heads to Cici's bedroom – the one closest to the tiled fireplace and closest to the Receiving Room.

The bedroom looks normal on one side but on the interior wall the edge is missing. Instead of a corner it's a convex arc, one part of the huge chimney hidden within, bulging, pushing itself into the room.

'Karin, can you put the kettle on, please,' says

Anna-Britta. 'Tuva, feel free to head home, otherwise I can order up an extra supper tray for you?'

There's no way Tammy wants to eat with me tonight. And I need to dig. I need more information.

'A tray would be good,' I say. 'If it's no bother.'

'What's one more mouth to feed when I have four-hundred and thirteen?' She's not wearing mascara and I can hardly see her eyelashes. 'And it's good to keep the kitchen busy. The more work around here the better it is for everyone.'

There's a lot of duvet throwing and sheet shaking and then Karin comes to collect Cici, who looks deathly tired now. Anna-Britta takes her into the bedroom and shuts the door. I've noticed commodes or 'piss-pots' as Dad used to call them, close to all the bedrooms, and in some ways these three women live like they're locked away securely in the past.

'I'll order your tray,' says Karin. 'Mother'll just forget.'

Karin calls down to the canteen.

The rabbit, the poor limping rabbit, is hobbling around in his wire hutch with a piece of lettuce hanging from his ear fur.

'Take him out,' Karin mimes to me, the phone to her ear, but I can read her better than she realises.

'Really?' I whisper.

She nods.

I open the wire gate and the rabbit, it's the size of a small dog, lollops out. I guess the Grimbergs do this, they let it run free around the Grand

Room for exercise. I see it head toward the knives under the long refectory table so I plant my foot in its way to make it divert. The white rabbit with its long floppy ears and its ridiculous tail brings some hint of the human, the normal, the familial, to this vast mouldy place.

Karin boils the kettle and lights a thick church candle with seven wicks. This is not like Tammy's flat, it is the polar opposite of Tam's flat; there are no cashmere throws or deep sofas full of unnecessary cushions, there are no fancy branded scented candles or dimmer switches on the lights, there's not a single photograph or piece of art. The family are the art, I suppose, the way they live is some absurd installation piece in an industrial gallery. There's a knock at the door.

Karin runs past me, her long black dress sweeping the floorboards as she goes, almost hovering, to the far side of the room. She unlocks the door and walks through and closes it. A moment later she brings through one tray.

'Can I help?' I ask.

She shakes her head.

The process is almost comic. She brings through a second tray and closes the door behind her and places it down and then opens the door and collects a third tray and closes the door and places it down near the others and then retrieves the final tray and closes the door and locks it shut.

'Now we're all in,' she says.

I help her carry the canteen trays over to the

knife table. Each one is covered in cling film and beaded with moisture. Karin peels off the cling film from one and I see the *Falukorv* stew: slices of anaemic sausage in overcooked cabbage. There's a glass of water and a knife and fork and one paper napkin. She takes it to Cici's room.

The rabbit's looking at me from underneath the cabinet of life. Its eyes are bright red and it's eating the piece of lettuce that was stuck to its ear.

'Let's keep the wraps on our trays until Mother comes out, else they'll get cold and then they'll taste even worse.'

'Are you ever tempted to get Thai from the van near ICA? Or a burger?'

She looks at me like I'm insane.

'Father always said, "if it's good enough for our workers, then it's good enough for us". We don't really cook as a family, never have. This is what we live on.'

'What a dreadful night,' says Anna-Britta walking toward us. 'Who's hungry?

'Sausage stew,' says Karin.

'Delicious,' says Anna-Britta. 'I'm pleased you're joining us, Tuva. Now you've come through the door you're almost a Grimberg.' She straightens her back. 'I'm sure you can understand why we're very private people, but now you're through the door you are very welcome.'

We sit down. Anna-Britta at the head of the table, me opposite Karin, the tips of my toes curled under my chair to prevent injury.

'Can I just ask, it's probably nothing, but I noticed you have a photo of me in your bedroom, Anna-Britta.'

Karin's eyes widen.

'I do?' says Anna-Britta, glancing over at her bedroom door. 'Ah, yes, I do. It's from the police, that's all. CCTV images from the clocking-in area the day Cecilia was pushed.'

'Am I a suspect?' I ask.

'Goodness me, no,' she says, gesturing for us to start eating.

The food is lukewarm and under-seasoned. It's godawful. But in a strange kind of way this feels like a family. Somehow I belong at this table with this sausage stew and since I had Christmas lunch on my own last year, in bed, most of it from a bottle, this feels okay.

There's more bindweed hanging from the lamp than before. It looks like blonde winter hair, my winter hair. The strands hang limp in the damp, cool air and they sashay gently in the breath breeze every time someone talks.

Karin reaches for her contact lens box. She unscrews the two lens-compartments: one blue, one white. I stare, I can't help it.

'Salt and pepper,' she says, showing me.

After she's doused the stew with her own personal seasoning she takes another pinch of salt and throws it over her left shoulder.

'Thank all the precautions the fire was just a small one, and just the root barns,' says Anna-Britta.

'And we hope our dear taster makes a swift recovery.'

Karin rubs her eyes and I can see ink all up one arm, not tattoo ink, she has that too, but it's further up where her mum can't see it. This is fresh ink.

'Have you been writing?' I ask, pointing to her arm.

Karin covers her wrists, pulling the sleeves of her creped, black dress down all the way to her first set of knuckles, the veins and tendons of her hand protruding like blue vines coiled around branches.

'Sculpting and painting,' she says. 'Something for Granny.'

'Can you set up the mirrors in the morning, Karin?' asks Anna-Britta. 'Cecilia needs to be able to see the family.'

'Of course,' says Karin, pushing her half-finished plate aside.

'I'll deal with these,' says Anna-Britta. 'Why don't you two go sit by the candle.'

I realise that when Anna-Britta says she'll 'deal with these' it's not like when a normal mum or dad would 'deal' with dirty plates on a kitchen table. She doesn't load a dishwasher or don Marigold rubber gloves, she simply stacks up the trays with all the leftover food and completes Karin's door charade in reverse. She opens the door and takes through a tray and closes the door. Four times.

We walk to the cold, unlit fireplace and I can see the rabbit cowering with fear under the cabinet of life, the soft flaps of his enormous ears shaking as Karin approaches.

The room's cool. I'm wearing long johns and a thermal long-sleeved T-shirt, a good one from the cross-country ski store, and tube socks and a micro fleece and a proper fleece and I am still cold. I think it's probably twelve degrees in here.

'Is Cecilia warm enough?' I ask.

Karin nods. 'Warmest room in the place, it's the heat memory of the chimney; it lingers in the old bricks. She'll be fine.'

Heat memory?

'What a night,' I say.

Karin stares at where a fire should be. 'Did you know Mother keeps her watch set at the exact moment my brother passed on. The precise second. This place is going to destroy her and she doesn't even know it.'

'Things will improve,' I say. 'Spring will be here soon.'

'Spring will not be here soon, it'll be here in three months and Mother may well be in the plot with the rest of the family by then. Which means it'll just be me.'

'Don't talk like that.'

'Easy for you to say,' she says, the seven flames from the seven-wick candle moving over her pupils. 'If I tried to sell this place then news would get out. It'd leak. Then this place, the workers, they wouldn't let me go, they wouldn't let me sell, they wouldn't let me leave the building. There's no way I'd make it out of this factory alive.'

CHAPTER 40

I keep my scarf wrapped around my face on the drive to Tammy's flat. Streetlights bleed into the empty, sparkling townscape. There's a murderer in Gavrik, a man or a woman with a weapon and a motive and it could be anyone. Locals are staying indoors. They're cancelling dates and they're sleeping with loaded guns hidden beneath their beds.

Gavrik is deserted considering it's a Saturday night, no queue outside Ronnie's, no cars driving thru McDonald's, no teenagers making their way to some house party intoxicated with what could happen.

Tam's not home. She'll be in her van, an electric blanket over her knees when she's not serving, some hacked TV show streaming on her iPad, fan heater whirring, her knives sharp and clean, her ingredients chopped and ready, her sauces steaming into the dry winter air. And a pistol by her lap.

I lock the Tacoma and then I realise I've left my phone inside. I'm not sure how it would cope with minus thirty so I unlock the door, the key sliding in with no problem, and then lift the plastic door-handle. Nothing. There's no resistance, just a flaccid flap of plastic rising and falling on its hinge. The cable connecting it to the door mechanism has snapped in two.

'Fuck.' I say, my face wrinkled into a knot. 'Fuck you, Arctic, Shitmobile potato-head piece of Toytown bullshit.'

And then I take a deep icy breath and feel better. I sidle round to the passenger side, a rock hard mound of gritty snow on this side, and gently open the handle. No problem. I take my phone and leave the truck unlocked like, 'oh, you're a thief in Gavrik in February with no key, good luck mate, she's all yours, you're very welcome, take her, be on your way, all the best, love, Tuva'.

The apartment's neat so Tam's been back since this morning. The blankets on the sofa are folded the way they always are, the frilly tasselled ends poking out. I sit down. My hand glides over the soft cashmere weave and then I lift it to my face and maybe I'm imagining it, who cares, but I can smell Noora's warm spiced perfume. I hold the pale blue blanket to my face, smothering my nose and mouth, and breathe her in, as much as I can get.

I take the rum from a cupboard and stuff it into a suitcase.

This place couldn't be more different from the Grimberg residence. This is normal size and it's filled with actual possessions and soft things you want to sit on and be close to after a tough day. There's a fitted kitchen with a half-fancy stereo attached to the wall. There's a TV for God's sake. I walk over to Tammy's bed and the top of my chest feels wrong. My eyes sting. There are three photos on her bedside table. One is of her mum and dad when they were young. It's a great shot of them on bikes in some Bangkok suburb outside their first house. It looks like a professional picture, but it was taken by Tam's uncle, the light was perfect, it was just one of those things, a quick snap by an amateur but the faces were pointed just right and the love was there and the image is beautiful. One of Tam and her mum from a few years' back, them out picking mushrooms together in Utgard forest, a short curved knife in Tam's hand, a basket in her mum's. It's a self-timed thing with the camera resting on a tree trunk. And then finally there's me. The smallest photo of the trio is me and her, our arms around each other, taken last summer down by the reservoir, the water twinkling in the background, best mates taking a true-love double selfie.

I ponder waiting for Tam to get home and I ponder apologising and talking it through but she's always so tired in the evenings. I'll see her tomorrow. I'll prioritise her and patch things up before I leave. I need Tam and I think she probably needs me.

My wash bag's still in the bathroom so I stuff it

into one of my three black suitcases, all three now waiting by the door where Tam left them.

The tasselled blanket draws me back to the sofa. I sniff it one last time and it feels like I'm saying goodbye to all the good things in my life. I start to cry and the soft blue threads take in my salt tears. I see a face and it's simultaneously Tammy and Lena and Noora in my mind's eye, all disappointed, all turning away. And then the face turns back to me and it's Mum and she has liquorice coins for pupils.

I fold up the blue blanket and take my cases, pushing one with my foot, and place my key on her coffee table. The door closes with a solid clunk. No way back.

The hotel door is locked and shuttered. I'm standing with three suitcases like a tourist who got the time zones mixed up. I feel light-headed. The only person around is the old hunched guy with the heavy stick and the oversize hood and he's on his way up to St Olov's with his Husky wolf-dog and an ICA plastic bag full of cans. Probably extra strong Norrland beer. I google Hotel Gavrik on my mobile and call and finally the owner-receptionist-waitress picks up and comes down to let me in.

'We don't admit guests after ten,' she says by way of greeting. I can't remember her name but she's wearing a onesie or a super long cardigan wrapped around her like a robe, and she's wearing sheepskin slippers and there's a pair of earmuffs loose around her neck like a lumberjack taking a pee break.

'It's me, Tuva, from the *Posten*. Sorry it's late but I need a room for two nights. I can pay up front.'

She sucks air through her pursed lips.

'Any room is fine,' I say.

'Police told us to be extra careful,' she says. 'Vigilant.'

'It's me. Tuva,' I say again.

She sniffs. 'We're refurbishing some of the rooms and most aren't made up. We don't get walk-ins, not in February, not even in summer, people usually book ahead over the telephone or the email address.'

'Can I come in, it's freezing out here.'

'Ain't much warmer in here,' she says. 'Twenty-nine under tonight and it may get colder still.'

She allows me in and then she shuffles off in her slippers to stand behind the counter.

'I'll see what I got.'

What you've got? How many people can be staying here?

'Choice of two,' she says. 'Either got the honeymoon suite – ain't really a suite, just a really long room – or I got a standard single with limited view.'

'I'll take the second one,' I say.

'Ain't been refurbished,' she says. 'I'm just being up front with you. I can do it for one-thousand-two hundred per night.'

'Oh, come on,' I say. 'You won't sell that room

tonight. Please, how about two-thousand for the two nights.'

'Got a hotel in Munkfors you could try, they're cheaper than us.'

I glower at her.

'Got the telephone number right here.'

'Fine,' I say, handing over my visa card. 'I'll take it.'

She checks me in and tells me the room's on the second floor at the back, and then she tells me not to open my door without checking who it is first. She says Gavrik's unsafe. I ride the tiny lift with my cases jammed in beside me. I slide my key card into the door and the light turns green and I sigh with relief and walk in. The cases pretty much fill the room. There's an empty minibar, warm, and a TV with a crack in its screen. The bathroom's a linoleum disgrace with one of those clingy shower curtains mottled with mould spores. It smells. I check the lock and I check the fisheye security lens, but someone's installed the damn door back-to-front so I can't see who's out there but they can see me. Tomorrow I'll stick a piece of gum over it. I double-check the internal door in the corner – I guess these are interconnecting rooms – and it's locked.

I take my rum from my case and climb into bed and pull over the extra blankets provided. They don't seem too clean but they might keep me alive tonight if the heating breaks.

From my bed I drink in smooth gulps, not sips, and look out of the window at the liquorice factory.

I'm in the middle of the action. I'm sleeping between my office, or rather my ex-office, and the cop shop – Noora in there, doing whatever she does – and the factory. I'm in the Toytown Bermuda triangle. And then there's a scrape at the door.

CHAPTER 41

I check the hall and there's nobody there. Must be mice. Or rats. Vermin. It's that time of year.

I sleep heavily and wake just after nine. The low sun's streaming though my window, beams of light cutting between the brick Grimberg chimneys and pinning me to my plywood headboard.

I stretch for a glass of water but there's just the rum bottle. I stay still, face screwed up tight against the light, my fingertips caressing the curved glass. But I'm not there yet, I'm not in that kind of trouble.

My skull's too tight. Doesn't fit. I rub my eyes and get up and open the triple-glazed window and freezing air pours inside like seawater into a breached submarine. I shower, if you can call it a shower, more like an anaemic tap spitting at my head, and then I take the lift down for breakfast with my aids turned low. A family of two extremely calm beige-wearing people, a red-faced man and a small no-make-up woman, take their temper-tantrum child, drag her, really, and leave soon after I arrive. Thank the lord.

The buffet is a joke, a crime, a lie. Tiny glasses

of watered-down juice, packets of cereal so small a hobbit would need four; sliced bread, the cheapest kind from ICA Maxi, the kind with no crust; maybe it's created that way, not baked, just somehow created.

I lost a clump of hair this morning when I brushed it. A big clump. I could really do without that two days before I start my new job. Down south I'll eat some raw green vegetables and drink gallons of water. Worth a try. At least I booked the sleeper carriage. Eleven hours on a night train rattling me from Toytown to the civilised, cosmopolitan south, eleven hours from minus thirty to about minus five, from relative darkness to relative light. I've checked the sunrise times online. There's an appreciable difference.

I have today to find a firm lead, something to help the police. Because if they don't make progress soon there will be another screaming, bled-out corpse found in this town, I can feel it.

There must be something to link Hellbom to Gunnarsson. I need to find out who's leaving the snow skulls around town. And who else was Gunnarsson bullying twenty years ago? Were there any other girls he was talking to?

Interviewing the Grimbergs is still my best bet. They have more to say, much more. Then tomorrow I'll tell the police whatever I've found out and I'll present my research to Holmqvist; emailed and in hard copy as requested. I'll say goodbye to Tam and Noora. Tomorrow night a taxi will pick me up and drive me to Karlstad station so I can catch the train at eleven-thirty. Yeah, I know a taxi's an extravagance but it's also my dream exit. It's what I've fantasised about for nearly four years, me in the back seat, everything I own in the car, one-way ticket. It's not Viggo driving me, don't worry. It's his new colleague.

I see Noora as I leave the hotel but she doesn't say hi. She's walking with Thord. I collect my interview gear and head through the iron gates of Grimberg Liquorice. There are other police here, police I don't recognise, and Janitor Andersson's shaking a shovel loaded with grit to make the ground safe to walk on.

'Oh, it's you,' he says as I walk over to him.

'Awful night,' I say.

'Them old root barns should've gone years ago,' he says. 'And now the fire hoses made it so Gavrik ice-hockey squad can practice back there; just look at it.'

The yard through the arch is a black mirror; white clouds dancing on its surface.

'All that hose water and almost minus thirty, look at it,' he says. 'The state of the place. More work. But it's the old mog-cat I feel for.'

'What?'

'You didn't hear? The old mog-cat met its maker last night. We found him this morning, blackened little thing, all bone and singed tufts. He was about twenty, maybe older, so it was about his natural time.'

415

'But what about the taster? The injured woman?'

'Oh, her,' he says, cringing. 'She's alive. Not good, but alive.'

Was the cat that awful high-pitched scream I heard? Or was that Great White?

'Bad way to go, fire,' he says. 'Bad way.'

I nod and I can almost taste the salt in his shovel grit. He's got his passport in his coat pocket, I can see the top of it poking out. Burgundy with gold lettering. A woman walks past us wearing thin latex gloves and then as she gets closer to the staff entrance she removes her hat. It's Red.

'Hates this place,' says Janitor Andersson, gesturing toward her.

'What?' I say.

'Told me once. She said how come Ma's sick and the Grimbergs still live here in luxury. She said it should be Grimbergs fading away not her ma who spent most of her life working her fingers to the bone here. But she can't quit because where else would she go? You know any other firms round here needs a liquorice stamper?' He shakes his head. 'Supporting her whole family she is. Making liquor on the side to top things up. Sells it in them foreign wine-boxes. Lethal stuff. Liquorice and liquor. One time someone tried to rob her, decent amount of cash she has on the weekends I expect, and she smacked him round the head with a sock full of pool balls. Almost killed the lad. Anyway, she's not got many good things to say about Grimberg Liquorice, that one.'

'Did she know the dead man, Gunnarsson?'

'Them two wasn't talking,' he says.

'They knew each other?'

'Could say that,' he says. 'She was the one that caught him talking to young Karin Grimberg years ago. She was the one that reported it.'

'Do the police know?' I say.

'How would I know?'

'But you know the Grimbergs well. You have a business relationship with them.'

'Oh,' he says, looking up toward the Grand Room and then down toward his basement. 'They told you, did they? Oh, that worked out real nice for them. They told you all about it, eh?'

'Would you prefer if someone new—'

He interrupts and bangs the wooden handle end of his shovel down on the cobbles.

'If they're moaning because I live down here then you can tell 'em . . .' He's almost shaking with anger. 'Forget it. Don't matter.'

'Go on,' I say, edging close to him.

'If they ever paid what I'm due,' he's almost whispering now. 'Then I'd be moving out double-quick to live someplace hot. With palm trees and outdoor dinners. They think I want to live down there?' He looks at his basement and then up to the Grand Room. 'I've had just about enough . . . They saying I chose it this way?'

'They don't pay you dividends?' I ask.

Andersson steps back from me. 'Must get on,' he says, and then he walks away.

417

I pass through the arch and what's left of the root barns is still smoking from random spots, melted tyre-rubber, slick and runny like asphalt in August.

To my right is the propane-gas device they used on Gustav's grave plot. It's on. Steaming. And it's placed this side, on the factory side, but close to the boundary, close to the family burial plot on the other side of the stone wall.

Behind the collapsed root barns, now just a few charred joists, there's a row of hideous snow skulls sitting on the wall of St Olov's. I suppose they've been there all along but the view was obscured by the barns and the delivery trucks until now. They're much bigger than the traditional skulls, these are marrow-sized. Or they were. Most are half melted from last night's heat, their faces as smooth and as featureless as Henrik Hellbom's. Their eyes must have fallen out, and what's left of each icy head is as gaunt as a never ending scream.

The snow mountains that were in the delivery van area have drained away and all that remains is the smell of charcoal and the ash-flecked ice beneath my feet. I can see Thord and Noora speaking with two official-looking women. I wait for them to finish.

'Bad night,' I say to Thord.

'Worse luck,' he says. 'They tell me bad things come in threes.'

I wonder which three he's talking about. The

suicide, the Ferryman attack, the truck crash, Cici's fall, or this. Are we past three yet? Multiples of three? Which events qualify?

'Can I get a quote for the paper?'

'Thought you'd left?' says Noora, her face expressionless.

'New guy starts on Tuesday so I'm still working until then. Quote?'

Thord smiles at me like he'll miss me. 'Your replacement's a semi-professional sailor, that's the rumour,' he says. 'Won't get much sailing done up here, will he?'

I laugh out loud and it hurts my head.

'You can write,' says Thord, 'that Gavrik police department responded to an emergency call at approximately seventeen-hundred hours. You can write that we discovered a fire in the corner of the Grimberg Liquorice site which was promptly extinguished by Gavrik Kommun fire service. You can write that one individual suffered second degree burns and is currently recovering in Karlstad specialist burns unit. You can write that Gavrik police are investigating the cause of the fire and that if anyone has any information pertaining . . .' He winks at me when he says pertaining, a word I think he's probably borrowed from Chief Björn, '. . . to this incident, please contact Gavrik police immediately.'

'Thank you,' I say.

'Off the record we're treating it as suspected arson.'

'Are you connecting this to the Ferryman murder?'

'No,' he says. 'But, and this is off the record, you get this many accidents in one place in such a short period and, I don't know, I have to figure if and how they're all linked together. There's a lot of grudges held in this town. Some of them decades old.'

I adjust my hearing aid, it's hurting my ear.

'Did you know that the red-haired stamper was the person who reported Gunnarsson years ago. She was the one who saw him talking to Karin.'

'We know,' he says. 'Some folks are asking us to impose a curfew.'

'Can you do that?' I say.

'It's February,' he says. 'We don't need to.'

'Can I ask,' I say, gesturing to the out-of-town women with my head, 'who are they?'

Noora and Thord look over to the women photographing the smouldering rubber glued to the cobbles. 'Arson investigators from Karlstad. More like rocket scientists than detectives, if you ask me,' he says. 'They've got a laboratory but I ain't never seen it. We were lucky to get them.'

'Lucky?'

'No fatalities, low-value fire,' says Noora. 'The Chief had to pull in a favour to get them here on a weekend. They're just finishing.'

I try to smell her breath across the chilled air that separates us but I can't.

Thord's radio crackles and I look down and see it on his belt with its holstered gun and black extendable baton. He and Noora say bye and leave in the direction of the station. I photograph the scene again, this time with my proper camera, the *Posten*'s camera, the expensive one; the one I need to return.

I walk through the factory floor wearing my shoe covers and disposable hat. I try to read lips but most of the workers keep their heads down. The machines are too noisy for me to hear much but I can make out 'insurance, always insurance' from a guy with a covered-up nose stud and I can make out 'twelve sets of summer tyres' from a guy with big attractive lips; kissing lips. I walk on to the stampers and tasters but they're not saying much. Red's there stamping away twice as fast as everyone else, the muscles in her forearms bulging. There are two guys and a woman leaning against a fork-lift in the packaging area, close to the loading bay. Two have their backs to me but the third, I can read him despite his goatee, he says 'melted most of her face off' and then he shakes his head and says 'within the month' and then the other two talk and I slow my pace and one says, 'that lawyer I reckon, and his partners'.

The canteen reeks of burnt matches and over-boiled spinach. I heave open the heavy door to the staircase and close it behind me, the noise of the canteen disappearing behind its oak heft. I stand where Cici landed. I walk up feeling dizzy, wrong, unsteady, and I brace myself against the banister and come face to face with a photo. It's

421

sepia but the woman in the centre, a woman being presented with some kind of shield, is the red-haired stamper. Or her mother. Or her grandmother. The man doing the presenting looks a bit like Hellbom. I photograph it with my phone and keep on climbing. Could Hellbom be related to the Grimbergs? A disinherited cousin?

'Hello,' says Anna-Britta from the top step. 'A word in my office, please.'

I go in.

'I'd appreciate it if you could make all reasonable efforts to keep the details of the fire out of your last article.'

'The injured woman?'

She nods.

There are official-looking papers in front of her weighed down by the bone-handled letter opener I saw before. I try to read the text upside down.

'I'll be sensitive,' I say.

Anna-Britta notices me reading and puts the papers face down on the desk, but I'm able to make out the letterhead. It says 'Third Way Publishing'.

CHAPTER 42

Karin looks stoic like a grieving mother holding it together for the sake of her surviving children. She stares at me from the top of the stairs, her razor-sharp fringe cutting her eyes in half, and leads me into the Receiving Room.

'Mother would rather you were her daughter,' she says. 'And Granny will miss you; the chats you two have.'

'I'll miss her, too,' I say, uncomfortable as I think back to the photo I saw in Anna-Britta's bedroom. The photo of me.

Karin opens the residence door and sweeps the heavy velvet curtain with her arm and lets me through. She smells of nothing at all.

'Ignore this,' she says, waving her arm in an arc at the room. 'We're expanding.'

I walk in and stop. There are strings of beads laid out on the floorboards in long lines, each string uncoupled; the beads making a kind of racetrack circuit of the room.

'Three done,' says Karin.

She means the circuit is three deep, three beads

423

deep. I can see cultivated pearls and pale-green plastic spheres and amber glowing warmly and then some black cuboid modern pieces. They're laid end to end with a huge space in the centre of the room.

She knocks on the door nearest the chimney breast and then walks away.

'Come in,' says a voice. I can't make out the words but I can guess.

'Hello, Cici. How are you feeling?'

'Like a mouse caught in a trap,' she says, and then she grins and bares her old lady teeth, and says 'I'm glad you came.'

'I'm leaving tomorrow night and I have a few more questions before I go.'

'You're leaving tomorrow?' she asks.

I nod.

'Before you flee, come and see me up here if you have time. I want to say goodbye properly and I want to tell you a very important secret.'

I urge her to tell me now but she shakes her head.

'You say you have more questions?' she asks. 'For the book?'

'If you don't mind.'

'We're under contract, darling,' she says. 'I can't mind.'

Via her complex arrangement of mirrors I can see a man outside – I think it's Janitor Andersson – and he's removing the propane device from the ground near the wall of St Olov's.

'Poor Puss,' she says. 'He was such a dear little

friend and protector of lilla Ludo. He'd follow him around, brushing against Ludo's bare legs, bothering him for a chin rub. Well, he never did that to any of us, nothing of the sort. They had a bond. They were spirit twins, Puss and Ludo.'

I see Karin walk toward the steaming ground, the propane contraption resting against the wall, the mirror framing her. Andersson digs a hole through the perspiring earth and throws the discarded soil up against the wall of the church-yard. Karin stands perfectly still.

'Pass me my opera glasses so I can see this, would you, darling,' Cici says.

I do as she asks.

'KK's heartbroken,' she says. 'It's hit her very hard indeed. Not the cat *per se*, she and he never saw eye-to-eye, but she loved Puss because he loved Ludo. That creature was the last link to her brother.'

Andersson places a large cardboard box into the hole and removes his hat and holds it flat to his chest. They stand there, just the pair of them, looking down into the shallow grave, the weirdest mourners in the world attending the weirdest burial. But it's not weird, it's touching. Lilla Ludo's only a metre or two away from that hole, no wall underneath the soil dividing him from his beloved pet.

'It's one way to go,' says Cici. 'Burnt alive in a liquorice inferno, it has drama at least, don't you think? I didn't know old Puss had it in him. No old cat's home for our Puss.'

I look back to Cici and smile and notice the rabbit foot around her neck. It looks misshapen this morning like she's slept on it or she's been over-fondling it. She keeps her eyes forward on the intimate ceremony. Workers arrive for their shift and they give Karin and Andersson a wide berth.

'We have a penchant for dramatic death, we always have,' says Cici.

'How do you mean?' I ask, switching on the 'record' function of my mobile.

'My father-in-law perished on a lake. He was ice fishing and we could never make our minds up. He either drowned or froze to death. Oh, look, Andersson's backfilling the hole.'

'And your husband?'

Cici drops her opera glasses to her nose and looks at me. 'Oh, Ludvig was the most impressive of them all. We still haven't found him.'

I frown and squint my eyes.

'His body, I mean. He left a note but really it was more like a bloody treasure hunt, fifty paces here, and my favourite colour this and that. They found empty pill bottles but they could have been weeks old. He just went off to die. Well, either he got something wrong or we weren't bright enough because we never found him.'

'Goodness,' I say.

'Badness,' she says. 'The insurance company paid out far less than we were due, and only after years of fighting. The family never really recovered. My husband was a frightfully smart man and a wonderful lover and friend, but a diligent planner he was not.'

We look back to the burial. Karin and Andersson have gone. It's about minus twenty out there and you can't stand still that long, it's not possible.

'The lawyer, Hellbom. Is he a cousin of Anna-Britta's or something? I can't help but see a family resemblance.'

Her face darkens. 'Nothing to do with me, that one,' she says. 'Who knows what he really looks like under all that surgery.'

'Per Gunnarsson,' I say. 'The Ferryman's victim. I know you see everything from your attics. Do you know who he bullied back in his schooldays? Can you remember any names?'

'I remember the name of my own son,' she says. 'Gunnarsson was a lout back in high school. Made Gustav's life very difficult. But apologies were offered and we all moved on. Gunnarsson tormented half his school, you see.'

'Is there anything else you want me to know?' I ask, hoping she'll tell me her secret now. 'Anything from your life you'd like included in the book?'

She snorts. 'First time anyone's bothered to ask me,' she says. 'Thank you, darling.'

I wait.

'Stick my motto in somewhere, would you do that?'

'All dressed up and nowhere to go?' I ask.

She grins, her teeth shiny and straight. 'These days it's more like all dressed up and can't go nowhere.'

We laugh together, proper belly laughs with hands placed on hands and tears in our eyes.

'Something funny?' asks Karin, passing the door.

'Oh, KK, come in, sit down.'

But Karin backs away.

'Would you talk to her?' Cici whispers. 'She says you're her one true friend.'

I watch Karin disappear out of view toward her corner room carrying a slim hammer and an oak-handled chisel.

CHAPTER 43

I find Karin in her corner bedroom. I stand by the doorframe and peer into the bathroom next door. She sees me and gestures for me to come in. We walk past her bed, past the chisel resting on the bedpost, and stand at the end window, the one directly beneath Cici's slanted attic window, the one facing the ruin of St Olov's.

'Woodwork?' I ask, pointing at the fine chisel.

'Clay work,' she says. 'Mother suggested I start a new piece, do something creative to clear my head.'

She looks through the window.

'We live here and then we die here and then we rest there,' she says.

The brown rectangle marking the cat's final resting place is fading; fine white snowflakes filling in the brown like someone high above us dusting icing sugar to finish off a poison cake.

'But you're leaving us,' she says. 'You get to go.'

She looks unreal with her coal-black hair and the mole above her lip, the one she darkens each morning with an eyebrow pencil. I feel for her. I like Karin a lot and if I was staying on in Toytown

I'd try to get her out of this place. To show her some fun.

'We're all chained to the spot.' She turns her head toward me but not completely, and then she crosses her wrists as if about to be handcuffed. She doesn't look me in the eye. 'We can't fly away. I thought I could, I managed one and a half semesters. Even then it was pulling me back. This monolith. This wet tomb of an inheritance. I felt its pull, even then.'

'Karin, come on,' I say, and then I feel bad for those two blunt words. Who am I to say 'come on' to anybody? 'It's been dreadful for all of you. I'm so sorry but things will get better. You're twenty years old. You can do anything, go anywhere.'

She looks down to the family plot, to her brother, to her cat, to her father. 'Perhaps you're right.' She turns to me. 'Or perhaps you don't really have any idea.'

'Of course I'm right,' I say. 'Why don't you come visit me in Skåne this summer? I won't know anyone down there. I'd be so grateful. What do you say?'

She looks at me, her eyes cut in half by her fringe, and smiles. But it's not a stable smile, her lips are quivering, the tiny muscles in spasm as she tries to hold it.

'I'll come back later tonight,' I say. 'I could bring Thai food?'

She laughs out loud and shakes her head so her hair swings around and makes a mess of itself.

'Come as you are,' she says. 'No takeout.'

I walk back to the office and Lena's sitting with her legs under my desk.

'You been demoted?' I ask, the bell above the door tinkling in my hearing aids.

She stands and helps me take off my coat and she hangs it up for me on a hook, something she's never done before.

'Not long now,' she says.

'Why did you hire Newboy? Don't you think the locals will feel alienated, with him being a professional sailor, Daddy's little rich boy and all?'

She pinches the end of her nose and my hearing aid beeps a battery warning.

'Four years ago Lars thought locals might feel alienated with me hiring a jacked-up chip-on-her-shoulder deaf bisexual Stockholm kid straight out of college.'

'He was right,' I say.

'It's healthy for them, they need shaking up. And you were good enough to handle it, and so, I think, is Sebastian.'

'You think?'

'I hired him, didn't I? When you applied for this position I only got three other applications and let me tell you they weren't very hot prospects. Washed-up cynics yearning for the good old days. When I advertised this time round I got seventeen replies. Because of you. Because of your Medusa reporting. A handful of them were excellent, people I'd have hired in the blink of an eye four

431

years ago, people that might one day be as good as you.'

'Maybe you could have given some other poor schmuck a chance? Someone whose father didn't buy him every opening in life?'

'You're quick to judge.'

'You think?' I say.

Lena sits up on Nils's desk, next to his yuppie rolodex.

'He's good, that's the first thing. Yeah, he looks like the crown prince of some central European country, but he's a good writer. His family had money once-upon-a-time but not anymore. Daddy went bankrupt. Mummy died from a brain haemorrhage. No warning, boom.'

'Shit,' I say.

'Shit,' she says. 'He's got two little sisters and he's been working multiple jobs all through school to help them out. His old man's not dealt with single parenthood so well. He's in a fragile state, signed off work sick.'

'Okay,' I say.

'He's a good kid.' She looks disappointed with me, like there's even more distance between us. 'Let's give him the benefit.'

I head back to my desk, subdued, a bad taste on my tongue. I print off all the latest work I've done for Holmqvist's book and then I write up everything else that's happened – the fire and what I've found out about Cici's life and the lake house. The fact they never found Ludvig's body. Every time I type a word starting with the letter 'N' it turns into 'Noora'. I see her name all over my screen. I say her name noiselessly in my head, rolling it over my tongue, pressing it to the roof of my mouth. Tasting it.

I'm giving Holmqvist most of what I have. The remainder I keep to myself. I'll hold it on trust for the Grimberg family, private matters and details that have no place in the end product.

And then I remember the letterhead in Anna-Britta's office. That publishing house, the one Holmqvist described as an imprint for one of the big New York outfits.

Third Way Publishing.

Google is my friend. Third Way have a nice corporate website; fancy photos morphing into each other, you know the type. I can see they've printed plenty of memoirs, many of them so-called 'misery memoirs'. I could write half a dozen.

There are testimonials on the site and they all look decent enough. I search for them on Amazon and see plenty of their books for sale and the pages look professional but the rankings suck. I mean, none of them are in the top ninety-thousand. That can't be a good sign.

I dig deeper. The first page-and-a-half on Google is all Third Way sponsored corporate crap and linked blogs. Then I find the negative news. The site is a self-publishing scam, according to a self-styled 'crusader', a guy with a penchant for semi-colons and capital letters. He calls Third Way a 'subsidy publisher' and 'essentially a vanity press'. I google 'Vanity Press'. He's basically saying they're not a real publishing house. He's basically saying that rich dudes pay Third Way Publishing to edit and format and print the books all for an outlandish fee.

Can't be. Holmqvist is paying me but they're paying him back. And they paid out an advance to Gustav Grimberg. Holmqvist said so.

I dig some more. I find some people who like dealing with Third Way; happy with their book and the service they got, nice cover designs. Maybe Holmqvist got a proper deal out of them because he's got such a strong track record?

One of the photos on the Third Way website is a dog book: *How to Train Big Breeds* – a non-fiction thing, and the photo that keeps attracting my attention is that of a German shepherd with an orange collar, heeling to its out-of-shot trainer.

I google 'dog breeders in Värmland'. I refine to German shepherd breeders and find two close to Munkfors, both in rural locations looking at their contact details. I call the first.

'Hello,' says a woman.

'Hi, I'm calling about your German shepherds.'

'We don't have none left, the last litter's all been taken.'

'Can I ask you, please, did you take in an adult German shepherd earlier this year or late last year?'

'Adult?'

'Yes.'

'We don't take in no adult dogs, we're not a kennel. We got Kalle the Giant and we got Macy-Anne Flop Ears and that's all the adults we need, all we can afford to feed, the amount them two eat.'

'Okay, sorry to bother you.'

'You want me put you on the waiting list?'

'No thanks. Bye.'

I call the other breeder and the line rings and rings and rings and then it sounds like a dog picks up. It's all barking and growling.

'Fredrik, that you?' asks a woman.

'No,' I say. 'My name's Tuva Moodyson and I—'

'Hold on a sec.' I hear dogs, sounds like fifty of them, barking and hollering and the woman who picked up is trying to calm them down and then I hear a door slam.'

'You say your name's Tuvasson?'

'Moodyson,' I say. 'Can I ask you about your adult dogs, please?'

'What for, you from the welfare? You an inspector, we gone finished our inspection in December, we got all signed off.'

'I'm trying to track a dog. I think he was adopted by you earlier this year or late last year.'

'You mean Philip?'

'Did you take him this year or last year?' I ask.

'First week in January, but he weren't no unwanted Christmas present. Fine dog.'

435

'I think my friend owned him before you. Did you take Philip from David Holmqvist up in Gavrik?'

'That's the one. He couldn't handle Philip eating up his nice car and such. Did us a big favour, truth be told. And he's gonna be a pappa later this year, how about that.'

'Philip, or David Holmqvist?'

She laughs. 'Philip got my new bitch pregnant almost soon as she got through the door; gonna be good strong pups I'd say. You want to go down on the list, better get in quick. Eight-thousand kronor and I ask a ten per cent deposit if it ain't no inconvenience. What's your name again, Tuvasson?'

I thank her for her time and end the call and hate myself. I suspected Holmqvist could have, I don't know, planted the dog tooth? For years, for most of his life, Holmqvist has been persecuted and bullied for being a weirdo. There are more rumours about him in this town than about anyone else, all because he looks and acts a bit different. I had images of him roasting his damn dog, eating the gourmet choice-cuts and somehow getting that tooth into Gunnarsson's neck. Now I feel sick. And guilty. And I need a drink.

Outside there's a man in a black suit with a long coat. He peers through the office window. Then he walks away and I go to the door and open it and cold air gusts around my neck. It's Henrik Hellbom, the lawyer. I can see his face clearly. It

436

looks like his skin's been poured onto his skull in liquid form and then left to set. He passes a file to Anna-Britta and then he walks, his back stooped, through the gates of the factory.

CHAPTER 44

Powder snow blows in through the open office door and melts on my indoor shoes. They look blotchy, sick, pocked. The thermometer on the window reads minus twenty-six and I can still see Anna-Britta and Facelift. He's wearing those tight calf-leather gloves and he's holding a battered briefcase. They walk through to the rear yard and there's something about the way they look at each other, the way they walk next to each other, their body language. There's an intimacy there. The iron hook above looks like a 'come hither' crooked finger, drawing people through that brick archway like an industrial pied piper.

I say bye to Lena and she asks if I'll pop by tomorrow and I tell her I'll try. She looks disappointed like this is not how she imagined my exit.

My right ear aches. I've been lucky with infections this winter, touch wood, but now I can feel one coming. The sofa surfing doesn't help. I tweak my aid and that relieves the pressure a little on my raw skin. I need new creams; something expensive from a Swiss laboratory.

There are no cars on the roads. People have left their dead Christmas trees in their gardens because it's too cold to deal with them and anyway, who gets visitors in February? Outside the Lutheran church there's a digger scooping up old snow and dumping it into a big ten-wheel truck ready to be carted away and left in some bleak permafrost field. I count six houses with casserole dishes outside their front doors as I drive out of town to the reservoir. Six. Probably sausage stew or slow-cooked pulled pork or maybe spare ribs, sticky with some kind of glaze. Moose-proofed. I need to start cooking once I get down south. One of about a hundred resolutions I've vaguely made to myself.

I leave Gavrik in my mirrors and the road is apocalypse empty. The night is black but it also has a grey glow to it, the snow reflecting what starlight can creep through the thick ice-clouds above. I park by the reservoir. Just me and one other truck.

The water's frozen and you'd think it was safe to drive on, or at least walk on, but you'd be dead wrong. We've had a quick freeze-thaw-freeze in the past week and the ice-fishermen and the hockey kids will wait another day or two before venturing onto the glistening flats.

I think about that couple, the couple Cici talked about, her best friends. They drowned together under this water all those years ago, the water I'm staring at now, the water beneath the untrustworthy ice; a couple weighed down with bricks and chains and with the sadness of their final bedtime embrace.

This is the closest thing to a sea or a horizon in Gavrik Kommun. Tam told me she overcame her fear of swimming in open water here one summer. Since then I've adopted it as my own. I've been here at least ten times since Mum died. Probably came five times in that first week. It's more relevant somehow than those side-by-side graves down in Karlstad cemetery. I always look up when I think of Dad, when I need a jolt of reassurance. But when I think of Mum, I look outward. I look at the water. At the distance. At the ice.

I'm here to say goodbye to Toytown for good.

There's a pain inside my chest. Something pulling. The lights come on inside the owner's house. They're faint and the smoke from the chimney's rising straight up, like a pencil line into a windless sky.

I need to make it up with Tammy. I've been a solid-gold bitch and she didn't deserve it. I need to lay it all out and apologise and hug the hell out of her. It feels good just acknowledging it.

There's a man on the edge of the reservoir walking his dog. I can see his breath.

I think about Noora, and stroke the inside of my forearm, the soft hairless skin under my wrist, and I'm back under those blankets. Her breath. Her fingertips gliding over me, over the unseen skin of my forearms and my lower neck and my legs. I need to see her again. In my mind's eye we meet and I tell her who the Ferryman is, along with some snippet of evidence everyone else has missed. I leave with a good taste in my mouth because I do my bit. I help stop the man who slit a jugular vein and jammed a fist-sized ball of liquorice into a dead man's mouth.

And then there's a wisp.

I sit up straight like a young me at the zoo. The northern lights flicker and go, thick cloud guarding them from mortal eyes. It was emerald green. I stare out and even with the blower on full and my goose-down jacket and fleece underlayers, it is cold. And then they flare up. I don't see much, just a fine spray between clouds, luminous and brightest green, the whip of a celestial horse's tail as it gallops away.

I look for more but get nothing. The man with the dog is getting close. He's wearing a heavy wool coat and backpack.

I pull back my gearstick to reverse and swing around and drive off toward the road. The man with the dog gets into his truck and blue-green lights flash in my rear-view mirrors; the Gods, my parents, a magnetic charge, the solar wind dancing and teasing, not showing itself straight to my face. I take my foot off the accelerator and watch the show. In my left mirror, green strips light up the sky, the clouds thinner now, the stars there as backdrop. The green reflects on the ice and snow, the whole scene glowing in my mirror. I turn my head and it dims so I look forward again, away from it, at my mirrors and only my mirrors and then it leaps, three bold stripes, curtains of electric light, swinging and cascading across the horizon. I think of Dad and the fact that I can't imagine reaching old age because he never did. I can't see that in my future. The green flashes leave me and everything darkens and I drive away, my chest at peace, my hands loose on the wheel, my breathing slow.

It's 6pm and one of the householders I passed before is retrieving his casserole from his garden. His snow shovel rests next to the wall ready for tomorrow. He's wearing huge, unlaced lumberjack boots and he's knocking off the brick securing the pot's lid and taking the thing inside to heat up in his warm kitchen with his loving nuclear family.

I drive past St Olov's, that darkest of places, and past the factory, the chimneys high and almost invisible in the night sky, and carry on up Storgatan. The man with the dog's close behind in his black SUV but he's keeping a good distance. The neon sign of Ronnie's Bar is dim. It is very faint. When it gets this cold the gases inside don't work as they're supposed to. The signage looks weak. It's straining. The blue has turned almost white and it's hardly glowing at all.

Tam's van has no queue, which is odd on a Sunday evening. ICA Maxi's quiet, but there's a dark green 4x4 in the far corner with its engine running. I drive past and park next to Tammy's van. It's locked. I have never once known her to close on a Sunday night, not once. Must be the extreme cold.

I park outside ICA Maxi, my tyres scratching along the hardened ice ridges. I lock up. This is an okay place for me. I've been shopping in ICA since I was fourteen, since Dad died, since Mum stopped being able to do it. I learned how to shop and how to budget and how to heat tinned food. I managed. But I never told Mum how I managed. I never told her I was sorry for her loss and for what became of her life. I should have said sorry for her silent bleakness, her angst. I should have told her I was sorry and thanked her for doing the best she could even though that wasn't much, and I should have given her some peace even though she never offered me any. I should have forgiven her for her sake. And for mine.

The doors whoosh open and hot air flattens my hair and pushes loose strands all over my face. I pick up a basket.

Four cinnamon buns, a princess torte cake, three bunches of roses, a scented candle, albeit a cheap chemical one made by the same company that manufactures toilet hook-ons. Goodbye gifts for Cici. For all the Grimberg women. To make their home a little more bearable. Three-hundred and fifteen kronor.

I drive to Tam's flat but she's not in. Maybe she's met someone? I try her phone just to check she's alright but it's switched off. I park back at the office and walk over to the factory gates and through the arch and up to the brown rectangle by the wall. I say goodbye to the cat that used to hiss at me and then I walk past the charred remains of the liquorice-root barns and into the building.

Skeleton staff.

Mainly clipboards and stirrers. One cutter and one stamper. The canteen's being cleaned, tables upturned on tables, mops and buckets and two twins with earphones doing their best to clean up. Bleach fumes burn the sensitive pink flesh inside my nostrils. I walk upstairs. Anna-Britta's in her office on the phone. The door to the residence is unlocked so I walk in and push past the velvet curtain. Cici's in bed asleep, her door ajar. It's cold up here. The vents are screaming their faint distant screams, whining and wailing up by the ceiling, and the refectory table has a box perched on the end of it. I walk past the cabinet of life, its doors wide open, some of its drawers pulled out by their milk-tooth handles. The box on the table is a red-wine box but someone's written 'red evil' on it in marker pen. I lift the lid of the box. The foil bag inside has been cut and resealed. Smells like vodka. The bag's empty.

'Karin?' I whisper, walking through to the kitchen. But she's not there. I place the roses and the cake down on the table and the rabbit-hutch door is wide open. They let it exercise in the evenings. Karin's bedroom door's ajar but I knock on the frame to announce myself and there's an envelope on her bed. I hear water in the bathroom but it's not a shower running or a tap dribbling. This is different. I knock on the door and it creaks open a little and there's water all over the floor.

'Karin,' I call out, louder this time.

I knock again and then push the door.

She's in the bath and the water is red.

CHAPTER 45

Her tattooed chest is rising and falling and red streams are running down her forearms.

I plunge my hands into the hot water and drag her up the bath. She's so heavy. My sleeves take on the colour of the bathwater.

'Help,' I scream, my voice breaking toward the end of the word. 'Help us!'

My ears buzz from my screech. I pull a towel from the rail and lift Karin's left arm and push the towel hard onto the vertical wound running up her skin. The towel reddens. Everything white to red.

'Help us, we need help!' I shout. 'Help us!'

And Karin looks at me and she doesn't smile exactly, but she closes her lips.

'Stay with me, Karin,' I say. 'Karin, you're going to be fine. It's okay. I'm here now, Karin. Stay with me.'

But her weight is pulling her back down into the water. I heave her up but she's slumped like a drunk or a newborn baby; some absurd and terrible creature, leaching out blood, her tattoos shimmering under the pink water, her fingers wrinkled.

'Help us!' I scream.

I can hear Cici, and she's crying and yelling something.

'Get help,' I shout. 'Cici, get help. It's Karin.'

Karin blinks but I can feel the life leaving her as the bathwater darkens incrementally with each second. I can't lift her out of the bath so I stretch my arm and pull the plug.

The water gurgles through the old pipework and the red drains away and Karin looks even more startling, even more fragile without the water to keep her warm. I take a new towel and press it to her other wrist.

'You're okay,' I say, my voice a mess, not enough hope in my tone, the towel's red, the left one more so than the right. 'I need to call help. I'll be back.'

I run through to the Grand Room and Cici's there on the floor.

'Is she alive?' she asks.

I nod and call 112.

'I'll get Anna-Britta,' she says.

'Hello, ambulance, right away, the factory, first floor.' They tell me to stay calm and ask the nature of the incident. 'Slit wrists,' I say. 'It's bad, come now,' and then I end the call. I want to run to Cici, sprawled there on the floor, dragging herself toward the Receiving Room, toward that curtained door. But I run back to the bathtub.

Karin looks so cold.

I take another towel, a large one with frayed edges, and lay it over her and keep pressure on the wrists. The knife's taunting me on the side of the bath. It's the antler one from beneath the table, the one with the Grimberg 'G' on its end. The blade's sitting there between a tea-light candle and a pair of liquorice coins.

Karin says something, her lips move a little, but it's a whisper of a whisper.

'What?' I say. 'You're okay, Karin, the ambulance will be here in minutes.'

'Tuva,' she whispers.

'I'm here,' I say, tears glazing my eyes.

'Help me,' she says.

My tears come stronger and time slows to the point where I know I must say the right words now. It may be the last thing she hears, God forbid, or the thing I'll forever remember saying to a dying girl, or the thing that brings her back.

'I'll help you,' I say, swallowing hard. 'Karin, I'm not leaving you.'

Her head lolls to one side and I hear a commotion from the other end of the Grand Room, Anna-Britta screaming like I've never heard anyone scream, the paramedics' boots stamping on the floorboards.

'In here!' I yell. 'Bathroom.'

A man and a woman open the door and edge me out of the way. They work on Karin but they speak to me.

'When did you find her?'

'Ten minutes ago.'

'Has she said anything to you?'

They bandage her wrists and the guy gives her a shot in her leg.

'She asked for help.' I take a huge breath in, the shock entering my body through my mouth, my heart too big for my chest.

'It's okay,' the woman paramedic says. 'We'll look after her now.'

'Karin!' screams Anna-Britta in the open door. She's staring down at her with that Edvard Munch face, absolute horror, the worst of all nightmares come true. She has the look of a woman who lost her husband and her son and is now watching her daughter lying flaccid and pale and naked and red.

'Johan,' says the woman paramedic. He takes Anna-Britta out of the room and sits her at the refectory table. I watch her stare at us through the open bathroom door, her face in her hands, her eyes wet through splayed fingers. She's quiet for a moment and then she wails.

'She's lost a lot of blood,' the woman paramedic tells me. 'But she's strong. Can you help us, can you unlock the archway door so we can get to the ambulance.'

'Yes.'

I run out of the room – Anna-Britta watching me go – and pass Cici, who's leant up against the cabinet of life, and I sprint through the Receiving Room and down the stairs.

449

'Door's open,' says Andersson. 'Unlocked. Snow's clear. What can I do?'

'Nothing, that's good.'

'The old lady?'

I shake my head and run back up. By the time I get to the Grand Room Karin's strapped to a stretcher, with a blanket and some kind of monitor attached to her. The roses I bought are scattered all around the table, some loose petals balancing on knife blades, other stems intact and closer to the kitchen, the pigment from their stamped-on petals bleeding into the bleached floorboards.

'Lilla Karin,' says Anna-Britta, her palm to Karin's cheek as the stretcher passes by. 'I'm with you.' The princess torte cake sits pristine in its clear plastic box atop the table, the fresh cream sweating beads of moisture which cling to the inside of the plastic.

Karin's mother follows the paramedics and the stretcher through to the Receiving Room. There's no 'don't look' this time.

I go to Cici.

She's sobbing and squeezing her rabbit foot in her palm, like it could burst at any moment.

'She'll be alright,' I tell her. 'They say it's not as serious as it looks.'

'It's more serious,' she says. 'It's got to her.'

Cici smacks her hand against the side of the huge cabinet of life, but it doesn't move or shake. I help her back into bed. She's sobbing, but she looks more angry than sad. I tell her I'll be back, and then I run down to the ambulance. Its roof lights are strobing off the glistening under-side of the brick archway, but its sirens are silent.

'We're going to Karlstad General,' says the male paramedic.

They drive away, the ambulance's studded tyres throwing up chips of salty ice in its wake as it speeds down an empty frozen Storgatan toward the E16.

A car pulls up.

'I came as soon as I heard,' says Stina Johanssen, the family GP. 'Where's Karin?'

'They left,' I say. 'Karlstad General.'

'Dammit.'

'But Cecilia's up there and she's not well, I think she's in shock. Could you check on her?'

We walk upstairs. Stina calms Cici, she's very good at that, and tells me she'll give her a pill to help her sleep.

'I might go to Karlstad,' I say. 'To the hospital.'

'I'll stay here,' she says. 'My daughter's skiing with her school. I'll stay here all night with Mrs Grimberg.'

I go back to the bathroom and much of the scene has now been washed away. Bottles of shampoo and cardboard toilet-paper tubes lie discarded near the sink. Plastic needle-wrappers and latex gloves. Gauze wrappers flap open and shut in the draught from the ill-fitting window. The colour's still there in the old bath. And in the towels. So much blood. A wasp sits drowsy on an old-fashioned bar of soap and another

451

buzzes close to the ceiling. I look into her bedroom and see the envelope on the bed. I pick it up. It's not addressed to anyone, not to her mother or grandmother, and it's not sealed. I open it. Inside is a compliment slip. It's a Henrik Hellbom Advokat compliment slip. I read Karin's writing.

'I'm so sorry. It was me.'

CHAPTER 46

Karin? Did she kill Gunnarsson? What did he do to her seven years ago? Why didn't anyone listen? I can't believe she's a killer. She must be apologising for something else. I cannot let my guard down. The Ferryman could still be on the loose.

I walk out through the curtained door, each squeak of the floorboards putting me on edge, every draught from the rotten windows making me stop and look around and look up.

I unlock my truck, and open the passenger side and then lean over to the driver's side and pull the handle and nothing. Dead. I try it again from the outside but the door is completely unopenable now, unlocked yet unopenable. Snapped inside and out. I have to scoot over the gearstick and plant myself in the driver's seat and then switch on the engine and then clamber out the way I came so I can scrape.

The E16 is a windswept ghost road. I call Thord and tell him to get to the factory, tell him about the note, tell him how Karin may have been angry with both her father and Gunnarsson, tell him

453

how she was probably frustrated with Cecilia for allowing Gunnarsson to keep his position, how she might have pushed her down the stairs.

I'm the only vehicle here, my tyres skirting over ice and through snow gusts blowing diagonally across both lanes. I hope to God that paramedic was telling the truth. I hope Karin's okay, because we still need her story.

A lumber wagon drives north past me and its pine load looks like giant liquorice-roots stacked in a long bale. It's weaving. I've scrubbed my hands but my nails are still red with Karin's blood, the skin dark and crusted, her haemoglobin deep under my cuticles.

This isn't something I've ever lived with. Suicide, I mean. Mum was depressed but that manifested in her living within herself for years on end. She imploded when dad died, collapsed, shrank, turned inside out. I'd try to coax her into hobbies, even just reading a book, but she shut down her whole life. She left it on standby mode until the cancer took her years later. I hate the idea of someone I love dying by suicide because I hate the idea that someone I love could be in that much pain. But the suicide itself, once it's been done, once Gustav jumped – I think you have to accept it. Cici's right. If they go through with it then there can be no talk of 'selfish act' or 'didn't think of the relatives' or 'took the easy way out'. Hell, no. It's never selfish when someone loses all hope. It is never not thinking about the relatives, it's despite how much this will hurt relatives and friends, I have no other option. It's never the easy way out. It must be the hardest thing in the world. I've seen Karin bathing in her own blood and I know that's not a decision she made lightly.

A snowplough up ahead takes up both lanes, scraping back fresh powder and dumping salt crystals on the asphalt. Must have joined at the last exit. Now my speed's limited to its speed and I feel like a parasitic cleaner-fish enjoying the protection of a larger species. A Mercedes jeep drives close behind me and its headlights aren't working.

And then I start to question why. Not why did Karin do it, but why didn't I spot any warning signs? Any hints she was weighed down with guilt? Any clues? Why didn't her mother spot them? As a journalist I need to see signals. Things other people miss. And as a deaf person I read body language all day long without even realising it. It's essential. It fills in the gaps.

The E16 turns into the E45 and the Mercedes is still there in my mirrors. I get to Karlstad and follow a familiar route to the hospital. Mum was here for about six months on and off. She almost died here but she didn't.

Parking's a charade. Me climbing over and through the truck twice and locking it and kicking it as I leave to walk through the big rotating front door; hot stale air blowing my hair and drying my already dried-out eyes.

Reception tells me where she is. I follow the blue stripe all the way to her ward and it's not intensive care so that must be a good thing, right? I catch a glimpse of myself in a window and I look like a corpse. I find the ward. It's sat between maternity and geriatric care, between the start and the end, the sapling and the final acorn produced before the oak comes crashing down.

It's a private room. Thank the lord for high Swedish taxes. I knock and Anna-Britta's by her side, her pink hand on Karin's white hand, her strength laying on Karin's needle-punctured weakness.

Anna-Britta smiles as I walk in. It's relief and appreciation and despair and exhaustion and terror and sadness all in one.

'She's okay,' she mouths to me silently.

I smile back at her. I want to tell her about the note but this is not the right moment. Karin's unconscious and medicated. She's not going anywhere. And Anna-Britta is a mother first and foremost, I need to remember that. I don't know anything for sure.

Anna-Britta breaks down crying. We hug each other, awkwardly at first, by Karin's blanketed feet and then she squeezes me, really squeezes my body in her arms. And I squeeze her back. We hold on to each other.

'They gave her new blood,' she says, pulling back from me, dabbing her eyes. 'And something to sleep and something else for the pain. They stitched her.' She cries again, her hands rubbing the tears from her cheeks. 'Her arms. Her poor beautiful arms, they're . . .'

'We can help her now,' I say, my hand on Anna-Britta's shoulder. 'Now we know, we can help.'

She nods. It's the nod of a woman who's lived with too much of this, too much for anyone to endure. It's the nod of a woman that says, 'yeah, we can help, but we can never be completely relaxed when she gets low, we can never let go of this when she goes back to college, we can never leave a hundred goddam knives under our dining table ever again'.

A nurse with red hair, she looks like an older version of the stamper, comes in and says there's a man downstairs and asks if we're expecting a visitor. We say we're not. She checks Karin's dressings and her heart monitor and asks if we'd like coffee.

We walk out into the waiting area. It's three long black-leather sofas and a flat-screen TV on mute and a stack of magazines. There's a shelf on the wall with well-thumbed novels, science-fiction tomes four fingers thick and romance novels with curled front covers. These are well-read books. These are stories that have helped loved ones to escape for a few pages, to offer some safety. I read a trilogy of fantasy novels waiting for Mum to die and those three books helped me more than I can say.

Two coffees arrive in plastic disposable cups with inappropriately small handles.

'I just don't know why,' says Anna-Britta cradling the cup in her hands. 'She could have come to me with her problems. I thought she was okay. I would do anything for my daughter.' She rips a sliver of flesh from her index fingernail. 'Absolutely anything.'

'It's been such a tough month for all of you.'

Anna-Britta looks up.

'They say you can't see it coming,' I say, and then I immediately regret those words, some nonsense from a magazine or a long-forgotten TV show. 'They say . . .' I'm sat in front of a woman whose husband just killed himself and I'm preaching about what 'they say' about suicide?

'I didn't see it coming,' says Anna-Britta, chewing at a hangnail. Biting it. 'She's only twenty. And she's the brightest of all of us, so much to live for, so much ahead of her.'

'She'll pull through,' I say, imagining Thord's handcuffs around her bandaged wrists. 'You can get her some professional help. She'll manage.'

'She's scared,' says Anna-Britta, sipping her coffee, blowing into the cup. 'Of our home, of the business, of old evil, of what might happen to our family.'

I smile a flat, crimped smile and wonder if what she's really scared of is justice. Punishment. Jail time. I remember the courses she's taken: Pathology and Taxonomy. The knife with the G stamped on the end. The fact that she's a sculptor. The finely-detailed snow skulls. And her access to the factory in its entirety.

'I feel like one of those tourists,' says Anna-Britta, her eyes on the TV. 'You know the ones you read about who drift out to sea on an inflatable lilo. They have no say what direction they travel in or if they live or if they die. The winds, the currents, they take them wherever they're going to go and all they can do is just hang on.'

She looks at me again.

'Or slip off.'

'Is there anyone you can speak to?' I say. 'About what you've been through? The Gunnarsson trauma? The factory business? Maybe not a sale, but a loan or an investment?'

'It's the book,' she says, eyeing the paperbacks on the shelf. 'That's our last hope. It's what Gustav told me, he was very insistent. The book has to be a success. It has to be gripping, to find a wide audience. It'll be out next year and we'll receive our royalty cheques quarterly.' She sips again. 'That's the difference, that's the key: ongoing income, a "revenue stream" as Gustav explained it to me, something to keep us afloat.'

'Okay,' I say.

A doctor in an ill-fitting white jacket walks out from the lifts and he must have a bad ankle or something, he's not walking straight.

'It's difficult to explain,' Anna-Britta says, crossing her legs the other way. 'We have a debt to pay. We were not always such a good employer.'

A patient gets wheeled through on a bed by two orderlies and he has his head bandaged. It seems like he winks at me but it could just be a blink because one eye's covered.

'In the early days, the mid 1800s, the first owners, the founders, we've taken down their portraits now, they exploited the locals. They worked them too hard and paid them too little, even by the standards of the day. The fatality rate in the factory was unacceptably high. The first year of the factory they paid high rates and then the worker's families relocated to Gavrik, which back then was just a new church and a ruined church and the factory and not much else. Then management reduced wages year on year.'

'It was different back then,' I say.

'Not really,' she says. 'The family became rich. They added to their wealth and expanded and we were the number two producer of salt liquorice for many years. They built the Manor on Lake Vänern with the profits and we've never been as successful since.'

An exhausted-looking junior doctor walks past us and nods to both of us, his stethoscope swinging from his neck, his white crocs squeaking along the rubberised floor.

'We're paying for their greed,' Anna-Britta says. 'They went too far and the town knows it. My father-in-law.' Her eyes darken. 'He went too far. Ludvig was a thug and he thought he was above the law, above the normal rules. The hurt that man caused. The kids he never acknowledged. We're still trying to make amends, and the factory

460

reminds us every time we draw up the annual accounts.' She points in the direction of Karin's room, tears in her eyes, and says, 'I hold her grandfather completely responsible.'

We both watch as the elderly doctor, the man with the bad ankle, shuffles into Karin's room.

CHAPTER 47

The doctor checks Karin's vitals and I drive north from Karlstad hospital in a trance. Too much to process. Karin. Her confession. Her broken skin. Her anguish.

I have a short text from Thord saying they're dealing with Karin's note. Thanking me.

It's too late to visit Cici so I park and lock up and there's someone standing outside Hotel Gavrik. It's a figure in a long padded black coat with a big hood. The figure's back-dropped by the hotel façade with its off-centre sign, and the hotel's backdropped by the dark factory and its chimneys.

Warily, I walk over.

The hood comes off and there's a balaclava underneath.

I stop walking, my heart booming in my chest.

'You got a key?' asks Noora, pulling off her balaclava.

The pressure I'm feeling inside my head, in my sinuses, bearing down on my shoulders, lifts a little at her words. I step closer and slip on an ice patch and she reaches out to steady me.

'Yeah,' I say, finding my key card and opening

the front door of the hotel. No night porters here, no bellboys with brass luggage-trolleys or night managers to say goodnight and call the lift for you. Just a key.

We step inside and the door locks behind us.

'Come,' she says, pulling off her duvet coat. She's wearing mascara and it's clumped a little on her thick lashes and her breath smells faintly of white wine.

We step into the lift and I press for floor two and the doors close.

She kisses me.

The doors open. My heart's racing so fast I might die right here on the second-floor corridor. I want to tell her about Karin and check what she knows about the note, about my theory, and I want to ask her why she's so weird around me in public. But I don't. I'm too exhausted. I open my door with my key card and jam it into the slot thing just inside the room. Noora looks at me, really at me, inside myself. She rubs her cheek softly against mine, her warmth gliding over my cold skin, her hands on my waist, mine at the back of her neck, her breath catching in my mouth, my lips brushing hers.

It's still dark when I wake up.

She's spooning me and curving her arm around my stomach. Not around, just resting there. This single bed is full. And it is warm with her, and the sheets are tangled and the blanket's pulled up as far as our necks. Out the window, I guess it's five am-ish, the chimneys are visible as grey vertical stripes against a grey sky. They taper as they rise, the white lettering easier to read in this half-light than in the middle of a summer's day. Grimberg Liquorice. Noora stirs and kisses the side of my face and her hands tighten around me and I turn to her and I kiss her.

I tell her how I found Karin. Sad, broken whispers from my lips to her ear. She knows the facts but I tell her what it felt like to find her. I pull her tighter to me and we fall back to sleep.

We jolt awake at same moment.

A rattle.

Someone's trying to open the interconnecting door in the corner of the room.

Noora gets out of bed.

She holds out her arm like 'stay there, Tuva' and then she picks up a glass vase from the desk and she listens at the wall. I watch from the bed as she tries the door handle. The door swings open and the room beyond is as black as a midnight forest. She peers inside and I feel like I need to back her up so I get out of bed and step over to stand behind her.

'Police,' she calls.

Nothing.

The dark room is freezing cold.

Noora steps in and tries the light switch but nothing happens. We don't have a key card for this room. The slot's empty. We walk a little way inside and the room's so long I can't see the end of it

464

and there's no light from bulbs or windows. Noora pulls me back to our room and closes the door and pushes a chair under the handle.

'Probably just housekeeping,' she says, but she doesn't look convinced.

I shower, Noora on guard duty. When I finish she's looking out of the window at the factory.

'That place,' she says.

'I know,' I say, drying my hair with a towel. There's an electric hairdryer bolted to the wall but it's faulty and sparks crackle if I try to switch it on.

'What do you think about the note? Will Karin be arrested?'

Noora looks at me. At my eyes and then my lips and then my eyes again, left eye, then right eye, her focus moving as if studying a painting in a gallery. I feel a little self-conscious but, to be completely honest, also exhilarated at the attention.

'Not sure,' she says. 'Thord's looking into it, checking her whereabouts on the day Gunnarsson was killed.'

'Okay.'

She touches my chin with her fingertip and then walks into the bathroom and leaves the door open.

'Should we eat first or go straight to Thord?' I say.

'Let's eat,' she says. 'Could be a long day.'

I feel completely at ease dressing in front of Noora. When I do this in front of a man, I feel, I don't know, not so much at ease. When we're both dressed I ask, 'Shall I go down and get some food and bring it up here?'

She chews the inside of her mouth and I think about how awkward she is when we're in public together.

'I could come down,' she says. 'We could eat together.'

'But everyone would see.'

'I know,' she says.

'You sure? You seem so private. Like you don't want anyone to guess.'

She swallows and nods.

I kiss her and we melt into each other again and have to pull ourselves apart.

'I'm here for a few years at least,' she says. 'Might as well face this head on.'

We go downstairs, our cheeks flushed, her hair still half wet, mine starting to frizz.

The breakfast room has four occupied tables. Three husband-and-wife tables, and one family table. The owner walks in with an apron tied around her waist and looks at me like I'm the Pope and I just stepped in with my new boyfriend.

'Morning,' Noora says to her. 'Breakfast for two.'

We sit down. Noora eats eggs and bacon with coffee and I eat toast and cereal and a lukewarm hot chocolate. We say nothing but we grin like idiots and our feet stroke each other under the table like it's a whole other realm down there.

I check-out with Noora at my side. The owner's

so damn squirmy we almost descend into a giggle fit but we hold it together. I leave my bags in the storeroom because it's too cold for them in the truck. I pay and we step outside. I want to kiss her but I just hold my nose against the softness of her cheek.

She tells me to head to my office and she'll update me when she can.

'I'll be back at the factory this evening,' I say. 'To say goodbye to the family. My taxi's booked at nine.'

'I'll wave you off,' she says, and then my old Hilux drives by, I'd recognise it anywhere, but it's not Potato Head in the driving seat, it's some old guy with a moustache and a high collar and a wide-rim hat. I turn to Noora.

We don't kiss on the street, we just blink at each other and slip apart, her to the cop shop, me, heart pounding, to my office.

It's about minus twenty and I am not cold. I'm not craving a drink and my ears aren't sore and I'm not anxious about the state of my bank account. I'm not even thinking too much about Mum. I'm okay. And I can still feel her on my fingertips.

Lena's in so I tell her about Karin and the note. I clear my desk and then at eleven she asks me into her office. This is our goodbye. This is it. My guts are torn in different directions, curious about Karin, thrilled to leave, cuckoo-gaga for Noora. Nils is still ice fishing and Lars has the day off so it's quiet in here. I step into her office and Lena looks tired and worried.

'I've got some news from your new job,' she says, her face sullen, stern. 'I'm really sorry. Wait here for a sec.' What? No. She leaves her office and closes her door and I'm left facing her side of the desk, her oversize monitor twisted half toward me. What's happening?

The door bursts open and it's Lena and then it's Lars in a reindeer jumper and then Nils wearing some kind of cowboy shirt tucked into his no-shape ICA jeans.

'Surprise!' yells Nils. He's carrying a bottle of Cava and Lars has a framed picture in his hands.

'You guys?' I say, astonished. 'You're both off today?'

'Sending you away in style,' says Lars, his bald patch freshly moisturised, it gets so dry in the winter months. Today it's glistening.

'We're gonna miss you, Tuva,' says Lena. I think there's a tear in one of her eyes, or the start of a tear, but she seems to will it back down into the duct. 'These are for you.'

'Too cold to fish,' says Nils, passing me the Cava. 'Don't drink it all at once.'

Lars passes me a framed page of the *Guardian* from last October. It's my Medusa story.

'My God,' I say, staring at them. 'Thank you all so much.'

'She paid for it,' says Nils, pointing at Lena.

'I'll miss this place,' I say, and I mean it. 'I'll miss you.'

Lars hugs me from a great distance. Nils hugs me like he'd hug a football player: hard taps on my shoulder. Lena holds me. She holds me and I hold her and she kisses the top of my head. 'You're welcome back here any time you like,' she says. 'Always welcome back.'

'What's the new employer news?' I ask.

'Spoke to Anders yesterday. He says you can write the occasional piece for me if you want, no problem at all. That north v south thing could be interesting to the locals. And if you want to write a one-off on the Ferryman case, once it's solved, we can accommodate that. Think about it once you're settled.'

I pack my book research into the Tacoma and see Thord knocking on Janitor Andersson's basement door, one hand resting on his holstered gun. He knocks on the window and peers in. What's that all about? I head in his direction but Thord turns to face me and he shakes his head.

I go past Benny Björnmossen's store at low speed and see Red coming out with a rifle case and two heavy bags. I drive on to the gas station by ICA and about three people stare as I slide in through the passenger side door and drive off. I can see Storgatan and the chimneys in my mirrors. One last trip there tonight to find out Cici's big secret and to say my goodbyes to Cici.

The junction with the E16 has some traffic, long-distance coaches and hunters heading off to the stalking grounds to kill elk or wild boar. I drive under the motorway. A Grimberg delivery van passes me at speed and I don't get a good look at the driver but he's wearing a bright orange shirt.

Utgard forest looks like a vast glacier creeping toward the rest of the world. It's high and white and it's too big for its own good. I pass the digger yard and remember Viggo and waking up in his locked taxi with that tea-light candle. A shiver runs down my spine. I indicate and pull off the ploughed salted asphalt onto the gravel track. The snow's deep but I can manage. It's so cold these days, never gets above minus fifteen even at midday, so there's a decent crust. Snow at zero degrees is the worst, no traction, especially in the Shitmobile. There's a warning light on the dash but I have no idea what it means. I pass hoarder's caravan. When I get to Viggo Svensson's torp cottage I have to slow to a crawl because the snow's too deep. Five kph. I look at the house and he's there. He's standing at a window. He's lit from one side only and he's wearing a woolly hat and no shirt and he's smiling at me. Hand on hips. Snarling. I can see scars on his arms. Small, round scars. Burn marks? There's a large crystal paperweight gleaming on his windowsill and if I was driving my Hilux right now I'd go twice as fast as this to get the hell past this guy. He holds up a hand, something tight in his fist, and then the Volvo in his driveway unlocks because I see the headlights flash twice. What? He can't follow me into the forest, not into it, he cannot do that. I accelerate and speed up the hill. The spruce trees at the top are laden with nights and nights of snowfall and their branches droop under the weight so they meet over the centre of the road in places forming an ice tunnel. I accelerate, my eyes flicking to my mirrors. Is he coming? I'm driving too fast for these conditions, too fast in this rental truck. I skid and my hands grip the wheel so tight my fingers hurt. The wood-carving sisters are busy packing demonic little pine trolls into their dark van and Alice, the quiet one, smiles at me as I go by.

I pull up to Holmqvist's house with its wrap-around veranda and mirrored windows. There's still a dog kennel in the garden and his car's parked very close to his front door and it's charging with one of those long battery trickle-cables. I'm sweating but there's no sign of Viggo's Volvo.

I lean over and clamber out the passenger door. I straighten my jacket and take the two lever-arch files and wonder what Cici's important secret is. I walk round the truck and my boots crunch.

'Tuva,' David says, opening his front door. 'Shall we?'

CHAPTER 48

Opera's playing on his tiny Bluetooth speaker. Something German. We go inside and he takes my coat and hangs it up as I pull off my boots and place them on his rack, just the way he likes it.

'Big day,' he says.

I put my lever-arch files down on one of his designer leather chairs and wipe the cold sweat from my brow. David's wearing leather slippers, monogrammed, and chinos and a mauve polo shirt. His arm hair's standing to attention.

'All set,' I say.

'Do they,' he points to my hearing aids. 'Do they work normally at these absurd low temperatures. Can they withstand a hundred-year Gavrik chill?'

'They're fine,' I say, glancing at the window to see if Viggo's outside. 'It's the wet they hate.'

'Ah,' says David, mentally recording that fact for his archive. 'Shall we see to business upstairs in my office? And then I've prepared a celebratory luncheon, just three courses.'

'Sounds good. But I can't be too late, I have

some goodbye calls to make in town and I want to visit the Grimbergs before I catch my train.'

'Naturally,' he says. 'In fact, do you mind if I visit the factory with you later this afternoon? I have the first half of the book ready for Anna-Britta to look over. It might be more,' he pauses to find the word. 'More palatable for them if I arrive with you.'

I don't really want him there with me but I can hardly say no.

'Fine.'

We walk upstairs, me behind him, and I can't stop looking at that strip of calf that exposes itself each time he climbs a step. He's like some wild thing under all the starched clothes.

My phone beeps. Reception is almost non-existent in this forest but three messages come through all from different people. Must have been queuing up until I got a signal. One's from Lena asking me to call her when I have a sec. One's from Toyota asking me to return the Tacoma to his garage and not leave it in ICA's car park like we'd agreed. He says the snowploughs need to clear ICA's lot tonight. And one from Thord. He says Karin's discharged herself from hospital. He asks me if I know where she is. I reply that I have no idea but the message fails to send.

'Here,' Homqvist says, pointing to a particular spot on the table. 'Lay out your work here and talk me through it if you would.'

I open my files.

Is Karin on the run? Is she on her way back to Gavrik?

'I'm in your debt,' says David flicking through my subject dividers. 'But not for too much longer. I intend to transfer the first half of your fee to your account immediately after we've gone through these.'

God knows I need it.

I talk him through what I have. Subjects with headings like 'Cecilia Grimberg' and 'The Vänern Lake House' and 'The Mobile-phone Masts' and 'Fire One' and 'Fire Two'.

'It's a record of what makes the family tick,' I say. 'What drives each generation and also the pressures they face, both from competition and from the community, but also from the site. Theirs is a story of endurance and sacrifice, but also guilt. They protect themselves in ways they've developed over generations, ways we'd laugh at, but they take very seriously. And I've interwoven the other stories through theirs, the story of Red, the stamper. The story of Janitor Andersson and his brother, the delivery driver injured when his truck left the road last week. But my main focus is Cecilia and how she's survived and how her husband, Ludvig, didn't. How they never found his body. How he never got a burial. And then Anna-Britta and how she's coping with the mammoth responsibility of managing the factory now she's alone. And, of course, how Gustav didn't manage. The place is dripping with loss, most acutely the loss of lilla Ludo who's buried just metres from where they all sleep each night.'

He nods and smiles, drinking all this down.

'Excellent material,' he says. 'This will inform the final part of the book, it'll really make for a fitting climax.'

'Good,' I say.

'And that will benefit the Grimbergs. You're helping them. They'll be subsidised by the royalties of this book for decades to come.'

'You really think it'll sell that well?'

He licks his lip from the scar at the centre to the left and then from the scar to the right.

'I hope so, for their sakes,' he says. 'Anna-Britta has talked more about marketing strategies and advertising and how to make the book stand out from competing titles than she has about Grimberg history. Gustav was always interested in industrial heritage, but Anna-Britta mainly talked about the need for a strong "hook". Hopefully the royalties will keep that ghastly lawyer from owning the place anytime soon. Honestly, the man acts like he's entitled to the company. Anyway, let me compensate you.'

He leads me through to his second guest room, his study. He sits at his workstation typing on his weird ergonomic split-keyboard. I think I hear a car outside but it's just his fancy computer booting up. The website for Handelsbanken appears on screen.

'Would you mind?' he says, holding up his digital security device.

'Oh, sorry.' I turn away to the books he's already written, books with other people's names printed on their spines.

'Okay,' he says. 'Ten thousand now and ten on the day of publication.'

'That's right.'

'Which should be next year sometime. I do hope you'll enjoy reading it.'

'I'm sure I will,' I say, and I mean it, especially the parts I contributed to.

'Go somewhere quiet and really enjoy it. Take your time.'

I nod. 'Not a cabin in the woods though,' I say. 'An apartment in the Med, perhaps, something warm with a terrace and a big sky.'

'All done,' he says, printing off the confirmation and handing it to me. 'Thanks again.'

'Thank you,' I say. 'It's been a fascinating project. I hope the Ferryman's caught quickly now and the town can have a few quieter months.'

'I'm sure it will,' he says. 'And it'll be summer soon enough. Can I get you a drink?'

Hell, yeah. Ten rum-and-Cokes. Line them up.

'That would be nice. Just a small one.'

We go downstairs and he's got a saucepan on his induction hob, one of those long hobs from a fancy brand, something that probably cost more than my monthly salary. He takes a bottle from his wine fridge and pours into two flutes. He changes the music on his little portable-speaker thing, the sound quality is amazing, and passes me a glass. Some kind of instrumental jazz. He's getting all pompous holding his glass by the base and straightening his back and clearing his throat so I sense a speech coming.

'This is a momentous day,' he says, and I swear his voice is almost breaking. 'I want to thank you for all your hard work. You've been an invaluable aide. You've made the Grimberg women open up and that is not a skill I possess. I would have written a far inferior book without you, Tuva.'

I nod and smile.

'To my book. *The Liquorice Factory*,' he says.

'*The Liquorice Factory*,' I say.

I move to chink glasses but he frowns and lifts his glass and drinks and sighs with pleasure. He must see the look on my face because he says, 'it's vintage, from '96, an exceptional year.'

I nod. 'Very nice.' It tastes like piss and the bubbles have all gone.

'The year my parents passed on, in fact.'

'It's very nice,' I say, and then I feel completely tactless for using those words after what he just told me.

'Hence the subdued mousse and the dark colour,' he says. 'Beautiful.'

Flat piss.

Then he turns his attention to stir whatever's in the saucepan. From the fridge he pulls a stainless steel tray lined with chicken drumsticks, each one coated with breadcrumbs. Looks edible at least. I want to call Thord about Karin discharging herself but I have no signal, not even on the stairs.

'Soup to start,' he says. 'Please be seated.'

I take my usual seat at his glass table and look down through it at my socked feet. Holmqvist brings over two glasses of water.

'No Pellegrino left,' he says. 'Please excuse the colour and the sediment, it's my well, it's all the wells in the village in fact. If you wait for a minute, it'll settle.'

I'm not going to miss this once I move to Skåne and everyone has municipal drinking water, all tested and homogenised and clean and filtered.

There's a bang outside the window and David says, 'Icicle'.

He brings two small bowls of soup.

'Borscht?' I say.

'Black soup,' he says.

Okay, I know what this is.

'In honour of your migration south.'

I stare at him.

'It's goose, don't worry. I'm not a philistine.'

So I take a spoonful of the goose blood, that's what this is, sure there may be some spices and salt and pepper and vinegar but it tastes pretty much like a cut finger to me.

'Nice,' I say.

'Isn't it, though?'

He eats with gusto and his lips have taken on a

dark hue on their innermost edges like lip-liner in reverse.

My mouth is all iron from the water and from the goose blood. It's silky and the taste isn't awful, but the texture . . . it coats the inside of my mouth like a heavy hot-chocolate and it's slightly too warm so I can feel it travel down to my stomach, blood hitting acid. I imagine what that looks like and all I can see in my mind's eye is a huge red clot.

I eat half and he clears away the bowls. I wash mine down with the expensive flat champagne and the well water.

The drumsticks are sizzling on the hob.

'Savour the champagne,' he says. 'Sip it slowly. We both need to drive later.'

'What are you cooking?' I ask.

'Not so easy to say.'

He lifts each drumstick with a pair of tongues and places it on a large wooden board. He sprinkles sea-salt flakes over the lot. The warmth of the house is making me tired, making my eyelids heavy.

'Himalayan sea salt,' he says. 'Lightly smoked.'

They look great; crispy fried things still sizzling.

'Help yourself,' he says. 'This is my death-row meal as some would call it, my favourite things in three courses.'

I lift two of them and place them on my plate. They're not chicken.

'What are they?'

'Divine is what they are.'

He takes five.

'Some think the term sweetbread refers to the thyroid gland. Others argue vehemently it's the pancreas. Some idiots talk of the windpipe or the spleen. These are what I consider the most delicious of the offal family. These are little thyroids, pig thyroids.'

Never a lamb chop here, is it?

There's a flash of white outside by the cars. Snow falling from a spruce tree.

I cut into a sweetbread and my knife sinks through the soft pink insides like it's liver but even more loose. I lift it to my mouth. And actually, if I can refrain from looking at Holmqvist's Adam's apple with its mole moving up and down, they actually taste quite lovely. Tender and delicate.

I ease into the meal. I drink a little more champagne and then I remember what the wood-carving sisters told me in the bank: don't fall at the final jump. I push the glass away.

'Quite so,' he says, removing his own glass at the same time. 'Water for both of us. Now, dessert.'

'I really am full.'

'But it's my favourite.'

I smile and he looks excited.

'Have you ever eaten *Casu marzu*, Tuva?'

I frown.

'No, I agree, I don't think you have.' He steps over to his fridge. 'It's a Sardinian delicacy. I've had it there twice over the years, just exquisite. Have you had pecorino?'

'Yes, I like it.'

'Good, well this is a kind of pecorino infested with the larvae of the cheese fly. They digest the surface of the cheese, breaking down the fats and creating the most delicious creaminess.'

No.

He brings out a tub of vanilla Häagen Dazs ice cream and a punnet of strawberries and a slab of dark chocolate with sea salt.

'I'm sorry,' he says. 'I couldn't resist. In fact, I do enjoy *Casu marzu*, but berries and ice cream is my favourite dessert, even when the fruit's so scandalously out of season.'

We smile at each other, him pleased with himself, me relieved.

The berries are a little hard, sent by airmail apparently, but the ice cream's delicious. The chocolate is that 90% cocoa stuff so I let him get busy with that.

There's a scratching or tapping noise. It's coming from the floor, maybe from the utility room. 'Can you hear that?' I ask, pointing over to that corner.

He looks worried.

'What?' he says.

'Something scratching?' I say. 'Knocking?'

'Mice,' he says, embarrassment in his voice. '*Rodentia*. They're in the walls I'm afraid.'

I pull a hair from my mouth and it drags tight against my lip. It's a bright red hair.

'Thanks for a lovely goodbye lunch,' I say, and I feel like I need a nap.

He looks almost sad.

'I have one last gift, just a small token of my appreciation.'

He picks up the little digital speaker and places it on the table.

There's a shadow at the window.

'Oh, you needn't have.'

'Close your eyes,' he says.

I close my eyes a little but I can see him take a dark blue jewellery box from a drawer. It has gold edges. I see him walk behind me with the jewellery box in one hand and his phone in the other. There's some static from the speaker and the music fades away. I hear sirens. Is he climbing the stairs? A door slams somewhere in the house, and the room begins to spin like I've had too much to drink but I haven't. And then there's a hand over my face. I struggle, my chair squeaking on the floor, my arms flailing, my shouts stifled. I kick against the glass table but a strong hand pushes me down into the chair and I can feel knuckles by my nose and a palm tight against my face. My vision blurs and darkens and I can hear Cici somewhere in the house and she is screaming for her life.

CHAPTER 49

I wake up shivering.

Blood in my mouth.

I'm thirsty in a dark, dark room, alone on the floor on some kind of mat. I rub my eyes and feel a balaclava entombing my head.

It's not mine.

I pull it off, dizzy, like I could fall but I'm already on the floor. The room smells damp and I listen. Nothing. Complete silence. I check my aids and they're both in, my ears sore, the hard skin at the top rubbed raw.

Wherever I am, I have to get out.

And then I remember Cici's scream. Is she here? Is Karin here? I try to stand but it's too difficult, my legs are like ribbons falling from a birthday balloon. I hold my palms to my cheeks to warm them. I have never been this cold in my life.

There's a noise by my feet, a rustling. I retract my knees under my chin and taste salt in the air, salt like they spread on the roads and the pavements. My right hearing aid beeps its final battery warning and I check my pocket for my key fob and spare batteries. I'm wearing my ski coat and it's zipped right up under my chin, higher than I like to have it, and my keys are missing.

I kneel and the room spins. I can't see anything much except a faint light bulb hanging from the ceiling, some low-watt bullshit that doesn't do its job. My feet are hot and my breast pocket feels warm through the material. I reach down and pull off a boot and there's a hot disc in there, one of those heating pads you stick in your gloves when you go skiing. I pull the boot back on and reach out. Nothing. No furniture, no TV, no door.

Am I in Holmqvist's attic? Some basement I never knew about? The memory of that hand at my face, the palm pressed into my nose, comes back and my head clears. I stand up and sway. The room feels wrong and the air feels wrong. Unfamiliar. A cobweb sticks to my cheek and I pull it off but it keeps on coming, some never-ending spider thread, and I pull and throw it away but it just comes back to me.

I crouch down.

What happened? I check my pockets again and my left hand's cut. My ankle hurts and my head hurts and my shoulders hurt. I feel like I've slipped on the ice and fallen on my backside, and there's a wound on my forehead. Hard, crusted blood. A bump. I've lost most of my things and gained plenty of somebody else's things but at least this is my jacket. In my right pocket is a pen and a folded piece of paper, and in my left pocket is another pen.

My hands are on a mattress.

I have to think now. I have to get out of here and I have to help Cici.

It's inflatable, quite flat, the kind of mattress you have under a sleeping bag; my God I wish I had a sleeping bag right now. I am so, so cold. I reach around and the room's carpeted. I can feel the tight hard weave underneath the mattress. I lock my jaw. My teeth grind together, scraping. I shuffle along on my knees to the end of the mattress and reach out for a wall but there's nothing. I brush my hands across the floor and touch something and recoil like a boxer evading a punch.

It feels like leaves or wet pieces of newspaper. Maybe tissue paper. And I can feel matchsticks. Or are they just sticks? Toothpicks? Needles? I won't put my hands there but I smell in that direction. It's musty.

I pull back and push my hands out in front of me like a zombie finding prey. There must be a door or a wall. I get to the other end of the carpet and it's uneven underneath, some papers stuffed down there, maybe cardboard. Is this a shed? A hut? A garage? I find the balaclava with my hands and pull it back on. It smells of a person and that person is not me but I need its warmth. I reach out my arms to the sides and there's a box and it is soft on my fingers. It's leather, I think. I open the lid and there are papers inside. I can't really see the box but I can feel it. Like a leather container for printer paper. And beside it are books, thin books. No, they're not books, they're cardboard, they're chocolate bars, the broad, flat ones, foil-wrapped, like cooking chocolate. Is this a basement kitchen?

I stand up and step off the mattress onto the lumpy carpet. It's uneven. I don't like it. I reach out and one of my hearing aids dies but the other one's still working.

No walls, no real floor. No heating, that's for damn sure. I get to the end of the carpet. I can feel its tasselled rim at my toes. A blanket? I feel like if I step off I'll fall a mile into darkness. I move one boot. Slowly. The floor is like an autumn park, a thick layer of leaves and something else. I reach out and my hands touch a wall and that's brilliant news. It is cold. Feels like an outside wall. It's brick. I reach along it to find the door. The bricks are rough; the mortar joining them together is missing in places and lumpy in others, nothing like the wet slime wall of the Grand Room in the factory. I move along the wall. It's curved. I move along some more and look up and feel the bricks at my hands and the light bulb on the ceiling brightens a little and it dawns on me that I am locked inside the base of a Grimberg chimney.

CHAPTER 50

'Help!' I scream, the noise ricocheting off the round walls and spiralling up and then back down to me. 'Help me!' I scream for minutes or hours, like a toddler wanting its mother. Needing her. I yell until my throat gets sore. I shout until my working aid rings with the abuse it's taking.

Nothing.

I bang on the concave brick walls and they just stand there. I have no idea how thick they are, how impenetrable they are, but right now I feel like I'm the bullet stored in the trigger end of an upended hunting rifle. I have no power. It's someone else who gets to fire the gun. I just sit here waiting, my face staring up at the pinprick of sky above me.

Is it still Monday afternoon? Tuesday morning? I'm hungry enough for it to be Tuesday.

I scream again, volleys of desperate pleas, but it's as though my voice can reach so far up this stack of freezing air, maybe ten metres up, maybe twenty, but then it weakens and floats back down to me here at the base. I check my pockets again. I need my phone but I just find the two pens. I pull them out. One's a biro, I can't see the colour. The other, the one in my left pocket, has a button on it. It's a pen torch. I click the button and a small beam of light hits the red brick wall.

I wave it around, starved for details of where I am and how I get out. It starts to slot together.

Oh my God.

I'm crouched on a thin mattress, which itself lies atop the circular carpet from Holmqvist's hallway. Under that is a layer of debris: old compacted ash mixed with twigs and leaves. The thing I touched before, the wet newspaper, is in fact a dead bird. It's mostly gone now but the beak is still pristine at the very tip of the sunken corpse. The ribs are as fine as curved needles.

The torchlight is so pathetic, the beam so concentrated, that it takes me time to fill in all the gaps. Like I'm looking at my surroundings through a huge sheet of cardboard with a pinhole cut out of it. There's the leather box. Looks expensive. Next to it is a silver bucket, the wine cooler from Holmqvist's house, and it's full of heat pads, hundreds of sealed chemical heating elements. I open two more and slide them down into my trousers. My thighs are too cold. My skin's starting to perish, ice crystals eating into my flesh. And then I open two more disc-shaped pads and stick them into my sleeves by my upper arms. I get my gloves and open another two and leave them inside to warm up. I should have mittens, not gloves, mittens are better. It's maybe minus ten down here. Or worse. The bird next to me is what I'll become if I don't think straight. The beak. The curved needle ribs.

The chocolate bars look frozen solid. It's dark chocolate with sea salt, the same as David served at lunch. There are maybe twenty bars, and behind them are three big green water bottles with heat pads sellotaped around them.

I'm being kept here, kept alive. He's keeping me here like Karin keeps that rabbit in the Grand Room.

I shine my torch around to fill in the darkest corners and I see a flash of white. A pile of snow mounded up by the bricks. I pull myself closer to it. It's round. Smooth. And it is far, far too big. This is human size, not snowball size. I shuffle closer and my torchlight picks out blonde hairs stuck to the back of the snow like the patchy ponytail of a month-old corpse. And there's something else. Something wrong. I scream with all my might and my voice echoes around this frozen column and sinks back down to taunt me. The top of the hideous life-size skull is flat. Like it's been operated on. A guillotine execution gone wrong. A scalping. The top is a sheet of centimetre-thin ice and there's something underneath it.

I approach from the side, my arms outstretched. The heat pad in my glove is scorching the skin on the back of my left hand. The skull, purest white, has a black rain beetle pressed into each eye socket. It has a piece of liver for a tongue, a bulging shiny offal tongue sitting in its mouth hole. And through the clear ice lid that caps its head I can see the unmistakable outline of a brain.

I'm starting to lose the feeling in my cheeks. I touch the skin and I'm numb. Numb in my fingertips and numb in my face.

I crouch down and lift the lid because how could I not.

The brain looks fresh. It's grey-pink and it has blood-filled valleys and troughs and a deep groove down its middle.

It smells like out-of-date steak.

I want to vomit. I want to die.

I'm being kept here, in this chimney, kept alive. What for? I turn my back on the skull. I cannot destroy this one. It's too human. I don't know who the brain belonged to. I try to ignore it. I turn my back.

There are packs of ICA Maxi batteries, the skinny triple-A type, next to the chocolate. I use the torch to look for a ladder or footholds but I just find two metal doors. I dart for them, the pen torch gleaming on their steel surface. They're locked. I pull on them and bash at them and yell, 'Help! Can anybody hear me?' and I scream a mad uncontrolled scream which only frightens me more.

How deep are the walls down here at the base? It's the thickest section, has to be to support the weight. Janitor Andersson did tell me. A metre thick? More?

It's night-time. Probably still Monday night. My train's probably leaving Karlstad right now, my cosy sleeper-berth empty. The Grimbergs will think I left without saying goodbye. Poor Karin, innocent Karin, the girl who asked me for help, she'll think I ran off when in fact I'm ten metres below her bedroom being kept alive on twisted life-support.

I try to slow my breathing.

There are two liquorice coins in the leather box. One for each eye. What the hell does he expect me to do?

I need to be clear-headed if I'm to make it out of here and make it out I will. I must. My God, they'd never even know it. They'd just think I left, no manhunt, no search. Just a skeleton. Two birds: one large one small. Two sets of ribs. Three brains. I have no family left to worry why I never get in touch, never turn up for Christmas dinner. Aunt Ida would just think, oh, that Tuva, she's an odd one, never calls, just like her mother. Everyone here believes I left for Skåne. I'll just freeze. And then, when the thaw comes, I'll rot.

He thinks he's so clever. When I do eventually rot the stench won't even bother anyone, will it? The stink of me and that pink-grey brain slowly decomposing will waft up through a chimney specifically designed to make sure odours and fumes drift away, well over Gavrik rooftops, away to the forests and the wild places.

The box is crocodile skin or snakeskin or

something expensive. I open the lid. Reaching in with my numb fingers I pull out the papers, the pen torch lodged tight between my chattering teeth. Two documents: one short, one long.

The first is a letter of sorts from David Holmqvist. The second is his printed manuscript, unbound, each page numbered, quality paper, double-spaced, Times New Roman 14pt. I take a sip of the ice-cold San Pellegrino water and I take a bite of salty dark chocolate, 90% cocoa, and read the letter.

CHAPTER 51

*B*y the time you read this I will be gone.

No. Oh, Jesus. Who's he told? Who knows I'm trapped down here? He mentioned to me once before about leaving the country, starting a new life, ghosting with a new identity. He hasn't told anyone I'm locked in here. He doesn't know anyone.

You must try to understand, Tuva. This was my one chance, my one opportunity. For a writer like myself to pen in the names of others is like a mother raising someone else's children, whilst yearning every day to give birth to her own, knowing she can conceive and carry the child and deliver it but finding no one to assist her. This book is my child.

What the hell have you done? What is this bullshit? What the fuck does he know about yearning to give birth?

I open two more heat pads and hold them in my hands while I read, the pen torch between my teeth, the air cold and dry inside my open mouth.

I've left instructions with Third Way Publishing; detailed instructions because I won't be able to contact them again going forward. The Liquorice Factory should be published next year. I've emailed cover design ideas, and my preference for the colour would be black, like a traditional Grimberg product. The end papers should be silver and I've insisted upon raised lettering. I think it'd be fitting. The chimneys should feature on the cover, perhaps with a black coin motif on the base of the spine.

I am shivering reading this. Chills run from my coccyx up my backbone, cooling each stiff vertebra, all the way up to my neck. I compact myself, huddling, bringing my limbs in closer, squeezing myself into a new shape. And then I smell smoke. Further up the chimney, maybe ten metres up, there's an angled opening from the right and smoke is rising into it. The tiled stove in the Grand Room. They can't light it, it's not safe, but they are burning something.

'Help!' I scream. 'Karin! Anna-Britta! Help me! Cici, help me!' My voice croaks and I sob. The air is faintly smoky and my tears roll down my cheeks onto my ski-jacket collar and I look up at the tiny white aperture above and plead to Dad. See me down here. Please see me, Dad. Help me.

I scream some more and then I stop. I keep on reading, incarcerated in the tallest, coldest jail cell ever conceived. Perhaps there's a clue, something to help me.

I am more similar to the Grimbergs than you might imagine. They're misunderstood by the Gavrik community. So am I. We've created something both historically relevant, and, vitally, commercially interesting. The book has intrigue, it's packed with it. I made quite sure of that. So copies will fly off the shelves and that will mean we save jobs. You and I, we'll keep the family in their home and we'll help this place thrive even though we'll no longer be living here to see it.

My lungs weigh deep in my chest like lead bowls full of ice water. I've been working for a fantasist so I could rent a decent flat down south. I sold my soul.

The snow skull's still there. Part-human, part-thing. I cannot allow myself to look at it or to think about it.

They're burning something upstairs, probably some kind of precaution. I can smell a herbal tone, maybe rosemary. My belly rumbles. Roast lamb. Reminds me of my mother roasting a leg of lamb in the years before Dad died. With crispy garlic potatoes. She was a very good cook before the accident. She knew how to judge meat.

I break a square of bitter dark chocolate. It snaps because it's frozen and because there's hardly any fat or sugar in it. It's not chocolate really. And I suck it whilst reading on, the pen light illuminating a few lines at a time, the rest of the page dark around the glow.

I've left instructions for your new notes to be assimilated into my work. Third Way are mercenary bastards and they'll follow my advice to the letter if they think it'll sell well. I've recommended three other ghosts to assist with the prose because you and I will be unable to continue.

495

'Help me!' I scream. I get to my feet and bang the metal doors leading out of this thing but they don't clang so much as absorb the impact, a dull thud each time they're struck. Tiny snowflakes of rosemary-scented ash float down from above and settle around me, on my face as I stare up at the miniscule shimmering light. I'm not usually claustrophobic, but this . . . I can run from one wall to the other in two strides. I can circumnavigate the area in less than three seconds. There's so much space but it's all above me. Teasing me. I'm a pea lodged at the base of some towering bamboo cane, with no hope of extraction.

I read on, snot freezing on my upper lip, the balaclava itchy against my cheeks.

I've helped this book evolve and events have assisted me along the way. I must confess all to clear my conscience. Please bear with me.

I shake my head.

The book was coming along reasonably well until Gustav's untimely fall. I had nothing to do with his suicide, I assure you of that, on my honour. He was exhausted. The burden, the overwhelming burden, had finished him off. Then the women stopped talking to me. Well, they hardly spoke to me even before. The historical elements were in place and all reasonably interesting, but I've written enough thrillers and romance mysteries and misery memoirs to know that you need hooks to really sell. So I had to manufacture some.

I rub my eyes, the heat packs clammy in my

palms. I'm supposed to be in Skåne right now, starting work at a quality bi-weekly, making a new life for myself, new hairstyle, new health regime, and I'm locked inside a chimney in the disused side of a death factory.

First, the tooth. The dog's alive, don't think that of me, he's alive and very jolly living on an arable farm near Munkfors, but his tooth fell out before Christmas so it would have been a waste not to use it. I knew it'd get the papers interested, what with Medusa and the missing eyes and all the publicity that generated. I'm so pleased I relocated the dog well before I left.

The chimney starts to spin. I drink water and my hearing aid beeps and switches off. So now I can't hear. If rescue services or Anna-Britta or Noora were to yell my name, I'd never even hear it. All I have now is the taste of chocolate and salt, the sight of a pinprick of frozen light, the feel of heat pads scorching my skin in certain places, the smell of rosemary smoke.

Shivering, I squint to focus on the pages.

Gunnarsson was a monster, you see. I know the local police force investigated him as a bully and a school tyrant, but they made one fatal error, thank goodness. They focussed on children in his year and in the years below. I was teased by Gunnarsson for years but he was far younger than me. He was a beast and when I was forced to up the stakes, he became the obvious solution. I took my pestle to the back of his head. I learnt a lot from Medusa – that case caught the national imagination, and do you know why? Because of the eyes and because of the trolls. There were three major book deals signed on the back of the Medusa murders. Three. All with big publishers and none of them offered to me even though, as my then agent made perfectly clear, I had the inside knowledge. Anyway, Medusa taught me that we'd need drama to make this book sell. And we'd need a hashtag. That's where the Ferryman came from. I waited for someone to come up with it but all I saw on social media was hashtag #LiquoriceMurder which was no good at all. So I got to work. I have twenty-seven separate Twitter accounts and eventually, after a night of hard graft, the hashtag began to stick. Then I researched automobiles; really I neither care nor know much about them. I researched corrosion of brake cables, what rodent damage looks like, how to saw through so that brakes work for a while and then shear away and fail. That story got some news coverage at least, some interest.

The curse. The precautions. They were against Holmqvist, not the factory. I want to scream up to Anna-Britta and Cici and Karin. I want my voice to carry on the delicate ash flakes, up and through their chimney flue to the tiled stove and around the internal pipes and out through the doors. 'It's him,' I want to say. 'You were right.'

The fire was all my idea. Something in the flavour of the Lake Vänern house fire, something to get people talking. Of course, I had nothing to do with the original blaze, and I made quite sure no lives were at risk from the root-barn inferno. I do feel bad for the taster. But she's alive. She still has a life to live. The fire bought me some coverage and cemented the Ferryman hashtag. It did its job.

I reckon I've been a full day now without real food. Only dark chocolate. I feel sick and I need to go to the toilet but all I have is this champagne cooler bucket and doing that in here feels like defeat, like I'm giving in to my fate. So I hold it.

Awful about young Karin, but that was nothing to do with me. It runs in the family. However, I did do something that never quite sat right with me, it's weighed heavy on my heart for some time. When you and I were in Anna-Britta's office and we heard Cici scream, we didn't actually hear her scream. What we heard was a recording of her scream, do you see? I pushed her down the stairs ten minutes before when you were in the bathroom, and I recorded her yelp on my mobile. Nobody else around. She'd talked before of being pushed at the lake house. I wanted to reopen that mystery, to leverage it. And also to divert suspicion away from me because I had an important book to finish, as you well know! The thick, archway doors and the sirens meant nobody heard the original yell. Then, when you came out, I played the scream back through my speaker. I'd perched it on the stairs, and then we ran through and saw Cici at the bottom near the arch door. Even though she's always looked down on me, I accept it was a step too far, and I regret it.

Bastard. How did I not see that at the time? Her lying there, her insisting she'd been pushed down.

You don't get to 'regret' that, David, and you don't get to 'apologise'.

We need sales, you see. Essential. For my legacy, my name. As I mentioned to you, this is my first book written in my own name, the spine will read David Holmqvist from top to bottom, I've asked for it to be in larger print than the title, The Liquorice Factory, *because I think it'll help sales once news of all this breaks.*

I open four more heat pads because the pathetic pinprick of light is fading and I'm getting colder and colder. I stick them inside my socks and long johns and then I open eight more for my sleeves and my back and my neck.

And the family need the sales, goodness, they really do need them. It's not easy to build an income stream from one non-fiction book, you know. This thing has to take off, it has to market itself, there's no advertising budget with people like Third Way, no help whatsoever. And this is my final strategy.

A grand finale.

The story of you, here, deep inside the liquorice factory.

CHAPTER 52

I thought the blank light above me was maddening, but now I'd give anything to have it back. There's still light up there but it's slush-coloured. I've seen a bird, I think it was a bird, maybe a crow or a goose, I only saw a wing tip, how can I judge its size from all the way down here?

The heat packs are keeping me alive. I have to ration them, not too many at once, not too many in one place, try to squeeze the last drops of heat from each disc before removing it and stacking it with the others in the corner. There are no fucking corners. I stack them at one point on the ground like a mound of clamshells by a grave. By my grave.

'Help! Can anybody hear me?' I just get a dull echo. I can feel it swirling around the chimney, my hoarse voice trapped down here close to the ground.

The book's actually quite good. I'm learning about the founding family and their children, about the difficulties they had sourcing the raw roots and signing trade contracts when political regimes were weak or in flux. Gavrik was much smaller back then, less than two-thousand souls. And the factory, the coffin I'm entombed inside of, was state of the art. It was mentioned in the press as far afield as Germany and Ireland. New machinery and stock systems and quality control methods. They were ahead of their time.

Not anymore.

I'm at the bottom of a dry well looking up at the cold, blank night. There are people close by at my level and people walking above my head, and the might of this chimney is keeping me from them and them from me. David Holmqvist's probably in France right now working on his new identity, or maybe in Vienna, I can see him there, living a high-culture existence on his own terms.

I change the batteries in the torch for fresh ones. The night freeze is draining their power.

Torch, carpet, manuscript, salty chocolate, water bottles with heat pads, a red pen I store in my pocket to prevent the ink from solidifying. And a human brain in an ice skull.

He's dedicated the entire book to me, the bastard.

Thanks to Tuva, my local friend and assistant, for your work and your belief.

For all his talk of legacy and immortality through prose, he's destroyed his literary reputation and taken my embryonic one down with it. I want to recall his email to Third Way Publishing and I want to burn this printed copy and dance on the embers.

I look up and there are holes in the brickwork.

They're not large. Not big enough to push something through. They're mouth-sized and a few metres above me and maybe they're just nooks, not holes at all. I direct my voice at them and scream.

Nothing.

I read on. I try to listen out for people calling my name, then scold myself for my stupidity. No aids, no chance. I get up abruptly and, holding the manuscript in both hands, my skin so sore it's bleeding, I beat the metal doors with the five hundred pages, over and over and over again.

I sit back down.

I'm exhausted. More salty chocolate. More thirst.

I have no sense of time. I start to panic, to breathe too fast, and then I close my eyes tight, so tight I can see orbs of light on the insides of my eyelids, and I think back to Dad, to his hands, his voice, his goodnight kiss, and my breathing slows and I quell the panic and I go on.

The sky, the tiny piece I'm permitted to see, is almost black. It's like the pupil of some mythical thing looking back down at me, inspecting me; Tuva, the bug pressed between glass slides and slotted into the base of a gigantic microscope.

What do you see, beast? An orphan? A lover? It could be Mum looking down, shaking her head at my stupidity, my blind ambition.

I discard my boot heat-pads and throw them on the pile. I snap open more. I probably have two-hundred left.

I count them.

Two-hundred and seventeen.

But how long will they keep me alive in this induced chimney coma? Is it better to stay warm and then just run out and stop, or to shiver on, rationing them for days or even weeks? I have enough chocolate to last me, enough water. And then I look at that silver champagne-cooler gleaming in the din.

The sensation of Gore-Tex and merino wool long johns dragging down my bare legs as I squat over the bucket is unbearable. Too dark, too cold. Hideous. The skull's there looking away, the rubber band of its ponytail holding its dead hair in place. I finish and wipe myself with David Holmqvist's dedication page because fuck you.

The smell sinks into the walls to join the others. It's not bad, it's too cold to be bad. You can buy freezer toilets in Sweden. I've seen them advertised in the *Posten*, next to my articles. You plug them into your cabin wall and then they freeze the family shit into neat little ice blocks for you to bury out in the nature.

I huddle.

I cup my hands to my cheeks.

No noises, just salt on my tongue and the yearning for a hot bath with bubbles, not unscented ICA soap, I'd take Tammy's fancy stuff, peonies and roses and peaches and froth. Lather. Hot water. So hot it'd numb my brain stem.

Sleep is difficult. It's not the mattress, that's fine as it goes. It's the fear of not waking. Makes a girl an insomniac, the lurking dread that you might close your eyes and only get discovered by some archaeologist three hundred years from now, theorising about the skeleton in the chimney and what it all meant.

So, I read.

How Grimberg Liquorice supplied the German troops in World War One. The Germans don't mind a bit of salt liquorice. About their exports to Holland, and, for a time, to the Minnesota region of the United States. And then he writes about the first suicide, the first one they know of. And the business problems starting in the sixties, issues around modernisation, the building of the new part of the factory.

Something catches my eye.

There's a mouse.

It's egg-size, plus tail, and it looks at me and scuttles around the curve of the chimney like I did when I woke up here and then it disappears into thin air. Poof. I scrabble around to investigate and find a hole the size of my eye. How the hell did it get through? I scream at the hole, crouching down, my cheek resting on wet leaf mulch. I get my lips so close to the damp old bricks I can taste them, the earth they were made from, the salt running through them. I scream and spit and holler into this tiny hole like Alice in Wonderland after she's had the 'eat me' cake, only this is a fucked-up new version where I'm a giant Alice and a miniature Alice all at the same time.

It could be the start of night, 4pm, it could be the end of night, 8am. I think it's late or very early, the air feels that way. But what is this air down here? A stale ancient unmoving cocktail pressed under a hundred metres of chilled fresher air higher up. The air down here could be fifty years old. I start coughing at the thought of it.

I look around for other holes but there are none.

The bird's over there, the dead carcass with the beak still gleaming and box-fresh. I decide I'll do the decent thing and give it a burial. I mound up fifty or so heat-pack wrappers above it like some sick Viking burial and then I look up to the grey dot and stand there in silence until I get dizzy.

I finish the book and I finish another bar of chocolate. Both things make me sick. I scream again, a strategic series of volleys aimed at the chimney vent above my head and at the mouse escape-hole down by the ground. If it's early morning this whole side of the factory, the old disused half, plus the residence above and the attics above that, will be silent. I scream more, yelling until my throat burns.

I take the red pen from my pocket. He gave it to me to make notes and editorial comments but I think I've done enough work, don't you? So I pull random pages from his bastard manuscript and I turn them over and I rest them on the leather box.

I need to tell a few people some important things. In case I never make it out of here. I never told Mum so now I must say these things. I must.

I write my first to Tammy.

I tell her I'm sorry. That I love her. I cry as I write the 'v' in love. I tell her she can have all my things if she wants them and that I'd like to, I break down properly now, tears flowing as I write, I can taste them, my vision blurred and shaky, I'd like to be placed next to Mum and Dad, next to Dad if possible.

I lay down and look up. Tears cooling on my skin.

I think I can see clouds pass in the grey February sky but it might just be me. My lips are dry scabs of baked desert earth and my hands hurt every time I move them. Whose brain's inside the *skalle*? How? I'm trying not to look through the ice lid or at the straw-colour ponytail stuck to the snow. Heat pads keep me going but my body is so cold it's starting to shut down. I think it's the darkness as much as the temperature. And the silence in these curved walls, this one curved wall, this cell.

If I had a match I'd burn the whole damn book and locals would say 'that's strange, isn't that the old chimney, the disused one' and 'must be testing it or something' and 'maybe it's another arson'. Someone might come.

But there are no matches.

I write a note to Noora thanking her. I write that I miss her. I write that if she needs allies in Gavrik she should turn to Lena and Thord and Tammy. I write that she made me feel wanted and warm. I write that I loved the time we spent together.

I write to Lena, a more upbeat letter, longer than the others, easier to write somehow, like it's an assignment for the paper or something. I tell her how much I owe her, how much I've learnt from her. I write that she's kept me whole these past years, especially during the weeks after Mum died and the weeks when Medusa coverage was too much to handle and the weekends when she let me stay at her place and she fed me meatloaf and mashed potatoes and hot tea and toast and fresh pancakes. She never asked me to speak. When I couldn't do my job she stepped in and did it for me, she demoted herself and didn't say a word. No complaints. She saved me. When I couldn't feed myself she fed me. Lena shrouded me in a thick, warm blanket of silent love, an unsaid gift, an unasked-for kindness. She let me live on.

And then I get a burst of energy from all the notes I've written, a surge, a realisation of what I have to lose. I stand and yell at different pitches, low grumbling roars and high-pitched wailing, anything that might get detected, that might trigger Karin to sit up in bed and ask 'what was that?'

I stop.

Nothing.

And then I realise Karin could still be in Karlstad and Anna-Britta's probably out looking for her.

I open more heat pads and put two in my armpits and two in my knee pits and four fresh ones down in my boots. My pen ink's frozen so I place that in my pocket with its own dedicated pad.

The bird burial-mound grows another centimetre taller like some hastily built memorial to a fallen mountaineer.

I take the printed bank-payment confirmation from my coat pocket and shred it and place the shreds on the burial mound.

The glass-like lid of the skull gleams in what little light there is and the brain sits beneath it like a body in a coffin or a sausage in a clingfilmed styrofoam packet.

I fall asleep but I don't mean to. It's the kind of shallow sleep you get on a long coach journey, heavy eyelids falling ever so slowly and then jolting open again, that numb sensation that you're caught floating between two worlds.

I dream or think, some mixture of the two, of Dad and then of Noora. We're watching TV together on a sofa, on Tam's sofa, blankets and feet touching.

My dream shatters as snow starts to fall on my face. I feel flakes melt on my lips and on my eyelids, the grey dot above me a dull white now, the walls around me brightening and glistening with flakes. Must be snowing hard up there for any to reach me at the bottom of this place. I pull up my hood.

I pass in and out of sleep. My body and my soul, they're both shutting down. Giving up. I didn't ask for any of this. I should be on a heated train. I should have gotten out of this town by now.

A spider uses my head as an anchor point for its thread and I just let it.

When I wake again my eyes are frozen shut and my hands are so cold I can't feel my fingertips. I panic, rubbing the skin together but it feels dead. Like rubber. Like a latex hand transplanted onto me as some sick joke. I gulp for breath. How long did I sleep for? I try to clear my eyes and then there's a vibration. It's not a sound, I can't hear anything, but something moves or the floor shakes in some way.

It's the metal doors.

'Help!' I scream. 'I'm locked inside, help me!'

The doors move slightly and I try to push them open but my fingers won't work as I want them to and the doors just rattle.

'Help me! Get me out of here!'

And then the right door swings open.

CHAPTER 53

I can see her lips, her tangerine lips. She's trying to tell me something.

'Cici,' I say, my voice weak.

I pull my balaclava off. I can't hear anything but I can just about read her.

'I thought . . .' she says. 'I thought I heard something in the chimney. Why were you . . .' I can't make out the last words. Too dark. And then her candle flares and she says, 'Come on, let me help you.'

'Don't look at the snow *skalle*,' I say as I crawl out through the brass doors and into the old furnace. It's big enough for us to crouch and shuffle through the ash and the century-old soot. We climb out through the doors and into the old factory, the disused half, the Ferryman's half.

She places the grave candle down and puts her hands around my face and I can smell lemons.

'Come here,' she says. 'Let me look at you, you're frozen solid.'

'I'm okay,' I say. 'How's Karin?'

Cici smiles and her face comes alive and her teeth shine in the dim industrial, winter light. 'She's doing well,' she says. 'She's talked to the police and she's doing well far away from this place.'

'She's not home yet?'

'I'm home alone,' she says.

My legs start to come back to life and we walk slowly past the old stirring vats, discoloured and hazy with cobwebs. The area where Gunnarsson died is clear. Bleached. Cici has a stick in one hand and me in the other.

'Let's get you something hot to drink,' she says. 'And then I'll call Stina to check you over.'

'I'm okay,' I say.

She's wearing a vintage fur coat with a hood and it's as moth-eaten as a mangy cat. She has a silver centipede brooch pinned to her lapel and it gleams as we walk past the old stamping tables, their surfaces warped with age and damp.

'I'll make sure Karin manages,' says Cici. 'I swear it on the granite we're built on. If I need to enrol myself at her art school for a semester I will, you know. I will.'

We hold onto each other for support and make our way slowly to the arch door.

'You have a key?' I ask.

She pulls a long iron relic from her pocket.

'I'm the elder around here. I have copies of all the building keys up in my attic resting on dried grapefruit-zest and beetle wings. Safest place for them.'

Snow's blown in under the arch but it's patchy. Frosted cobblestones shine and the veins of sand in between them lock the ground together and keep it all whole.

As Cici comes into the light I see her bruises from the fall and they're purple like elephant hide.

'What time is it?' I ask. 'Which day?'

'Six am on Wednesday the nineteenth of February,' she says. 'We thought you'd left town.'

'Cici,' I say, still shivering. 'What's your secret? You said you had a secret?'

'Never mind,' she says, flicking it away with her fingers. 'Let's get you some sweet tea.'

'What did you want to tell me?' I say.

She steps closer to me, holding my arm for support. The heating pads up my sleeves are cooling down but I can still feel them. Cici opens her eyes wide and says, 'That you'll find your own way through life.' She rubs my arm as if to warm me but her touch is too light. 'That you alone will shape your future and you have every right to be happy.' She swallows. 'And that even though you didn't tell your mother you loved her she still knew deep down. Because you were there. She knew, Tuva.'

I mouth 'Thank you'. Then I almost collapse with it all.

'I need to tell the police,' I say, turning left out of the arch.

And then I see his boots.

Swinging.

Swaying in a liquorice breeze, Storgatan out of focus behind his chinos.

I release her and run through the snow to the boots and then I look up.

'Help!' I yell. 'Help! Someone!'

I try to support Holmqvist's weight, my hands pushing up into the soles of his boots, my arms weak, pathetic, useless.

'I'm coming!' shouts Andersson.

'Quick!' I scream, and others join us, two clipboard guys on their break. I'm aware of passers-by, people on their way to work or out walking their short-legged dogs, dragging them through deep snow.

'I'll cut him down,' says Andersson, suddenly at my side with a stepladder and a pair of bolt cutters. 'Mind yourself.'

The two men and I prepare to catch David Holmqvist, as Andersson cuts through the rope just above the noose knot. He's swinging from the iron hook beneath the Receiving Room window and the window's open and its flapping on its hinges. He has a bound version of his manuscript tied around his neck and he has a cross of duct tape covering each eye like two Xs.

Red runs out and she doesn't say a word she just throws her bag down into the snow and positions herself shoulder-to-shoulder with me under Holmqvist's feet. They're all talking but I can't hear the words. The body comes down and Red and the two men do most of the catching. I'm too weak, too cold.

'An ambulance is on its way,' says Cici from the archway, her lipstick catching my eye.

He's wearing a suit jacket and chinos and the hairs on his shins are bristling in the wind.

We rest him down on the snow.

One of the clipbopard guys takes off his coat and folds it and pushes it under Holmqvist's head and then I sense sirens. A crow passes over me on its way to St Olov's churchyard. Andersson's checking for a pulse and narrowing his eyes like he might be detecting something.

I look at this man: ghostwriter, liar, imprisoner, monster. He lies in the exact same spot where Gustav Grimberg died. Red sand under cobbles under snow under Holmqvist. Red from two weeks ago. This was Holmqvist's escape, his final strategy to make the book sell, to make his name live on forever. Snowflakes fall. The climax, his climax, wasn't me dying in a chimney it was him dying with the saviour manuscript hanging from his neck.

Thord and Noora run through the gates from Storgatan.

I rip the tape from his eyelids. Each one has a liquorice coin attached. I look at Holmqvist's hideous bulging eyes and I want to scratch him. For killing a lonely man and for hurting all of us. Karin, especially. I believed in him when nobody else did and he betrayed my trust. People are gathering around us and I suppose he's a victim too in all this. A town full of victims. Victims of each other.

I crouch down and swallow hard and my cheek

515

brushes the powder snow and I put my dry, cracked lips close to Holmqvist's ear. I take a breath and close my eyes. It's like it was with Mum. My chest tightens and hardens. His chest convulses. I move my lips closer to his ear and I try to whisper but no noise comes out. It's too difficult. His face is dark red and his skin is cold and a piece of tape that's still stuck to his temple flaps in the breeze. He reminds me of Mum in her final moments. He's slipping. I know what I have to do. My breath catches in my chest and I move closer and my lips brush his ear and I force myself to whisper, 'I forgive you'.

CHAPTER 54

The taxi smells of pine-tree air freshener. There are about twenty cardboard trees hanging from the rear-view mirror. The driver's called Linda. Hair shaved at the sides and long on top.

We pull up to Karlstad train station.

I thank her and pay and she helps drag my three black bags to the platform. Lena had offered to drive me but I wanted the headspace of a taxi after what happened. I wanted to leave the way I'd always dreamt about, a taxi on the E16 headed south, everything I own in the car, a deep breath and a new life.

There's a truck in the station car park getting jump started and the red jump-lead looks like a thick cord of Valentine's liquorice against the dirty, grit-laden snow. Behind it is parked a Volvo taxi. Viggo's taxi, I recognise his number plate. It's in long-term parking.

The screen tells me my train will be one minute late and it tells me the temperature is seven below.

I haven't slept since the chimney. Not much, anyway. I try to think of Aunt Ida, of the things we might do together later in the year, the bonding time, the new relationship. Those thoughts soothe me but I keep waking as soon as I drift off, panic attacks in the middle of the night. Like I'm trapped. Frozen. Suffocating.

The train approaches in the distance and I see its lights in the gloom growing brighter, growing larger. I can't hear it yet. I still need to see Tammy. She's away in Stockholm, some kind of family emergency, her cousin's in trouble.

The train comes closer, its snowplough front edge slicing through fresh powder, and then it slows and stops and about thirty people shuffle off, collars raised, wheelie suitcases dragging salted snow and depositing it near the taxi rank. I am hollow. This was always going to be my moment. I'd played it out in my head: the send-off, the new job, the dream of an apartment not too far from the sea. The act of moving on. But I feel empty and twisted inside. Too many deaths too close to me. Too much hurt.

Karin's note was apologising for an argument she'd had with her father the week before he killed himself. And for not clearing Gunnarsson's name because all he ever did was chat to her. He was lonely, that's all. Karin felt guilty all that time. Especially about her dad. Sometimes you don't get to choose the last words you say to someone.

I step up and in and pull my bags one at a time and store two of them in the train luggage area.

One bag doesn't quite fit so it sticks out like a crooked tooth ruining a smile. I find my sleeper berth. I have it to myself and I am so completely grateful I could cry. I need to be cradled to sleep by this thousand-ton locomotive, I need to be held by it and soothed to a proper slumber.

The snow skull contained a cow's brain. Smaller than a human brain but I didn't know that. I still recoil every time I see a snowball or a snowman in a front garden.

The goodbye with Noora was a disaster. I'd given my official police statement to Chief Björn and Thord, and when it came for me to leave, my taxi waiting outside the cop shop, Noora and I had to do everything, say everything, in front of them. Thord turned away, bless him. But the Chief just stared at us. I tried to communicate through my eyes and I could tell that she tried as well but we had too much we wanted to say and it was not what it should have been.

There's an announcement. Two minutes until departure.

I offered to donate the money Holmqvist paid me to Karin, for a holiday or a break for all three of them. But Anna-Britta said no. She said the Samaritans and the Swedish Childhood Cancer Foundation needed it more than they did.

A loud whistle and someone enters my little sleeper cabin and for a moment I think they have a reservation in here with me, but no, their mistake.

519

The police found the murder weapon in Holmqvist's house. A 7cm German-made chef's paring knife. And a granite pestle.

My guts are a mess. I feel like I shouldn't be leaving like this but I can't stay. I need to survive my own life, to thrive, to find a way. I need to.

Police discovered that Holmqvist had applied for an emergency passport. David knew the net was closing in on him and he knew he'd never survive prison. He's not the type to do time. So he took the only other option available to him.

There's a blur at the window.

I pull off one hearing aid and put it in its plastic overnight jar.

As I reach up to remove the other aid I see Tammy at the train window holding a blanket.

Tam?

'Tam?' I say.

She knocks on the double-glazed window and I stand up and knock back. She gestures toward the door and I run out.

'Doors will be closing in one minute,' says the announcer.

'Sorry I was away,' she says, down there on the platform, her head at the level of my knees. 'I should have been there for you.'

'No,' I say, my breathing fast and desperate. 'I was an idiot.'

She nods her head and bursts into tears and I jump down to the icy platform and hug her. We hold on. We both squeeze and tighten our arms